PRAI

"Beautifully written, weaving past and present, *Zulaikha* is a tense and touching novel you won't soon forget."

–Anita Kushwaha, the author of *Secret Lives of Mothers & Daughters*

"A hauntingly moving and brilliant book that paints a portrait of longing, heartache, love and hope. *Zulaikha* is an ambitious and powerful debut novel from a brave new voice bringing attention to the politics in Iran and how lives are affected, especially the lives of women. With sensitivity, Niloufar-Lily Soltani weaves a tale of courage, betrayal and forgiveness. Fast-paced and well-written, this story captures you from its first page and carries you along like the achingly beautiful notes of the oud."

–Sonia Saikaley, author of *The Allspice Bath*

"Epic and intimate, *Zulaikha* contains the great sweep of a life lived against the backdrop of history. It is a rare pleasure to read a novel so perceptive and so wise."

–André Forget, author of *In the City of Pigs*

ZULAIKHA

ZULAIKHA

A NOVEL
Niloufar-Lily Soltani

Toronto, Ontario, Canada
www.inanna.ca

Copyright © 2023 Niloufar-Lily Soltani
Except for the use of short passages for review purposes, no part of this book may be reproduced, in part or in whole, or transmitted in any form or by any means, electronically or mechanically, including photocopying, recording, or any information or storage retrieval system, without prior permission in writing from the publisher or a licence from the Canadian Copyright Collective Agency (Access Copyright).

We gratefully acknowledge the support of the Canada Council for the Arts and the Ontario Arts Council for our publishing program. We also acknowledge the financial support of the Government of Canada.

Cover design: Courtney Hellam

Zulaikha is a work of fiction. All names, characters, businesses, places, events and incidents in this book are either the product of the author's imagination or used in a fictitious manner.

All trademarks and copyrights mentioned within the work are included for literary effect only and are the property of their respective owners.

Library and Archives Canada Cataloguing in Publication

Title: Zulaikha : a novel / Niloufar-Lily Soltani.
Names: Soltani, Niloufar-Lily, author.
Series: Inanna poetry & fiction series.
Description: Series statement: Inanna poetry & fiction | Includes bibliographical references.
Identifiers: Canadiana (print) 20230532934 | Canadiana (ebook) 20230532942 | ISBN 9781771339568 (softcover) | ISBN 9781771339575 (EPUB) | ISBN 9781771339582 (PDF)
Subjects: LCGFT: Thrillers (Fiction) | LCGFT: Novels.
Classification: LCC PS8637.O4472 Z43 2023 | DDC C813/.6—dc23

Printed and bound in Canada

Inanna Publications and Education Inc.
210 Founders College, York University
4700 Keele Street, Toronto, Ontario, Canada M3J 1P3
Telephone: (416) 736-5356 Fax: (416) 736-5765
Email: inanna.publications@inanna.ca Website: www.inanna.ca

To Nina, my infinite hope

PREFACE

KHUZESTAN, THE SITE OF MUCH of Iran's oil reserves, is the most strategically important province in the south of Iran. Like many other provinces, Khuzestan is multi-ethnic. Arabs and Lurs comprise the primary workforce, though neither benefits much from oil revenues. Khuzestan's proximity to Arab countries and its long, shared history with Iran give the culture its unique flavour. In addition to Arab and Persian influences, Khuzestan is also influenced by the British, who discovered the oil reserves at the beginning of the twentieth century.

In 1951, the Iranian government, led by the new Prime Minister, Dr. Mohammad Mosaddegh, nationalized the oil industry. Signs prohibiting Iranians from entering British territories were removed. The British no longer ruled the city. However, two years later, the coup arranged by the American government through Operation Ajax returned Mohamad Reza Shah Pahlavi to power. Mosaddegh's influence remained: Khuzestan was no longer subject to British control.

Imitating British suburbs in the heart of tropical Abadan, the British designed the architecture for the National Oil Company's senior staff living quarters and built beautiful, fully furnished houses in the Beraim and Bovardeh neighbourhoods, complete with patios in their back yards.

Many oil company workers and other citizens lived on a long boulevard with numbered bus stops, which stretched from *Istgah Yek* to *Istgah Davazdah* and further.

The British and, later on, the Americans, worked for the National Oil Company of Iran as consultants and senior staff. With the 1979 revolution, which ended Mohmmad Reza Shah's regime, they left the country.

A year later, Iraqi forces invaded Iran. Saddam Hussein's main objective was to capture Khuzestan. From 1980 to 1988, Iran was a war zone, with most fighting concentrated in Khuzestan. Khorramshahr, Abadan's twin city, was invaded first. When the war ended, it had claimed the lives of approximately one million people with more significant losses in Khuzestan.

Zulaikha—pronounced *Zuli-Ka*—is a figure, most likely historical, known in the Middle East. It was the name of the exotic and sensual wife of Potiphar, the Pharaoh's guard. Her obsessive story with Yusef or Joseph is told in the Quran, Bible, and Torah. Persian poet Jami (1414–1492) has a book of poetry named *Yusuf and Zulaikha*.

CHARACTERS AND NAMES

Madineh: Mother

Hessam: Zulaikha's younger brother

Gholam: Zulaikha's older brother

Assef: Zulaikha's husband, Sohrab's father

Sohrab: Zulaikha's son, Hessam's nephew

Abbass: Hessam's best friend

Abu: Abbass's father

Kia Chaharlangi: Hessam's friend

Jamshid Chaharlangi: Kia's father, also an old friend of Abu's

Maryam Chaharlangi: Jamshid's wife

Habib: Madineh's husband, Assef's friend

Mrs. Sara: Zulaikha's next door neighbour in Abadan

Sheikh Ahmed: Zulaikha's first husband in Bahrain

Aliah: Sheikh's first wife

Najwa: Abbass's fiancée

Abdul: Zulaikha's friend and lover

Kobra: Gholam's wife

Mousa: Gholam's son (Zulaikha's nephew and Sohrab's cousin)

Dr. Matlab: Prison guard, later a member of parliament

Nasim: Zulaikha's friend in Tehran

The Alipours: Zulaikha's employers and friends in Tehran

Reza: The Alipours' son, Sohrab's friend

Sheila: Sohrab's girlfriend in Holland

FARSI WORDS

Amu: Uncle (In Khuzestan, a stranger is called Amu to show respect and closeness)

Azizam: My dear

Bandari: Port-related (Bandari dance and music style belongs to Khuzestan and Hormozgan provinces.)

Azhir: Siren

Bastani: Ice cream

Bibi: Grandmother (Old Farsi)

Bebakhshid: Forgive me

Chador: A long cloak covering head to toe

Eidi: Gifts, of cash or otherwise, traditionally given to family and youth for Eid.

Ey Khoda: Calling God (Oh Mighty)

Faloodeh: Sorbet

Havoo: Second wife

Istgah Yek: Stop One

Istgah Seh: Stop Three

Istgah Haft: Stop Seven

Istgah Davazdah: Stop Twelve

Jan: Soul. Equivalent to *dear* when addressing loved ones (see *Azizam*)

Joon: An informal and modern version of *jan*

Kadu: Gift

Khanum: Lady, Madam, Ma'am

Khasteh Nabashi: An expression showing gratitude for another's hard work, wishing them to not be too tired

Khoda: Creator, God

Maman: Mum, used in contemporary times

Manteau: French word for a coat women wear as Hijab to cover themselves from neck to legs

Narges: Daffodils

Nowruz: New Day (Persian New Year's Day)

Pahlavan: A warrior, hero

Pesar: Boy, son

Sabzi: Herbs

Salaam: Hello

Shah: King

Shahr: City (In Khuzestan this word means downtown too.)

Shirini: Sweets and pastries traditionally distributed during a celebration

Soghati: Souvenir

Tajlil: Tribute

Tabrik/Mobarak: Congratulations

Tasilat: Condolences

Velgard: Stray

Volek: A slang term for "buddy," used by people in Khuzestan

Zahr e mar: Snake poison (A phrase used to insult)

Zereshk: Barberry

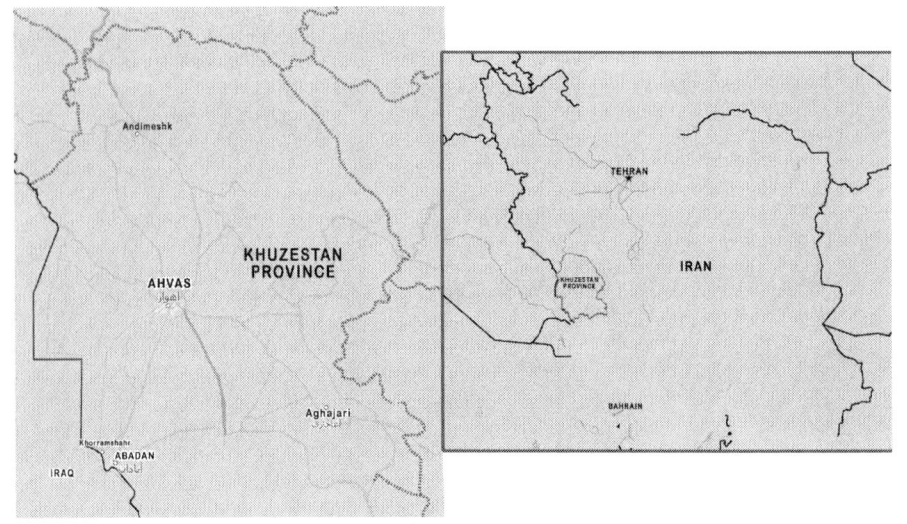

PART 1

Two Airports

DECEMBER 2007

*Someone with his silence,
took me to the endless desert of madness.
Someone with his gaze,
took me to the vast sea of blood.
Return me!
You, who threw me to the end,
Resume me!*

–Hamid Mosadegh

IT WAS PAST THREE IN the morning. Tehran spread out beneath Zulaikha's airplane. Flying above Mount Damavand, covered in snow from top to bottom, she knew that Tehran must have seen a cold winter. Watching Tehran as the underworld, she wondered which would be safer, floating aimlessly in the air or landing in a city where you know you are in trouble.

Yesterday, before leaving Amsterdam, before feeling excited about returning home and sleeping in her bed, everything suddenly changed. A ghost of her past appeared in Europe, in a crowded airport as her pleasant vacation was about to end.

At one point in her life—she couldn't remember exactly when—she had wanted her ghosts to rest in peace and let her live without them, without Abbass's beauty and art, without Hessam's care and presence. She had managed to close their files and move on. But it was always enough to mention their names or ask about them: Abbass, her murdered friend, or Hessam, her missing brother. Enough to bring them back and let them haunt her. Yesterday, someone called their names. Someone asked about them.

This was her first visit to Holland after her now thirty-four-year-old son, Sohrab, left Iran six years ago. He lived in a small town, Haarlem, thirty kilometres north of Amsterdam, and drove a cargo semi-trailer truck for a living. He took two days off—all he could get, and he felt bad, but that was all Zulaikha expected from her son: to make his supervisor happy. "Driving a big truck requires skills. You're in demand, Sohrab," she said. "I'll be fine."

Thanks to their recent Skype video chats, Zulaikha was not too shocked when she first saw her son at the airport. He had shaved just the way she had always told him to. Clean-cut.

When she first entered Sohrab's flat, the window to his front street looked welcoming. As she stepped forward, she recognized a book of poetry on the far end of the window shelf—a collection of poems and paintings by Sohrab Sepehri. She looked away, back to the street and then to Sohrab, as if remembering those poems would open their life story. She didn't go all the way to Holland to open that book. Not anymore.

On their first weekend, they caught a train to Amsterdam. She refrained from asking if Sohrab borrowed money to take her to Madam Tussaud's museum. While he worked long hours, she cleaned, cooked Sohrab's favourite meals—a celery stew and rice or beef cutlets and fries—and walked around Haarlem, staring at thin wooden houses lining canals. She had learned the direction from Sohrab's place to the town's main square path and even dared to enter the stunning Groke Kerk Church. She loved walking. In Tehran, too, she often walked to the old Pepsi-Cola factory and then back to the path to Nasim's bookstore. It was Nasim who had told her, "You would need to entertain yourself there. Trust me and take a few books. I read more when I visit my daughters in Canada." So, Zulaikha had brought a few magazines that occupied her with crossword puzzles. Two romance books, too.

When Sohrab got home, he kept apologizing before falling asleep on his sofa.

"You were right—the Christmas songs and the decorations—that church down the street—I'm having a good time," she said.

"Nice try, *Maman*," Sohrab said. "Still not a good liar. You're bored to tears. We'll take the Amsterdam Canal tour next weekend. You'll love it."

Zulaikha made a face. "Maybe you're bored. Not me."

Sohrab managed to take her to the Canal tour just a few days before her departure day. How she enjoyed watching the historic buildings from the water and listening to her son explain the city's history.

Sohrab had accompanied her as she got her boarding pass. His puffy brown eyes looked tired—but the puffiness was him—Sohrab had said people mistook him as part-Japanese or Korean. She had heard that when he was a child, too. He was now a young man standing beside her in the lineup to another separation.

He was once her eight-year-old boy who didn't want to part from her—nevertheless, he had walked to the Basij Range Rover, his tiny body obeying her demand, but his eyes betrayed him. They mirrored his pain. She'd had to send her child to a safe place far from the war zone. His eyes questioned everything. They especially questioned her decision.

Sohrab glanced at her passport. "I know I left you alone too much," Sohrab said. "Next time, I'll take some time off. I promise."

He put her suitcase on the scale and helped her to check in. The airline clerk pointed to the right with a smile. They had three hours to kill before the flight to Tehran. She could use this time to stay with Sohrab that much longer, but instead, she said, "I think I'll just go through security and find my gate. You go back and get good rest tonight."

"You sure?"

She stood on her tiptoes to reach his height and kiss his forehead. "Very sure," she muttered.

"This was great, *Maman*—especially all the food."

"At least I know you have food for a week."

They both laughed and held each other.

"I'm working tonight—I'll sleep on my way home," he said. "Ask Reza to call me when you land in Tehran." Reza was his old friend.

She nodded.

As Sohrab reached the airport's sliding doors, he turned around and glanced at her. There she was, feeling confused and empty, as if a microbe was attacking her immune system, making her thirsty and nauseous. Then the doors closed, and his presence faded from her sight.

Zulaikha followed the path toward her gate, and a few steps further, she joined a crowded lineup. She showed her documents to the security guard, who said hello and directed her to line number two—it was shorter than the others. Carrying only a handbag and her coat made going through security smoother, but the thirst still bothered her.

A bathroom and a water fountain were just a few steps away. Zulaikha searched in her bag and found her asthma inhaler. She often ensured it was there even if she didn't need it. After washing her face and drinking some water, she could see better, but still, the airport was like a full suspension bridge where she stood with so many other strangers.

Her boarding pass showed her gate number. She could read the number eight on it, and down the way, she saw a sign to her gate. She should be fine.

A man was approaching her. He looked familiar.

He might be another passenger, a friendly countryman who wanted to help a lost woman.

"Are you Iranian?" he asked.

Her heart shifted in her chest.

It was Kia. Only now, with grey hair. He looked shorter than she had remembered.

What should I do? Shake his hand? Kiss his cheeks or hug him?

It had been almost forty years since she last saw him. Long enough to erase many details from her memory, except the retained distasteful moments.

He spoke her name. "Zulaikha?"

She walked toward him, still trying to understand the situation. His hands held her arms as if trying to shake and return her to reality.

"Unbelievable! Isn't it?" he said with joy in his voice.

Did he still have his Khuzestan provincial accent, or was it a sweet American one he had developed all these years? Or both?

"What are you doing here?" Kia asked.

"I was visiting my son. What about you?" How embarrassing this heat was. Her cheeks must have been flushed.

He looked stunned. "Your son?"

Why is he asking me with surprise?

"My son, Sohrab. He lives in Haarlem—near Amsterdam. He just left. He had to go back to work," she said. "What about you? Are you flying to Tehran?"

"Yes, I'm going to—" He coughed. "Well, it's my father's funeral."

The word "funeral" echoed in her head. Jamshid, that strong, tough man, was now a corpse. A harmless corpse.

"*Tasliat*, God bless his soul," she sighed. "It's hard to believe so much time has passed, and *Amu* Jamshid is gone."

Kia thanked her for her blessing as he looked at his watch. "I think it's time to go to our gate."

Walking beside him, Zulaikha was careful not to show she was curious about his appearance or how he aged. She kept her gaze away and looked straight ahead.

Kia asked about her son's father. "Do you and your husband live in Tehran now?"

He's curious about my life, about Assef.

"Oh, we aren't with each other anymore. It ended long ago—even before the war—before I moved to Tehran."

"Who was he? Did I know him?"

"No, you didn't. My mother got married a couple of years after you left Iran. He was her husband's close friend. He lives in the Emirates now—sometimes in Dubai, sometimes in Kuwait."

"So you're still in touch. That's a good thing."

"We still talk on occasion. You know how it is when you have children. Do you have children?"

Kia told her about his life, his daughter Sherry and his separation from her mother. They both lived in Los Angeles, but Kia resided in Canada, in Vancouver. She had learned about Vancouver in recent years. Nasim's daughters had lived there.

A few drops of sweat cooled her forehead. She rummaged through her purse and opened a Ziploc bag. She used her passport and paperwork as a fan.

"So, your mother remarried?" Kia asked.

"Yes, she did."

"And she's well?"

"She passed away a few years ago, and her husband was killed in a car accident long before that."

"I'm sorry," he was louder than before. "You've been through a lot."

Silence reigned for a time. She was searching for a short sentence that did not sound like whining, words sharp enough to express that it did not matter anymore. Something like, "You left, but life did not stop," or, "While you were away, so much happened to all of us—not just me, but to your friends, too."

Instead, she said, "Yes, a lot is an understatement. Did you hear what happened to my brother, Hessam, or his friend Abbass?"

Kia stared at her for a few seconds. "I did." He looked at his watch again. "I'm very sorry about all of it."

They continued walking side by side and stopped at their gate. "My father wrote to me about Hessam and his disappearance—about Abbass, too," Kia said. "It was devastating for me. I always wanted to know how you and your family coped with it. I knew how close you were, but you know how it was back then." He stared at the flight display. "My father wrote to me about people—as if he read my mind and knew what I wanted to hear. He wrote to me that you were married too."

Perhaps it was Jamshid's guilty conscience writing those letters. Before that fateful night, almost forty years ago, when Jamshid knocked on their door in Abadan, Zulaikha had always respected him. He was a senior National Oil Company staff member—he always wore a black tie and white shirt. But that night, he wasn't wearing a tie. He was wearing brown Luri attire. Perhaps looking cozier would help manipulate his subordinates. That night he told Zulaikha's mother that he had a proposition for them. Some proposition.

Kia must have a first-class ticket and would separate from her soon. She would remain in her seat without thinking about him or the past, only planning for after her arrival: finding a taxi, sleeping, showering, and living her life. Kia, with his charm and politeness, and Jamshid, as a dead man—both seemed harmless. But what she remembered from them was far from harmless. She checked her bag for her inhaler one more time.

They noticed a commotion at the departure gate beside them as a KLM airport worker made an announcement. Zulaikha only understood the words flight and Tehran. She glanced at Kia. "What did they say?"

"Our flight was cancelled," he said. "What's wrong with you? Do you have asthma?"

"Yes, but it's under control." There was no point in telling him how she got her illness. The illness that had become a part of her identity.

She followed Kia to the front desk of their gate, where the blond woman from KLM was.

"All flights are cancelled due to security reasons." Kia translated it for Zulaikha.

"My son will be worried about me if he doesn't hear from me tonight."

Kia lent her his cell. "Call him."

She dropped a few items while searching for her journal in her purse. Kia helped her put them back, making her feel like a fool. She found the notebook and dialled Sohrab's number a few steps away from Kia in a more private corner.

"Do you want me to come back?" Sohrab asked. "We can hang out in Amsterdam tonight."

"There're many of us here—I think every passenger is Iranian, so I'll be fine. Not to worry, I can talk to people around me."

"Whose phone are you using?"

She did not tell him about Kia. "I borrowed it from another passenger here at the gate. I'll call you as soon as we're okay to fly or in Tehran."

When she returned the cell phone to Kia, a KLM employee gave all passengers directions for a shuttle to a hotel. Zulaikha followed Kia and the others, in part feeling lucky that he was there like a relative or friend to tell her what to do or what they were saying. Another part of her was annoyed and uncomfortable that the closeness had reasserted itself, even decades later. But every moment she walked beside him, the pain he and his father had inadvertently caused her so long ago became closer. Sharper.

In the hotel lobby, Kia asked her about her room number. "Let's have tea later this evening," he said. "It's so strange to see you here today right when I'm going to my father's funeral. Don't you think?" He hung his coat on his carry-on bag's handle and didn't wait for her answer. "I'll come to get you in a couple of hours—"

"Maybe it's best that you get some rest. It'll be very busy when you get home with your family and the funeral." She hung her handbag around her shoulder. It felt heavier than before.

"I know I won't be able to sleep. It's been days since I've slept. I think this may be an opportunity for me to explain things to you a bit."

"Explain?" She pressed the elevator button.

"Yes, about when—I mean—after I left Iran."

She glanced at him. He was still handsome and charming. Remembering her younger self's infatuation with him felt funny. "It was a long time ago. Do we have to?"

They entered the elevator.

But this would finally give her a chance to ask him questions—not just about what happened between them but what he heard about Hessam's disappearance.

"No, we don't—but I think—oh, this is my floor,"

"Okay, I'll wait for you," Zulaikha said.

■ ■ ■

Being in this luxury hotel was far from her reality in Tehran, yet as she showered, the scent of soap and shampoo was familiar. She had not thought about this smell for a long time, the aroma of Abadan's Kuwaiti bazaar. Running into Kia was awakening long-buried memories.

Figuring out how to make a cup of tea with the coffee maker was a feat. The room was quiet, and television programs were in English or Dutch. Her eyelids drooped, and she surrendered to the sleep enveloping her body.

A knock on the door startled her. She sat up and looked around, disoriented. Her half-filled cup, and the scent of shampoo and soap lingering in the air, helped her remember where she was and who she was waiting for. But why was Kia knocking so harshly? She looked through the peephole, expecting to see Kia. Instead, three men were on the other side of the door, two Caucasians and one man who appeared Middle-Eastern, perhaps Iranian. "Yes?" she asked.

One of them spoke Farsi. "Please open the door. We're from airport security."

"Is something wrong?"

"Ma'am, we just want to ask you a few questions. We are showing our ID cards. Please let us know if you see them." Two of the men held their identification cards up to the peephole. She couldn't read them and relied on the interpreter's speaking on their behalf.

She opened the door, panic rising in her throat.

"What's happening?"

The Iranian introduced the two men as his American and European representatives. "It's just a procedure, nothing to worry about."

"A procedure for what?"

"We'll explain. It won't take more than a few minutes."

"But I was about to see a friend. He's in the same hotel. I just ran into him before the flight."

The two men looked at each other. "Don't worry, Ma'am, you'll be back very soon," the translator said. "We'll leave a message for him."

They escorted her into a black BMW parked in the hotel loading dock. She tried to communicate with the Iranian fellow as they drove, but he didn't sound friendly. "Listen, Ma'am, I'm only an interpreter and not supposed to chat with you, so if you don't want more trouble than you already have, just sit back and keep quiet."

I am in trouble. But why?

"I just have to know what's going on. Translate this: I want to contact my son right now."

The two men listened to the interpreter as he translated her words. The American permitted her to call her son using his phone.

"I called to say—where are you?"

"I'm at work, driving, *Maman*. Anything wrong? Did you borrow another phone again?"

She paused for a few moments. "Yes, I did. Nothing is wrong. Sorry, I forgot you're working a night shift."

"Did they tell you when you can fly?"

"Not yet, but I just wanted to say I'm still here. Is everything okay with you?"

"Since we talked? Yes, I'm fine. You should get some rest."

The American glared at her.

"You're right. I should. Drive safely."

They arrived in the Amsterdam canal belt—Sohrab had taken her on a cruise there a few days earlier.

Disrupting her reverie, the strangers ordered her to leave the car. Taking the elevator up two flights, they entered an enormous office, surprisingly busy with people wearing earphones, talking in different languages she could not discern. It only gave her a lonely feeling. They passed through one office into a hallway.

"Here. Take a seat," the interpreter said.

A tall blond female officer at a desk gave her some forms in Farsi to complete and took her picture and fingerprints. She led her down the hall to a bare room and asked her to wait. The room had no windows—a wooden bench rested against one wall, and a chair stood in the centre. Four video cameras pointed toward the chair. She sat on the bench and looked down at the floor. Her ponytail still smelled of shampoo.

The two men and the same translator entered the room a few minutes later. The translator sat beside her, a bit too close. She moved slightly to the left, giving him space to make notes. The first question came from the American man.

"Sorry, Ma'am. This will only take a few minutes. I'm from

the U.S. Homeland Security, but I work in Europe. Our job is to prevent any suspicious activities or shipments to or from my continent." He glanced at the translator and paused for him to translate.

Zulaikha was about to ask what was suspicious about her when the American spoke again. "What is your occupation?"

"My occupation? I'm a housekeeper. Why?"

"What is your relationship with Mr. Kia Chaharlangi?"

"Did something happen to him?"

"Don't answer the question with a question. He's fine. Now, answer the question, please," he asked sternly.

In a flash, she remembered a bearded Iranian interrogator who had once told her, "Don't answer the question with a question."

"I ran into him in the airport a few hours ago," she swallowed. "I know him from a long time ago. He was my brother's friend."

"Your brother?" inquired the European man. "Where does your brother live? Here in Holland?"

"Why are you asking?"

"We just asked you not to answer a question with—"

"But your questions are strange. What difference does it make where my brother lives? He went missing in the war a long time ago."

"Which war?" the American asked.

Was the Iran-Iraq war already forgotten?

"Which war? The Iran-Iraq war, obviously. How many wars has Iran had in recent history?"

The men did not show any emotions. The translator looked down, trying to make minimum eye contact with her.

"How about your son's occupation and status in Holland?"

"What is this about? Can I go to the bathroom? I have asthma—I need air—I need my medicine."

Zulaikha could tell they were used to doing this, frightening people—putting a person's life under their microscope. But she was experienced, too. She should be firm with them. "I said I want to go to the bathroom and call my son again right now," she shouted.

The men glanced at each other. The Euopean man opened the door, and the translator followed her out.

"Who do you think you are?" She turned and yelled at the Iranian translator, "Are you following me to the bathroom or want to hear my conversation with my son?"

"Calm down, *khanum*. This isn't Iran."

"Oh, Iran sounds like an awful place to you?" she said grimly. "Why are they asking about my son's job? He's a hardworking driver. Tell them that."

"Keep your voice down," he said. "I thought you needed the bathroom."

The female Dutch officer, a broadly-built woman in her forties, approached them. She asked Zulaikha something with concern in her eyes. Zulaikha pointed at the telephone on the desk and tried to show her that she wanted to call someone. The officer put the phone in front of her.

The Iranian translator frowned and said something to the officer.

She dialled Sohrab's number and said, "Sohrab, *jan*. Salaam—don't worry, I'm okay, but I need your help—hold on—Can you hold, please?" She gave the phone to the officer. "Can you talk to him?" Then she said in English, "Please." Her desperate look worked. The woman spoke to Sohrab and then hung up, offering a kind smile.

"I think we should go back to the room," the translator said. "They're waiting for us."

"I need to go to the washroom—I've said that how many times?"

She went toward the sign of the female toilet in the hallway, and when she looked back, she saw the female officer talking on the phone.

As Zulaikha washed her face, she tried to understand her situation. *Why am I in trouble here and concerning Kia? They seem to be making a stupid mistake thinking we have any connection.*

She walked back to the Dutch officer's desk. The interpreter was no longer there. A tall, young woman with long wavy dark-brown hair was waiting for her. From the helmet she held in her hand, Zulaikha assumed that she had biked there.

"My name is Sheila. I came as soon as Sohrab called me," the young woman said in Farsi as she held her hand.

"Sohrab called you?" Zulaikha shook her hand.

"Yes, he did. I live close by. I work here. You're safe with me now. Don't worry."

Sheila greeted the same female officer in Dutch.

"This policewoman says she thought you were having problems with these men and their interpreter," Sheila said.

Zulaikha had been in Holland for three months, but Sohrab never mentioned this beauty. It was not the place or time to ask her about that. "You're a godsend," Zulaikha said.

As Sheila smiled, Zulaikha noticed the corners of her mouth. Her lips were upturned naturally, giving her the semblance of a smile even when she wasn't. "Don't worry too much. The Dutch government is afraid of scandals involving immigrants."

"Can I speak to Sohrab again?"

"Of course," she said. "He may be talking to an immigration lawyer he knows. Let's go and see what these gentlemen have to say to us."

Zulaikha followed Sheila back to the interrogation room, where Sheila told them she was a Dutch authority and gave them Sohrab's immigration lawyer's phone number. They made a call in the hall, and only the British man returned to speak to Sheila before leaving.

"Where did they go?" Zulaikha asked.

"Back to their offices—wherever the hell that is. They said you can return to Iran on the next flight."

"Return to Iran," Zulaikha repeated as if she had an option never to return. "Do you think they might report it to Iran, too?"

"I doubt that. The West's relationship with Iran is cold. But the Iranian aviation authority may ask why the flight was cancelled or passengers were kept for questioning."

"This can't be real," Zulaikha muttered.

"What's the matter?" Sheila asked.

"You know how it is there."

"Let's hope nothing happens."

"I don't know what would've happened without you," she said.

"I'm glad I could help. Would you like me to find out how your friend is faring?"

"My friend?"

"Yes, the gentleman you were with. Mr. Kia. Sorry, I forget his last name."

"I think he'll be fine without a translator. He's been in North America for a long time."

"Let me get you something." Sheila brought her a cup of tea and a chocolate bar. "Sorry, I couldn't find anything better."

The hot tea was an enormous relief. "I don't want to keep you."

"Don't worry. Let's wait for Sohrab."

They sat and chatted about Zulaikha's visit. "It's quite strange that I'm just meeting you now. I wish Sohrab had told me about you before," Zulaikha said.

"It's probably because we haven't been in touch for a while." Sheila used a rubber band to tie her hair up. "We met here when he was a newcomer. But then Sohrab found a job and moved to Haarlem—we were both too busy to keep in touch." She got up from her seat. "I think I'll leave you to rest a bit. You must be exhausted."

Zulaikha leaned back in her chair and stretched her arms. "So sorry." She yawned.

Sheila went to chat with her colleagues.

A tap on her shoulder woke her up. Sohrab was with another man—he seemed to be from Pakistan. "Wake up, *Maman*. We can go now. This is Kamal," Sohrab said. "He's my lawyer friend I told you about. I pulled him out of a Christmas party."

Zulaikha, still feeling groggy, got up to shake the man's hand.

"Don't worry," Kamal said in English.

Sheila put her helmet back on, and this time, she hugged Zulaikha. "So sorry we met under these conditions. You should visit again soon."

"I feel I've found a new friend," Zulaikha said. "We should keep in touch."

"For sure," she then glanced at Sohrab. "Let's go biking soon."

"After winter, anything you say," he hugged her. "You be careful out there. Okay?"

Even in the midst of her dilemma, Zulaikha noticed the spark between Sheila and Sohrab.

■ ■ ■

Kamal gave them a ride to the airport hotel in his red BMW that smelled of cologne. He didn't say much in the car, perhaps because of their language barrier, or it was too late to be chatty—it was after midnight. Zulaikha's flight was rescheduled for early the following morning, so they walked to the airport and sat in a coffee shop. Over tea, Sohrab told her what he'd heard about Kia.

"He travels to the Middle East and the US a few times a year—probably he buys and sells oil equipment," Sohrab said. "These days, with the sanctions against Iran, they seem to keep an eye on people like him. Those men had asked about my bank account," he chuckled. "They suspected he sends loads of money to us or he's in some illegal business with you. Some joke."

She rolled her eyes. "I'm an expert in all the troubles of the world."

"But, *Maman*, this man Kia, how far back did you know him?"

"I know him and his family from childhood, long before you were born."

"Were you close?"

"No." She answered abruptly. "Why do you ask?"

Sohrab leaned slightly forward with his elbows on the table. "Why don't I remember you ever talking about him? Was he Uncle Hessam's friend?"

What could I tell you about Kia and his family? That they killed my baby?

"Yes, he was your Uncle Hessam's childhood friend. You never met him."

"But I remember most of my uncle's friends. I remember Uncle Abbass like it was yesterday. But nothing about this man, Kia."

"Something happened between Kia and Uncle Hessam in the past. Their friendship ended."

"What happened?"

All these years, Zulaikha had managed to eliminate Kia from the list of friends her son should know about. What could she share in this airport just a couple of hours before leaving?

"Something very personal had happened between our families—I'm too tired, and it was a long time ago."

"Don't you think he was in contact with Uncle Hessam before or after his disappearance—if they were that close?"

Zulaikha felt dryness in her throat. "No. I don't think so. You've started investigating again. You never give up, do you?"

Sohrab patted her hand. "Don't be upset, *Maman*. I was just wondering."

She was eager for a subject change. She smiled mischievously. "It's my turn to ask you a question now."

He raised his eyebrows in anticipation of what she might be getting at.

"Why didn't you tell me anything about Sheila?"

"We're just friends, *Maman*. I met her here in the immigration office when I needed a translator four years ago."

"Just friends can change. Can it not?"

"You have a flight to catch, and I think they'll give you your new boarding pass soon. Call me from Tehran, okay?"

Zulaikha hugged him again. She hadn't cried when he'd dropped her off at the airport the first time. She refused to show her tears to her son, but now she couldn't restrain herself.

"What's the matter? Everything will be fine, *Maman*."

"I don't know. I'm suddenly worried. I don't want to be questioned again in Tehran."

"Hopefully, nothing will happen. I'll call Reza to give him a heads-up. Just call me when you get there." He kissed her cheek.

It was almost half past three in the morning when her flight landed in Tehran. She remained in her seat for a long time, until there was nobody left on the plane but her and the flight attendants. She was in no rush.

PART 2

Untimely Sunset

1950s TO THE 1990s

Like the moon, you appeared from the heart of darkness,
You created a world of love inside me.
Alas, by an untimely sunset,
You dragged me into the pit of darkness.

–Fereydoon Moshiri

CHAPTER 1

After the Coup

KHUZESTAN IN THE 1950s AND 1960s

That early summer of 1958 was the end of childhood for thirteen-year-old Zulaikha. In school, they called her Zuli *Siah*, meaning Black Zulaikha, for her dark skin. Most people in Abadan were dark-skinned, too, though her skin colour was the most prominent part of her, shades darker than her mother, Madineh, and her brothers. On the last day of grade six, she walked home with her mother, happy and proud of her excellent report card. They entered their courtyard when Madineh told her this was her final school year. Zulaikha sat in the corner of their yard, held her school bag, and cried.

"School wouldn't do you any good," Madineh said and went inside. In Madineh's world, no man would marry a girl with an education. Zulaikha was supposed to marry and leave home eventually, but she was still too young. Until then, she should work and bring home some money.

That summer of the beginning of adulthood, Zulaikha accepted her fate. No school from that year on. But it was too early to give up childhood. She wore sleeveless dresses—she loved her dark blue skirt with white polka dots. She borrowed her younger brother, Hessam's bike and rode from Co-Fay-Sheh and the

Arabs' bazaar to buy groceries. But something was different. Boys stared or whistled at her when the wind blew under her skirt, making a big circle of white polka dots. She had no idea how to react to such attention to her developed curves. She smiled at boys all through the bazaar. Sometimes Zulaikha sat outside a coffee shop alone and enjoyed a treat. An icy Coca-Cola or Pepsi tasted like heaven. If she forgot about the people around her, the neighbourhood boys told her older brother or mother that she sat before them licking ice cream. Then Zulaikha would get in trouble at home.

"A decent young lady would not behave like that in public." Her older brother Gholam shouted at her with his angry face so close to her she felt the urge to push him away with her two small hands. "Leave me alone, you big bully. I didn't do anything."

When Zulaikha was ten, her father, an Oil Company worker, suddenly left them. She remembered the day he packed and kissed her and Hessam and then held Gholam as he cried. But her father's image was fading from Zulaikha's mind—only a slim man with a moustache remained in her memory. He was always tired when he was home but kind to her. When he stroked her hair or held her arm, her mother, Madineh, shouted at him. "Don't go near children smelling like alcohol." His behaviour scared Zulaikha when he punched a door or broke a glass in front of their mother. A year after he left Khuzestan, they heard he died in Kuwait of a heart attack.

Madineh found work in the houses of British Oil Company employees in Beraim as a cook and housekeeper. She found Zulaikha a job in a British man's house in the same neighbourhood. But before she started her job, her mother had presented Zulaikha with a list of things to avoid doing in front of men. Laughing was at the top. "Do not laugh in front of men, especially foreign men."

"Why?" Zulaikha fixed her hair in front of the mirror.

"They will take it as a sign of flirtation."

She had learned flirtation meant inviting a man to come forward and touch her. It was a filthy word.

■■■

Before entering her new employer's house on the first day, Zulaikha gaped first at their lace-curtained windows opening to the street, then at the pink rose bush before the entrance door. Zulaikha's employer, a middle-aged man with a difficult last name she could not pronounce, took Zulaikha and Madineh to the patio in the backyard.

"Call me Mr. John if it's easier," he said in Farsi with his funny accent.

Zulaikha gazed at the daffodils, the *narges*, in the garden, desiring to leave the adults, sit on the grass and smell the flowers.

When Mr. John had parties, Zulaikha worked overtime and enjoyed dressing up and serving his guests. Most of them ignored her presence—they only saw her tray of food and drinks. Mr. John had a cook, a local man in his sixties who was very friendly with Zulaikha. She learned the English word "chef" and called him *Amu* Chef. He taught her to make a few appetizers, like a caviar plate with pickles and bite-sized rolls, which she hated. Funny, rich people ate them with such gluttony. Mr. John invited Ali, the neighbour's gardener, to help when needed. Ali was around thirty, and he worked shirtless on most hot days. He teased Zulaikha for her skin colour or full lips.

"Where you come from? Africa?" he said, "There—let's taste this together." He put his finger in the caviar bowl to taste it.

Zulaikha hated the way he smiled with his gaze at her lips.

It was *Amu* Chef who usually came to her rescue. "When are you going to grow up, Ali? You're not her age anymore. Put that in your mind, will you?"

Then, one Wednesday afternoon, Mr. John told Zulaikha to get permission from her mother to stay late to prepare for a big party the coming weekend. She had to clean the house and set up the backyard for the guests. Abadan's summers were always hot, but it was near fifty degrees Celcius some days that year. Zulaikha was watering the lawn when she saw Ali, the gardener, watching her. She ignored him and went into the kitchen to scrub the kitchen floor. She still had the patio table and chairs to clean, so she returned with a bucket and cloth after twenty minutes. Ali was not there. She relaxed and began cleaning.

"Do you need help here?" Ali mumbled from behind.

She straightened her posture. "Salaam," she said.

Ali took the cloth from her hand and came closer. Zulaikha stepped back and retreated to the kitchen. He followed her inside.

She stood by the sink with her arms grasping its two sides. Ali touched her arm—she could smell him—his hands reached her breast. She let him. But then he pulled her dress up. He wanted more from her.

No, why does he think he can do this? She pushed him outside and closed the door. Her heart beat faster.

She finished her work feeling distracted and guilty. Madineh had told her that people would say it was always a woman's fault if a stranger touched her.

Is it, though? Zulaikha wanted to ask, but Madineh read her mind. "People always win, Zulaikha. Right or wrong. People can crush you. Be careful out there."

When Zulaikha returned home that afternoon, her mother was not there. Gholam was in their bathroom opposite the entrance door in the courtyard. The door was open, and he was shaving. She muttered a hello and stepped toward the living room.

"Hey, *khasteh nabashi.*" Gholam was always in a better mood when their mother was not around.

Hessam, her younger brother, was not home yet. She assumed he was playing football in one of the neighbourhood alleys. In the kitchen, a pile of dishes was waiting for her.

Gholam appeared in his uniform. After dropping out of high school, he served his conscription in the local police station. Now he was off to work.

"Where's Mother?"

He shrugged. "How would I know?"

Gholam had come home two weeks ago, suspended for three

days for punching another soldier. The soldier had caught his father kissing their maid, Madineh. Then he spread the word that Gholam's mother slept with all kinds of men for money. "Tell me it's a lie, Mother," Gholam said with teary eyes. "You were like this to our father, too."

Madineh slapped his face. "I'm not a nun, but I won't let you question me."

Zulaikha wouldn't have been so disappointed by her mother's absence if it had been a different day. She wanted to tell her mother she did not want to go to Mr. John's house anymore. She crafted many stories to convince Madineh that she should not be working there but couldn't come up with anything better than telling her that she was not feeling well.

After washing the dishes, she took a shower and let the water wash away the sweat and fatigue from her body. The image of the gardener in her mind gave her a disturbing shock that she didn't understand. She was changing in their bathroom when she heard Hessam from the courtyard calling her name and asking for some food.

"Where's everybody today?" Hessam asked.

She stepped into the living room. "At work—where else?" she said. "Go wash up. You stink."

She gave him some of the leftovers she had brought from Mr. John's house the night before.

Hessam enjoyed the sausage cocktails and French-style bread. "Where's Mother?" he asked again.

This time she shrugged. "No idea."

"What's wrong with you? Why aren't you eating?"

"I ate already," she lied.

Hessam went to the rooftop to study and sleep. The roof, with its view of the city lights and the palm grove, was Hessam's oasis. She brushed her hair, went to the bedroom she shared with her mother, lay down and closed her eyes. But the recurring feeling of the gardener touching her breast struck her like lightning. She opened her eyes and sat up, then lay down again. Under the sheet, she touched her own breast. It didn't give her the same pleasure she felt that afternoon at a stranger's touch—until her finger touched her erect nipple. No, she shouldn't be doing this. She turned to her side and let her heartbeat slow down.

The familiar voice of the radio program woke her. Her mother listened to a program called *The Night Story* every night at ten. Madineh was smoking in front of the open window. She wore a tight beige blouse and black skirt, and her dark wavy hair was shorter than ever. Her silhouette in the moonlight was chubbier than before. Zulaikha noticed a new golden watch on her mother's wrist. She smelled a cloying sweet perfume.

Madineh never asked her about her daughter's day at work, but why? Did she think everything always went smoothly, nothing happened? Zulaikha did not understand Madineh for many reasons, but she knew that even if her mother did ask, she would never share anything that would create more trouble. When Madineh wanted to discipline the children, she became grumpier or left them alone at home longer. She once grounded Zulaikha when she was in trouble for talking back to her school principal. She locked Zulaikha in their attic for almost an hour. Zulaikha hated that attic because of the lizards that lived there.

"You cut your hair," Zulaikha said.

Madineh smiled in response but hushed her and continued listening to the radio program. The program ended, and her mother hummed a Vigen song as she changed into her nightgown:

> *My spring is past*
> *The past has passed*
> *And I am on a quest for destiny.*

Zulaikha couldn't resist saying, "I think you have gained weight."

Madineh threw a pillow at Zulaikha's head. "Did you see Gholam today?"

"Yes, he's kinder when you're not around." Zulaikha stretched her arms. "What's wrong with you two again?"

"He's still sore with me," she said. "He blames me since your father left. He treats me like I'm a criminal."

Zulaikha watched her mother as she brushed her hair. Madineh went to sleep quickly, but Zulaikha couldn't. She went to the rooftop. Hessam was sleeping with an open *Youth* magazine on his face—she gently lifted the magazine and covered her brother with a light sheet.

∎∎∎

The next day Zulaikha went back to Mr. John's house around noon. She wore a short sleeve top and a pair of dark jeans. She had put her dress in a bag to change into later for the party. *Amu* Chef told her that the guests would arrive after six. The gardener joined them later in the afternoon. He did not meet her eyes and acted like nothing had happened the day before. Zulaikha dusted the dining room, washed the patio, and tidied all the areas where she knew he wouldn't be.

"This area is spotless now. Come give me a hand in the kitchen," *Amu* Chef said. "Take those out, will you?"

Zulaikha bent to pick up the garbage bag. Ali, the gardener, offered to help with two. Her knees trembled as Ali walked behind her closely.

Later on, she changed, washed her face, tied her hair up, and made herself presentable for serving. The guests were four National Oil Company seniors and an American, all of them with their wives. She knew of Jamshid, a respected Lur man who used to work with her father. When Jamshid came to the kitchen to chat with *Amu* Chef, he recognized Zulaikha. "Zulaikha *jan*, is that you?"

She said, "Salaam," and looked down, clasping her hands over her lower abdomen.

"Look at you. You're a young lady now. How are your mother and brothers?"

"They send their regards," she muttered.

Jamshid gave her two tomans tip. Zulaikha shyly tried refusing it, but he insisted.

"Finish up and leave before dark," *Amu* Chef said after the party. "Come back next Wednesday, not earlier."

She grabbed her bag of leftover food. The gardener's indoor shoes were in the corner of the walk-in closet beside her shoes. He must have gone home already.

Her mother didn't come home for three days, as Gholam worked away in his post. She and Hessam enjoyed fancy leftovers. She biked to the corner store near Bahmanshir Bridge and bought a *Youth* magazine with her earned tip. She and Hessam solved an entire crossword puzzle. The gardener's images had begun to fade from her mind.

When she went to work the next week, *Amu* Chef was sick and resting in his room on the other side of the house. Mr. John sent Zulaikha to do the shopping. Ali was in the kitchen cleaning. He grabbed the shopping bags from her as their eyes met. She picked out the apples and placed them in the fridge. He held the fridge door. His eyes injected fear into her body. She turned away and brushed through him, but he stopped her.

He pushed her to the wall—his fingertips gently brushed her lips. "Don't be afraid of me—I know you enjoy this." He pulled her toward his chest and kissed her neck.

Zulaikha couldn't move, nor could she try to stop him.

He smelled like a spice that reminded her of her mother. They did not hear the footsteps of *Amu* Chef approaching the kitchen.

"Go home at once, Zulaikha!" *Amu* Chef shouted.

She ran out the door to her bicycle and rode back home as fast as possible.

She entered the house with teary eyes and found her whole family home.

"What's wrong?" Gholam asked.

"*Amu* Chef sent me home. I didn't do anything."

Gholam pulled her hand. "Take me to Mr. John's house."

"You calm down. This isn't your goddamned police station," Madineh demanded.

Madineh and Gholam had seized this opportunity to get back at each other.

"You're right," Gholam said. "Why in the world do I care about you or her? I'm out of here." He stormed outside.

"Yes, you go to hell," Madineh shouted as her eyes followed him.

"What's this about, Zuli?"

Zulaikha shook her head. "I don't know."

"Let's see what they have to say." She picked up her purse.

Amu Chef must have already explained to his boss the scene he had witnessed, but Zulaikha kept quiet. She herself had no idea what had happened so quickly.

Mr. John didn't sound like he knew the details. "Your daughter didn't get along with others in the household, Madam." Mr. John lit his pipe. "My chef wants to bring one of his friends in. He's more comfortable working with a boy than your teenage daughter."

"But she needs a job."

"Madam, you'd better find her a job in a more feminine environment, like in a sewing factory or for packing cookies," he said. "She's a hard worker—I wrote her a reference." He passed her an envelope.

"My son is a police officer. He would want to know what happened here. She was crying when she got home."

How odd. She's suddenly proud of Gholam.

"There, here's a month's wage." He passed her another envelope from his desk drawer as if he wanted to give it to them only if they objected.

On the way home, Madineh looked satisfied with the money. "I told you to be careful." She looked out the taxi's window.

Madineh, *Amu* Chef, and Mr. John reacted peculiarly that day, but it went rather well—she wasn't grounded. The evening breeze on her cheeks was pleasant. Too bad they had no leftover sausages from last week.

■■■

After Gholam was transferred to Ahvaz the following year, their house became more peaceful. Madineh did not tell them where she was going or who she was seeing. Zulaikha had become the cook and took care of errands. She went to the market for groceries through a path beside a field of wild daffodils that reminded her of Mr. John's backyard. Rats running along their alley always made her walk faster, so she could get to the boulevard, where she strolled or biked toward Bahmanshir Bridge and watched the river. *Istgah Haft*, where they lived, was not too far from Beraim, but felt as though it belonged to a different world.

When Madineh was home, she seemed more pleasant—she did not question them for every little thing, brought them good leftover food, sang songs, and listened to her night radio. Hessam spent lots of time with his friends, Abbass and Kia. Zulaikha knew Abbass but nothing about Kia, only that he was the son of Jamshid, the generous man who'd appeared at Mr. John's party.

Abadan's fogs in early spring were thick on the water, hiding the surface of the Karun River. Hessam had finished his homework, closed his book, and stood up to go outside when his mother stopped him.

"Where to? It's foggy tonight."

"Abbass's old man will return from sailing tonight. Abbass needs me."

"Needs you for what?" She stretched her arms and yawned.

"To stay with him on the shore and wait for his father to return."

"It's a school night. I'm sure he'll understand." She glared at Zulaikha, who was washing the dishes in the kitchen as if she expected her to say something in her defence.

"I don't want to stay home with you women—it's a foggy night, and Abbass wants to stay in the harbour, giving signals to his father. What's wrong with helping a friend?" he said. "Plus, his father will give me a big fish." He raised his eyebrows to charm Madineh.

"Okay, go, but stay out of trouble. I don't want to hear people saying that Madineh doesn't know how to keep her boys at home."

Hessam kissed his mother's cheek and winked at Zulaikha as he left. Zulaikha shook her head.

Madineh was about to bathe when they heard a knock at the door. Madineh let Zulaikha open the door as she stepped into the bathroom.

"Salaam, *Amu* Jamshid. Something wrong?"

"No, no, nothing is wrong. I'm just—"

Madineh hid her towel behind her and invited him in, but he preferred to stand in the doorway. "What's the matter then?" she asked.

"My son, Kia, he never returned from school today—we didn't know what to do," Jamshid said with a shaking voice. "Have you seen him?"

"Hessam went to the harbour to wait for Abu. Maybe all three boys are together?"

Jamshid suggested looking for them in the harbour. "I asked a neighbour to give me a ride here. He can take us there, too."

"You've told a whole lot of people about your son being late, and it's not even eight o'clock, *Amu* Jamshid."

She turned toward Zulaikha behind her and rolled her eyes. "And my kids call me controlling," she muttered.

Jamshid looked down.

"Can I come too?" Zulaikha asked. "I think I know where they are." Only yesterday, Hessam, Zulaikha, and Abbass gathered to watch the sunset. Abbass's father anchored his boat nearby—that would be the spot they would wait for him.

"Alright! Show us where to go."

The fog horns were repeatedly roaring. Jamshid's neighbour pulled over where Zulaikha told him to. They saw a small fire and three boys sitting around it—one was playing a drum, and the other two were sitting idly in the sand. Jamshid recognized his son and called his name, "Kia!"

Hessam saw them in the car and recognized his mother. He ran toward them. "Salaam, *Amu* Jamshid." When he received no answer, he asked Madineh, "What's the matter?"

Abbass stopped playing his drum.

Kia stood up and said hello politely. He looked too innocent for such a fuss. Zulaikha and Madineh both greeted him at the same time.

"You didn't tell your mother you would be late," Jamshid said.

"Sorry, nobody was home. What could I do?"

"You could have left a note. You know how to write, don't you?"

Hessam intervened. "It was my fault. I was waiting for him outside of your house. I think he was rushed because of me."

"This isn't what I call staying out of trouble. Didn't I tell you?" Madineh said.

Jamshid frowned. "What trouble?"

"*Amu* Jamshid, please forgive him," Abbass begged. "For my father's sake. It was just a mistake. We're all worried for him tonight. Look how foggy it is, and he's not back yet."

"How is your father these days?" Jamshid asked.

Everybody always calmed down for Abbass's father, Abu.

"He's okay. He wants to work."

"Soon, you'll be going to the sea instead."

"I will if he allows me," Abbass responded, holding the drum on his side.

"Don't stop playing your music. Go back to it."

Jamshid asked his neighbour to drive the ladies home and tell his wife they were in Khosrowabad harbour waiting for Abu's boat to return.

Zulaikha, like the others, was relieved by the peaceful ending of the father-son quarrel and reluctantly left. As the car drove away, she saw the boys running barefoot to the shore. Abu's boat was anchoring. Zulaikha smelled the saltiness of the harbour on her skin. Stars were breaking through the fog. She put her hand out in the air and wished she and her mother could ride in the car for a long time. This was the first time that Zulaikha met Kia. She did not say anything to him except a hello. He looked annoyed, but neither the thickness of the fog nor his disappointment could hide the beauty of his features.

∎∎∎

Zulaikha watched Kia stroll into their house like some Hollywood celebrity—his black hair lustrous against his light skin. He came over three times a week to study or play soccer. She waited for them to return from playing in the alley and found ways to impress Kia, but he did not seem to care for her.

Today, they were on the rooftop. She went up there twice to hang laundry, then took a basket of fruit and a glass of lemonade.

"Why didn't you call me for these?" Hessam said.

Kia said nothing—he didn't even glance at her.

She shrugged and went back downstairs.

She drank lemonade while listening Oum Kalthoum's long song, "*Laylat Hob*" on Radio Baghdad. She saw her reflection in the window and enjoyed dancing to the music for a few seconds until her tired mother returned home from work.

"It's a night from hell," Madineh said. "I walked six blocks in this heat." Zulaikha stopped dancing reluctantly and greeted her mother. She gave her a glass of icy lemonade and turned on the cooler.

The music was still playing, and Madineh hummed along and smoked a cigarette. "You know, I saw Oum Kalthoum performing on television. It was spectacular." She watched television at the home of her employer.

"When can we have a television?"

Madineh leaned back and puffed her smoke. "I should buy a lottery ticket. There's a winner every Wednesday."

After Kia left, Madineh heated leftover rice and chicken kabab while Zulaikha made a salad. At dinner, Zulaikha made Hessam tell her all he knew about Kia's family.

Hessam spoke about Jamshid's family with so much admiration. "You have to see and smell their Istanbuli rice—full of lamb, turmeric, and saffron. You should see how Kia's parents dress up to go to the National Oil Company Club."

"Why are you asking so much about them?" Madineh frowned.

"I only want to picture a glamorous family in my life."
Madineh sighed and lit another cigarette.
"Can you not quit smoking?"
"Don't annoy me, Hessam. I am too tired."
Hessam continued talking about Kia's family. "They bought a television a few days ago."
Madineh went to sleep shortly after that, but brother and sister took the radio to the courtyard and kept talking about the happy life out there, far from them—a life they could both have one day. "*Ahwak*," another beautiful song from Abdul Halim, came on the radio.

I love you.
And I wish I could forget you,
And forget my soul with you.

"Look at the stars tonight. Do you think there's any sky more beautiful than the Abadan sky?" Zulaikha said.
"I don't know. Maybe in America."
"America?"
"Yes, Kia talks a lot about going to America."
"That's really the other side of the world."
Hessam told her that Jamshid had made plans for his son to go abroad for a university education in England or America.
"Maybe it's better this way after all," she said.
"What way?"
"That we can't go too far from each other."
"I don't know. We have to leave and live our lives one day, too. Look how Gholam is right now. He doesn't live that far, but he doesn't care about any of us."
"I don't think I can ever be like Gholam. Even if I went to America, I would want to know how you are." Zulaikha folded her arms under her head.
"You? America?" They both covered their mouths and tried not to laugh aloud.
That night she had a dream about the gardener. He had been

out of her mind for many months but he appeared again. He touched her legs and slowly reached for her breasts. Her eyes were closed, feeling his moist kisses on her chest, but when she opened her eyes, it was Kia's beautiful face close to hers. She imagined him beside her, touching her naked thighs. "Stay. Don't go." She heard her voice.

The next morning, her mother was awake before everyone. Zulaikha took a shower and came into the living room, which doubled as the dining room. The morning radio was on. Zulaikha was drying her hair with a towel when she noticed Madineh glaring at her behind her tea.

Could she know about my dreams?

"What was wrong with you last night?" Madineh asked. "You moaned as you tossed and turned."

"Nothing. It was just a bad dream."

Madineh came closer to her. "Nothing?"

"What's wrong with you—first thing in the morning, Mother?"

"Were you crying over a boy?"

"What boy?"

"I'm not stupid. A mother knows that a girl cries about her sins when she doesn't talk about them."

"I'm not like you."

Madineh's look was stony. Her eyes demanded her daughter take back the insult. It was too late. Zulaikha could not undo what she had said to her mother and a burning slap struck Zulaikha's face. A slap to reposition the boundary between mother and daughter.

Madineh did not wait to see Zulaikha's reaction. Without looking at her, she grabbed her purse. "That was for thinking that you're better than I am." She slammed the door behind her.

Zulaikha wept by herself in the corner. The radio was still playing a song she thought she would hate forever. A song her mother loved so much.

Where are you, fairy?
Wouldn't you show your face?

*Why won't you open the door
to the hidden paradise?*

■ ■ ■

Almost one school year had passed, and summer was coming. Zulaikha learned about the World Cup in Brazil from Hessam that year. Playing soccer connected Kia and Hassam's separate worlds, leaving Zulaikha alone at home most days. She had lost touch with the girls from school—except Mahtab, who told her last week that her parents wouldn't allow her to hang out with Zulaikha any longer. She was not the right friend because of her mother, or because she was not going to school. Some days Zulaikha visited Abu and then strolled to the harbour to see Abbass. The harbour was the best place to cool off, where Abbass worked almost daily on his father's boat.

Abbass was always happy to see her. "Is Hessam playing soccer with Kia again?"

Zulaikha nodded.

"Kia is a good kid—never mind his issues—I hope Hessam doesn't look up to him too much."

"Why?"

"Does Hessam study like he used to?"

"Hessam is smart. He always catches up closer to finals."

A boy she recognized approached them. "Your key." He gave Abbass some money.

Zulaikha was curious about what just happened between them, but she didn't ask anything.

Hessam's absence didn't bother Zulaikha as long as he came home and told her about Kia's life. Madineh was out that night. An old friend, Habib's wife, had passed away and Madineh attended her funeral, which gave Zulaikha and Hessam some space to freely talk about Kia's family, about their things, their house. She imagined it to be even nicer than Mr. John's.

"Kia's mother, Maryam *khanum*, is obsessed with Persian carpets," Hessam said at dinner. "She can tell every region's

design. They just bought a silk Kashan pattern."
"Is Maryam *khanum* beautiful?" Zulaikha asked.
"Yes, not as much as our mother, but—"
"But what?"
"Well, she has nice things—sometimes—" Hessam scooped some rice. "Never mind."
"I know what you mean."
"Remember last week when they let me and Kia go with them to the National Oil Company of Iran senior club? I heard *Amu* Jamshid tell her that she looked like Ava Gardner."
"I would turn heads if I wore her expensive high heels, too." Madineh stood at the door threshold.
"Salaam," Zulaikha said. "How do you know what shoes she wore?"
"I just know. Look at these, for heaven's sake." Madineh bent over to take off her shoes as if she had been in pain all night. "I need some luck more than anything."
Zulaikha went to the kitchen to fill a big bowl with water.
"Maybe I should find a job." Hessam glanced at Madineh's blisters.
"No way, and no hanging out with Kia if your scores are low. The report card is tomorrow. Isn't it?"
"Let's go to the courtyard. You need to rest your feet in this," Zulaikha carried the bowl outside. "I think you're the prettiest woman when you're less grumpy, *Mother*." Zulaikha winked at Hessam. Neither could deny their mother's beauty—nor her lack of luck.

The next day, Madineh and Hessam went to his school together, but Madineh returned alone. Hessam's scores were good, and he had gone to Kia's house to spend time with him.

Madineh was in a good mood and told Zulaikha they should go to *shahr* to shop. She needed new shoes, and they could have ice cream. They were about to leave when Hessam showed up with a long face.

"What's wrong?" Madineh asked.

"Kia's scores are low. His father isn't happy."

"Who cares? We wanted to go for some ice cream—come with us."

"No, you two go. I haven't seen Abbass for a while—I need to wash my face," Hessam said. "Buy me something good—like some sunflower seeds." He went inside.

■ ■ ■

Zulaikha and Madineh had a good time downtown. Madineh bought a pair of white sandals. They sat in a tiny café and had *bastani* filled with pistachios, saffron, and rose water. They caught the bus to *Istgah Haft*. When they reached their door at the end of the alley, a man was there waiting. Jamshid had sent a messenger to tell her he wanted to see Hessam in his office.

"Oh really?" Madineh unlocked their door. "Would you tell him he should first ask my permission?"

"Mother," Zulaikha muttered. What if her mother's abrupt answer offended Jamshid?

The messenger smirked. "I'm sure it's good news. He speaks highly of your son, Madineh *khanum*."

Madineh's tone suddenly changed. "It's hot here. Have you been waiting for a long time?"

"I'll get you some water," Zulaikha ran inside to bring him a full glass of icy water.

Madineh let him finish the water. "Tell him I'll think about it."

When Hessam came back, he went directly to the shower. Madineh didn't wait to break the news to him. She stood behind the bathroom door on the other side of the courtyard.

"Do you know why Jamshid wants to see you? He sent a messenger."

"No, I don't." Hessam began humming a song.

"Can you leave him alone for a second?" Zulaikha said. "I'll go get some bread. Get some rest. We've been out in the sun all day."

Zulaikha had prepared a bowl of yogurt and cucumbers for dinner. She wasn't feeling well. She had cramps in her legs, but it was such a good day. She managed to hide her pain.

"Is this the dinner?" Hessam dried his wet hair with a towel. "I thought we were celebrating tonight."

"It was too hot in the kitchen. Do you want eggs?" Zulaikha asked.

"It's okay," he dipped a slice of bread in the yogurt.

"You didn't tell me what Jamshid wants," Madineh said.

"I haven't the faintest idea. I have to go and see what's going on, on my own. Maybe there's something wrong with Kia."

"I don't understand why he sends someone here. You're not an orphan—"

"I said I don't know, Mother." Hessam slammed the door and went to his space, the rooftop.

Madineh asked Zulaikha to go and fetch him.

"Tell him I calmed down."

Hessam and Zulaikha were excited to hear their mother's verdict.

"I'll take you to Jamshid's office, but will stop at the gate and wait for you. There. That's my decision. Take it or leave it."

Zulaikha lay back against the wall behind her.

"What's wrong?" Hessam asked. "You look pale—what did you two eat today?"

"Go lie down," Madineh said. "We'll go to the clinic tomorrow."

■■■

The first thing the next day, Madineh took Zulaikha to the clinic two blocks from the refinery and told Hessam to meet them there.

When they tested Zulaikha's urine, they asked her to lie on a bed. She was too dehydrated and needed a serum.

"Oh no—it was supposed to be a good day. I'm ruining it for everyone."

"What's the good news?" the nurse asked.

"My brother got good scores. We were going to celebrate."

"Don't worry, young lady—you'll be fine before you know it."

Madineh frowned and began pacing the room. "I'll wait

outside," she said ten minutes later.

It took almost an hour for the electrolytes to work. Zulaikha felt better, and she asked the nurse if she could go.

"Where's your mother? She needs to sign this."

Standing at the entrance door, Zulaikha looked outside. Madineh was sitting under a small tree. She got up when she saw Zulaikha.

"I think you need to sign something," Zulaikha said.

Madineh went inside quickly.

The sun was sharp. But nothing seemed to be as crucial as Hessam's news for Madineh. They walked back toward the refinery.

Hessam was running toward them. He looked as if he had won something. "I think we have to go for *faloodeh*. Next time I will buy—I will have money soon."

"What happened there?" Madineh asked.

"He offered me a tutoring job for Kia. What was wrong with Zulaikha?"

"Nothing. I'm okay." It was Hessam's day.

"I knew he could never find anything bad about you." On their way home, they bought a vanilla and rosewater *faloodeh*. It was exactly how Zulaikha liked it. Hessam would bring some money and tell her about Kia, their house, their food, and all the other colourful things she didn't have.

Zulaikha's intuitions were correct. Things were going their way. That year, in 1958, Hessam brought home their first fourteen-inch television—a gift from Jamshid for Hessam's hard work tutoring Kia.

■■■

Television changed Zulaikha's life. She now knew what Ava Gardner looked like, how she walked and how she kissed men in the movies. Zulaikha discovered beauty in the foreign actresses, yet she compared their hair, neck, and how they walked with women she knew, like her mother. Madineh was now in her early forties, still stunning, although chubbier than she had been—chubbier than those film stars. And lately, she'd had some health issues.

Zulaikha didn't go with her mother to the doctor, but saw Madineh's medicines on the counter. "What are these for?" Zulaikha asked.

"Just for my blood pressure."

Zulaikha stared at the bottle with disbelief in her eyes. "You're still young, Mother. Maybe he's wrong."

"The doctor says I should quit smoking."

"He's right about that one, though." She was longing for clean air in their living room.

Someone pressed their buzzer, but Madineh didn't let Zulaikha go this time. "I'll get it—it must be Habib." Madineh stepped outside, but she paused. "But come with me. I think he's bringing us groceries."

Zulaikha was comfortable when Habib was around. He was an old friend of her father's. There was something about Habib's manners. Madineh was kinder around him, too. She had been seeing Habib for a while. Zulaikha suspected it was after she reunited with him at his wife's funeral.

Beside the car, Zulaikha peeked at the contents of the bags. "Chicken?" Zulaikha said. "I'll make this tonight."

"You and Hessam have dinner. Leave me some leftovers for tomorrow."

"Let them eat all of it—good woman," Habib said.

Madineh put her hand on Zulaikha's arm. "Okay, don't stay up too late with Hessam watching television. The doctor said it's not good for your eyes."

For a moment, Zulaikha assumed her mother wanted to hold her. She couldn't remember the last time they had hugged. But this touch, this kind of look, was worth the world.

Zulaikha and Hessam ate fried chicken legs with potatoes that night, cleaned and set a small space in a corner for snacks—sunflower seeds and almonds. They were settled in, watching a dubbed American sitcom, *I Love Lucy*, when they heard Madineh turning her keys in the front door. Zulaikha didn't expect her to show up that night at all.

"What's the matter, *Maman*? You look pale," Zulaikha went to the fridge to bring everyone lemonade.

Suddenly Madineh was beside her.

"You should be more careful about what you're wearing in front of your brother. Do you understand?" Madineh said.

Zulaikha looked down and noticed that her mother was right. Her pyjama dress was above her knees. "But I don't have anything—"

"Wear my skirts from now on. Okay?" She was now a bit louder.

"Here we go again," Hessam muttered and went to the courtyard with his small radio he'd brought from Kia's house.

Zulaikha turned off the TV and went to their bedroom to change.

Madineh joined her there. She lit a cigarette and sat beside the open window. "Let's go to the Kuwaiti bazaar tomorrow."

"Really? To shop?" Zulaikha needed a better wardrobe, but why there? The Kuwaiti bazaar was usually for window shopping. But it was always fun to go there and watch wealthy tourists from the Gulf Emirates.

"Why not? Maybe a couple of dresses for you—you're taller than me now."

Zulaikha would be happy with a soap or small perfume, but now she would get dresses. Did something happen between Madineh and *Amu* Habib tonight that resulted in a shopping plan? "How was *Amu* Habib?" Zulaikha lay on her side to face her mother. Madineh's dress was too big.

"He was okay until his daughters' families meddled," Madineh said. "So I left early."

"They—his daughters are not nice to you?"

"I don't know—they spoke and sobbed for their mother in Arabic. I hardly knew the woman." She put out her cigarette. "He drinks—like your father. It frightens me," she muttered.

∎∎∎

The next day, as Zulaikha and Madineh were browsing the market, Zulaikha found a little boy crying in the corner of the bazaar. She took his hand, and they led him to the nearest police station. The boy's mother was already there. She screamed his name, "Rafi," when she saw her baby. From her gold and jewels, it wasn't hard to guess that she was an Arab Sheikh's wife.

Madineh and Zulaikha knew a little Arabic, and the woman, Aliah, spoke Farsi. She was from Bahrain and frequently came to Abadan to visit relatives. Madineh invited her for lunch the next day.

Aliah appeared to be in her thirties, slim and tall. She entered their house like a queen and sat on the floor with her three children, Hashem, Saba, and Rafi.

Madineh placed a cushion between Aliah's back and the wall and asked Zulaikha to bring her coffee. Aliah, excited by the warmth of their hospitality, said, "Come sit down with me, *habibti*. Let's get to know each other."

"Don't worry, *sayidati*. We'll be done in a minute." Madineh tasted the stew as if she was the head chef and Zulaikha was the cook. "It needs twenty more minutes—more tamarind paste, too," she muttered.

"Why don't you go and sit with her?" Zulaikha frowned. "I don't need you here."

Zulaikha served *ghalieh mahi*, a special Arab Khuzestani seafood stew and rice.

"Why didn't you marry after your husband?" Aliah asked Madineh.

"I didn't want a stepfather for my children."

"Good for you. Men can be problematic."

"What about yourself? Where's your husband?" Madineh passed a dirty plate to Zulaikha.

"He's in Bahrain. I married him when I was very young—I'm tired of him."

Madineh laughed and offered Aliah a smoke—they went to the courtyard together.

Zulaikha glanced at the children. Saba, the girl, went to sleep. She turned on the television for the boys and let them watch *Tom and Jerry* on a Kuwaiti channel. She looked out into the courtyard. It was a cloudy day—a bit cooler than other days. She didn't want to sit with Aliah and her mother and hear them talking about men. Besides, all that smoke made her dizzy. She made more lemonade and put some Danish pastry on the plates while waiting for them to finish smoking.

"How delicious!" Aliah said. "Would you like to come to Bahrain with me?"

This must have been only a joke. "Me? Of course, I would." She put a small plate of Danish down and glanced at Madineh. *Why does she look so serious?*

"I was just talking to your mother about my life in Bahrain," Aliah said. "I want to propose on behalf of my husband. You'll look after him and our children and be my friend, too."

"Mother?"

Madineh showed no reaction.

"He's a good man," Aliah said. "Girls marry like this. Trust me, it's not only you. I'll give you a good life there." She glanced at Madineh, expecting her to elaborate.

Zulaikha stood near the door to the courtyard with a steel tray in her hand. Hessam and Kia were planning to swim with Abbass today. The sky was cloudy—a good day for them to swim and not get burned. She glanced back at the kitchen sink and the pile of dishes she had to wash. She might as well start doing the dishes.

"This is very nice of you, Aliah *khanum*," Madineh said. "We feel honoured. Right, Zulaikha?"

Zulaikha kept rinsing the dishes as she stared at the running water on her hands, cooling her uprising temperature.

"More lemonade?" Madineh asked Aliah. "Do you, by any chance, have any pictures to show us?"

Aliah opened her purse and showed her a family picture

inserted into her passport. Madineh looked at it with satisfaction as if it was she who was to marry the Sheikh. She called Zulaikha, but she ignored her. She kept tidying up the dishes on the counter. "My hands are wet. Don't you see?"

Madineh apologized for her daughter's rude behaviour.

"No need to apologize." Aliah got up and returned the picture to her purse. "Think about it as a responsibility toward your family, Zulaikha *jan*." She dressed Rafi to leave and told the others to get ready.

What kind of mother would plan like this for her daughter?

As Zulaikha glanced at groggy Rafi, the little boy, then Madineh, leaving this house didn't feel too tragic.

"She's old enough to understand," Madineh said.

"No, *habibti*, she's just a child. We both know that."

This stranger suddenly sounded more reasonable than her mother.

"How about if I take you to the market so you feel better about us? I think my kids like you already."

Zulaikha grinned at the children.

"I'll make sure she's ready for tomorrow morning."

"I'll be here around ten," Aliah winked at Zulaikha.

"Please come for lunch after that," Madineh said.

"Oh no, we've been too much trouble for you already. We'll bring you food from a restaurant. How does that sound?"

"God bless you." Madineh hugged the woman and kissed her cheek.

Zulaikha couldn't sleep that night. She climbed the stairs and looked for the geography book she had stored with her other schoolbooks in the attic.

"Who's there?" Hessam was sleeping on the roof again.

"My geography—I'm sure there was a map to Bahrain."

"What's going on, Zulaikha?" Hessam's eyes were half open.

"Nothing," she said. "Mother wants to send me to Bahrain to marry a man."

"Maybe it's her trick to make you obey her more, Zulaikha. We'll sort it out tomorrow. Go back to sleep."

She found her book. Bahrain wasn't that far. It wouldn't be hard to visit Abadan, maybe for the *Nowruz*. By then, maybe her mother would regret her decision. A lizard moving fast on the wall startled her. She hoped she wouldn't share a space with a lizard in her new house. Instead, she hoped she would find a friend she never would have made in Abadan. But it wouldn't be easy on such a tiny island.

■ ■ ■

In the early morning on the day of Zulaikha's departure, Hessam was still asleep, his face covered with a blanket. She bent down and uncovered his face. He opened his eyes and asked, "Is it time?"

She nodded.

"Yesterday while you were out shopping with that lady, I asked Mother why you had to go, but she told me to shut up. She screamed at me, asking how much longer she could keep working. She said girls should get married and asked me to grow up in a hurry, too. Can you believe it? She thinks I can get bigger if she yells at me."

"Hurry up, Zulaikha," Madineh shouted from the courtyard.

"I wish you were bigger, too, Hessam," Zulaikha said. "Get bigger and taller fast, so no one can force me against my will. Okay?"

"Then I'll send for you. Would you come back to this hell hole?"

She kissed his forehead. "I think I would." She ran outside.

■ ■ ■

When Zulaikha and Aliah arrived at Bahrain's international airport, a man in a white *dishdasha* was waiting for them. Aliah introduced her to her soon-to-be husband, Sheikh Ahmed.

"Salaam," Zulaikha said as she would to any older person.

He wasn't as old or as bad as she had imagined. He had suntanned skin, a long forehead, and a bony nose. He only nodded and held one of the children—the boy, Rafi—and walked ahead of them.

He could be older than Amu Habib.

They all sat in the back seat of his Chevrolet. He drove along a boulevard that resembled Abadan. But their house—a few stairs at the front and its dome windows—was nothing like Mr. John's house. The facade was open to a field with no other houses in sight. Sheikh Ahmed spread a blanket out underneath a big tree. He lit a pipe and let Aliah take the luggage inside.

A narrow hall led them to the courtyard with a small pool in the middle. The children ran to their bicycles as if they had reached a finish line.

"Let's go change, Zuli *jan*," Aliah said. "You're not tired, are you?"

It was hardly a two-hour flight. Zulaikha shook her head.

"Cheer up. It can't be that bad," Aliah said. "Let me show you your room." They passed the hall again and faced two closed doors side by side. "There—and this is the children's room."

Her room was like a walk-in closet opening on to the children's room. There was no window and no bed—only a drawer and a closet for her clothes. A few folded mattresses were on the top shelf. She was supposed to sleep on the floor—like the children. She hadn't come to a palace, after all.

"This part is for you to have some privacy," Aliah said. "But you will stay in the master bedroom most nights."

This was what she feared.

"Which one is your room?" Zulaikha asked.

"Right here." Aliah opened the door to a bedroom—the one next to the children. She had a single bed and a dresser.

Their kitchen was the most impressive. It was larger than her room, with a big refrigerator and a door to the backyard. There was a small building on the other side of the house.

"Is that your bathroom?" Zulaikha asked.

"Yes, do you need to go?" Aliah opened the refrigerator door. "We need to go to the *souk*—there's nothing here."

Having a separate bathroom outside the house reminded her

of her own home. A good place for her to sing on good days and cry on bad ones.

"Go freshen up if you want. But be quick. Ahmed will take us to the town," Aliah said. "By the way, we should wear *aba*. I'll have one for you in my room. Come see me there."

Aliah had worn her *aba* since they met—a black cover from head to toe. The sleeves made it more comfortable than the other ones some Iranian women wore. Madineh preferred them to chador—she put one in her purse for attending a funeral or cemetery. Zulaikha tried her new *aba* in front of a mirror in Aliah's bedroom. She didn't like the way it made her look.

"You'll be safer with it—trust me, you'll see."

Zulaikha began to chuckle uncontrollably. Aliah had deceived her from day one. Her pleas to trust her were beginning to sound more like a joke.

"What's so funny?" Aliah asked.

"Nothing."

"I'm glad to see you can laugh finally."

She had no idea how Zulaikha only wanted to run away from her to find a corner to cry in.

Ahmed called Aliah from the courtyard—one of the kids was crying. They must be hungry now. When did they expect her to do her job? What was her job? Being their maid or babysitter? Or a companion? She would soon know.

■ ■ ■

Aliah wanted to go to the market before the shops closed. She left the kids alone. Hashem, Aliah's oldest, would watch his siblings—so Aliah said. It was a short drive into town, and Ahmed would return to stay with the children soon.

Zulaikha had seen Arab men in their *dishdasha* before, but here in Manama, there seemed to be many of them, and them exclusively. She spotted a few European women tourists walking near a mosque, but to Zulaikha, the rest of the population seemed to be only men on that day.

They bought vegetables and meat. Aliah lifted the heavy bag of groceries and placed it on her right shoulder.

"Let me try that." Zulaikha learned this lifting and walking that day. They switched the bag between them as they walked until they caught a taxi.

They sat on the floor to eat, just like in Abadan, but their dishes looked fancier—chinaware and crystal glasses. Aliah had made the dinner, an okra dish with mushy rice. Hessam would laugh at it if he were there, but they all ate heartily. Zulaikha helped with the dishes and cleaning.

"Would you like to learn to make coffee? We drink coffee—I know you Persians like tea more."

Zulaikha enjoyed making their strong, bitter coffee. It turned out well. Sheikh Ahmed glanced at her several times as he drank it, but she looked away.

"Stop staring at her," Aliah said in Arabic. "You're scaring her." She sipped the coffee. "*Ahsan*, good coffee, you smart girl. You understand Arabic, don't you?" Aliah glanced at her husband, as if she meant to show off that she brought him a girl with skills.

"A little bit. My friend—" She hesitated. "My brother's friend is Arab."

How will Abu and Abbass react when they hear about her sudden move to Bahrain? She wished that Abu would yell at Madineh, the same way he would sometimes yell at her, demanding to know why Zulaikha looked so thin or why she was working so much. But her mother would always win the argument when she said that she brought home the bread—not them.

As they sat, Ahmed smoked a pipe and said nothing in response to Aliah. He didn't talk much, kissed his kids, and went to bed as early as the children.

Zulaikha wasn't scared of him that night—they were not married yet. She slept in the closet next to the children.

■ ■ ■

The following day, after a light breakfast of tea, bread, and cheese, Aliah gave Zulaikah a white and baby blue floral dress and a small *surma* container. The dress was slightly oversized and made of soft cotton, but Zulaikha couldn't deny she was proud of how she looked that day with her glowing skin and the *surma* eyeliner Aliah helped her to use.

They drove to a notary public, where a mullah married them after reading a line from the Quran and asking them who would witness their marriage. Ahmed's partner, a man in a black suit and white shirt, stepped forward. Aliah and all three children sat behind them.

When Ahmed put a ring on Zulaikha's finger, she turned to glance at Aliah, her light brown dress was peeking through her *aba*, which covered her head to toe. She blinked and nodded with a smile to show Zulaikha that she was content. The children were strangely silent, as if they were competing for who could be the quietest. Only the older son, Hashem, asked his mother, "Is she our aunt now?"

"Yes, you could say that," Aliah said. "She's family."

Aliah let Zulaikha sleep in her closet next to the children's room that night. "I'll tell him you got your period," she said. "But you know we can't keep lying."

■■■

Zulaikha could not eat much for days, but she wanted to be polite and helped Aliah in the kitchen. Time went faster when she swept the floor or cleaned their fridge. But when she was tired and on her own, she cried uncontrollably. One afternoon, Aliah caught her crying in the bathroom. "Try to think about good things," Aliah said. "You'll buy things soon and send them to your mother. Dry your tears. Let's go to the Manama *souk*."

Browsing in the market, Zulaikha desired jewellery, nice dresses, French-scented soaps, and perfume. Why not? She had given up her miserable life in Abadan—a miserable life she was born to, a life she had no idea was so precious until it was taken.

So far, Aliah had bought Zulaikha nothing that expensive or shiny. Aliah tried on a pearl necklace Zulaikha had her eye on. She put it down when the merchant named its price.
"Believe me when I say I understand you. I was just like you when I married him."
"He was younger when you married him."
"I know, but I didn't know him. He was a stranger to me, too. As soon as you let me know you are ready to be with him, I'll give you money to send to your mother. Maybe even this necklace will be yours."
Zulaikha looked at the pearls and then at Aliah. She smirked in disbelief.

■■■

At the end of the second week, Aliah, having grown impatient, told Zulaikha to go to his room after dinner.
"I made him a promise I must keep. Do you understand?"
Zulaikha nodded slightly. Aliah couldn't postpone the new bride's duty any further.
Zulaikha took a long shower and managed not to cry, instead she hummed the tune to *"Ahwak"* until a knock at the door startled her.
"Open the door. I brought you something."
Aliah passed her a kit—hair lotion, lipstick, perfume—and a pink satin nightgown.
Zulaikha wrapped a towel around her chest and let her in.
Aliah helped her dry her hair. "You do it this way to activate your curls. There—it looks much better."
The dryer burned her skull, but she didn't react. The strange numbness in her hands and feet could have gone to her head, too.
Aliah took her to Ahmed's room, kissed her forehead and left.

■■■

Zulaikha was sitting on the mattress in the middle of the master bedroom when Sheikh Ahmed entered. He looked skinnier in his white robe. He was clean and smelled of strong cologne and tobacco. She hid her body under the comforter, lay on her back, and stared at the ceiling. He came near and patted her hair.

He spoke Farsi with a thick Arabic accent. "Have you learned some Arabic words?"

She nodded.

"Good girl. Is Aliah nice to you?" He slid under the comforter beside her.

"Yes, she's very kind." Zulaikha let him touch her breast.

"Good. I'll be good to you, too. You can teach me more Farsi, and I'll teach you Arabic. Can you dance?"

"A little."

Aliah had left the fan on, but Zulaikha felt heated under that thick comforter.

The man climbed onto her stiff body and looked into her eyes.

She had not expected him to be so heavy. The room was not quite dark. She closed her eyes to make him disappear.

"Aliah is a good woman, but she's getting old," he muttered. "She doesn't like me anymore. But you—young and beautiful." Parting her closed legs with his knees, he crept further.

She squeezed her eyes more tightly shut. "Please don't hurt me." A burning pain developed in her lower abdomen. She let her mind travel. She was biking—she always dreamed about biking beside Abadan's evergreen hedges. A warm wind blew her hair and polka-dot dress. A group of street boys whistled at her. Kia was among them, but far back. She wanted to wave at them but she thought she might lose control of the bike and fall. A nasty, painful fall. What was this heavy weight on her chest? Every push into her body made her heart beat faster. She wanted to push him off her. How dare this man allow himself such pleasure from her body? How invasive. She began sobbing.

The man moaned heavily, gasped, and stopped. He lay on his side and shouted, "Aliah!"

Aliah entered the room almost immediately as if she had been waiting outside.

"Take care of her," the Sheikh said. "She's bleeding."

"All girls bleed the first time," she muttered. "Didn't your mother tell you that?" Aliah walked her outside to the bathroom.

A frightening rustling sound made Zulaikha turn her head toward the tree near their door. "Can I sleep with you or the children? Please! I beg you."

Aliah gave her a pad she had kept in a cabinet and let her return to her room. The bleeding did not stop that night.

■ ■ ■

Zulaikha took care of Aliah's three young children, and even missed them when they were not home. On Fridays, their day off, she played with them and watched them climb the tree in the front yard as if she was their older sister.

At night, beside the Sheikh, she wasn't a child anymore. Her experience with men was limited to the gardener making passes at her and her fantasies about Kia. She wanted to remove the gardener's sharp and crude gaze at her breasts from her memory and keep Kia alive forever instead. His hair, smile, and voice. Sleeping with this much older man with his strange manner was her bitter destiny. She wanted to throw up.

Aliah had taught her to take one birth control pill before bed. To carry on each night, after taking the pill, she would plan to distract herself from what was about to happen. It was not just the man she wanted to isolate from her thoughts, but also her own unwanted pleasure, a pleasure that felt so natural yet so wrong. It was legitimate—like a job—to sleep beside him, to let him teach her things she wanted to know about her body. And his body. But the pleasure she felt was inhumane.

He should not see past me! No, he can't look into my eyes! Close your eyes. His lips are touching your lips. Turn your face, let him kiss your neck only. Wait until there's no weight on top of you. You are light now. Turn to your side and breathe, go to the bathroom and wash. He'll be asleep when you return—maybe even go and check if the children are asleep yet. If not, read them a story from one of their books.

A few nights ago, Aliah had asked her to stay with the middle child, Saba. She was unwell all day. After Aliah went to Ahmed's bedroom, Zulaikha drank hot milk with Saba in the kitchen and turned on the radio. She managed to find Radio Iran. "Kiss Me," the Vigen song Madineh liked, was playing.

In the morning, Aliah was colder with Zulaikha. This was the first time she had seemed jealous of Zulaikha. By the afternoon, her mood had improved.

"What was wrong with you this morning?" Zulaikha asked.

"Oh, ignore me," she said. After a moment's silence, she spoke again. "Okay—I admit, I didn't expect him to ask about you. He sounded like he's getting attached to you."

He probably said, *What the hell are you doing here? Where's the younger one?*

"And what did you say?"

Aliah had again brought up the same excuse: that Zulaikha had gotten her period. Zulaikha never imagined getting her painful period would be like going on vacation, away from the smell of tobacco and sweat.

■■■

Aliah had rented a big room from a friend, only a block from their house, and used it as a beauty salon. She and her friend, Leelah, mainly threaded women's faces and eyebrows, but sometimes they cut and coloured hair, too. The first time Zulaikha visited was on a sunny, autumn day after the children had gone to nursery. Zulaikha, on Aliah's request, walked to a nearby pastry shop to buy Aliah's favourite rose water and vanilla bean cupcakes.

The windows of Aliah's beauty salon windows were papered over with pictures of Indian actresses to hide the women working inside. Zulaikha entered the salon shyly. Near the entrance door, a waiting customer said hello to her. A magazine with a picture of a gorgeous woman on the cover caught Zulaikha's attention. The radio played a familiar song by Abdul Halim. Aliah and her friend were talking and laughing with their customers.

The salon smelled like hair spray and lotion, reminding Zulaikha of those days in Abadan when she waited for her mother to finish her eyebrows and hair. People would compliment Madineh, "Oh, look at those hazel eyes! Now, with those thick black eyebrows, you should watch out—men will drop dead for you." Madineh was aware of her beauty, without a doubt. Zulaikha often wondered why she did not resemble her mother. Was it a curse? Or was her mother's beauty a curse? Madineh always told her that such beauty never brought her happiness. Happiness might have made her a better mother— one who wouldn't ship her daughter away.

Zulaikha greeted the working ladies as she put aside the box of cupcakes. She browsed the magazine and learned the beautiful actress's name was Sophia Loren. Madineh used to bring magazines home from her employer's house. She had told her children that she'd been in school but had forgotten the alphabet. Madineh picked the articles with pictures she liked and would ask Zulaikha to read them aloud and tell her all about the world out there.

Leelah looked younger than Aliah. She had a long ponytail and a black headband that Zulaikha thought made her face look spectacular. Like Aliah, Leelah spoke a southern Farsi dialect. They were *Ajams* of Bahrain who knew both Arabic and Farsi. Aliah broke Zulaikha's thoughts by saying, "Come here—don't be shy. Make us some coffee. It'll be good with the cupcakes."

Zulaikha served coffee and cupcakes happily and listened to them chatting and laughing about their men, how the world had changed, and why women should learn to be independent.

"I've heard so much about you." Leelah sipped her coffee.

Aliah tells her about me. I wonder if she says I'm the trophy wife or the girl she saved from a miserable home.

"Aliah is very kind to me," Zulaikha said.

Leelah kept talking to Zulaikha as she worked on a woman's

hair colour. "Yes, you're lucky, darling. You see, she picked you to be her *havoo*, her rival. Not all women do that."

Zulaikha knew that had it not been her, Ahmed would have married another girl by now, anyway. Some days when Aliah found Zulaikha sad, she would share stories to calm her down. "A family member told me he was looking for a young wife. It would happen sooner or later—then that day when you found my boy—it dawned on me, who'd be better than you?" Aliah wanted to be innovative, to find someone who would serve her and her children, too.

Zulaikha poured coffee and glanced at her reflection in the mirror.

Aliah now addressed Leelah. "Ahmed is nicer to me since Zulaikha started living with us. Look what he bought me yesterday." Aliah showed off her new golden bracelet. "It must be magic she knows." She winked, and the women giggled.

"For heaven's sake, share some of that magic with us, too," Leelah said. "We could use some."

"She never shares, at least not with me. Maybe you'd have more luck," Aliah said.

Zulaikha picked up a cupcake and ignored them.

Aliah looked at Leelah playfully, as though they had been scheming. "Come—Zuli—take a seat here. We're not that busy today. Let's give you a make-over."

They threaded her face and eyebrows and cut a bit of her hair.

"Look at you," Leelah said. "Aliah had no idea how you would transform when she picked you," Leelah muttered in her ears.

Zulaikha liked her reflection in the mirror. She hadn't noticed her black eyelashes before. The atmosphere and attention pleased her even more. She should call home soon and let her mother know that things were not bad for her anymore. From that day on, whenever she was bored while the children were at nursery, she went to the salon to help Aliah. She became interested in doing women's hair and makeup. Soon, she started to work more hours and even earned some tips.

Aliah didn't only work for fun and independence. Some days

she whined about money problems and called her husband lazy. Sheikh Ahmed complained about fatigue. He didn't eat much and had lost more weight. They never fought, but now Zulaikha understood he did not have as much as Madineh had believed. He was a small-time merchant selling textiles in Manama.

■■■

It hadn't rained once the three years Zulaikha had lived in Bahrain. The sound of thunder startled them on that winter night. The Sheikh said that he was tired and went to sleep early. Zulaikha tossed and turned, and when she heard the children and Aliah talking in the kitchen, she joined them. None of them could sleep that night. They made coffee while the children drank milk and snacked on cookies. By then, her Arabic was better, though she still spoke with them in both languages.

"I am proud that my children have learned Farsi," Aliah said as she poured milk into her coffee. "I owe it to you—they'll have a better future in Khuzestan."

Zulaikha stopped eating her cookie. "Really? You see a better future in Khuzestan?"

"Of course! It'll be much better there for my children. At work, I listen to the radio news about Iran's oil resources, the country's relationship with America, and Shah's different plans for improvement. What do we have here in this small hole?"

Zulaikha shrugged her shoulder and yawned. It was getting late, and Aliah asked everyone to call it a night.

When Zulaikha returned to the bedroom, Sheikh Ahmed's sleep seemed peaceful and deeper than usual—he was not even snoring. She lay beside him. Another crack of lightning brightened up the room. She thought back to rainy days in Abadan, playing with Hessam in the courtyard. Their mother would call them to come inside, but they'd refuse. They'd keep playing until the rain stopped and they were soaked from head to toe. Madineh would laugh when she saw them. How was it that their mother could be so kind some days? What could Zulaikha do to keep her that way? That night, it dawned on her that Madineh was kinder when it was raining. Maybe it was walking back home from work in the heat that made her cranky.

The room felt cold. She turned her back on her husband and closed her eyes. When she woke up in the morning, the room was too quiet. Ahmed was there beside her but no breathing or snoring sound. "Ahmed?" she called his name and gently shook his arm but received no response. The Sheikh was dead.

When Aliah heard Zulaikha's scream, she opened their door abruptly and stepped inside with fear in her eyes. She muttered his name as she sat and pulled his motionless head, and rested it on her chest.

"Go to the other room and stay with the children," Aliah ordered her with a shaking voice.

"What are you going to do?" She felt nauseous as she stood up.

"He's gone, Zulaikha—I must find the coroner and take care of the funeral. I don't want the children to witness all of that. Do you understand?"

Zulaikha nodded. Before entering the children's room, she heard Aliah mourning and sobbing. "What am I going to do now without you, *habibi*?"

Saba and Hashem were staring at her, expecting an explanation. "*Baba* is sick, isn't he?" Saba asked.

Zulaikha felt a painful lump in her throat. "I think so. Let's pray—can you pray?"

All of them sat down in the direction of *Qibla* and read *Alfitah*, the only sura from the Quran she had memorized. "…*Ihdina'sarat'al mostaqim.*" Guide us to the straight path.

■■■

The funeral and mourning passed quickly. Zulaikha inherited one hundred dinars, not a penny more. The money was enough for her to rent a room for six months or to save for a rainy day. Aliah allowed her to have the Sheikh's old radio but told her to behave and avoid listening to music. In Muslim tradition, they would remain in mourning for forty days.

On a chillier winter day in that year, Zulaikha switched to Radio Tehran while cleaning the kitchen and listened to the enthusiastic voice of the news anchor reporting about the Shah's impact during Iran's White Revolution. She stopped working and listened more carefully.

"Soldiers serving as schoolteachers in villages have reduced illiteracy in the rural population. These soldiers are our Army of Education, *Sepah e Danesh*."

That afternoon she wrote to Hessam and told him she had heard about this new plan.

> I just listened to the news about *Sepah e Danesh*. Let me know if this means you can teach in a Khuzestan village as a conscript instead of serving in a faraway city.

A month later, she received Hessam's response.

> My Dear Sister:
> My assignment is strictly military, but thankfully, not too far. I am going to serve in Bushehr. Kia, on the other hand, will go to Rasht in the North. He will be near the Caspian Sea. *Amu* Jamshid tried his best for both of us. Mother doesn't say it, but she misses you a lot. She is very upset about you becoming a widow. I think she wants you back. Keep writing to me.
>
> Hessam

A week before the forty days curfew, Aliah no longer wanted to wear black. She, Zulaikha, and the children all went to the market, and Aliah bought new garments for her children and herself. She picked a green dress for Zulaikha. "Green is nice on you. I no longer want us to look sad in front of my children. Go and try it on."

Zulaikha tried on the dress and examined her reflection, looking carefully at the size of her waist and breasts in the mirror. "Does this mean you want me to stay in Bahrain?" She showed the dress to Aliah.

Aliah sat down on a small ottoman in the corner and sighed. "You can stay, but I need you to work in the salon. Otherwise, I may not be able to afford you anymore."

Zulaikha hugged her, and they went for ice cream.

Working in the hair salon and being the housekeeper made her tired, but she didn't mind any of it. Things changed, though, when Aliah told her, "I'm thinking about renting your—I mean, the children's—room out. Life is getting a lot harder. If you want to stay, I can reduce the rent from your wage."

"But then I can't send my mother money."

"What about your brother? Why do you have to take care of them?"

"My brother is a conscript. They don't pay that much to soldiers." She agreed to pay her rent and send less money to Iran.

Two weeks later, as she was leaving the house to go shopping, she found a letter from Madineh. She began to read it as she walked.

> **Enough of disgrace. That woman lied to me about her husband from day one. I didn't send you there for slavery. There is no reason to stay there unless it's your way to get back at me. All I did was for your own sake.**

Zulaikha put the letter in her purse and walked to Manama's Fishermen Port. She stood in front of a fence that opened to the ocean. Abadan was just on the other side.

As always, Madineh was mean in her letter, but she was right—there was no reason for Zulaikha to stay there anymore.

On one of the final days of that winter, Zulaikha returned to Abadan. As her airport taxi pulled away from Aliah's home, she glanced over at Aliah and the children standing beside the tree, waving at her. Rafi was crying loudly. She was leaving behind a life of unwanted sex as a second wife, taking care of children, and experiences in a world away from Abadan. She would miss the children—mostly Rafi. She would miss working, dressing up, and laughing freely with her friends in the beauty salon. With Hessam being away, she would be with Madineh most of the time. Perhaps Madineh would try to find new men for Zulaikha to marry, or she might complain all day long. Regardless, she longed to hug her mother when she arrived in Abadan.

■ ■ ■

Hessam also came home in early spring to celebrate the Nowruz with them. Gholam didn't, but Hessam said they wrote to each other. He had visited him in Bushehr. "Gholam is getting married," Hessam said before the Nowruz ceremony.

Madineh's look changed. "He's so ungrateful. Who is she?"

Hessam and Zulaikha exchanged a look. Hessam passed his mother a small gift box. "Maybe it's better to give him the space he wants. She's a nice girl. Her name is Kobra."

As the radio announced the exact time of the vernal equinox, Madineh kissed Zulaikha and Hessam's foreheads, giving each a coin as *eidi*, and opened her gifts—Hessam's gift was a Fidji perfume. Zulaikha had brought her soaps and cosmetics and pillowcases from Bahrain. Hessam's gift for Zulaikha was a white headband. "I saw a girl wearing something like this and thought of you," he said. "But you look so different now."

"A girl?" This time Madineh and Zulaikha exchanged a look.

Zulaikha hadn't thought about Kia, or anyone else for that matter, until that afternoon when Hessam dressed up to visit Kia's house and show his gratitude to Jamshid's family. He returned with English cookies and said Kia was also visiting his parents.

After lunch the following day, Madineh suggested they visit Abbass's father. Abu, the sailor, was now home after another back injury, unable to return to the sea. Zulaikha wore her green dress. Hessam and Madineh were waiting for her in the courtyard. They were just about to leave when someone knocked. She heard a man's voice from the other room. It was Kia.

"I'm sorry for barging in—you all seem to be leaving." He looked more mature than she remembered.

Hessam tapped his shoulder and suggested he accompany them. After all, they all knew Abu and his son.

Abu's house was in Bahman Shir, on the other side of the city, where the fishermen lived. It was a small house, kept clean and organized mainly by Abbass. Their small courtyard smelled like jasmine in springtime. Feeling uneasy near Kia, Zulaikha stared at their garden. Abu asked her about Bahrain and told her that he was sad when his son told him about her husband's passing.

"Living in Bahrain was not easy at first, but I was getting used to it—then he died." She glanced at Kia, wishing his face would be the one to replace her dead husband's image in her dreams.

Abu turned to Kia. "Young man, you're Jamshid's son. Right?" he asked.

"Yes, sir."

"You have turned into a handsome young man. Are you serving in the military now?"

"Yes sir, but I'm in *Sepah Danesh*," Kia muttered shyly.

"At least you're not serving at dangerous borders. You teach little children. Where do you serve?"

Zulaikha and Abbass served plates of cookies and tea, and that was when her eyes met Kia's. They spoke of desire. She turned away but looked again a moment later. On that early spring afternoon, she was rejuvenated like the wild clovers and pansies of the valley blossoming near Abu's house.

■ ■ ■

Abu in Arabic means Father. Everyone called Abbass's father *Abu*, as if it was his real name, as if being father to Abbass was his identity. Abu and Jamshid had been childhood classmates. Abu had never applied to work for the National Oil Company, as many others did then. He remained a fisherman.

Madineh had told Abu's story to her children enthusiastically several times.

"Abu married Ableh, my childhood friend, when he was only twenty and she was fifteen—they had Abbass five years later."

Madineh sounded envious. Now, Zulaikha was filled with the same envy for others' love stories. She asked her mother to tell her about their stories again.

"They loved each other like school kids. She welcomed him with open arms whenever he returned from his long fishing trips. He bought their tiny house and cared for his wife and son. After Abbass, they wanted more children, but no other child came. No one knows why. Ableh died from liver disease when Abbass was only ten years old. Until the last month of her life, no one knew she was ill. We just saw that her eyes were turning yellow. Even after her death, Abu still had to go to sea to feed Abbass. Neighbours and acquaintances insisted that he marry again, but he refused. He told people that he did not want his son to be raised by a stepmother, but the truth was that he could not let the dead woman go. He felt responsible for her death. Once, he told me he did not love the sea as much as he used to—he even despised it. Abu was the master of the sea, and as he got older, he did not even fear the storms. One day when I was visiting him, Jamshid made an appearance, too. He told Abu, 'I heard about your boy being alone and out of school—you don't have to do this. I could put in a good word to the Oil Company, get them to hire you.'

"Abu said, 'I am my own man, Jamshid. I am no servant of the British. I belong to the sea.'

"'We are all servants,' Jamshid had told him, 'Servants of someone. Just look at your boy. He is dropping out of school so soon.'

"'We live our lives the way we want, Jamshid. My boy will turn out fine. Mind your own business.'

"The night Abu fell, he had not felt well for days. Stubbornly, he'd continued working but felt worse on the sea. He'd fallen and injured his back, hauling nets onto the boat. He was never the same man after that accident."

Zulaikha resumed going to their place and helping Abbass clean and cook meals. Abu strolled along the riverside with his new wheelchair some days. It was rather strange how tidy their home now was—some cookies on the plate on the counter—as if it was a small motel. One day, a young couple opened the door when she was leaving. Abbass must have given them a key. They were startled by Zulaikha's presence.

"I was just leaving," Zulaikha said. Outside, she chuckled. Abbass had found a sneaky way to take advantage of Abadan's rich kids.

■ ■ ■

A few days after their new year's visit, Zulaikha offered her help to Abbass when she heard he needed a hand with Abu. After lunch, she gave him a prescribed painkiller and left him to sleep. She was washing the dishes when Kia appeared unexpectedly.

"What are you doing here?" she asked.

"I came to see you," he muttered.

"How did you know I was here?" She avoided looking at him.

"Abbass told me."

"And you told him you would come here to see me?"

"Of course not. I saw him at the port and asked him about his father. He told me you were with him."

"This is not right." She rinsed a plate.

"I know—but I can't keep you out of my mind."

It was strange how easy it was to have him there near her. He came closer and held her wet, trembling hand. A curtain dividing the rooms stirred gently in the warm air. Abu was in a deep sleep. Abbass's single bed was in another corner as if calling to her. She pulled Kia toward her and sat on the bed. Kia sat on the floor and touched her thighs underneath her skirt. How different his touch was. Nothing else in the world mattered but this touch. His hands worked their way to more sensitive parts. Their lips met for the first time—Kia unzipped his pants and pushed himself inside her slowly. Their bodies intertwined so tightly—distinctly different from the way her late husband invaded her. She put her hand on his mouth when he came. His body grew rigid, then slowly relaxed.

It was like Zulaikha woke up from a blackout. They were on Abbass's bed. "You'd better leave," she muttered.

He ran outside and left her there. She had not experienced the same release as Kia. Her skirt was soiled. She went to the bathroom, washed, finished a couple of dishes, and sat beside Abu. He was awake now.

"Your tea is in the teapot. Your son will be here soon. I must go now."

Following that first encounter, Kia and Zulaikha went to Abbass's house whenever they found a minute, whenever they could escape from their homes and affairs. One day Kia had just got there when Abu asked for some water. Kia startled by Abu's loud voice, dropped his Ray-Ban glasses, but he picked them up quickly, and hid in their tiny courtyard while Zulaikha ran to the fridge, poured Abu some water, and took it to his bed.

"You're here often these days, Zulaikha. How's your mother?" Abu's greying beard had covered his wrinkled, weathered face.

"She's good. Abbass told me that you would like to have company. Besides, I like your garden."

"That's nice. Who's here with you?"

"No one. Abbass asked me to come and clean your kitchen—was I too noisy?"

"You did not have to, young lady—" He tried to sit and drink the water. "If you need to be away from Madineh, I can talk to her."

She heard Kia leave. Abu's swollen eyes noticed something, too. "What was that?"

"Let me see." She pretended that she had checked the other room. "It's nothing—just the wind. I'll make some tea. Will you have a cup with me? I found some cookies in your cupboard, too."

"God must be on my side today. Yes, dear. It's been so long

since I had tea with an elegant lady like you."

He calls me elegant.

After tea, she helped Abu take a walk outside. Zulaikha watered the jasmine tree and washed the courtyard. When she was done, she returned inside to pick up her purse beside Abbass's bed, where she and Kia had made love. She tried to make the bed look perfect. The sheet still smelled like Kia.

She was about to leave when Abbass returned from fishing. He remarked on the fresh smell of detergent. "Oh, no wonder. Zulaikha's here."

"She's been keeping me company. We just had tea," Abu said.

Abbass glanced at the plate of cookies.

"Having company is nice," Abu coughed. "But why do you tell her to clean the kitchen and wash my garments?"

"Did I do that?" He glared at Zulaikha. "I don't remember."

"It's no problem, Abu—I've got to go now."

Abbass walked with her outside. "Everything okay, Zulaikha? I didn't ask you to clean. Did I?"

"No, I'm sorry. I shouldn't have said that. I thought it would be more convincing—you know how he is." She had to walk away faster, or she would have to lie more and more.

She strolled a longer distance than usual. She stopped by the telecommunications office to make a phone call. She gave the destination phone number to a clerk and waited for the clerk's announcement that a telephone cabin was free. There weren't many cabin cubicles available, and the wait could be long, but she was in no rush to go home and face her mother. She filled out a small form requesting to make a call to Manama. After a ten minute wait, she spoke to Aliah and Leelah. They made her laugh and cry with their excited voices telling her about the salon, and then they asked her to send them shampoos and perfumes they couldn't find there.

"Wait a minute, ladies," Zulaikha responded. "I'll need money for this upfront."

It was about time she showed some boldness.

"That's fair," Leelah said. "Maybe you should become one of

our salon's suppliers. We hear Abadan is the Los Angeles of Iran these days."

"Yes," Zulaikha chuckled. "You can't see me right now, but I'm in a short dress." The connection began to break up. "The signal is weak——hello? Oh, give the kids my love." She hung up but froze for a moment as she recalled finding Rafi, Aliah's youngest child, in the bazaar. They had developed a bond since that first day. It took her weeks to get over the image of Rafi sobbing in his mother's arms, reaching for Zulaikha's taxi as she'd left for the airport.

At the bus stop across the street from their home, she ran into Hessam.

"Hey. You won't believe what just happened," Hessam said.

"What?"

"Abbass had found us on the football field. He was so angry. He asked Kia for his key," Hessam said. "Where have you been. Is everything okay?"

"I went to Abu's, then to the telecom office to call Bahrain."

"Oh, you still talk to that lady—Aliah?"

"Shouldn't I?"

"I wouldn't. I would cut her out of my life—but we're different—"

She glanced at him. "If I wanted to stop talking to all the people who had hurt me—Oh, never mind. What happened there on the football field?"

"Abbass was acting strange. I asked him what's wrong—you know what he said?"

Zulaikha swallowed. "No, what?"

"He said it's between Kia and him. Can you believe this? I haven't even been away an entire year, and already I'm a stranger—"

"No, it's not about you. Kia's been away, too. Something must have happened between them."

She didn't intend to give him any hints, but it wasn't fair to hurt Hessam. If only he knew their fight was about her.

"Maybe you're right, because when I asked Abbass to tell

me—" Hessam stopped walking as if he was putting two and two together. "He told me to give him some time."

They got to their front door. "I don't want Mother to know about this," Hessam said. "She would make a fuss."

Zulaikha could not agree more.

∎∎∎

Zulaikha's period was already two months late, but until the morning sickness started, she was too scared to tell anyone what might have happened. She had been home from Bahrain for almost eight months. It was impossible that the baby was Ahmed's child. She wrote a note to Kia.

> **I must see you. Please don't ignore this message. I will explain.**

She wanted to send him the note by messenger, but who would take it without reading it? Who could she trust? She had no courage to ask anyone for his mailing address, either.

Madineh was the first to figure it out. "You must tell me who the father is." She was beside the bathroom door in the courtyard.

Zulaikha said nothing.

"You're such an idiot. Weren't you taking pills?"

She had considered buying pills, but she had no idea who would sell them to her. Everyone knew their family—Abu's family, too.

"I don't know what you're talking about," Zulaikha said. They did not speak of it for days, as if hoping the problem would disappear.

A week later, Zulaikha was handwashing the laundry in the courtyard when Madineh passed Zulaikha silently. She was dressed up. "Where're you going?" she asked.

"I'm going next door. Mrs. Sara has invited me for supper."

Mrs. Sara was from Shiraz, where she had met her husband, Parviz, an ex-oil company worker. Parviz was unhappy with his job—there was too much of a gap between workers and senior staff. So, after a few years, he quit his job and opened his own plumbing business. According to Madineh, Mrs. Sara was a gypsy. She was always dressed in long skirts and baggy blouses. She had a chin tattoo and wore large gold dangling earrings. She had very long hair and always wore it in a ponytail. Mrs. Sara was entertaining. She knew how to read cards and tell fortunes from coffee grits. She worked as a customer service receptionist for her husband, kept his calendar, and answered his phone. They were one of the first couples she knew to get a phone.

"I'll come with you," Zulaikha said.

"They have connected a new phone. I want to call Hessam to tell him about my ordeal—this shame—that's what I'm up to," Madineh said.

"What can he do?"

"Do you have a better idea?" Madineh opened the front door to leave. "I won't tell him on the phone in front of Mrs. Sara—I'll tell him you're sick or something." She slammed the door.

When Madineh returned, she said Hessam would take leave as soon as possible.

"I can hide somewhere until the baby is born," Zulaikha said.

"Like where?"

"I don't know—I can rent a room in Khorramshahr, Ahvaz, or a village."

"You're mad," replied Madineh. "What are you going to do with the baby?

"I don't know—I'll pretend it's Ahmed's baby."

Nothing Zulaikha said made sense.

■■■

When Hessam arrived, Zulaikha was in the shower in the corner of the courtyard. She joined them in the living room. The air conditioning was on. Hessam rose to hold his sister. She longed for some peace.

"She doesn't deserve your kindness," Madineh said.

"Stop being so mean," Hessam yelled.
"Shut up, Hessam. You know nothing," Madineh shouted back.
"See, now you're being mean to me, too. I just got here."
"Am I? You don't know why I asked you to come—what she's done."
Zulaikha burst into tears.
"What's going on?" Hessam glared at Zulaikha.
"Your sister is a pregnant whore. Don't just stand there. Do something."
Hessam paused for a few brief moments, trying to process what he had just heard. "Don't call her that," he said grimly.
Zulaikha had never seen him like that before.
"Are you taking her side? Do you understand what can happen to us in this situation?"
"No, I don't, and I don't want to. Maybe I should leave you, too, just like Gholam did."
Hessam picked up his bag.
Madineh approached him and pulled the bag off his hands. "Don't be a coward," she screamed.
"What do you expect me to do? Beat her?" He yelled as he went toward Zulaikha and grabbed her arm.
Zulaikha had no time to fight back. All she thought in those brief moments was to protect her belly. Hessam was too strong—he pushed her to the floor, but Zulaikha couldn't tell if Hessam meant to hurt her or let her arm go to control his anger.
"I thought so highly of you, Zulaikha. You don't care about any of us, do you?"
Zulaikha's head was between her tucked knees. She refused to look at them anymore. Her arms wouldn't cover her ears tightly enough. She could still hear them.
"Happy now, Mother?" He picked up his bag again. "I'll be at Abbass's house for the rest of my stupid leave before you make a monster out of me—call me whatever you want, Mother."
Hessam's slam of the door sent the room into darkness; their voices were gone; only a hiss remained in Zulaikha's ears. She had no control over her trembling legs. She fainted.

■■■

When she opened her eyes, Zulaikha was in the clinic. Madineh was sleeping beside her on a chair. She looked around the room. A picture of a nurse gesturing for silence was on the wall, and another patient slept in the next bed. She glared at her mother's face and prayed that either she or Madineh would die. There would be no other way out of this disgrace. She climbed out of the bed and looked outside the ward. She recognized the young receptionist—she had seen her before with Abbass who, as luck would have it, was already standing in front of her desk with Abu. Abu must have been sick.

Abbass glanced at Zulaikha through the open ward door. He approached her. "What's wrong? Doesn't Hessam know you're sick?"

"She's just tired from working outside on these hot days." Madineh had woken up and followed Zulaikha to the ward. "She fainted after Hessam left."

Zulaikha switched her look between them.

"This heat is killing everyone. Go get rest." Without looking back at her, Abbass went to Abu with his head down.

Abbass was the only person who knew about her and Kia.

■■■

Fifteen weeks into the pregnancy, Zulaikha, with her slim figure, could no longer hide the bump in her tummy. Madineh had tried different ways to discover the father's identity, but Zulaikha's lips were still sealed. She was still thinking about ways to disappear. She had little money, even thought about stealing some from her mother, but couldn't find the moment.

One day, Mrs. Sara came over. "I came to cheer you up a bit, if I may."

Madineh frowned. "Cheer us up?"

"You both are tired—we can hear you arguing. Let me take you on a trip. My husband bought a new car."

"*Mobarak*," Zulaikha said.

They drove to Khorramshahr and stopped by a new pastry café for a bathroom break while Parviz stayed in the car. The café was like heaven, with fresh pastries and the smell of vanilla and cardamom. It had been days that Zulaikha craved a piece of cake and milk. She browsed the window as Madineh stared at her.

"Let's go. Parviz is waiting," Mrs. Sara said. "It's hot."

"You go. I'll be there in a minute." Madineh ordered a small vanilla cake and a bottle of milk.

Zulaikha put her hand on her mother's arm. "*Merci*," She muttered.

Mrs. Sara grinned when they returned to the car. "Didn't I tell you? You should get out sometimes."

■ ■ ■

Madineh's eyes were kinder at home when she opened the box and picked up two plates.

"I'm not as evil as you think I am." She poured a glass of milk. "We can't go on like this, and you know it."

"What do you want me to do?"

"Just tell me who the father is. If he's a loser, then I'll arrange to send you to a village as you wish."

"What if he's not? A loser—I mean."

"We'll go and demand that they marry you, Zulaikha. No one would want you to be like this," she said. "Now drink this milk—you poor thing."

"Okay, I'll tell you." She took a deep breath. "It's Kia."

Madineh looked relieved. "That pretty boy, hah?"

Zulaikha cut a slice of the cake.

"Did you bring him here?"

"No, don't ask more questions."

"Where, then?" Madineh asked, but as if she was talking to herself.

"Why does it matter?"

"Right. We'll get to that later. We should visit Jamshid, but not today."

"Then when?" She asked.

"When their pretty boy is back for a visit. I'll go to Abbass to find out when that is. You rest assured now."

"Abbass?"

Madineh picked up her purse. "I wasn't born yesterday, Zulaikha. You visited their house too many times—that wasn't all for Abu, was it?"

"Stop it. Why don't you ever stop policing me?"

"Because I have to have proof, you idiot—I can't just go to Jamshid and say hey, your son got my daughter pregnant."

Zulaikha's legs were numb. She leaned against the wall. "But Kia knows—"

"You think he'll admit it?"

"He's not like that." Suddenly Kia's innocent eyes came to her mind.

"You dumb girl. Don't faint on me again," Madineh said. "Finish that slice. Eat for your baby."

■■■

They heard that Kia was home from his teaching post. Madineh and Zulaikha dressed nicely and went to Jamshid's house uninvited. Jamshid himself opened the door. Surprised to see them, he called his wife, Maryam. "Look who's here." He led them to the living room. "Welcome, welcome. Take a seat there." He showed them the couch at the far end to show his respect for special guests. "To what do I owe this visit?" He was still standing.

Madineh sat on the couch, but Zulaikha remained in the doorway as if she were about to watch a staged play.

"*Amu* Jamshid, I am here to tell you that your son got my daughter pregnant," she said.

Jamshid sat down on a chair.

"We cannot hide it from people anymore. There must be some

passion, love, or whatever to do such a crazy thing without considering the consequences. I am asking you to let these two young people get married."

Zulaikha's head hung down with embarrassment and disappointment. She looked around for a second. They discussed her as if they were the law and she was a criminal.

With her elegant hairdo and pink lipstick, Kia's mother, Maryam, stood beside her husband. "How do we know the baby is Kia's child?"

"Ask Abbas—or their neighbours," Madineh said. "He'll tell you how often they went to his house together."

"Find Kia right this instant, Maryam *jan*," Jamshid said. "Wherever he is!"

Maryam left the house to search for their boy.

They waited in the living room as Jamshid paced with a cane, mumbling something like a verse from Quran. Zulaikha's eyes followed him.

Strange. He was walking perfectly when he got to the door. Why does he need a cane?

Maryam, out of breath, entered the living room first. Kia muttered a Salaam with his head down.

"No salaam, but *zahr e mar*." Jamshid slapped his son's face. "Do you know how hard it is for us to plan to send you overseas to become somebody? And now this girl says she's pregnant with your child." He pointed the bottom of the cane at Zulaikha.

Kia turned to leave the room, but his mother stopped him.

"This girl?" Madineh screamed. "Who the hell do you think you are? My son was your stupid son's tutor. Remember? If he becomes somebody, it'll be because Hessam taught him the math."

Maryam's cheeks were red. The elegance was fading from her movements. "Everyone, calm down, please," she shouted.

Jamshid looked enraged. He pressed his hand to the cane handle. "I am a decent Muslim man, Madineh *khanum*. Please go home and let us try to find a mature solution to the problem." Maryam poured him a glass of water from a jar. Jamshid shook his head as if drinking the water in front of others would prove his vulnerability. Maryam stood beside him with the glass of water in hand.

Zulaikha's head was still down. She glanced at Kia, searching for a sign. He was not even looking at her. There was no way to presume his feeling toward her or the baby. His only apparent emotions were shame and fear.

Zulaikha and her mother left the house, trusting Jamshid would find a solution that would satisfy everyone.

■ ■ ■

That evening, Abbass came over to tell them that Hessam had been staying with him for a week, but he was about to return to his post in Bushehr. "He's trying to transfer to Abadan—he might be able to do that with his good behaviour."

"Come in—sit down here beside me, Abbass, dear," Madineh said.

Abbass ignored her and remained standing beside the door. He glanced at Zulaikha. "Abu talked to Hessam and calmed him down—this isn't the end of the world."

"Yes, Abu is right. Jamshid is a powerful man. I don't want my son to be resentful of him," Madineh said. "He was so angry—he pressed that stupid cane on those delicate carpets."

Zulaikha frowned. "Maybe he's still pacing their room with that cane." She found half a chicken she had made yesterday in their fridge. Reminding herself she should eat for her baby, she cut the meat.

"I heard Jamshid went to Ahvaz refinery," Abbass said. "Who knows what's he up to, but my father thinks it might even end up being a good thing for everyone if Kia married Zulaikha, even for a little while, until the baby's born, and then divorced her and sent her home."

Zulaikha passed Abbass a small bag. She wished life for her and Hessam would return to the way it was.

"What's this for?" Abbass asked.

"Some chicken and pickled cucumbers. Hessam loves pickles." Abbass chuckled. "I know."

"Hold on, put this in the bag, too. It's a new hand towel and pillowcase." Madineh said as she went to the courtyard for a smoke.

"Please tell him I didn't mean to hurt him," Zulaikha said. "He shouldn't cut me out of his life."

Abbass's eyes were illuminated. "He told me what happened when he was here—he shouldn't have raised his hand to you. I told him that was uncool," he paused to swallow. "But he keeps saying it was an accident."

"Was it?" Zulaikha muttered.

"Have hope, Zulaikha."

Hope was like a sleeping creature inside of her that needed a nudge. She needed to learn to wake it up more often.

■ ■ ■

A week later, Zulaikha was next door at Mrs. Sara's. She was helping to make tomato paste in their courtyard when she was startled by Jamshid's voice. Madineh greeted him loudly for Zulaikha to hear.

"I've got to go, Mrs. Sara. I'm so sorry—"

"Go, dear. I think you have a visitor."

Zulaikha turned the key quietly and waited behind the living room door. Zulaikha heard Jamshid speaking.

"I have thought about this a lot. I've spent much money and time preparing Kia to go to America for his education. I cannot destroy his future. He's still a child."

"He doesn't look like a child to me," Madineh replied.

"Let me talk," he said. "Zulaikha is a beautiful girl, and I will help her to settle down. If you agree to abort the child, I can offer one hundred tomans."

"No," Zulaikha yelled as she entered the room. "My baby is moving in my stomach. You can't do this."

Jamshid would not look at Zulaikha at that moment. He turned to Madineh. "Do you and your daughter realize that this child results from sin? I will pray that God forgives us all, but I cannot ruin my son's life to let a bastard child live. Do you understand?"

"I would understand better if you were more generous." Madineh stepped forward with an evil look in her eyes. "Your wife collects the nicest carpets." She had been talking about their carpets since yesterday.

"What are you doing, Mother?" Zulaikha yelled.

Madineh demanded one of the most beautiful ones—the one Hessam had told her about. "How about your silk Kashan carpet and the money?" she said.

Jamshid looked downward as if this demand had crushed him. He rose to leave.

"A fruitful barter trade," Zulaikha said. "Pray that God forgives you both. I won't."

Jamshid did not look at her again but gave Madineh a piece of paper. "Go to this address tomorrow and see a nurse named Marsha."

■ ■ ■

Zulaikha resisted, begged, and cried. "No, please! Don't let this happen, Mother. Do something. I know you can. Please, it's my child."

"What should we tell people?" Madineh suddenly began slapping her own face.

"Stop! Have you gone mad?"

"You have no idea." Madineh hit her own head on the wall so many times that Zulaikha had to jump up and grab her mother's hand.

Mrs. Sara pressed their buzzer. "Let me in. What's happening here?"

Zulaikha let go of Madineh to get the door.

"I'll scream if you don't do as I say, Zulaikha. Then I'll tell everyone you did this." Madineh scratched her own cheek like a wild cat and drew blood.

Zulaikha squatted down to hold Madineh's hand again. "Okay—just calm down. I'll do anything."

Zulaikha greeted Mrs. Sara at the door. "We're fine," she told Mrs. Sara. "Mother hit her head on the cupboard and fell—but she's fine. Not to worry."

"You sure?"

She nodded and closed the door. She put her hands behind her back and leaned against the door as she looked at the sky. It was nearing dusk, and a pleasant breeze played on her cheek. She thought about reopening the door and reaching out to Mrs. Sara, shouting she needed help. But what if Mrs. Sara also blamed her? Her mouth was dry, and her legs were trembling. Suddenly she felt a gentle kick in her belly.

Madineh was standing in the room with a belt in her hand and her hair in her face. "Give me some water and get ready," she said. She began to whip her own back with the belt. "Or I'll do it again until I pass out. My blood is on your hands."

■ ■ ■

They caught a bus to Khorramshahr to the address Jamshid had given them. It was a private clinic with a funny name, Women's Well-Being Clinic. It was past six in the evening, and all the shops were closing. The entrance opened to a stairway. Madineh struggled to climb the stairs, and pressed a buzzer at the top.

A nice looking blond woman opened the door and greeted them.

"You, Marsha?" Madineh asked.

Marsha knew how to speak Farsi very well, with a sweet English accent. She asked Madineh to wait and led Zulaikha toward a room in the hallway. Zulaikha was the only patient. She had never seen an empty clinic before.

"Sweetie, it'll be okay, don't worry. I'll do it quickly, and you won't feel a thing," she said. "Don't think you're the only one—I've done it many times."

What was this woman smiling about? If all the other women

she talked about were forced the way she was, this world needed a saviour.

Marsha gave her a shot. "You see! I'm the wife of Mr. Jamshid's close friend."

"I don't care who you are, Ma'am." Zulaikha stared at the needle.

"You must be angry at everybody. But think about all the bad things that could happen to you. I've seen women in your condition beaten by their fathers or brothers. I can see that no one has touched you, sweetie."

She hadn't seen Madineh beating herself. Obviously, that's a new method no one had tried. Her mother should teach them all a lesson.

A sharp pain she had never felt before spread in her lower abdomen.

"You can grab this handle if you want—or shout, darling. Breathe hard and push. It will help you."

Zulaikha sobbed. "I don't want anything to help me. I want to die. Do something so that I die, too."

"You've got to help your baby not to feel anything. Don't you want to do that?"

Zulaikha shouted from the deepest part of her throat. She gave birth to a boy. The infant was alive for a few minutes. His eyes were closed, but his tiny legs and hands moved slowly as if he wanted to grab something—to hold onto something that helped him stay in this world.

Zulaikha stared at Marsha as she wrapped the baby in a white sheet and took him away.

She came back in a few minutes. "Don't worry, dear. You're very young. You can have a lot of babies."

"It was a boy, right?"

"Yes, it was a boy. He didn't feel anything."

"What are you going to do with him?"

"I don't know what the clinic will do. Now, try to think about your own health. Go to sleep." She injected her with one more shot.

When she woke up, Madineh was beside her bed. She looked

sad, as if Zulaikha had died and she was mourning for her. Maybe she had realized that a part of Zulaikha had died on that bed.

Marsha was still giving her a lecture on self-care. "You'll be weak and have to rest for a while."

"I would prefer to die—didn't I tell you that?"

Marsha glanced at Madineh. "Treat her like she's given birth to a child. She must rest and take vitamins—here are a few—"

Marsha's voice sounded like babbling as Zulaikha changed into her skirt and shirt. Zulaikha had never before experienced the hate she felt for Marsha, her baby's murderer.

It was now dark outside. The temperature had cooled down and she could feel a nice breeze on her cheeks. She looked at the sky and saw many shining stars. Why did the stars come out on such an ugly night? What happened to those thick fogs or sandstorms that blinded everything in Abadan? Why not now?

She was bleeding heavily. Madineh hailed a taxi and helped her daughter in. When the cab turned into their alley, it was quiet and dark. The rats and lizards were resting in their homes. It was autumn, the time of year she loved Abadan the most: Abadan without rats and lizards.

■■■

The first lesson Zulaikha applied from Marsha's self-care lecture was throwing the vitamins into the garbage. When Madineh opened her mouth to object, Zulaikha looked straight into her eyes. "Don't talk to me, or I'll—" she paused. "Just don't speak to me ever again."

"Whatever you say," Madineh muttered.

The next morning, she returned to Mrs. Sara for the unfinished tomato paste making. She strolled every afternoon and returned home hungry, but no food tasted like it used to. She had no interest in cooking either, especially for her mother.

During the night, she woke up from sweating or a chill. It could be a fever, or maybe she caught some sort of disease. She didn't care to do anything about it. Living didn't matter to her that much anymore.

Madineh began to disappear some days. It had been a few months since she hadn't talked about seeing Habib. Zulaikha didn't care where she was as long as she stayed away. Sometimes she even wished that someone would bring her news that her mother had died somewhere, like in an accident, or drowned in the Karun River. Then she would know there was a God somewhere.

Almost two weeks after Zulaikha lost her baby, Hessam arrived home before noon. He finally managed to get a transfer to Khorramshahr's naval force. Zulaikha didn't hold him as she used to. She only said hello and stared at the television. Those days, television—especially Umm Kulthum's concert on the Baghdad channel—was the only companion she kept.

"Where's Mother?" Hessam noticed there was nothing in the fridge.

Zulaikha didn't answer.

"I'll go to get kabab and rice. Do you want anything else?"

"Nothing for me."

He squatted beside Zulaikha and told her that Madineh had called asking him to expedite his return. "She's worried for you, and I see she had a point—"

"Don't make me laugh, Hessam. Not you." She coughed. Her urge to cough felt to her as though there was no air on Earth anymore. She couldn't breathe. This was the moment she had prayed for. She was about to die, to close her eyes, and that would be the end of it.

Hessam was looking at her with worried eyes, saying something she could not understand. He carried her to the courtyard and put her on the ground. Was that Madineh screaming and asking her to forgive her? No, that was the memory of a dream she had last night.

After a few moments, blurry strangers in white uniforms appeared, blocking her view of the stars. Something brought the air back to her. There. An oxygen mask. She was in an ambulance, pulling away from the alley in *Istgah Haft*. Suddenly a strange sensation occurred to her as she began breathing normally. She could love this life again the way she did before.

When she woke up, she heard Hessam's voice. "They say you have asthma. Do you know what it is?"

"Not really. Am I dying?"

"No, we won't let you." That was the doctor behind Hessam carrying a file of her X-rays.

■ ■ ■

When Zulaikha and Hessam returned home that evening, Zulaikha recognized Jamshid's car. A man with a large hand-knotted silk carpet was at their door.

"What's this for?" Hessam asked.

The man said, "I am not sure, sir. I was told to deliver it. I work for Mr. Jamshid."

Hessam stared at it with disgust in his eyes.

"Just leave it there," Madineh said.

The man put the carpet in the courtyard and left.

"Sometimes you make me really ashamed, Mother." Hessam glanced at Zulaikha.

Zulaikha shook her head. She pitied the artist who had created this unwanted gift—this beautiful work of art with its deep red central field and green and yellow flowers.

"Be ashamed as much as you want," Madineh said. "I didn't do it for money—"

Zulaikha rolled her eyes.

"I wanted to take away a cherished belonging from them. I just wanted to hurt them. That's all I could think of. You say you are ashamed of me. I say the whole thing is a shame, and all of us are part of it, not just me."

"I don't want to see this—hide it somewhere," he said. "I swear, if you ever want to see me again, get rid of it," Hessam demanded.

Zulaikha began to sense a pattern in Hessam's angry moments

that frightened her. He threatened them that he would disappear from their lives, like her other brother, Gholam. She wondered if Hessam had the heart to ever do that to them.

■■■

Ten months after the abortion, one Friday morning, Zulaikha woke up noticing that she had slept all night. She had not woken up even once. Last night she had not been lost in Beraim neighbourhood outside Mr. John's house, or in Manama's fish market holding Rafi's hand. She was not a barefoot vagabond the way she had been in those dreams—until she saw two little feet, an infant, or a nurse in a white uniform hushing her. Last night brought relief from that reoccurring nightmare.

The house was quiet. She had recently resumed speaking to Madineh—a couple of words here and there. Madineh pretended nothing was wrong between them. She told her it was a nice day, how about doing this or that, she needed a haircut or a good face and eyebrow threading. When Zulaikha ignored her, Madineh gave up for the day.

They had guests that Friday and Zulaikha had a lot to do. Abu was feeling better, so Madineh invited him and Abbass for lunch. It would be a fun day, but Zulaikha was worried they would talk about what had happened to her—about Jamshid and his family. She appreciated that Abu and Abbass were protective of her, but she didn't want to go back to those days. To her nightmares. They had only stopped last night.

Hessam helped Abbass walk Abu as he carried his new musical instrument, an *oud*, and a large box of English cookies.

Zulaikha asked if they wanted the usual black tea or milk with cookies.

"I'd like milk, but I serve milk and tea for everyone today. You sit down," Abbass said. "Stop playing with TV channels, Hessam. Give me a hand here, will you?"

Hessam glared at him. "It's my day off work."

"I didn't want those cookies," Abu said. "Abbass said to bring them here."

Zulaikha glanced at Abbass.

"Here we go again," Abbass muttered as he rolled his eyes.

Abu began telling them about Jamshid's recent visit. He had come to explain things, to ensure that what happened would remain between their families.

Madineh was eager to hear all the details, even though Hessam and Abbass tried to change the subject.

"I told him we'd keep Hessam's secret, not yours," Abu said. "Hessam is like my son's brother. We said no word, and no one will hear a word from us, but not because of you and your canned fruit and English cookies."

"Good for you, Abu," Madineh said.

Why wouldn't they stop talking about it?

"Jamshid brings up the Quran to explain his stupid choices—the holy book," Abu said. "I'm glad I never lived my life according to any book."

Abbass asked his father to calm down.

"I'll be right back. I forgot to do something." Zulaikha went to the courtyard for some fresh air. She started to water the new plants she'd recently bought when someone knocked on the door.

The same man who had delivered the carpet had two bags of lamb meat to deliver this time. "What's this for?" Zulaikha suddenly felt she needed her inhaler.

"*Amu* Jamshid sends his regards," he said. "This is in honour of his son, Kia, finishing his military service. Please accept it."

A sheep must have been sacrificed in the Muslim tradition, and the meat shared among the neighbours and the poor.

Zulaikha shouted Hessam's name. "Please come to the door. There's someone here." She ran to fetch her inhaler.

Abbass noticed Zulaikha's distress. "What's wrong?"

"Jamshid—I mean *Amu* Jamshid sent *ghorbani* meat—"

"Hessam, you can take it if you want, but we won't eat it," Abu shouted so he could be heard there at the entrance door. "You tell him to give the meat to a poor family."

Abu's angry voice didn't comfort Zulaikha this time. Unlike the other times she appreciated his loud and clear support, this time it bothered her strangely. She went back to the door. The delivery man turned to go back to his car. "Wait, please." She brushed passed Hessam and got the bag off the man's hand. "Thank you, sir," she said.

The man nodded out of respect in response.

"Where are you going?" Hessam asked.

Zulaikha ignored Hessam and walked a few steps alongside the delivery man outside. She pressed the buzzer next door.

"We have too much food, Mrs. Sara. Would you accept this? It's from an old family friend."

"Sure thing, love. How nice. Would you like to come in?"

"No, we have guests. Enjoy it."

Zulaikha glanced at the delivery man as he drove away.

Hessam was still waiting for her.

"Don't tell them what I did."

"Okay, but don't you want to come inside?"

"In a minute—would you tell them not to talk about them—I mean, Kia's family—anymore?"

Hessam nodded.

She returned to watering her plants. The anger inside her had been replaced with a strange emotion. The look in the delivery man's eyes as they rejected the gift in his hand, then Abu's slim, ill body but his strong and firm voice she always envied. Where was the balance? She wanted to return to who she was before this ordeal.

Abbass was playing a familiar tune. The sound of music invited her back to her party.

■ ■ ■

The year was 1966 when Kia left Iran. Hessam was released from military service and brought home good news. The Navy had offered him a permanent accounting position stationed at Khorramshahr.

CHAPTER 2

Assef and Zulaikha

KHUZESTAN IN THE 1970s

> *Call my name.*
> *Your voice is pleasant.*
> *Your voice is the greenness of the strange plant*
> *that grows in the deep end of the sincerity of sorrow.*
>
> **–Sohrab Sepehri**

Hessam grew a moustache after an American navy officer told him he reminded him of Omar Sharif, the Egyptian actor who became a Hollywood star for his role in *Lawrence of Arabia*. With him working in Khorramshahr, things improved financially for Zulaikha's family. On the first day of each month, he left some money from his salary on the kitchen counter, one-third of which was for Zulaikha. She wore better clothing now and could save some for the future.

Like their mother, getting gifts fascinated Hessam. Zulaikha suspected that Hessam had a relationship with a well-off woman who was giving him the things he brought home, things they could never afford, like Ray-Ban glasses or expensive wallets and belts. But also like their mother, he was secretive about the identity of his lover. Zulaikha was the only open book in her family. Her experiences must have been a lesson learned. He appeared to be careful about his relationships.

One day, while helping him to pack for a trip, Zulaikha decided to ask him why he had never mentioned any girls.

"Girls want babies and marriage."

"So, what then?"

Hessam looked away and zipped his expensive brown leather bag.

"A married woman?"

Hessam was not giving anything away, but he didn't deny it either.

"You be careful, Hessam. Affairs with rich women in a small city can get dangerous." She expected him to say, look who's talking about being careful, but he didn't.

"I am. Don't worry," he muttered.

On weekends, Zulaikha enjoyed going to the movies with Hessam and strolling near the Karun River. She would watch other families from their neighbourhood having picnics, playing ball, and barbecuing liver and kabab. They played *Bandari* music, danced, and laughed. Looking on these scenes, she felt that something was missing from her life. While grocery shopping, she would observe the people around her. The strangers in the marketplace looked kind from a distance. She preferred strangers. If she could only make one good friend or companion, she would make it right this time.

At home, she could not hide her resentment toward her mother. Madineh was sick of her, too, and was probably already looking for another husband for her. Zulaikha did not tell anyone when she wrote to Aliah that she was considering returning to Bahrain to work at the salon. Impatient, she went down to the telecommunication office. They had added five more booths in the last couple of years, but the front seats were all taken. She sat in the back and browsed her *Zan e Rouz*—"Today's Woman"— magazine.

"Bahrain, cabin two." The microphone behind her announced.

She rushed to take the call, afraid to lose it, before she reached

the booth. "Hello, Aliah?"
"Yes, this is she."
"This is Zulaikha calling from Abadan."
"How are you, Zulaikha *jan*. I just received your letter. I was going to reply tonight."
"How are your children? Is everything going well?" She inquired.
"All good here—I may get married again soon."
"Really?"
"Yes, I've fallen into that trap again."
"Good. Are you sure you don't want to find another wife for him?" Zulaikha asked cheekily.
"No, no, no, not this one!" Aliah replied vehemently.
"I'm only joking."
"I know," Aliah laughed. "How are you? What's going on? You sounded sad in the letter."
"It's a long story. I can't talk for too long. I beg you to accept me again—For all I have done for your children—" She hesitated. "For your family."
"You can come and work, but things are different now. I can send you the employment letter you wanted for your visa to the embassy, but you must make your own money, rent your own room. It's hard to make ends meet. My new husband has four children, and I can't expect too much from him."
"Four children? You'll have a full house."
"Oh, no. His first wife died a few years ago, and he has a sixteen-year-old daughter who can look after the other three children."
Poor girl.
"I'll work hard. Please send me the letter of employment as soon as possible."
"Okay. I'll do it right away."
"*Shokran*, Aliah. I'll make it up to you."
"*Shokran*, Zulaikha. You have done a lot for us already."
Walking back, she passed the Cinema Taj roundabout. Hessam had been telling her that he got two passes. She crossed the street

and stopped by the cinema's window. No one was there, but the weekly program was on the window. Hessam was discreet about the movie passes. "A colleague got them from an oil company employee." Only oil company employees were allowed to Cinema Taj.

She called his work from a telephone booth.

"Can we still go to Cinema Taj? Do you still have those passes?"

"Tonight?"

"Yes, I just saw their program. They're showing *Sultan e Ghalbha* (*The King of Hearts*)."

Hessam put her on hold for a minute. "I'll pick you up at five."

She put on a blue dress, wore a pair of fake pearl earrings and put her hair up. One of Hessam's colleagues gave them a ride to the roundabout. She looked out of the window to avoid his eyes checking her out in the mirror. Any man with the slightest connection to her brother would be a lousy idea. She wasn't interested.

Inside the cinema, the cloth-covered seats were so neat she didn't want to leave. The movie was a dramatic Farsi film, and most women were in tears when they exited the building.

The air smelled like night-blooming jasmine and was perfect for walking.

"I've something to tell you," she said.

Hessam stopped walking.

Zulaikha hooked her arm around her brother's. "It's not bad. I'm thinking about going back to Manama. I want to work with Aliah again."

"Was I so incompetent you decided to leave?"

"It's not about you, Hessam. I have no reason to stay here."

"Are you sure?"

She told him she had made plans and asked him to help her with money and the ticket.

"Of course," He said. "I'll do anything."

"One more favour." She glanced at him. "You have to tell our mother—I'll make you *Ghalieh Mahi*."

Unexpectedly, their mother seemed indifferent. Her only advice to Zulaikha was that she find a rich man this time.

■■■

Zulaikha did not tell Aliah about her pregnancy or abortion. She had moved there for a fresh start. It must remain her secret forever. But she told her she had a fling with someone from a different class who left Iran. Aliah treated her gently, especially after discovering she now had asthma.

Aliah's children were now teenagers. Hashem and Saba had gone on a school field trip. Only twelve-year-old Rafi, who stayed with his stepfather's family, visited her one afternoon for tea. He was wearing a bow tie and a baby blue shirt. He had a camera strap around his neck and brought her a rose bouquet, making her cry.

"You're a young man, Rafi," she said. "I can't believe it."

He was almost Zulaikha's height.

"My mother always tells me you found me when I was lost," Rafi said. "I wanted to meet you and thank you."

"That was my pleasure," she said. "That's a nice camera. Are you a photographer?"

"Yes, I'm learning it. I brought it to take a picture with you. Shall we?"

"He's serious about his camera," Aliah said as she took a picture of Zulaikha and Rafi standing side by side, smiling for the camera.

In her dreams, Rafi had remained a two-year-old child that Zulaikha would lose and search for. His image melded with that of her own child. Once, she even called her dying infant, "Oh, Rafi." But Rafi had grown older—so should those stupid dreams. No one could ever find her lost child for her.

■■■

Two weeks into her stay at Aliah's place, before the children returned from their trip, Zulaikha found a room to rent on the second floor of a small house. Its walls were cracked, but the window overlooked a field with wild *narges*. The first thing to do was wash the window. She made the window gleam like crystal and sighed. "This little space is all I wanted."

She worked most days, and each passing day was a little smoother than the last. After work, she would walk home along the shoreline watching the deep blue sea. She loved the sandwiches at the deli near her house, listening to Arabic music, reading Farsi magazines at night and taking long showers. In the morning, she dressed up to be presentable at work. One day, she was in the back of the salon mixing hair dye for her client when Leelah told her she had a visitor.

"A visitor?" she asked.

"Yes, it's a man. I haven't seen him before."

She glanced in the mirror at her large hoops and fixed her white headband. Bahrain's humidity and sunshine had made her hair wavier than ever.

Her visitor was dark-skinned with puffy eyes. He carried an envelope and a plastic bag.

"Can I help you? I'm Zulaikha."

"My name is Assef. Your mother sent these." He handed over the envelope and a plastic bag.

"How do you know my mother?"

"Oh, I'm a truck driver—I work with Habib. Do you know him?" He looked younger than her and spoke Farsi with an Arabic accent.

So Mother had been seeing Habib again.

"Yes, I know him. You're from Abadan?"

"No, Ahvaz. Doesn't my Farsi scream Khuzestani Arab?"

Zulaikha chuckled. "It's a sweet accent. I learned some Arabic here." A strange tension built between them. Zulaikha didn't want him to go, but she didn't have much more to say.

"*Amu* Habib told me a lot about you and your mother."

"He did? I hope good things."

"Of course."

Aliah and everyone else in the salon was staring at them.

"I'm going to go back to work," Zulaikha said, aware of their audience.

"Oh, me too." Assef turned around to leave, but then he stopped. "I'm only here for two days. Can I see you after your work? Do you have time to show me around Manama?"

"Is it your first time here?"

"No, I've been a few times, but—"

"But?" She prompted.

He was looking for proper words. "But every time just for a day. I'm always too tired to be a tourist."

Zulaikha gave him a coy smile. "Okay. When can you be here?"

"I'm done by five."

"I'll be waiting."

They met that night and walked along the seaside. Zulaikha took him to the deli she always went to for lunch. They ordered two mortadella sandwiches with plenty of pickles and a couple of Pepsis and sat on a bench near the water to enjoy their meal. Zulaikha told him how she first met Aliah and her marriage to the Sheikh. Assef told her about his family—his sister in Ahvaz.

At the end of their date, Assef leaned in to kiss her on the cheek. Her reflexes pulled her back, before she tilted her head and let him.

"Can I see you again tomorrow?" he asked.

She blinked and nodded.

Zulaikha had turned into a reserved woman afraid of a man's touch. She was fearful of people and what they could do to her. Bahrain was a haven for her, and she didn't want to lose that sense of security. But in her room that night, when the darkness shrouded the field of *narges*, she longed for the thrill Assef had given her a few hours ago.

The next night, he took her to a restaurant near his motel. The server greeted them warmly and seated them at a table facing Manama Harbour.

When he paid their bill, he asked her to wait for a minute while he ran outside with the takeout box. She watched him from the window giving the food to an older man sitting on the bench outside.

"That was very nice of you," she said. "Do you know him?"

"He works in my motel—I like him." He had checked out, and his bags were in his trailer truck.

"Do you want a ride with my buddy?" he pointed to his truck.

It was her first time getting into a giant truck while wearing a dress. He put a tape on and hummed to the song as he glanced at her. She had missed this liveliness.

Before he left Manama at the end of that night, a striking hope awakened in her. No one could see them share a lengthy kiss in the cabin of his truck.

The next morning she woke to the song of a sparrow on her windowsill. The colourful bird did not fly away when she approached the window.

She finally opened the letter from her mother that she had left sitting on her night table for a few days. Habib had asked her to marry him—such good news, she wished she had opened it sooner. Habib was the only man who could control Madineh.

■ ■ ■

Assef returned to her every two weeks. He would stay a day then leave. That week he showed up unexpectedly at the beauty salon around noon. She took a break, and they went to the bakery in the marina and sat on the patio under an umbrella where Assef brought up Madineh's marriage.

"Let's have a banana and coconut milkshake." She didn't like to talk about her mother.

He came back with two milkshakes. "Why are you so distant from your mother? She seems to be a lovely lady."

Zulaikha looked away and sipped on the beverage—the flavours were a perfect combination.

"You're alone here, and Manama is so small—you're always working. Your mother has Habib now. Think about yourself a little bit."

"Myself?"

"Yes, yourself!"

Zulaikha sighed.

"What happened back there?"

Why won't he let me enjoy this milkshake?

"Nothing," she said. "I love Abadan, but Abadan does not love me. It always pushes me away."

"I know you got married here, and your husband died. It's been a while now, and I wonder if—"

"If what?" she asked defensively.

"Nothing! I'm having trouble understanding your being so distant. Did your mother do something?"

"Did she tell you how old he was when she sent me, a teenage girl, here?"

"No." He paused. "That's awful, Zulaikha. I had no idea."

"Of course you didn't. My mother doesn't share the awful stuff," she said. "Do you see them often?"

"Habib invites me over sometimes. I've met Hessam, too."

It was a long time since she'd heard from Hessam. "Are you close to my brother? How is he?"

"Oh, he's fine. He and his friends go out after work. He's having a good time."

"Does having a good time mean drinking with you and Habib?"

"Come on now. Don't be like that."

"My mother once told me *Amu* Habib drinks, like my father, and she's scared of men who drink."

"There's no problem with having fun." Assef's milkshake glass was still half-full, but nothing was left in hers.

"I need to go back to work now," she said. "When are you leaving?"

He stood up and put both his hands in his pockets. "Wait a minute," he swallowed. "I'm going to ask your mother and brother to give me their blessings to marry you—and you should prepare for me to come and get you next time."

She looked up and shielded her face from the glaze of the sun. A team of geese was flying away.

"You won't ask me? You just order me?"

"I thought I did not need to. Did I?" He sounded dejected.

"I should get back to work." She walked away in disbelief. Glancing back, he was still in the same spot under the patio umbrella. She stopped a moment before turning back towards him. She gently held his hand. It was a public place, and they couldn't hold each other, but he dared to kiss her hand. "Wait for me, Zulaikha. Just wait." He sounded genuine.

Her heart beat faster the closer she got to the salon. *I am being a fool again! How am I going to break this news to the girls?*

∎∎∎

She did not hear from Assef for nine weeks. Her new friend, the little sparrow, was also gone. Then, on a Friday evening when she got home from work, she found a letter from her mother. Zulaikha anxiously searched for a word about Assef but found nothing.

> **I am happier these days, but you act distant and cold. What have I done to deserve this? I am your mother.**

She tore apart the letter.

Murdering my child is so trivial that it could be forgotten so quickly.

Assef's silence made her feel like a fool, but she consoled herself by remembering that before Assef, she was living her life. Still, this stranger's absence sucked her energy.

Aliah and the girls at the salon kept asking her what was wrong. She shook her head and said, "Nothing, just tired," and kept working, but that didn't stop them from commenting: "Maybe you should forget about him. Maybe he was only a passerby."

Finally, on an early morning two weeks later, when the sparrow returned, Zulaikha decided to tell Aliah that she wanted to visit her family.

Aliah stopped working for a moment. "Go find your man, Zuli.

But always remember that this is your second home."

■ ■ ■

Her small plane landed at Abadan airport in the evening. Hessam was there to welcome his now twenty-seven-year-old sister warmly. Hessam's moustache was different, and he sported a big afro.

Zulaikha laughed the moment she saw him. "What's that?"

He picked up her suitcase. "What's wrong? Not cool enough for you, Sister?"

Abbass was waiting for them beside his pickup truck in the parking lot. It took Zulaikha a few seconds to recognize him. He was taller than she remembered. His shoulders must have grown broad from the work and swimming. His hair was tied in a small ponytail.

"You look so different." She kissed both his cheeks.

"Yes, I tell him to stay away from me," Hessam said. "I look too ugly walking with him."

"Shut up." Abbass took the luggage from Hessam and put it in the back.

How she had missed them both. Abbass's truck had only one wide seat at the front. She let Hessam get in first, so she could take the window seat. She wanted to see everything. "It hasn't been that long, but everything looks different."

"If you're not too tired, we can drive around the city," Abbass said.

Zulaikha turned around to view Hotel Karevansara from different angles. American and European tourists wandered among the nightclubs, bars, and casinos. She had never noticed Abadan's nightlife before that day.

■ ■ ■

Madineh had moved to a small house with Habib, so Zulaikha stayed in the old house, which was messier than ever. But getting rid of the clutter, cooking, and cleaning made her feel more productive and less like a burden to Hessam. She still had some savings, but without a steady income she worried about her future.

After Hessam went to work the next day, she sat on the stairs in the courtyard with a big bowl of soapy water, handwashing Hessam's shirts. Madineh came over unexpectedly. "Is the washing machine not working?"

"His shirts are delicate—handwashing them is better."

"Let me help you."

"No, it's hot. Go inside."

"What am I supposed to do inside? You clean all the time. What's left to do?"

"Okay," Zulaikha said. "Help me rinse this one."

"Have you heard from Assef?"

Zulaikha shook her head.

"I know that he proposed to you."

"How do you know?"

"He told Habib. We haven't seen him for more than a month. I know you like him, but you should be careful with him. Remember how he met you in Bahrain? He meets other women in other places, too."

Zulaikha stopped working. Her forehead was wet from sweat. "You know what? I wish you would learn that if you don't have something good to say, don't say anything at all."

"Don't be upset. I want the best for you."

"You? The best for me? Don't make me laugh." She scoffed.

"Maybe I'd better leave. I just came to invite you and Hessam over for dinner. Habib wants to see you." She closed the door behind her.

Zulaikha stared at the door. A part of her wanted to go after her, tell her to stay—they could watch a show or listen to the radio and make lemonade. But there was a cast iron door between them. She was safer if it remained closed.

Zulaikha finished hanging the laundry to dry. She spent the rest of the day switching between Iranian TV's new dubbed American series and her old Emirates programs.

When Hessam got home, he inhaled the fresh smell of detergent. "Good to have you back, Zulaikha."

She had prepared a small dinner. Hessam sat down and waited for her to serve. "It smells wonderful here, but it worries me. I'm going to miss you a lot more this time when you leave."

"Who said I'll be leaving?"

"You've become a temporary occupant, a visitor," he replied.

"And what have you become?"

"I don't know." He looked for words. "The man of the house?"

"Well, man of the house, you should start taking care of this place. It looked awful before I got here. You wear expensive shirts, ties, and shoes but the house stinks. We'll start painting and buying a few things tomorrow."

Hessam frowned.

She scooped some rice to put onto his plate. "I won't take no for an answer."

■■■

When Zulaikha and Hessam arrived at their mother's new house, Habib had already started drinking. Zulaikha recognized the carpet that Jamshid had sent them in the middle of their living room.

Habib must have noticed her disgusted face. "You alright? Why are you always sad and quiet, girl?"

"I'm fine," Zulaikha said. "*Tabrik, Amu Habib.*"

"This time, when Assef comes back, I'm going to keep him here until he marries you," he said.

Is he drunk already?

"Coffee, Zuli *jan*?" Madineh had made coffee for Zulaikha with the right amount of sugar and milk. "Where the hell is Assef? Hopefully, not already married in Kuwait."

Hearing Madineh disrespect Assef, Zulaikha wished she could drink, too.

"Now, don't make up stories, good woman," Habib said. "His

sister needed him to be there in Ahvaz. Their old aunt was sick. He doesn't know Zulaikha's here. If only he knew." He had another sip of his drink.

Hessam munched on walnuts and gulped some *arak*. Zulaikha didn't want to look at either of them anymore. She asked her mother to turn the television on. Abdul Halim Hafez's concert was on. She turned her back to the others and sat in front of the TV.

■■■

The next day, just before sunset, Habib and Madineh came for a visit. Zulaikha offered tea or a cold drink.

"Nothing for me," Madineh said. "This alley is so filthy. Why don't people clean their front door anymore?"

"We do, Mother—our neighbourhood is too low class for you now." Madineh and Habib now lived in *Istgah Seh*, a better neighbourhood than theirs.

"Didn't you tell me you wanted to visit your next-door neighbour?" Habib told Madineh. "Go and pay your visit while I talk to your girl for a few minutes, will you?"

Madineh gave him an alluring glance and left. Watching her mother's submissiveness toward Habib was amusing. She left the room slowly like a tame animal, calm and obedient.

"We have Canada Dry in the fridge, too, if you prefer."

"It's a beautiful evening—let's sit in the courtyard," Habib suggested.

Zulaikha took two bottles and some almonds outside. They sat on the brick step before the courtyard. "Zulaikha *jan*, you've known me for a long time, right?"

"Yes, *Amu* Habib."

"So, you know I want nothing but the best for you and Hessam." He lit a cigar. "I know you aren't so content with your mother—I'm not here tonight to preach."

Where was this going? Mother had found a partner in plotting my future. Couples talk to each other about their family secrets. But had she also described her own role in hurting her daughter?

"What's wrong, *Amu?*"
"Nothing to worry about. I wanted to talk to you about Assef."
She looked down.
"Don't be embarrassed, Zulaikha *jan*," Habib said. "You're both two beautiful souls with feelings for each other. Assef is like a son to me. I just wanted to tell you a few things about him."
"Is he alright?"
"Yes, dear, nothing is wrong with him," he said. "I met him when he was a child. His father was a good friend of mine. His mother died when she gave birth to his sister Rhianna. Did you know about it?"
"Yes, he told me he was raised without parents."
"Shortly after his mother's death, his father, a truck driver, died in an accident. Assef and that poor girl became orphans too soon. A relative, a grand aunt, raised them, but it wasn't easy. Assef is a runaway, my child. He doesn't stay in one place. He doesn't want to attach to anyone or anything. He ran away from home a few times and his aunt gave up on him. I finally brought him here, to Abadan from Ahvaz, gave him a job to assist me in my truck until he was ready to drive a truck, too."
"He has told me about most of this but not his running away."
"I knew he wouldn't. He thinks it's like a sickness in him. He's ashamed of it. He thinks he'll be cured with you, but I'm not so sure—not so quickly."
"Has he told you that?" Now, she could look Habib in the eyes.
"Yes, he has. If you want to marry him, you have to know this. He runs away—it is not about you. Can you deal with something like this in your life?"
"No one is perfect, *Amu* Habib. I am a damaged soul, too."
"Whose soul is not damaged, my child? Don't think you must marry him because this marriage will heal you. You can wait longer. You can marry again, maybe to someone more mature, someone older than you."
Assef is only a couple of years younger. Now I'm suddenly an older woman falling for a boy.
"It's not easy to be a widow, *Amu* Habib, a fatherless widow. I'm

a burden to my brother now. I don't want that."

"Assef will take care of you. But remember that I warned you. He has not had an easy life—neither have you. Being young is not easy."

Habib's closeness to Assef warmed her heart. He was close to Assef and influenced his decisions. She wanted him to keep telling her about Assef's habits, hobbies, and flaws. But a sudden bang startled her. Madineh entered the courtyard. "Are you two enjoying a picnic without me?"

She got up and offered her spot to Madineh.

"Hessam and Abbass will be coming over for dinner. Will you stay?" Her invitation was genuine.

■ ■ ■

Assef returned to Abadan a few days later. Just as Habib promised, a small wedding was arranged for them. Zulaikha was too shy to buy a wedding dress even though she hadn't worn one for her first marriage.

She was in her late twenties—with Assef three years younger, she was careful not to come across as an older woman.

"Who cares what people think?" Assef said. "You're my bride, and you should dress like one for me."

She ended up buying a white dress from the Kuwaiti bazaar.

Hessam and Abbass made all the arrangements. Hessam handed her two small jewellery boxes—her wedding gifts.

She shook her head in disbelief. "Two?"

"One of them is from Gholam," Hessam said.

"You see Gholam?"

"He calls me sometimes," Hessam said. "I told him about you getting married. He sent you this."

Assef glanced at the turquoise pendant in Zulaikha's hand. "That's nice. We should go meet him soon."

"Help me put it on, Assef."

Hessam had bought her a gold bracelet. Abbass's gift was his performance. He brought a friend—they played Bandari music with *oud* and drum. All of them, even Abu, danced until the bride and groom went to the tiny house they had rented in *Istgah Davazdah* from Farah Abad.

■■■

Their balcony opened out onto the palm grove. She changed into her white, lacy nightgown and went out to watch the stars while Assef was freshening up. An airplane was flying somewhere high above. Not long ago, she would have wished she was in that airplane flying far away, to a place where no one knew her, somewhere to start a new life. But in that moment, where she was standing was the best spot on earth. A spot to start anew.

She heard Assef's breathing behind her as he held her hand gently. "Let's go inside." He pressed his hand on her back, and she followed him. They sat on the bed. "Everything went well—" He was nervous and shy. "I mean the wedding. Don't you think?"

She didn't answer his question. She put her arms around him and rested her head on his shoulder. They lost themselves to each other's touch. How foolishly love had struck her. This time, not just her body, but her entire soul swallowed this delicious energy. She hadn't known this sensation called love until that night.

She stayed awake to watch Assef sleep, to make herself believe it was all real. Assef's closed eyes, long eyelashes, bony cheeks, and slim naked legs were all so real and so near to her. The sound of crickets gave her a familiar thrill.

In the morning, the tall palm trees still stood outside of her windows. Everything was real last night. Paradise couldn't be more peaceful than the palm grove outside her balcony. She made a big breakfast.

■■■

The night before Assef left for his next trip, he asked her if she wanted anything from Ahvaz.

"Like what?" She asked.

"I don't know. You name it."
"I can't think of anything," she replied.
"Come on. I'll tickle you if you don't."
"I want a baby."
"From Ahvaz?"
She hit him with a pillow gently. "I want us to have a baby. That's all I want."
"I haven't taken you anywhere. You sure?"
She nodded. They cuddled.
"You want a baby to be sure I'll come back?"
"I hadn't thought about that until you just said it. You asked me what I want—"
"I know, Zulaikha. It's okay if you want to trick me into keeping me. I want you to."
She held him tight but avoided his eyes. She didn't want him to know how terrified she was.

■ ■ ■

Zulaikah's asthma made her pregnancy challenging this time. The vomiting and headaches did not help either. When Assef worked in town or drove between Khorramshahr and Ahvaz, he helped with everything at home. She was twelve weeks pregnant when Assef told her with excitement that he got a deal with a company in Kuwait. "Don't look upset, Zulaikha. We'll have more money for the baby."

The money was good, but now that Assef was away, Madineh frequently visited her and ensured that her daughter ate and rested. Hessam brought gifts for the baby or took Zulaikha out to stroll along the Karun River. He didn't know anything better.

"How is Assef doing?" Hessam asked.
"Do you want the truth?"
Hessam stopped walking. "What's going on?" He shielded his face from the sun.
"I don't hear from him much—that's the truth," she said. "But I'll kill you if you tell Mother. She keeps asking me—every single

day."

"I'll try to find a messenger. This doesn't seem right."

Karun River was smooth that day. A boat with loud, laughing European-looking tourists left the shore. She didn't want to send for Assef. If this baby didn't keep him, nothing would.

■■■

Zulaikha was due in four weeks when Assef returned. She felt that his absence could not be entirely excused by money and his job. Was there another woman? To tell him about her insecurities could end badly. He would tell her yes, there was another woman, and then what? She decided it best to wait. The baby would change everything.

Assef brought a suitcase of baby soaps, shampoo, lotions, and other necessities. He had a gift and a letter from Aliah, whom he had visited while in Bahrain last weekend.

Zulaikha called Aliah from the telephone cabin the next day and asked about Assef's visit.

"He didn't tell me that he had left you alone for so long," Aliah said. "He said he was working in Kuwait—I assumed he was only working there a few weeks and rotating between Kuwait and Abadan." Zulaikha was quiet for a moment too long. She heard Aliah say, "Hello. Are you still there?"

"Yes, yes, I can hear you."

"He visited the salon on the weekend to tell me about the baby."

"I don't know what to think, Aliah. Why is everything always so hard?"

"He loves you, Zulaikha. Maybe he's just used to being on the road."

Maybe Abadan was too small for Assef.

On her way home, Zulaikha thought about all the maybes and possibilities. In the end, Assef had won. There were so many excuses for him and no reason for her to stay bitter.

When she got home, Madineh was visiting. As usual, she had

plans, and today was the worst day to discuss buying the child's furniture.

"I saw a pink and blue children's bedroom set. I wanted to take you there."

"Today is not good, Mother." She gulped some water.

"The baby will be here any day. We should also go and make the appointment with the hospital."

"We will—just not today. I'm not feeling well."

Madineh frowned and turned to Assef. "There's this private clinic in Khorramshahr—it's so clean."

Is she talking about that same damned clinic?

"Will you stop?" Zulaikha shouted. "You don't need to be worried about those things. We can manage."

Madineh glanced at Assef. "I guess I'll leave you to it then."

Assef saw her to the door and apologized. "It's probably because of me. She'll feel better when she gets some rest."

Assef turned around. He stretched his arm as always, inviting Zulaikha to hold him. She didn't move.

"What are we waiting for?" She picked up her purse. "Let's go. The baby needs a clinic. Furniture, too."

"Wait. Just sit down a moment. I've got to rent a truck. It'll take a minute."

"No, I'm sick of waiting for you."

■■■

They stopped into the new women's hospital near Khorramshahr to book an appointment. Zulaikha was quiet the whole time.

"What did I do wrong, Zulaikha?" he said as he drove the rented truck full of blue baby furniture.

"Nothing. It's just that I'm out of tricks to keep you."

"Too bad I can't smoke." Assef sighed. "This thing you're doing right now—it's a good trick to repel me." Suddenly he drove over a speed bump. She pressed her hand on the window as a stabbing pain entered her spine.

"I didn't mean to," Assef said. "Forgive me."

She glanced at him and put her hand on his. He kissed her hand and continued to handle the truck.

Fear was a gift from the devil. A limitless one. She had to stop feeding it. It was growing in her.

■■■

Zulaikha gave birth to her son a week later, a year after her marriage. As Nurse Marzi, a chubby woman with a husky voice, pushed Zulaikha's stretcher into the hallway, Assef, Madineh, and Hessam clamoured around her, yelling *mobarak*. "It's a boy!" Nurse Marzi didn't wait for them to ask about the child's gender. "Now get out of the way," she yelled.

Assef and Hessam held each other as if they had won the lottery. Zulaikha glanced at Madineh, who bent to say something to her, but she couldn't hear. Her mother was in tears. Madineh never cried.

Two hours later, Zulaikha held her newborn, kissed his small forehead and thought about the resurrection of her dead son. She couldn't remember how her first baby looked. She only remembered his tiny legs and hands moving before someone took him away. Zulaikha's constant coughing while breastfeeding her newborn worried everyone.

Nurse Marzi took her baby from her hands. "Don't fuss." She frowned. "He'll be fine."

Zulaikha could trust a tough lady like her more than a pretty, smiling one.

Nurse Marzi came back a minute later to give her oxygen. She asked Hessam and Madineh to leave the room. "Only her husband can stay."

She has a talent for mind-reading, too.

As Hessam and Madineh left to buy *shirini*, Zulaikha called Hessam and said to ask Nurse Marzi what kind of sweets she liked.

Now, finally alone with Assef, she said in a weak voice, "I'm going to name him Sohrab, like it or not."

"It's a good name," he agreed readily.

She tried to stay seated and gain more strength. "Of course, it's good. What did you think? That I'm going to give him an Arabic name? One Arab man is enough around me."

Assef sat on the edge of her bed. "Zuli *jan*? It's not like you to talk like this. Our son is Arab because he's my son."

"Why aren't you asking me when I came up with Sohrab?"

"Why does it matter? I like it."

"All those months when I was alone, reading magazines and cleaning our place while I waited and waited for you, sometimes Hessam would visit me and take me to see a show or shop. He showered me with gifts as though they could make me forget everything. One day I went to visit him, and he was reading a book. When I asked him about it, he read me a poem by this poet, Sohrab Sepehri. You know me, I'm not even sure what the entire poem meant, but I will never forget these lines:

> *If you come to me,*
> *Come, but gently and delicately,*
> *So, my thin glass of loneliness,*
> *Never gets fractured.*

"And that was when I decided our son's name."

"Oh, so our Sohrab is not based on the Rostam and Sohrab epic."

Rostam and Sohrab were fictional Persian warriors whose stories Zulaikha had learned in school and from radio programs.

"No, because Sohrab, our *Pahlavan*—he searched all his life for Rostam, his father." She glanced at Sohrab, the baby boy. Suddenly she felt herself become as brave as a real warrior. "Where were you staying all that time in Kuwait?"

Assef's hands comforted her, touching her hair, travelling down her arm and gently pulling her body toward his chest. "I ignorantly felt more useful making money in Kuwait," he said. "You know I must support my sister and aunt in Ahvaz, too."

Zulaikha lay on her side—Assef was almost falling off the edge of the bed. He stared at the blood on the sheets. Assef stood up calmly, pushed a button beside her bed and left the room to ask for a nurse.

Nurse Marzi and a young orderly immediately changed her sheets and checked her blood pressure. "Your husband will bring you some juice. We want to discharge you tomorrow, you're doing fine, but you shouldn't look so pale."

Sohrab was sleeping in a tiny bed beside her. Assef returned to the room with a few packs of apple and orange juice. She fed Sohrab and fell into a deep sleep.

■ ■ ■

Assef stayed in town caring for her and the baby. He drove between Khorramshahr and Ahvaz every week. Aside from her sleep deprivation, Zulaikha was happier than ever. Sohrab also brought peace between Zulaikha and Madineh. Although Zulaikha was still cold with her mother, Madineh took any chance to take care of Sohrab. She often visited them uninvited.

"Last Friday, Habib and I went to Cinema Rex and watched a movie with Doris Day. You two should go and see it. I'll look after Sohrab." She kept reminding her daughter to think about having fun. "Come on! What are you waiting for? Get ready. The show will start at seven. You two need some time to yourselves."

One weekend, Assef got a pass to the National Oil Company Club for dinner as a gift from a client, a senior oil employee. It was the first time Zulaikha was allowed to enter this park she had always imagined was a paradise. She saw Jamshid and his wife. Maryam still looked glamorous with her side chignon hairstyle, orange lipstick, and beautiful yellow dress. She did not even look at Zulaikha. Jamshid approached their table, however, and greeted the couple warmly. "I'm so happy to see you, Zulaikha *jan*. You look healthy and happy. Is this gentleman your husband?"

Unbelievable! He acts as if nothing happened between us.

She was proud to introduce Assef.

"We heard that you have a son now."

Yes, another son. "Yes, his name is Sohrab. Thanks for asking."

"Send my regards to your family. It was very nice to meet you, young man."

Assef stood up out of respect as Jamshid left their table. He asked her who Jamshid was.

"His son was Hessam's high school friend."

"Do I know him?"

"He's studying in the US now."

"Jamshid seems to be a nice man," said Assef.

Zulaikha looked away. She began talking about how she had always imagined the club just the way it was: the pool, the fountain, and the trees. The American and European guests danced to the live music.

At home, Zulaikha was quiet. Running into Jamshid and his wife opened an old wound. Sohrab was sleeping soundly, but she couldn't. She poured herself an icy glass of water and stood on her balcony. The palm grove at night had a pleasant soundtrack. Crickets chirping, dogs barking, and the breeze cooling their room. This peaceful silence was heaven with Assef near her, and it would be frightening as a nightmare without him. She glanced at Assef sleeping as she crawled under the sheets. "When will you leave me with my thin glass of loneliness again?" she muttered.

Six weeks later, Assef lit a cigar on their balcony one night watching the grove, his back to her. Zulaikha didn't like the smoke and stayed inside.

"I have to leave for a job in Kuwait tomorrow," he said.

She stayed idle on the bed.

Assef turned to her. "I can't refuse a lucrative job, Zuli—we need money."

Zulaikha held Sohrab in her arms. "Did I say anything?"

"Your silence is louder than any scream," Assef said. "You have no idea how much it hurts. I prefer that you shout at me."

"How long will you be away this time?"

"Probably for five or six weeks."

"This time, sometimes call, or at least write."

"That's a promise." He came inside and held her and Sohrab. "You and this little one are all I have in this world."

Zulaikha would have to explain his absence again and react to judgmental comments implying his unfaithfulness. Sometimes she ran out of ideas to defend him, making her doubt whether she trusted him. But her little boy would perhaps make their separation tolerable this time.

■■■

Hessam's weekends began every Thursday afternoon. After tutoring Abbass and Zulaikha, he would head out to gallivant downtown. Abbass and Zulaikha were trying to improve their Farsi. Abbass wanted to get a high school diploma, and Zulaikha wanted to read books in her free time when Assef was away. Sometimes, on their break, Hessam talked about things he had heard at work, the revolutionary movements in Northern Iran or the suspicious deaths of the famous writers Samad Behrangi and Forough Farakhozad in the late-sixties. Zulaikha enjoyed learning about the world outside of Khuzestan. One day, she noticed a few new books scattered around Hessam's place and tried to organize his clutter. When Hessam caught her smelling one of his books, he laughed and said, "I like the smell of new books, too."

Abbass joined them.

"I like the musty smell of old books more," she said. "They remind me of my schoolbooks. These smell new. Why do you buy so many books all at once?"

"A campaign against censorship was announced on the news," Hessam said. "I even saw Maxim Gorky's novels in a downtown bookstore. You never know. They may change their mind and ban them again."

"You should buy a bookcase then. Lend me a few, but only the ones with a love story."

"Love story?" Hessam shook his head and glanced at Abbass, who was reading and not paying attention to them.

"What did I say wrong?" She glanced at Abbass. "Okay. Find me a forbidden love story, then." Hessam's rolled his eyes and Zulaikha responded by making a face with her tongue out.

■ ■ ■

Whenever Assef arrived in town from a long trip, Zulaikha would prepare a big meal and invite her family. It was February of 1974 and Assef had just returned. Madineh and Habib were out of town visiting Isfahan and she asked Hessam to come over for lunch, but he refused. He and Abbass planned to watch the live broadcast of Khosro Golesorkhi and his friend Keramat Daneshian's trial. They were convicted of a plot to kidnap the King's son. It was the first time in Iran's history that a political prisoner's prosecution would be televised live.

Assef went to Hessam's house to bring them over, promising they would watch the program together.

Zulaikha had made cinnamon-flavoured green beans and rice—*lubia polo*—but no one had an appetite. Each prisoner bravely defended himself and told the court that the Shah's National Intelligence and Security, called SAVAK, had tortured them. They were imprisoned only for their ideas—they were journalists—they had not committed any crime.

"Are they going to kill them?" Zulaikha sat beside Hessam.

Assef fed Sohrab and did not participate.

"After what they said today? I don't think they expected that to happen."

"You and Abbass, are you careful?" Zulaikha asked, but no one answered her question. She repeated louder, "Hessam, answer me!"

"We're hungry. Where's the food?" Assef said playfully.

Sohrab giggled at Assef and Abbass, who were making funny faces.

After they left, Assef searched for an Emirates channel. "Let's cheer up a bit. I can't breathe—I need music."

Suddenly Zulaikha heard Googoosh's voice. "Stop it right

there." She pointed at the television.

Assef began to move his body and hummed with the song.

"You like her, don't you?" Zulaikha said as she put her hand on her hip.

"Who doesn't?"

A few days later, Assef rose before sunrise, kissed Zulaikha and Sohrab, and left to be on the road again. Zulaikha couldn't sleep anymore. She turned on the radio. Before switching the news channel, she heard that the two prisoners were executed yesterday. She switched it off and stared at the ceiling for a few minutes.

Hessam must be devastated.

She needed to run a few errands. It was windy that day, leading the palm trees to dance and her hair to blow. Sohrab walked closer to her. She heard two young men talking in an aisle as she was looking for sunflower oil. She heard the word "strike," but they stopped when they saw Zulaikha. They looked scared, but why? Suddenly the store owner yelled at them. "No politics talk here. Get out."

The men glared at him and left the store.

Zulaikha picked up the oil and approached the cashier. "What was that about?"

"Nothing!" He gave her back some change and grinned at Sohrab. "Every idiot in this town is Che Guevara these days."

She had seen a book about Che at Hessam's the other day. Her hand trembled as she held Sohrab's hand.

She couldn't wait to see Hessam and ask him what he knew—what was changing in the country.

Hessam would know the answers. He should. He reads all those books.

She gazed out of the window as she cooked a spicy spaghetti dinner. When the storm stopped, she packed and placed it in her basket bag.

"Let's go see Uncle Hessam," she said.

Sohrab was playful—he had a drawing to show his uncle.

Hessam looked tired and wasn't excited about the drawing or

the spicy food. He didn't talk much, either, not even with Sohrab. She put the dish in the fridge. "If you have a Golesorkhi book or any banned books, let me take them to my house. I'll keep them for you."

"Leave me alone," Hessam said. "I don't need protection—not yet."

She said goodnight and opened the door to leave.

"Wait!" Hessam said. "This poem is by Daneshian, the quiet one." He recited:

> *And may this lash, this slavery,*
> *And may this burden of poverty, this futility,*
> *In every form,*
> *May these be abolished all over the world.*

Zulaikha was even more confused now than she was before asking Hessam for answers. Her brother just implied that she was a slave to poverty and futility. She closed the door without another word.

■ ■ ■

Sohrab was almost four years old, and Zulaikha had a few steady years with Assef. They still lived in the same place but talked about moving to a bigger one, maybe buying a small house and having another child—even her asthma was under control. She had bought newer furniture, a brown buffet hutch that she decorated with nice chinaware and crystal. They had travelled to Ahvaz, Shiraz a few times, and even visited Gholam's family in Aghajary once. She still enjoyed reading magazines and romantic books and watching late-night shows and old movies. She did not work, but when her acquaintances or neighbours needed her, she did their hair and makeup. When there was a wedding, she was invited by the families who owed her for her services. When Assef was absent, she would take Sohrab and Madineh with her. She didn't call Aliah as often as she used to except when she would dream about her, Leelah, or Bahrain.

"I dreamed about you last night," she said. "How are things with you?"

Aliah told her about the children—now irritating teenagers. She always asked Zulaikha what she saw in her dream.

"We went to the deli and bought a sandwich. Suddenly a seagull swooped down and stole it from my hand, and you laughed." She didn't tell her that Sohrab was with her in those dreams but never Assef.

One night Sohrab asked her in Arabic, "Where's my father?" She responded in Farsi that he was working and would return soon. Sohrab was learning both languages from Assef and Abbass. She enjoyed their unique bilingual conversations. Madineh and even Hessam criticized her for letting Sohrab learn his father's tongue simultaneously.

"Sohrab should learn his first language first," Hessam said when they took Sohrab to the swimming pool in a taxi.

"Sometimes you sound and act like our mother. Did you know that?"

"No, I don't. Why do you say that?"

Sohrab was staring at her. She was determined to find the right place and time to tell Hessam openly that she expected more from him. She didn't respond to him; instead, she grinned at Sohrab.

Sohrab was still sleeping in his parents' bed. When she thought about moving to another house, it was the balcony that she didn't want to give up. She recently noticed the cacophonous, distant sounds of shotguns. Though too far away to wake up other people in the neighbourhood, they still interrupted her peaceful moments with the grove.

"Did you hear that?" Sohrab was startled.

"Nothing to be afraid of. The police are chasing thieves." She tried to grasp if it was in her mind that the shotguns were now a part of the voices of the grove. She blamed watching too much political news, cautioning the increasing fragility of peace in Khuzestan. Suddenly she heard another single shot. This time from an even closer distance. "They're real," she muttered. She closed the balcony door and turned the ceiling fan on.

■ ■ ■

Early autumn was the best time for a picnic in Abadan, when the sun gently enveloped the Karun River and people could breathe again outside of their houses. Zulaikha noticed a change in her mother's behaviour. She used to be the one to fill the cooler with beer bottles, but not anymore. That day, Madineh sat in a corner beside Hessam and leaned against a willow tree. When Habib asked her about his beverages, she said, "Sorry, I forgot them."

He shouted, "No, you didn't."

Assef was happy to intervene. "I have enough for all of us. Where's Abbass by the way?" He looked at his watch.

Zulaikha and Sohrab were playing on the other side of the willow tree. She heard Madineh and Hessam's conversation.

"I'll talk to him," Hessam said.

"With Assef, he drinks even more. He's not himself anymore."

Still sitting with Assef, Habib asked Hessam, "What's the matter? Why are you looking at me this way? What's your mother been telling you?" He was now having a Coca-Cola and seemed sober. Assef was having a nap.

Hessam went closer to Habib. "With all due respect, *Amu* Habib, we had something good going in our family with you, but you're ruining it for all of us with your excessive drinking. This has to stop—especially when women and children are around."

Assef opened his eyes and sat as he hugged his knees. "Look who's talking."

Habib chuckled.

"I'm not against drinking, but *Amu* Habib, you're our elder. You always give us life lessons. This scene near my sister and her child is not right. Is it, Assef?"

"I didn't know we were being inappropriate."

Abbass greeted everyone and explained that his truck had broken—he had been stuck in an auto shop. "I've borrowed a new Paykan—" He sounded excited but noticed the intense atmosphere. "Have I missed anything?"

"Can you give us a ride?" Zulaikha asked. "We should go. Sohrab is tired."

"Yes, keep your husband away," Madineh muttered. "He's bad news."

Zulaikha heard her but continued her way toward the parking lot. Abbass took her picnic basket from her hand as Assef carried Sohrab.

Assef sat in the front seat, complimenting Abbass's borrowed car. They spoke Arabic, with Sohrab in the back seat, too. Typically it was fun to see the three of them being so close. Today, they all irritated her. "Can you stop speaking Arabic when I am around?" she asked. "It's rather rude."

Abbass looked into the mirror and apologized to her, but Assef looked out of the window until they got home. He asked Abbass to wait for him while he helped to bring the picnic bag, Sohrab, and the blanket to the door. He didn't go inside. "I'm going for a stroll with Abbass—I need to clear my mind."

Her knees trembled as she went inside. She had forgotten this extent of fear, now suddenly rushing through her body.

■ ■ ■

Madineh visited them often to see Sohrab, whom she would bring toys or treats, a box of cookies or chocolate. She didn't talk about how things were between her and Habib. When Zulaikha asked her how *Amu* Habib was doing, Madineh would only answer, "Like always!" Both women were dealing with the same thing—denying that something was wrong with their relationships with the men they loved.

Abadan was mysteriously beautiful in the fog in the winter. The mist spread throughout the city, obscuring the sightlines but making the view more enigmatic. Near dawn, Zulaikha was woken by someone knocking at the door. Assef had gone out with Habib and some co-workers after work, but he wasn't back yet.

She put her ear to the door. "Who's there?"

"It's me—your mother. Habib is not home yet."

Zulaikha opened the door.

"Something must have happened. Habib always returns before midnight."

"You stay here with Sohrab. I'll go find them." She put on her clothes.

"Where are you going?"

"I don't know. I'll go to Hessam's first. Maybe we'll go to their depot. Just stay here with Sohrab, will you?"

"I want to come, too," said Madineh.

"No, we can't leave Sohrab, and we can't carry him with us. You came to ask for my help. Let me help."

Hessam was alone and had no clue about their whereabouts. Zulaikha and Hessam caught a cab to Habib's depot. From a distance, they saw an ambulance and two police cars. Their taxi driver slowed down, when one of the officers gave him a signal to pull over. Hessam and Zulaikha got out of the car and looked around.

Zulaikha found an acquaintance and asked him what had happened.

"We all went out for a few drinks after work—as we were on our way back, we were all teasing Habib because he was so drunk. Assef bet him that he couldn't cross the street without falling. Habib stepped into the road—it was foggy. The approaching driver couldn't see him. The truck didn't hit him hard, but *Amu* Habib lost control and hit his head on a street pole. It all happened in an instant."

"But he's alive, right?" Zulaikha asked him, sick with fear.

"It happened too fast—" The man sobbed. "We all loved him like a father."

"Where's Assef?" The thought of what she had just heard was like ice creeping through her veins, numbing her hands and feet.

"He must be in the police car over there."

She ran toward the police car. "I want to talk to him," she

shouted. "That's my husband."

"Step aside, ma'am. We just want to ask a few questions. He'll be home soon."

Inside the police car, Assef's head was down. Zulaikha tapped her fingers on the car's window as she called his name again. Still, Assef would not meet her eyes.

"Zuli *jan*," Hessam said. "You must let them do their jobs." He stroked her arm gently.

They returned to Zulaikha's house, where Madineh was sitting on the street waiting for them. Seeing her, Zulaikha burst into tears.

"Could you wait here?" Hessam told the driver. He approached Madineh and held her tight as he told her the news. "There was an accident, Mother," he said. "We lost *Amu* Habib."

"You witch," Madineh swore at Zulaikha. "You and your endless hatred for me, you cursed me—you and your no-good husband."

"Take her home," Zulaikha said. "And leave me alone, Hessam."

Inside the house, Sohrab, too, began to cry.

Zulaikha tried to make Sohrab go back to sleep. She whispered a lullaby while her mind went to the day that Habib told her about Assef's problems. It was as if he was in the room telling her, "Be prepared, my child. He will run away."

Assef returned a few hours later. Zulaikha held him in her arms and told him everything would be okay if they had each other. Assef looked at her and said, "I can't stay here, Zulaikha."

"Why?"

"Why? I could've prevented this. I can't face Hessam and your mother. I need to go away."

"Where are you going?"

"I'm going to stay with my sister for a while."

"But you will come back soon, won't you?"

"I only know that I need some time away from here."

"We'll come with you."

"No, Zulaikha. I want to be alone."

"What's happening here?" She cleared her throat.

Where did I put my inhaler?
"I have never been a good husband to you, Zulaikha."
"Stop this now."
"Your mother is right about me. She's always been right."
"You don't believe that." She held the inhaler in her mouth for a few seconds. "Stop it. Don't hurt me like this, Assef."
He packed his bag and gave her some money.
"Go. Take the time you need, but come back," she pleaded.
At the door, avoiding the look in her eyes, he held her and Sohrab, then left.

■■■

Zulaikha visited her mourning mother sometimes to make sure she ate or there was food for Hessam. Madineh was suffering, but she was the reason for Zulaikha's unhappiness once again. Madineh constantly complained about Habib's drinking, but she also served him trays of *arak* and sometimes joked that he was happier and funnier when he drank.
"Why do you come here?" Madineh asked. "You didn't even come to his funeral."
"Who would take care of Sohrab?"
"Good excuse." Madineh had resumed smoking.
"Judge me as much as you want, Mother. But Sohrab shouldn't see scenes of sobbing people like that. You shouldn't want that either."
The truth was that she avoided the scene of her mother's mourning. She had wished for Madineh's suffering for a long time, and now she was. To feel anything for her mother was unbearable.

■■■

After three more weeks without hearing from Assef, Zulaikha finally decided to find him in Ahvaz using an old address from Rhianna, his younger sister.

It had been a few months since some of their neighbours had gotten telephone lines installed. Zulaikha pushed Hessam to apply for a telephone line but he replied that he was being careful about their expenses. He still shopped in the Kuwaiti market for his wardrobe, though. "The real reason is your laziness if you ask me," she told him.

When she couldn't get a hold of Hessam at work, she called Mrs. Sara.

"Hessam said he was going to Kharg Island for work," Mrs. Sara said.

"Really? I just called his work. They didn't know."

"I don't know, darling. He gave me the key to water the plants and told me he was going for a few days. That's all I know."

That was strange, but she had more important things in mind than monitoring Hessam's whereabouts. She packed and got a bus ticket, and four hours later, she and Sohrab were in Ahvaz. She had no appetite to watch the scenery as the bus entered Ahvaz, but she couldn't ignore the migrating birds flying above White Bridge, *Pol-e Sefid*. They overwhelmed Sohrab. He stood on his seat with his tiny legs, humming bird-like sounds. At first, Zulaikha tried to calm him, but then she went along. They made funny sounds together, ignoring sleeping passengers. And then they were at the bus station.

Upon arriving at Assef's home, she asked the taxi driver to wait a moment to ensure the address was correct.

Rhianna opened the door and greeted her warmly. She held Sohrab and said, "Finally, I get to see my nephew. Come in. Welcome." Rhianna was quiet, but Zulaikha was sure that she knew everything. She played with Sohrab and kept saying to him, "You, my brother, or my nephew?" Sohrab laughed as if he knew she was teasing him for his resemblance to his father.

"Do you know where Assef is?"

Rhianna certainly was a mature nineteen-year-old. "He'll come back to you. He loves you," she said.

"I want him to let me into his world."

"He's hurt. *Amu* Habib was like a father to him. We always lose people. There's something about us. When we love people, they either die or go away."

"That's a scary thought. Please don't tell him that."

Rhianna smiled and walked with Sohrab toward the kitchen. "Just give him some time."

Zulaikha followed her but kept her eyes on Sohrab. "What can a woman do to keep a man?"

Why am I asking her? She's just a kid.

Rhianna showed Sohrab a stuffed animal and made faces as if she had not heard Zulaikha.

Zulaikha's throat was dry. She had not had anything to eat or drink since the morning.

Assef came back to his sister's at night. Zulaikha asked him to return to Abadan with her. "It'll be the fortieth day of *Amu* Habib's passing. I need you, Assef. I've been crying since he died, but I'm no longer sure if it's for him or me. The deceased deserve for us to pay attention to them. You don't let me do that."

"You think it's easy for me?"

"No, I don't. But easier for you to be here than with your child and me. That's for sure."

"Think whatever you want. I can't go back there again," he said. "I don't want to stay in Khuzestan anymore. Do you remember telling me that you wanted to stay in Abadan, but Abadan did not want to keep you? Now, I feel the same about Abadan, about Khuzestan."

"What about our child?" She was resigned to the answer she knew she would hear, but despair forced her to ask it anyway.

"I'm not a good father to him. Don't worry—I'll keep supporting both of you."

"Supporting us?" A line of sweat trailed down her neck. "I thought you'd come to your senses when you saw Sohrab and me. I wanted to take you home. Now that I see you like this, I want to run from you. You're a coward."

"Don't say things you don't mean."

"I can't find any other word to describe you better."

She gently pulled Sohrab's hand.

Assef brushed passed her, but Zulaikha shouted, "No, you don't need to leave. I'll leave this time." She grabbed her bag.

Rhianna intervened. "Zulaikha *jan*, please. Just for tonight, for me. I want to have some time with my nephew."

As soon as Sohrab was soundly asleep, Rhianna left the tiny house. "I'll go to stay with a friend. We had plans to watch a movie together."

The road trip had been exhausting. Zulaikha took a shower, changed into something comfortable and went to bed. She could hear the TV from the other room, even though the volume was down. Warda was performing her relatively new song, "*Esmaony*" (Listen to Me). They had watched this together a few weeks ago—she had danced to parts of that long, mesmerizing song.

She awoke to Assef's body close to her, watching her face. She looked into his eyes and let him kiss her neck and then her mouth. Their bodies entangled again, as intense as their first time. She wrapped her arms around his lower back. He had lost weight. She pulled his body to the side and led him to lie on his back. Now she kissed his neck and chest. Only their moaning from pleasure broke the silence in that room, but that song, "*Esmaony*," was in her head. She could hear the end of the opening music, and with her broken Arabic, she could grasp the lyrics of the first lines: *people who love, before you judge me, listen to me, listen to me*. She would leave him tomorrow. She was out of tricks to keep him.

■■■

For days, she avoided Madineh and Hessam. Their sympathetic *I told you so* looks were more humiliating than comforting. Her bond with Abbass and his father became closer, though. Abbass might know about Assef's whereabouts. His youthfulness attracted little Sohrab. Sometimes they went to the harbour, and Zulaikha watched them playing at the beach, then they sat and listened to his music. Often she wondered how Sohrab would turn out in the future without Assef's presence. Despite the heartbreak, she still wanted Sohrab to become like his father in many ways. Sohrab had taken Assef's looks, but would he inherit his humour, the way he walked, his voice, and all she had missed?

Six months later, there was no sign of Assef, except every three months, a messenger showed up with an envelope containing three or four hundred tomans—enough for food and shelter.

Madineh was getting better. She visited Sohrab once a week. She was busy dealing with Habib's estate. Habib had two daughters from his first marriage. He had a will that said Madineh had a small share of his house. Habib's son-in-law bought it from her, and she moved back to their old house.

Hessam asked Zulaikha to help with unpacking of the boxes Madineh had moved back. "She keeps sleeping and when she's up, she's smoking," he said. "Please come at least unpack those boxes she had brought back. They're in the middle of the living room."

When Zulaikha went to the house, Madineh was smoking in the courtyard, just like how Hessam described her: messy hair and puffy eyes.

Zulaikha was beginning to place the dishes from a box in the cupboard when she heard Madineh. "I've heard about Assef," Madineh said. "You should stop working. You're going to need to sit down for this."

"Don't tell me he has a girl," Zulaikha said.

"You got that right—an Arab girl in Kuwait."

Zulaikha picked up her bag and went to the door.

"Where are you going? You just got here, for heaven's sake."

Zulaikha found her inhaler in her bag. "I need fresh air. I'll be back. You stay with Sohrab. I need two minutes."

Abbass was taking Abu out for dinner when Zulaikha showed up at their door.

"Have you heard about Assef?"

They invited her in, but she didn't go inside.

"Why, Abbass? You know him well. Tell me why? Was I not Arab enough for him?"

Abbass dropped his car key. He squatted down to pick it up. "I honestly don't know what to say," He looked up. "Maybe he didn't feel he belonged here—"

Zulaikha burst into tears.

Abu shouted, "Stop it. Don't blame yourself. You didn't deserve to be abandoned—neither did Sohrab." Abu asked Abbass to drive her home.

Sohrab and Madineh were both sleeping when she got home. Hessam was up watching TV. "What's going on?" he asked.

"Happy now? He proved you right. Go celebrate." Zulaikha threw her wallet and key on a shelf.

Hessam frowned at Abbass, who made a "be quiet" sign with his index finger. She went to bed, knowing that she would have another sleepless night.

■■■

It wasn't the norm for a young single woman to live alone. Hessam finally broke the silence between them.

"I don't want you to be a second wife anymore. I couldn't do anything the first time—I was a child, but now I'm not so I go on and say it, it's time you divorced him."

"I still need time. Besides, how can we divorce without his presence?"

"It shouldn't be hard—he's been absent for how long?"

Assef's absence for over a year would make it legal for the woman to divorce.

"Who would marry a second wife in this country, Zuli?"

Talking badly about Assef still made her uncomfortable.

Next Friday morning, when Hessam was off work, she and Hessam went to a divorce notary public together. No one was there but them. Zulaikha suspected that Hessam paid them extra money not to ask questions or pry into Zulaikha and Assef's history.

Hessam had hidden a gift-wrapped box that he gave her that night after dinner. "What is it for?"

"Just to bring a smile to your face," he said. "Open it."

"I'm not celebrating my divorce, if that's what you mean. Take it back."

"Give it to me." Madineh and Sohrab opened it playfully. It was a yellow purse she had wanted for a while but was too expensive.

Zulaikha cancelled her lease and moved in with Hessam and their mother. They all lived together in *Istgah Haft* once again.

■■■

Sohrab was five years old. Despite taking after his father's looks, his character was different. He was lively and energetic but, thankfully, not too curious. He didn't ask too many questions about why they moved or where his father was—perhaps he considered Hessam a father figure—which made things smoother for Zulaikha.

That Friday afternoon, on the final hours of his weekend, Hessam took a shower and dressed up to go out. Zulaikha was feeding Sohrab and watching television. Madineh and Mrs. Sara had gone grocery shopping. Everyone in Abadan was talking about *Gavaznha—The Deer*—a new Iranian movie. Hessam told Zulaikha that he would take her to see it if she'd like.

"What's it about?" She turned the TV's volume down.

"It's about someone who runs from the police and takes refuge at an old friend's house. The friend is Behrouz Vossoughi."

"Sounds like a movie for men. Is there a love story in it?"

Hessam chuckled. "I don't think so."

"If you'd like to see it, go watch it with Abbass. I'll make dinner—bring him over. I'll put aside some food for Abu, too."

"Okay. I'd better run to catch the early show. I heard this movie sells out quickly."

"Wait, Hessam. Call Mrs. Sara next door if you go to the late-night show so we don't wait up for you."

He was on his way out when Zulaikha asked, "By the way, which cinema is the show playing at, The Oil Club's?"

"No, it's at Cinema Rex."

"Okay. Have fun, Brother."

For dinner, Zulaikha cooked white fish and a herbed rice dish made with cilantro and dill, *sabzi polo*. She set the table with her chinaware, and when there was no sign of Hessam and Abbass, they ate as they watched television. After another hour had passed, she began to feel anxious. "I'll check with Mrs. Sara if Hessam has called."

Hessam had not called Mrs. Sara, but he was always late and rarely kept his promise to tell them where he was. Still, she had a bad feeling. Abbass would never leave his father alone for too long. She told Madineh she would take some food to Abu and return quickly. Sohrab was sleeping. "Keep an eye on Sohrab. I'll be right back."

It was a hot August night, and Abu's door was open. Ambulances and police sirens were waking up the city, but she tried not to let her mind wander. She stood on Abu's threshold while greeting him and bringing in the dishes.

"Why are you troubling yourself for me, Zulaikha *jan*, at this time of the night?" Abu said with kindness as always.

"No trouble, Abu. I thought Abbass forgot to leave some food for you since he was supposed to have dinner with us."

"They are late. It's almost midnight." He lifted his head carefully. He could also hear the sirens.

"Don't worry. I heard there was a late show tonight. Hessam said that if the earlier movie was sold out, they would catch the late show," she said. "It's an excellent movie."

All of Abadan seemed full of piercing sounds. "Something must be wrong," Abu said.

Zulaikha did not know what to say. "What should we do, Abu?"

"We'd better listen to the news on the radio."

The local radio announcer said there was a big fire at Cinema Rex. "Fire broke out half an hour ago. As yet, we have no information about casualties."

Abu looked at Zulaikha with fear in his eyes. "Go and find our boys, Zulaikha. Go quickly."

Down the street, people were outside of their homes. Everyone was running. The smoke got thicker and thicker as she approached the cinema—she ran all eight blocks alongside a massive crowd of people moving toward Cinema Rex when she recognized Abbass running with a shovel.

"Abbass!" she yelled.

He stopped. "Zulaikha? Have you heard?"

"Where's Hessam?"

"He's okay. He went to find a phone booth to call your neighbour."

"What are you doing with that shovel?"

"I'm volunteering to help. There must be survivors. They locked people in the theatre and burned them alive—just like that."

"Who did?" she asked.

"Nobody knows. Go home to Sohrab."

"You'd better go home, too. Abu's very worried for you. I was just there."

He shook his head. "No, I can't."

"Yes, you can. Don't do this to him."

"Would you go and tell him I'm okay then?" he begged.

As soon as Hessam approached them, Zulaikha grabbed his arm. "What's going on?"

"I don't know. They say more than four hundred have died."

Zulaikha covered her open mouth with her hand. "Did you call Mrs. Sara?"

"Yes, she said she would go and tell Mother we're fine."

"You two let my father know I'm okay. I have to stay here and help if I can."

"He won't believe us," Zulaikha insisted.

"Let's go, Zuli," Hessam said. "He's as stubborn as Abu. You can never convince him of anything."

They walked back toward Abu's home. "Why didn't you phone?" Zulaikha asked. "We waited for you for a long time."

"Well, Abbass brought his girlfriend to the movie."

Zulaikha stopped walking. "Girlfriend?"

"Yes, he's a human being, you know."

"I know, okay, and then?" she asked impatiently.

"After the show, he wanted to walk her to her house. So we got there, and she offered us tea and cookies, and we stayed a bit."

"You forgot about me waiting for you?"

"No. I kept telling Abbass I had to call you, and he kept saying okay, in a minute, and then we heard the sirens and ran back to the Rex to help people, but we were too late. It was already blazing."

"You two could have been killed tonight." She breathed faster—she was scared of any asthma attack symptoms her doctor had warned her of. "I need my inhaler. I'm going to be sick." She ran toward a group of people standing outside of their house watching the crowd. She asked them to let her use their bathroom.

No one ever solved the mystery of the Cinema Rex burning. The horrifying thought of burning people alive in that cinema damaged the soul of Abadan and that of the whole country. The images of those last hours, the victims' families in mourning, and their stories were the topic of Iran's media, the *Keyhan* and *Ettela'at* papers, and local daily news. In coffee shops and cashier line-ups throughout the city, people offered their views about the burning of Cinema Rex.

"It was SAVAK's doing. They wanted to warn people not to go to movies portraying political messages."

"You're awfully wrong. Shah would never let something like this happen. There's a new Islamic movement. Have you heard about Mojahedin? This is their work."

"Damn Bolsheviks. This is what the Soviet spies are doing to this country. They want to weaken the kingdom and take over."

A few days later, The National Oil Company workers of Abadan went on strike against the regime.

Abadan wore the black of mourning that hot summer of 1978.

CHAPTER 3

Iran and Iraq War

SEPTEMBER 1980 TO AUGUST 1988

Madineh shouted, "How can they be so happy? How can they celebrate like this?" Shah had left Iran. The TV news showed people celebrating on the streets of Tehran and all over the country as Madineh shed tears for the King.

Zulaikha read the *Ettela'at* paper every day. On that day, January 16, 1979, *Shah Raft*, the King is Gone, was the headline. Mohammad Reza Shah had become an outcast, a man with no country. He flew for hours and days to find a leader who might accept him—let him land on foreign soil.

When Shah's picture appeared on the screen, Madineh sobbed, "He was so charming—so handsome, we didn't deserve him. *Ey Khoda*, this migraine is killing me."

"Snap out of it, Mother." Zulaikha was fed up with Madineh's constant whining. "Since when did you fall in love with the King? Why can't we be happy like other people are right now? It may be a good change."

"You'll see about that. You and everyone else."

Trying to distract from Madineh's depressing mood, Zulaikha said to now six-year-old Sohrab, "Let's go and buy some aspirin for Bibi Madineh. Maybe we can get some mortadella for tonight to make sandwiches for dinner, too. How does that sound?" Sohrab loved mortadella sandwiches. He ran to his room to change.

They walked through the quiet alley. The crowd must be gathering downtown. "How about going downtown and having a nice milkshake?"

A big toothless smile blossomed on Sohrab's face. A taxi driver warned her that the streets were too busy and he would take them a few blocks only. He was right. They walked the rest along with the crowd. She picked a piece of candy off a tray a young man was offering and handed it to Sohrab.

"Whose birthday is it?" Sohrab asked.

"Nobody's—we're celebrating—" She searched for words that would make sense. "—a new thing."

"What thing?"

"We don't know yet, but it'll be good."

It was easy to convince Sohrab. He held the candy in his hand.

Not long ago, the same streets were filled with angry demonstrators, refinery workers on strike, and soldiers with guns enforcing the evening curfew. Now, flowers, cookies, smiles, and beeping car horns had taken over. Such a happy city it appeared to be!

But no, there was still anger. Another group at the next intersection was passing and shouting, "Down with America, death to the Shah, death to capitalism."

"They don't look happy, *Maman*," Sohrab said.

Maybe it hadn't been such a good idea to bring Sohrab into this mob. The pharmacy was at the corner. She bought a few packs of aspirin, some chocolate bars, and a bag of chips. When they left the pharmacy, the sidewalks seemed less crowded. She spotted a woman across the street carrying a big picture frame, maybe a work of art. She looked familiar. She wore a lacy green scarf and a dark blue suit.

Sohrab distracted her. "Where are we going? You forgot the mortadella."

The woman entered a shop—a carpet shop. She was Kia's mother.

"Sorry, *azizam*. Let's wait for the crowd and noise to calm down."

"Can I have a chocolate bar?"

She conceded, letting him have a treat. She held on to her son's hand as they crossed the street and entered the carpet shop without knowing what she was doing. "Let's see some of these frames. You'll like them."

Maryam was talking to the shopkeeper. She seemed stressed. It appeared that the man had expected her—she sold her artwork to him and received some cash in exchange.

"Be careful out there—it's not safe for a woman to be alone right now," said the shopkeeper.

"My husband is waiting for me in the car," she said. "You know him—he's too proud. He doesn't want to be seen selling anything."

As she turned to leave the shop, Maryam glanced at Zulaikha and Sohrab, browsing the walls in the other corner. She left the shop hastily.

Zulaikha approached the cashier to see her artwork. The carpet frame portrayed a young girl sitting beside a river in the woods. "Is this that lady's handmade work?"

"Yes, Ma'am. She makes these and sells them to send money abroad for her son."

"*Maman*, it's beautiful. Can we buy it?"

She grinned. "I think it's too expensive for us, *azizam*, right Sir?"

"She makes them by hand, and they're precious," he said. "Hopefully, when you finish school and work, you can come and buy one for your mother."

Sohrab nodded.

She was still staring at the portrait of the woman who resembled the artist.

"I wish I could find a customer for it in this situation," the shopkeeper said. "I couldn't refuse her. She's been an excellent customer for a long time."

Perhaps the carpet my mother got for the blood money of my murdered child was from this shop.

A few demonstrators were shouting, "Death to capitalists.

Down with the USA."

The man opened a pack of cookies and offered it to Sohrab. "You see—I should show them I'm delighted." He glanced at Zulaikha. "Otherwise, I'd be taken as a capitalist, and heaven knows what would happen to me." He went outside his store and stood beside his door like a guard with the pack of cookies. Zulaikha and Sohrab remained behind the window watching the crowd. When the noises disappeared, they left the shop.

When they got home, Hessam, Abbass, and the neighbours were outside, celebrating, dancing, hugging, and distributing *shirini* in the neighbourhood. She could not get the image of Kia's mother and her artwork out of her mind. It had been years since she'd given any thought to Kia and his family. Only one moment was enough to take her back to the pain she suffered. They killed a baby just to prevent their family from mixing with hers. Did other people on the city streets experience the same pain and humiliation? Why didn't she ever scream about an injustice like that? These angry faces and fists aimed to destroy anything in their way. But no such plans for reconstructing or recovering. Something was wrong. Hate was a creepy monster taking over the atmosphere. She shook her head.

"What's wrong? Did something happen?" Hessam asked.

"Nothing, the crowd and noise," she said. "Will you keep an eye on Sohrab? I got something for Mother's migraine."

Sohrab shouted, "Uncle Hessam, we have mortadella sandwiches for dinner tonight."

Hessam leaned over and touched Sohrab's shoulder. "Really? Let's go and get a few Pepsis." He turned and glared at Zulaikha's stunned, frozen face.

This monster she was afraid of, this hate and resentment that looked so ugly on other people, was nested inside her for years. She knew nothing better.

■■■

In the next few weeks, when people finally felt relief and

freedom, they gathered in cafés and other public places to talk about their lessons learned. Some suddenly turned exceedingly religious and quoted the Quran for everything they did, even their bathroom habits. Zulaikha observed that Hessam and Abbass often talked about it. Was it better to lean left toward communism, or was it more practical to wait and see what the government would do?

Madineh was skeptical about the mullahs more than anyone else. "A mullah's job should be limited to preaching at funerals, not running a country." She was sure that everything would die down soon. "It's just a power game. It was the same when Dr. Mosaddegh's coup happened. We must be careful not to get mixed up in with the games of the British."

Zulaikha was silently eager to know what would change for women. Would they still allow a child to become a second wife to an older man, or would an unwanted pregnancy end as tragically as it did for her?

Four months later, in early April, a month after the Persian New Year, when Abadan smelled like jasmine again, the papers printed a naked picture of Amir Abbass Hoveyda's dead body—he was executed the night before. He was the last prime minister in Shah's regime. Zulaikha never had any affection for him, but killing and then displaying him like that disgusted her. This time he let her mother curse them as much as she wanted.

Shortly after, people saw pictures and heard the names of supposed anti-revolutionists, who were promptly executed. It was as if wild animals were unleashed and had no other instinct but killing for survival.

Zulaikha ignored the news and kept working in the house and caring for Sohrab. Because of the political upheavals, the schools were often closed, like many other institutions in the country.

Madineh and Hessam listened to the news all the time. They were becoming lazier and lazier, even in cleaning up after themselves. One morning, she grabbed the radio from her mother's hand and told her to bathe.

"This is going too far. Go on—move—I'll come and wash your

back."

Madineh walked reluctantly toward the bathroom in the courtyard as Zulaikha switched the radio to an Emirates station and watered her plants. She wanted to listen to Vigen again, singing "*Mara Beboos.*" She wanted their everyday life to return.

The radio playing a familiar song, "*Esmaony,*" froze her. Once again, she tried to figure out the lyrics.

Our hearts suffered, we melted, one night they asked him about me, asked him my name, about my love, he said he didn't know me.

But there was no place for sentimentalism anymore. Madineh yelled from the bathroom, "Where are you, girl? You said you'd wash my back."

■ ■ ■

For Sohrab's seventh birthday, she hosted a dinner party to cheer up everyone, complete with a small cake. Assef had sent Sohrab a gift—a toy car she had hidden to give him today. Preparation for the party was tiring, mainly because neither Madineh nor Hessam helped her. They constantly switched back and forth between the BBC and Radio America. Zulaikha asked Hessam to buy some tomatoes for the salad, but he lazily refused. She decided to do it herself after finishing her stew. When she returned to the living room to pick up her purse, Sohrab was trying to show Hessam a funny caricature in a magazine. Hessam and Madineh both hushed the child.

"Later, I'm listening to this," Hessam said.

She asked Sohrab to show her the cartoon—she sat and looked at the magazine with him. "Why don't you and Bibi Madineh go to freshen up?" She glanced at Madineh.

She waited for a moment to confront Hessam, contemplating some mild vengeance. Lately, she missed Assef. Assef had issues, but her family wasn't that innocent, either. Madineh's resentments were evident, but Hessam did nothing to calm her or intervene.

Hessam went to the kitchen for a cup of tea.

"What's up with that beard?" This was the moment she was

looking for. "Why don't you shave it? It's disgusting."

Hessam saw through her insult. "What's your problem? Why are you so cranky with me these days?"

Her brother's identity had been confusing her for some time. He had become an intellectual, and recited complicated poems to her or told her things she didn't know in his condescending tone. But what happened to her fun-loving, outgoing brother? What happened to his nightlife and secret lovers?

He now only hung out with people in mosques and unknown friends' houses to discuss the latest news about the new government—whether a coup would happen or if people would say no to the Islamic regime.

"I feel you want to be someone else—someone I don't recognize anymore—from that beard to how you talk."

"Maybe you're not yourself, either." He frowned as he sipped some tea, showing it burned his tongue.

Maybe he was right. She was changing into an ignorant person who did not care about what was happening to other people. "Excuse me." She brushed past him to go to Mrs. Sara's and borrow a few tomatoes.

The radio was off when she returned to the kitchen to wash the tomatoes.

"Come on now, Zulaikha. What's happening between us?"

"I asked you a simple question. Why are you growing a beard and going to the mosque? I want to understand."

"Don't you see what's going on in this country?"

That condescending tone again.

"I was known as a communist. Up to a few weeks ago, everyone thought the communists or the nationalists would get the power. Now things shifted. Everywhere I go, I feel I don't belong anymore. I want to make everyone comfortable with me. Don't you think having a beard or hanging out with them in the mosque would make them believe I am not the enemy?" he implored.

Pressuring him might have been selfish. He wanted to blend in with those whom he did not understand. Was he able to fool the extremists, though? He was not one of them. Their values were not his. But what if, through closeness, he became one of them?

Hessam returned to the living room and sat on the carpet pillow. He glanced at her, expecting her to say something. But she continued stirring the pot.

Madineh and Sohrab entered the room. "Bathroom is free now, Hessam. Go shave your beard, for heaven's sake."

"Seriously? You too?"

Zulaikha chuckled. "Yes, we're an anti-beard team in this house."

"What's this smell, *Maman*? What did you cook?" Sohrab asked.

"I'm making that okra dish that you like. Are you hungry?"

"Yes, very. When will it be ready?"

"Wait a bit, darling. We have guests. Have some fruit to tide you over."

She checked the cooler's switch. "Why isn't this cooling?" she muttered.

Hessam took out the cutlery and plates from the cupboard. "Growing a beard is the same as if they asked you to wear Hijab."

"It's not the same," she said. "They're trying to force us to wear it." She made a fan from a magazine as she glanced at Madineh, expecting her to comment. But she was occupied with her new hobby of card reading that she was learning from Mrs. Sara. "Isn't Sara coming?" Madineh asked.

"She will, after dinner," Zulaikha said.

"So, you're saying you will wear it only if they force you to?" Hessam asked.

"I won't wear it—just like I don't now."

"I bet you would if one of them came to our house. Things are different now."

"Maybe I would, just to avoid confrontation, but not to blend in with them. That is different."

Her guests Abbass, Najwa, his fiancé, her son, Jalal, and Abu arrived.

Abu's condition had been improving. Maybe because of the

care he was receiving from Abbass's fiancé, Najwa, he was even walking with the help of a cane—he ate and slept better. Najwa had a son from her first marriage, Jalal—a bit younger than Sohrab. It would be good for Sohrab to spend time with a boy his age. Sohrab had not had any friends over for a long time. Zulaikha needed a friend, too. It had been ages since she had some girl talk, the way she did with Aliah and Leelah in Bahrain.

Abbass's *oud* once again made her realize how much she missed music. The love songs she used to listen to, romantic love scenes she watched and cried over, things that would tell her that life was beautiful. Those were replaced by the gunshots or the footsteps of the revolutionary guards.

After dinner, Mrs. Sara came over and made them coffee. They all had Turkish coffee and cake, as Zulaikha gave Sohrab his gifts. He opened them with excitement. Her gift was a sketchbook with colour pencils. He was over the moon when he opened Assef's box. She kissed Sohrab and told him to play with Najwa's son.

Hessam was quiet again, confusing her as to whether it was about the same issues he had been talking about or if it was about Assef's gift.

"What's going on?" Abbass asked.

"They had a fight," Sohrab piped up. "My *Maman* and Bibi Madineh don't like my uncle's beard."

Abbass chuckled. "What about you? Do you like your uncle's beard?"

Sohrab whispered, "No, I don't."

"You see, Hessam, *volek*, we are all voting for you to shave tonight. What do you say?"

"Leave me alone." There was despair in Hessam's voice.

"Do you want to hear some music?" Abbass asked Sohrab. Sohrab and Jalal sat and watched him play. He allowed them to touch the *oud* and make some sounds. Then he played his music and sang an old Arabic and Farsi song about which they had a long-running debate. Hessam believed that it was an old Farsi song, but Abbass disagreed. "It was an old Arabic folk song called *Al Bint El Chalabiya*. I also heard the Lebanese singer, Fairouz, sing it."

Najwa brought a plate for Abu and sat beside him. She was tall and slim but not stunningly beautiful. Zulaikha had always wondered who would be compatible with Abbass's striking features. She wanted to get to know her better. After years of going to the same clinic, Abbass had made friends with the staff. Najwa was the clinic's new orderly. They met at her friend's, a clinic nurse's wedding. Najwa was also coaching adult swimming part-time. That was why she was in such good shape.

Zulaikha couldn't help envying her for living independently, having a career, and, best of all, having a musician lover. Her thoughts went far away to her world with Assef when he'd watched her dance, admiring her moves and curves.

Abbass played his *oud* and sang in Farsi:

> *My beloved, comb your hair less*
> *For in its waves and tangles*
> *my heart is nesting*
> *You bruise my heart*
> *Every time you comb your hair*

The song's origin was a mystery. It was nested in the heart of the Middle East with its various adaptations.

■ ■ ■

A rigid knock on the bathroom door startled Zulaikha under the stream of the shower. "Hurry up, Zulaikha," Hessam shouted. "There's a war outside." He'd left for work just an hour ago, and now he was back suddenly.

She needed a minute. Last night she woke up thinking she dreamed an earthquake shook the room. She blamed hearing too much news from Madineh's radio.

It was another beautiful September day—the Monday morning of September 22nd, 1981. She planned to see Najwa, and then they would go school shopping for Sohrab and Jalal. This would be their first year of school.

She stepped out of the bathroom with a towel covering her head. "I thought I heard something last night."

"It's not just the air attack, Zuli," Hessam said. "They've invaded Khorramshahr—even people's houses—"

"What's wrong, *Maman*?" Sohrab was beside the tiny garden, holding his toy car.

"Where's Bibi?" Hessam asked him.

She was practicing Turkish coffee reading with Mrs. Sara, but now she opened the door to the courtyard. She had already heard the news. "Did you hear? *Ey, Khoda*. That monster, Saddam Hussein, he always wanted Khuzestan," she said. "Didn't I tell you mullahs should only preach about how to wash our asses in a toilet? What are we going to do now?"

"Calm down," Hessam said. "We need to plan."

"Let's go to the alley—see what neighbours want to do." Zulaikha didn't wait for anyone. She knocked on Mrs. Sara's door and asked Sohrab to buzz all the other neighbours. Sohrab ran playfully as if this was a new game.

Neighbours gathered in front of Mrs. Sara's place. Distant sounds of men calling to one another spoke of their confusion. Men agreed to gather in the neighbourhood mosque to plan. A minute after the men left, the anti-aircraft guns began shooting. Mrs. Sara offered their basement for shelter as she carried her small radio.

"Won't we go to see Jalal anymore?" Sohrab asked.

"Let's wait a bit. We'll call them soon."

The news broadcasted a report about identifying *Azhir e Ghermez* (Red Siren) and what they should do.

She couldn't find Najwa when she called her number in the hospital in Khorramshahr. Zulaikha tried not to show too much anxiety to others, especially Sohrab, but this was a different worry. Death was flying above their heads. It could take one of them away at any moment.

In addition to the radio, mosques used loudspeakers around town to announce siren modes.

"Attention, attention. The alarm you are hearing now is the danger or red sign, and it means the air attack is about to happen. Leave your workplaces and take refuge in a shelter."

When the red mode became white, they returned to their homes, to breakfast, and to watch the news.

Abbass stopped by, but he couldn't stay. He only wanted to tell her that Najwa was fine. They had found a shelter, too.

That was the first night they slept underground and understood the meaning of the red siren mode.

Hessam attended extensive training with Basij forces calling for volunteers the following days.

When the war intensified a week later, panicked, Zulaikha sent a telegram to Aliah about the state of the war and asked if she would accept them in Bahrain for a few months. She would do anything.

Aliah had called Mrs. Sara next door as soon as she got the telegram. But Mrs. Sara had guests. "Forgive me. Everybody comes to my basement these days, and they don't leave," Mrs. Sara said.

"Did Aliah say anything?"

Mrs. Sara nodded. "Yes, yes. She said she could use your help in the hair salon but could not do anything for Sohrab or Madineh."

"That's all she said?"

"Wait, no, there's more—she said this way you could save money and later arrange for your family to join you."

"Are you sure she said that, not you?"

Mrs. Sara chuckled. "Well, partly me. Think about it, Zuli."

It was a ridiculous suggestion. Sohrab was only seven. She couldn't leave him alone with Madineh.

■■■

Abadan's October always felt like a fresh spring, with the occasional rain washing away the dirt and bringing a cool breeze. That autumn became the ugliest season. In October, the

Iranian forces lost control of The City of Khorramshahr, Abadan's glamorous twin city. Najwa's eyes were swollen when they met in their children's new school. There was a war, and everyone was distressed, but Najwa had kept her brave caring smile before that day. "My cousin," she said. "An Iraqi soldier attacked her in her courtyard—he was on top of her—when her brother stabbed him in the back."

Zulaikha's stomach was cramped. "Where are they now?"

"They left the city. I think we should, too. We can't stay, Zuli jan."

They raped women, much like the city itself. Teenage soldiers, who'd crawl under enemy tanks to detonate hand grenades, became war heroes.

"Abbass is going to take me and my son, but please go and move Abu from the danger zone, please."

Abbass's house was near the captured sections' border in the danger zone. There was no fishing business anymore—Abbass moved people out of town with his old truck. When Zulaikha went to Abu's house, Abu was in his wheelchair in a corner. She helped him to change. "Get up, Abu. We need to get out of here fast."

Abu, like a sick old tiger, obeyed anything she asked of him. She packed a few things in a plastic bag and asked him to wait so she could find a ride. "Be patient. I'll be back for you."

Not too many cars were on the road. It took almost half an hour to stop a Basiji Jeep and shout for help. Basiji soldiers helped Abu to get in the car.

As they drove, she had no courage to look around. Her head was down as Abu leaned on her shoulder like a baby. When they got home, Sohrab ran outside and helped his mother. The Basiji man saw little Sohrab and said, "You should evacuate the city tonight. Can you do that?"

She swallowed and didn't utter a word.

The man said, "I can help to get you out of town. You have a child and this elderly gentleman. You shouldn't stay here." He surely didn't know about Madineh also being inside.

Zulaikha thanked him and asked where she could find him. He gave an Islamic Revolution Committee's address and a name.

"Wait, please," she begged. "I need to write it down." Her hands were tied, holding the bag and Abu's arm. The man faced Sohrab and repeated the address.

"Did you get it?"

Sohrab nodded.

"Now go and write it in a paper, you brave boy. Will you?" Sohrab ran inside.

Inside the house, the local radio news announced help needed—blankets, water, blood.

Madineh stopped cursing for a moment to welcome Abu. Zulaikha told Sohrab that he should go to Mrs. Sara's basement. "I need to go and find your uncle. We have to make a plan to leave this city as soon as possible. Do you promise me to do that?"

"What about them?" He pointed to Madineh and Abu.

She squatted down at his eye level and held his hand.

"I know what you're thinking, but you need to think about saving yourself first and asking for help because you are a child. You're the first to be rescued in any war in this world. Do you understand?"

Sohrab burst into tears. She held him and asked Madineh to help calm him down. Zulaikha put on her sneakers, a pair she had bought before the war. How much she had run around lately in these sneakers.

Luckily, that day she knew where Hessam was. Every morning she asked him to tell her where he was going.

"I have to know, and you can't refuse."

He was in a mosque where the Arab People of Khuzestan held a meeting. She asked a messenger at the door to go and fetch him—women weren't allowed in men's gatherings.

"Something happened?" Hessam asked.

"You need to come home. We have to save Sohrab and Mother before it's too late."

"How many times did I tell you about moving to Tehran? All

roads are now closed."

Hessam had told her the government had created dormitories for war refugees around greater Tehran. He told the family about it, but neither Madineh nor Zulaikha wanted to go. Who could leave Khuzestan? They would no longer be themselves if they left.

"Don't argue with me, Hessam. Do something," she said. "Let's call Gholam. His town is safe. Isn't it?"

The telecommunication office was open. Zulaikha and Sohrab were beside Hessam at the long-distance phone booth. She struggled to gather Gholam's reaction.

"Are you being serious?" Hessam said. "They need to be safe and away from here," he retorted furiously.

They had a heated conversation, the tension building as Hessam furiously tried to make him understand their situation, but finally, Hessam hung up. He was calm.

"He says he would only accept Sohrab and Mother—he can't afford all of us," Hessam said. "He asked me to send him money—my salary is already delayed. I shouldn't have called."

"Wait a minute," Zulaikha said. "Maybe I should go to Bahrain again. I must call Aliah."

Sohrab, in a corner, only said one word, "*Maman!*" Sohrab was crying out for attention and consideration from his mother.

Zulaikha held him. "Don't worry. Nothing has happened yet. I'm here."

"But you want to leave without me. I want to come, too. You said yourself—children are important to rescue first."

Zulaikha held his hand.

"We need to get home fast. Before another air attack," Hessam said.

They couldn't catch a taxi and walked most of the way. When they got home, Sohrab ran to Madineh and hugged her. Madineh glared at Zulaikha expecting an explanation.

"He's upset, because Gholam said on the phone that he'll only accept you and him."

In those days, Sohrab had become closer to his grandmother,

and her words strangely became more convincing. "You'll stay with me," Madineh said. "You'll help me not feel too lonesome there, and I'll tell you a story every night."

Sohrab asked his mother to give him a pillow. He went to sleep without eating dinner.

At night when Sohrab was sleeping, Zulaikha confessed to Hessam, "Even if Gholam invited me, I wouldn't want to go there. I'd rather die here."

"You can't be serious."

"She's serious," Madineh said. "I feel the same. I'm only going because of Sohrab."

■ ■ ■

Zulaikha wept as she packed. Hessam had found the Basiji Jeep driver at the address he had provided. The plan was to pick them up at 4:00 AM, before sunrise.

Sohrab was sleeping when Hessam carried him to the car, a green Range Rover.

Madineh strolled toward the car with a small box in her hand. "Send for us as soon as possible. Don't leave me in Gholam's care. You know he hates my guts."

"What's that in the box?"

"Mrs. Sara gave me these playing cards last night—I forgot to pack them."

Zulaikha held her. "Oh, Mother." Madineh never failed to surprise her. Those cards would hopefully keep her quiet, and she wouldn't annoy Gholam too much.

Sohrab tapped the car window. "*Maman*," he called her. Zulaikha sat beside him and, one more time, promised him that she would come for them as soon as she could.

"I'll buy you many things from Bahrain—they have good shops there. I'll write, too." She got out of the car and stood beside his window.

As the Basiji soldiers helped Madineh get in their Range Rover, she looked at them with the immunity provided by her older age.

"Happy now with your masterpiece revolution?" she said.

The soldiers glanced at each other stunned, but she continued her vulgar language, "You shat all over this country!"

Zulaikha shouted, "Mother!"

The soldier ignored her, climbed up the car and started the engine. Sohrab was waving to her as the car pulled away. She knelt on the ground and watched him go. Two months ago, the thought of this separation was laughable.

A few hours later, she called her brother, Gholam, from Abadan to check if they had arrived.

"I'm begging you, Gholam," she said. "Our mother is not young anymore—please bear with her. I'll bring them back here as soon as I can. I promise."

Gholam's voice sounded smoother than she remembered. "I won't let them suffer, Zulaikha. Think about your own safety."

Was it the war, as bad as it was, that made people closer to each other? How long could people live in a war with a neighbouring country? This would end soon. It must.

■■■

Madineh did not hide Gholam's comments from her daughter. "He asked how could you leave Sohrab with me—like you were going to be the princess of Bahrain."

Zulaikha did not care too much. She suspected that Madineh might have expressed her own thoughts but quoted Gholam.

"He says you could do people's eyebrows here."

"Tell him it's not fun here—most of my days go by hiding with Abu in Mrs. Sara's basement. Does he want Abu and me there as well?" Zulaikha retorted.

"When are you leaving for Bahrain?"

"I don't know. The airports are not safe. Hessam will tell me when. He's checking every day."

With Abadan's airports closing, Abbass helped his father and Zulaikha leave Abadan. He found a shelter for Abu and booked Zulaikha a flight from Ahvaz to Bahrain. A bomb exploded near

Abbass's house and destroyed part of it a few days after Zulaikha sent for Abu.

During their last phone call, Madineh did not complain too much about Gholam to Zulaikha. She had brought Sohrab with her to the telephone cabin, so his mother could hear his voice. Madineh had a kind voice that day—a kind tone that Zulaikha always knew was only for Sohrab or because he was near her. "He got bored sitting and waiting for our names to be called, but he's wonderful Zuli *jan*. Don't you worry one bit."

Zulaikha could not help but cry. "Maybe I should have come with you. Maybe Gholam is right, and I could find a job there, too."

"Did I say Gholam said that?"

"Yes, you did—"

"I made that up, girl—he didn't say that—he's fine," Madineh said.

"What?" Zulaikha chuckled.

"The town is full of unemployed refugees from Abadan and Khorramshahr—who would go to a hair salon?" Madineh explained that Sohrab was now attending an elementary school and had quickly adapted to his new situation, happily accommodating his school, classmates, and most of all his cousin, Mousa.

"Every day he asks if the war is over. Here, talk to him."

"*Maman*." It was Sohrab. "Bibi Madineh said you would send me good stuff from Bahrain."

Zulaikha wiped the tears from her face and tried to sound calm. "Yes, make a list, okay?"

Madineh heard Zulaikha's weeping tone. "Don't be a cry baby, Zulaikha. Go make some money there and come to our rescue. You know what I mean?"

"You just said Gholam is fine."

"I know, but we can't stand each other most of the time. Besides, I miss Abadan the way it was."

That miserable life we had wasn't that bad after all.

She promised and heard a click before she finished her

sentence, before she could tell Madineh she was grateful to her.

■ ■ ■

As she arrived at Bahrain's airport, the endless blue ocean, tall palm trees, cars driving by, and people walking and shopping made the welcome signs, *Ahlan Wa Sahlan*, all around the city more and more appealing. Aliah was waiting for her at the airport. When they hugged, Zulaikha couldn't help but cry in her arms.

"First thing we do is your eyebrows and upper lip, my dear," Aliah said. "It's too obvious you're returning from a war zone."

Zulaikha had caught sight of herself in the plane bathroom. Her facial hair, eyebrows, and sombre outfit made her look older than ever.

They laughed and went home to catch up on the past seven years. Aliah had divorced her second husband for infidelity. Hashem, the oldest son, was a naval engineer and lived in Kuwait. Rafi became a professional photographer, met a British model, and they moved to London. Saba, now almost twenty-six years old, couldn't believe how much Zulaikha had changed. She picked up a magazine from their coffee table. "Doesn't she look like Samia Gamal?"

"The dancer?" Aliah glanced at the dancer's picture and then at Zulaikha as if making a comparison.

Zulaikha peeked at the back of the magazine advertising *Shaft*, an American movie. Suddenly she thought about Hessam and how much he loved American films and longed to be up to date.

How long has it been since he has seen a film in the cinema?

"You have kind eyes, Saba. I wish I looked like her."

Aliah and Saba still lived in the same house, but it was renovated and looked different than she remembered. This time Zulaikha was allowed to stay in Hashem's old room.

Nothing, not even the peace, felt the same without her family. She had lived without them before, but now she was in exile.

When Zulaikha asked her son and mother what they needed

the most, Sohrab always had something to ask, but his demands were curious and often too small, such as a ball or Adidas shoes. He was a war refugee living in a small town. What else could a little boy ask for? She often wondered what her son did for fun in a town surrounded by oil refineries.

■ ■ ■

Less than three weeks after her arrival, Assef visited her. When Aliah told Zulaikha that he was coming to see her, she asked, "Why?"

Aliah retorted, "Why what?"

"Why does he want to see me? How does he know I am here?"

"Come on, Zuli. He's been calling me about you much more after the war began. He cares about you and his son. Don't be so stubborn."

"Stubborn?"

Aliah shook her head. "Well, he told me he never wanted to divorce you—your family made you—"

"He married another woman, Aliah." She resisted saying that being a second wife might not sound so bad to Aliah, but she had had enough of it.

She had parked questions in her mind about what she did wrong in her relationship with Assef for quite some time. It didn't matter what happened back then anymore. Now their son lived in a country at war. He was Sohrab's father, and he had rights. Tomorrow, she should be careful.

She left the salon early and barely slept that night.

When Assef went to see them at the salon's door the next day, she was wearing a black dress to show him her grief. Assef looked reserved. They didn't hug or touch each other. Only robotically walked two blocks toward the old deli they used to go to together.

"Why are you here, Assef?

"To talk about Sohrab—why is he not with you? Why is he there with your mother?"

"Did you have a better idea?" Zulaikha asked.

"You have left our son in your mother's care. Knowing your relationship with her, it's strange. Why don't you move to Ahvaz—It's safer there, and I still have a house there—I'll provide more—for both of you."

"You were not there. Don't judge me or anyone in my family."

"I'm not here to fight. I take the blame."

"I don't care why you came here."

"You could have contacted my sister—"

"In times of war, people's plans might seem unusual to those who only hear about it from afar."

"I want a chance to take care of Sohrab."

What is he trying to say? That he would take Sohrab away from me and Iran?

He could take custody of Sohrab by law. She had never expected this side of Assef.

"Are you threatening me?"

He lit his cigarette. "You've changed a lot, Zulaikha."

"Or maybe you never knew me that well."

"There's something else I want you to know."

This could not be good. "Can you not just leave me alone?" She turned back to walk away from him.

"I have a daughter."

She stopped walking—her back was still to him. "I don't want to hear it."

Assef continued as if the news he just gave her was unimportant. "I moved to another city, married a different person, had another child, but nothing changed in me," he said. "I still hurt people who love me."

She turned around. "What do you expect me to say? You should stay away from me then—that's the only way you won't hurt me—goodbye, Assef."

He'd told her that his new woman and child did not change anything for him. She let her malicious wish for her rival sink in: she'd gone through hell with the man she'd stolen.

She did not stay at work for too long that day. Feeling nostalgic, she called Mrs. Sara to see if she could talk to Hessam. Mrs. Sara went and knocked at their door, but no one answered.

The next day at the hair salon, Aliah had an envelope for Zulaikha. She stared at it in Aliah's hand.

"Come on. It can't be bad."

It was a note and four hundred US dollars.

> This should cover the cost of a plane ticket to find a new home for you, Sohrab, and your mother. I am sorry about yesterday. I still don't know how to speak. I didn't tell you how stunning you look. You are the best mother a son could wish for. Thank your mother for me, too, and please have Sohrab call my number some time. He has it.

She sat down and used her inhaler. Aliah lost her patience and grabbed the note. "Give that to me." She read it fast and shouted joyfully, "Didn't I tell you? He's a fine man."

■ ■ ■

It was almost the end of the week, and she was about to close up the salon for the evening when Madineh called. "Gholam and his wife don't want us here anymore," she said. "There isn't a day he doesn't ask me about your plans and when you'll come for your son. The other day, I caught her hiding a package of cookies so Sohrab wouldn't eat them—I pay them most of what you send me. I'm tired of it."

"Let me think. I'll give Gholam a call." It had now been almost six months. Long enough for a family to want their space back, but Sohrab was a good boy. Madineh and her demands, on the other hand, were hard to handle.

"Don't take sides, Zulaikha," Gholam yelled. "You should know by now that our mother is an ungrateful witch. How is it that my children are nothing to her, but your Sohrab must get so much attention? Who the hell do you think you have raised? A prince?

No, he is just a—"

"Calm down. He's just a boy away from his mother."

"You'd better get here—you or Hessam, as soon as possible before I throw them out in the street."

She had made things worse by calling Gholam. Now, knowing their mother had reported everything to her, he would go home and treat them worse. She called Mrs. Sara and asked her to find Hessam.

"Please ask him to move them back right away." She told her everything about her conversations with her mother and Gholam.

"I always take your messages without questioning anything," Mrs. Sara said. "But Abadan is not safe—there's no school—"

Zulaikha began crying.

"I'll tell him to call his brother or go there—maybe he can rent a place for them."

A week later, when Zulaikha called again, Mrs. Sara didn't pick up. For weeks there was no response. No connection. Only news about bloody battles for Khorramshahr.

Iran liberated Khorramshahr at the end of the second battle in May 1982.

■■■

Zulaikha returned to Abadan in 1983. This time she planned to move to Tehran. This war would not end. The world had forgotten them.

Abadan was now the ruins of the city they'd once known. Poverty was eating at the flesh and blood of the city. Those who had no place to go, mainly the Arab population, suffered the most.

Gholam had arranged with two conscripts to drive Sohrab and Madineh to Abadan in a police ambulance. "You raised a good boy, Zulaikha. He was excited. They'll be there in two hours—max three," Gholam said. "Mother doesn't look that well, though. You may want to have her checked out in Tehran. She wouldn't listen to me."

Zulaikha stood across the alley on the boulevard facing Bahmanshir Bridge. Gholam was right. The approaching ambulance siren was ringing. It stopped and Sohrab got out and ran toward her. He was now ten years old, taller, and with a face more like Assef's.

Madineh had a hard time climbing out of the ambulance. She noticed Zulaikha's glance. "Don't you dare call me fat!"

"I thought you said Gholam didn't feed you."

Sohrab chuckled.

The ambulance conscripts stared at the three of them embracing as though they had never seen a display of peaceful kindness. Zulaikha approached them. "I don't know how to thank you."

"It's nothing for our Chief." They meant Gholam.

He must have been treating these young men well.

Hessam volunteered part-time at the Abadan Basij headquarters. He said the shortest route to Tehran was through Ahvaz by train.

Zulaikha paid some of her savings to a driver to get them to Ahvaz. They all packed and were on their way, this time to Tehran, the city they dreamed of visiting one day but never wanted to live in.

The night before they left, Mrs. Sara asked Zulaikha to cut her long hair for the first time in many years. "I can't handle this hair under the scarf—cut it short—but I still want my ponytail."

"Come with us to Tehran, Mrs. Sara. Let me talk to Parviz."

"We talked about it last night," she said. "We have no kids—if Abadan dies, we'll die with it."

"You sound like those musicians in that movie—"

They had watched *A Night to Remember* together.

"Right, Abadan is now our Titanic," she said. "Wait. I have something for you."

She pulled something from her skirt's pocket. It was a pair of gold earrings.

"Oh no, I can't," Zulaikha said.

"You should. You've always been like the daughter or little sister I never had. Go wear them and find love again. Call me here and tell me all about it."

Zulaikha wore the earrings as she glanced at both of their reflections in the mirror. Mrs. Sara's hair was now shoulder length—she could still wear it in a ponytail.

■■■

While migrating from Khuzestan, Zulaikha and her family stayed with Abu and Abbass in Ahvaz. Through a referral from Najwa's brother, Salem, a high school teacher, Abbass became the school janitor, and they occupied a small suite in the corner of the schoolyard. Abbass now tutored students who liked to learn music. He had grown his hair. His striking clean-cut face and glossy black ponytail caught others' attention quickly.

They had just arrived that afternoon and were tired, but the empty schoolyard tempted the boys to play. Najwa helped Madineh lie down and rest. After a few minutes of the ladies catching up and talking about their new lives, Zulaikha picked up a jar of icy water and a few plastic cups to take to the men. Najwa stopped her and gave her Abu's hat. "Put this on his head, please. He shouldn't stay in the heat too long."

"You're always nursing, Najwa. I love that about you." They hugged.

A game of soccer ensued in the yard. Abbass, Jalal, and Salem formed a team against Sohrab and Hessam. Abu sat in the shade under a palm tree to applaud them, or act like he was a referee. Zulaikha interrupted the boys and gave them water, then sat beside Abu and watched them play.

"The war is separating us," Abu said.

"We'll come back, Abu. Hopefully, for Abbass's wedding."

"Take Hessam to Tehran, too. Don't let him stay in Abadan."

"He says he has to apply for a transfer. He needs to keep his job."

"It's not all about that. Hessam's too attached to us, Abbass and me, to Abadan," Abu said.

Zulaikha spotted a boy sitting and watching them on the other side of the yard. Salem called him over to join them, "Hey Omid!" The boy seemed to be shy. Zulaikha stood up to go back inside. A van parked in front of the school gate, and a man wearing a green uniform entered the school.

"I sense trouble," Abu muttered.

Everyone stopped playing.

The green-uniformed man grabbed the schoolboy's hand and pulled him harshly. The boy obeyed the man who seemed to be his father. As Omid glanced back at Salem and Abbass, the man hit him in the back of his head.

Abbass stepped forward to intervene, but Salem and Hessam stopped him. Their soccer game ended bitterly.

When inside, Abbass explained that Omid was a talented student interested in poetry and music but terrified of his father, who was a high-ranking guard.

"You should be careful, son," Abu said.

"Careful about what? What can he do?"

Abu glanced at Zulaikha as if looking for support.

"I think you care about the child, but when his father is so stubborn, you can't do much," Zulaikha said. "Parents can be dangerous when it comes to their children. Remember that."

The night before their departure, they had an early dinner. Abbass and Salem served the takeout kabab and bread with a heap of basil. Hessam read a poem and Abbass played the *oud*. Even Abu and Madineh hummed an old song as the women danced. They enjoyed a night away from their troubles.

Madineh couldn't contain her emotions. She held Abbass, kissed his cheek, and said, "When will we celebrate your wedding? What are you two waiting for?"

The couple looked at each other. Abbass explained that Najwa's mother had passed a few months ago. They wouldn't celebrate before the first anniversary of her passing.

Maybe I will find love again. Perhaps something good will happen to me in Tehran. But where is Assef at this moment? How is his life without me?

Sohrab was staring at Abbass. "Uncle Abbass, you look like an American movie star."

Abbass's cheeks flushed. He patted Sohrab's head.

"Some students call him Messiah, some Che," Jalal said.

Abu looked proud of his son even though he seemed stressed.

That night after dinner, someone knocked on the door. The same boy from earlier, Omid, returned a music book. He looked inside to find Abbass, but Abbass, Hessam, and Salem had gone for a walk around the block.

Sohrab invited him in.

"My parents are waiting," Omid said. "I can't stay." Najwa was standing behind Sohrab. "Thanks for returning this," she said. "But you shouldn't have come here without your parents' permission. Understand?"

Omid's head was down.

"You know your father is a powerful man," Najwa said. "He could make trouble for my brother and Abbass. Please understand."

When Najwa closed the door, the look in her eyes frightened Zulaikha.

"Abbass is not careful enough," Abu said. "This boy is trouble."

Everyone was tired and preferred to let the situation be. "Don't worry too much, Abu," Zulaikha said, refraining from saying he should rely on God. That would make Abu mad.

They had a long way to go tomorrow, so they went to bed early, right after Najwa, Jalal, and Salem left.

They said their goodbyes in the early hours of the morning and took the train to Tehran.

At their stops along the way to Tehran, as they got some distance from Khuzestan, Sohrab and Zulaikha saw children running and playing. The mother and son kept pointing at the scenes outside their windows. "Look, *Maman*," Sohrab said a few times, filled with joy and hope. But Madineh was exhausted and could only ask how many stops were left.

■ ■ ■

When they arrived in Tehran, they went to a mosque that was receiving refugees. The volunteers welcomed Zulaikha's family and let them take a spot in the corner of a big hall covered by machine-made carpets. Their first meal was a tasteless plate of rice and lentils. Sohrab looked at Zulaikha with disappointment.

"I'll make you something good once we settle," she said. "Just eat and be thankful. It's food."

After the meal, the volunteers distributed tea and fresh dates from Khuzestan's palm trees—the palm trees that were not standing tall anymore. They were hurt and destroyed, like everything else in the war.

Zulaikha held up the date and told Madineh and Sohrab, "See? Somewhere dates are still growing."

Zulaikha and Sohrab had brought books and magazines and a crossword for Zulaikha. Only Madineh's hobby, playing cards, was problematic and *haram*. Together they played the *Esm-Famil* (Name-Family) game. Sohrab wrote a list of categories in his notebook that included name, family, animal, city, and food. Each person was to come up with a word for each that started with their selected letter *beh*. Entertaining Madineh amused Sohrab, and his chuckles brought joy to Zulaikha.

They slept in the mosque that night. Zulaikha went to the Foundation of War Refugees the next morning to ask for help. Surprisingly they were quick in their arrangements. Their next home was a dormitory in Palestine Square, which used to be Palace Square before the revolution.

The building was old and creepy. The rumour was that it had belonged to SAVAK for interrogations. They issued one large room for the three of them. The kitchen was fifteen stairs down into a dark and humid basement. They had to share a bathroom with three other families on the same floor. After what they'd experienced in Abadan, no one complained. They had embarked on another temporary stage of their lives.

Neighbours talked to one another and made a schedule for taking baths. Each family had a fridge and a small portable oven and used the kitchen in turns. There was a fridge in the creepy kitchen that everyone agreed to use for unwanted leftovers.

Zulaikha cleaned the large kitchen by herself—she swept the stairs, bought cheap curtains for the windows and tried to make the dorm a home for everyone. She registered Sohrab in a nearby school and started looking for a job.

The government gave them a small allowance every month and coupons for rice, cooking oil, and a little meat. Her experience at the hair salon had made her good at making friends. She bought a second-hand chair and mirror and invited the ladies of the dormitory to come to her for their eyebrow care and haircuts. The money was little, but being productive made her happy. She highlighted her hair and put make-up on to look clean and friendly to her new female customers. In the public area, she was careful with her Hijab.

She could tolerate her new life as long as she was inside the dorm, no matter how creepy and stinky the building was. Dishes spiced with unique flavours from Abadan, tamarind paste, red pepper, and garlic would make everyone hungry. Sometimes neighbours gathered together in a circle, played *Bandari* music, and a good dancer would jump into the middle to perform a shoulder shimmy dance. To keep the Revolutionary Guards away, they kept the music volume as low as possible, and the young men playing soccer in the yard would keep an eye on the gate.

A small simulation of Abadan had been shaped in that dingy dormitory. But when she interacted with people outside, reality hit her. She was not in Khuzestan anymore. People were colder and sadder. The war had not directly hit their city yet, but their men and sons were at the front, or in prison for objecting to it.

Zulaikha still thought about Assef sometimes. She ran their last meeting in her mind many times. On that day, Assef implied that his new life was not so happy, but it did not matter. Tehran was a lot farther from the Emirates than Abadan. He was so out of reach. Soon, Assef would call Mrs. Sara and ask about them, but when? Sohrab hadn't asked about his father for a long time.

Love for Zulaikha was as complicated as a crossword she didn't want to try to solve anymore. She wanted to learn to have fun with men without overanalyzing them or giving her heart to anyone. There was a much younger man who wanted her. He lived on another floor and drove a taxi cab in Tehran. His name was Abdul, and he limped because of the remains of an exploded grenade in his leg that the doctors couldn't completely remove. Zulaikha dated him whenever she could find a minute away from her mother and son. Everything, even having a lover, could be dangerous. She wanted to be smart about it this time.

One day, when Abdul drove her to a shopping centre in now Vali-Asr Square, a guard asked them to pull over. They were in trouble for laughing and looking at each other intimately. They each got out of the car from their respective side.

"Cover your hair," the guard screamed at her.

She did, wondering how he noticed her hair when his eyes were on the ground as if he were speaking to someone else. He was obeying the rules of Islam, which forbade him from looking into a woman's eyes when talking to her.

"What's going on between you and your female passenger?"

"She's my neighbour—not just a passenger."

The guard slapped him in the face. "She's your neighbour, so you think you can act like a pervert?" the guard said. "Do you know I can take you to the Committee, and have you lashed for acting against Islamic rules?"

Abdul apologized. "*Bebakhshid*, Brother. It won't happen again." His head was down.

Zulaikha wanted to say something in Abdul's defence, but it wouldn't be well-received. She could have said that her brother was in the war, or that they had been through so much, and it wasn't fair to treat them like garbage. But before she could say anything, the guard noticed Abdul's Southern accent. "Are you from the south?"

"Yes, Brother. We're war refugees."

"My brother is there fighting to keep your city, and you're having fun here?" The guard said as he searched their trunk, then he pulled Zulaikha's bag from her hand and opened it.

"I was wounded at the beginning of the war and was exempt

from the service," Abdul said.

The guard glared at him. He showed no sign of regret for humiliating them but let them go.

On their way home, Zulaikha was quiet and didn't dare to look at Abdul the entire way.

"I'll make *aush reshteh* tonight and bring you a bowl." She stepped out of his car beside the dorm gate. "Don't be upset. They're not worth it."

She heard about others in such situations—some had been taken, lashed, and humiliated even more. She had seen their patrols in crowded places, checking cars and warning women. But now it had happened to her. She had to be more careful. How would she explain it to Sohrab?

■ ■ ■

Palestine Square, where the dormitory was, belonged to an upper-class neighbourhood. When Zulaikha dropped Sohrab off at school, she noticed the cars and outfits of the other children's parents. Sohrab refused to bring his friends to their poor dormitory room when she said they could sleep over. One day she went to a school event and met some of the mothers. One of them, Mrs. Alipour, was very friendly to her and told her that Sohrab had been to their house a few times. Sohrab shared his lunch with her boy. "Reza, my son, raves about your cooking all the time."

"Why don't you and Reza come over for lunch this Friday?" She didn't anticipate that her invitation might embarrass Sohrab. "You should have asked me first," he said to her later that day. "You haven't seen their house, so you don't know, *Maman*." Sohrab sounded like Hessam talking about Kia's house many years ago.

Where was Kia? He must know about the war. Would he do something for his parents?

"*Maman*, are you listening to me?" Sohrab's voice brought her back to reality.

But the lunch on Friday didn't turn out to be that bad. Reza and Mrs. Alipour came to their poor room in the dormitory, sat on the floor with them, and enjoyed dill rice with lamb shank.

"I want to ask you something," Mrs. Alipour said in the yard near the gate. "We have a big house with a section for a caregiver—would you consider—"

Zulaikha stepped closer to Mrs. Alipour. "It's not up to me," she muttered. "Let me talk to my man." She nodded toward Sohrab, who was showing the yard to Reza.

"Why don't you come over for a visit tomorrow? He hasn't seen that part of our house."

When Sohrab saw the basement where they were to live, he was convinced that his mother's working for his classmate's parents could be okay after all.

Zulaikha told Madineh she got a job, the house was nice, and the family would take them all.

"No, I'm good here," she said. "I sit with the neighbours in the yard. We talk about Abadan. We shouldn't lose this room."

"I'll come to see you, Bibi," Sohrab said. "Every day right from school."

■■■

Madineh told her she hadn't heard from Hessam for a few days. "Mrs. Sara keeps saying he's not home. I don't know why, but I have a bad feeling this time."

When Zulaikha called Mrs. Sara, he wasn't available.

"Zuli *jan*, not to worry you, but I think he's now at the frontier," she said. "He'd told my husband."

Zulaikha swallowed.

"Hello? You there?" Mrs. Sara asked.

"Right," Zulaikha said. "What is he doing there? He's not a militant."

"Parviz said they're using him as a guide because he knows Khuzestan."

"How am I going to tell our mother?"

"Don't," she said. "I'll tell him to write to her as soon as he's here. Give me your number—the place you live—you said they had a phone."

Zulaikha didn't share the news with Madineh or Sohrab for a few days. "I couldn't get a hold of them," she lied. "Nobody picked up."

Hessam's letter and a picture came a month later. He was in a Basij uniform with a long beard they disliked. The school authority had fired Abbass and Salem from the school because of a report about that boy, Omid. They had said the janitor, Abbass, was not allowed to teach music without his parents' permission. Salem defended him, so they both were let go. Abbass had repaired their house, and they moved back. Najwa and her son still lived in Ahvaz.

■■■

Iraqi missiles finally reached Tehran in 1984, a few months after they had left Abadan.

One weekend, before visiting Madineh, Zulaikha and Sohrab went to a bakery and bought a box of Danish pastries. The telecommunication office was across the street. Sohrab was excited to talk to his uncle after a long while.

Mrs. Sara sounded unusually sad when she picked up. "Zulaikha *jan*, I don't think Hessam will come to the phone today."

"Why? What happened to him?"

"He's fine. He's at home, but just—"

"Is he wounded?" she asked.

"Something really bad happened—not to Hessam, but to his friend, the young man who was always with him."

Zulaikha cried, "Abbass? How?" A pain washed through her lower abdomen and back as though she got her period suddenly.

"He was shot in downtown Abadan yesterday afternoon," Mrs. Sara sobbed. "He died instantly, poor kid. How beautiful he was."

"What? Shot? Who did this to him?"

"Who knows? He was shot in the middle of the day not once but a few times."

"But I need to speak to Hessam. How is he coping?"

"He's not going to work. He knew you would call. He told me to ask you to wait for his call."

"What's wrong, *Maman*?" Sohrab took the box from her trembling hands.

"How can I tell you this? It's about Abbass."

"Is he hurt?"

"Yes." She trembled. "Someone killed him." She squatted down as she heard her own voice.

"*Maman*—" Eleven-year-old Sohrab helped her to get up. He walked along with her quietly.

"Actually, I need to go to the bathroom. Give me a minute. Will you?" It was only two weeks after her last period, but the bleeding had returned.

At home, Madineh screamed. She slapped her own face a few times.

"Stop it," Zulaikha sobbed. "I have no energy left in me for you."

"I want to feel the pain," Madineh shouted. "*Vhy*, *Vhy*, how could they do such a thing? Abu will die now, too. He will die."

Abdul knocked on their door. Weeping for family and friends was not too shocking in those days. Abdul held Sohrab's hand. "Let's give the ladies some space." They left the room.

"Hessam is next," Madineh said.

"What?"

"There's no question—he's next."

Zulaikha was out of words. Madineh had a point.

"Don't stand there. Do something before it's too late."

The next day, she caught a train to Ahvaz and a bus to Abadan.

■ ■ ■

Slender and pale, Hessam lived in the remains of their house.

She put her bag down. "Tell me all you know. I'm dying." She unveiled her scarf as if it was choking her.

"It's that boy's father," Hessam wept. "He killed Abbass or paid someone to do it for him."

She stepped forward to be closer to him. "What boy?"

"The boy he was tutoring. His name was Omid. Don't you remember?"

She did remember him and Najwa's frightened eyes after he left their place.

"Abbass told me he was being followed. Omid was obsessed with Abbass. His father threatened Abbass to leave him alone. He didn't know what to do. Omid is only fourteen years old. He hates his father's Islamic rules."

"What about you? Are you also in danger?"

"I don't know. He hates my guts, too. His son is a runaway now. He suspects I hid Omid."

"Where is Abu? Let's go to their house. Hurry up. I won't let you sit here and be useless. We don't have any time for this."

"What are you going to do?"

"I don't know. I can't let him die in that house. I'll take him to Tehran. One more person wouldn't kill us."

When they saw Abu, he had trouble talking and looked confused. He didn't recognize Zulaikha for a few minutes, but when he did, he asked her if Abbass was still working in his boat. She walked to the nearby clinic and begged for help. Two medics went with her to Abu's house, but when they saw his condition, they transferred him to the hospital, where they found that Abu had suffered a mild stroke. He kept asking for Abbass. "There's a storm tonight at sea. He'll be lost. Can anyone find my boy?" Zulaikha left him after he went to sleep with the help of drugs.

At night when she returned to their home, she sat in the courtyard beside Hessam. "What's your plan, Hessam?" she asked.

He did not answer. He seemed disoriented. "What day is it? Wednesday? When did you say you were leaving?"

"I'm staying for a few days. Why? Come with me to Tehran. Stop this madness. This is not our war anymore."

"What about our house? Should I abandon it after all these years?"

"Yes. You'll find a job in Tehran. We'll find a new home."

"I will have to report to my superiors in the navy, so I can possibly get a transfer. Don't you want to go to bed?"

"No, who can sleep?"

"I don't feel like talking. There's so much in my mind right now."

"Okay. I'll leave you alone. Please don't plan anything foolish, though."

"I was born a fool, Zulaikha. That's why I'm alive. Smart people like Abbass are in their graves. Don't you see that?" Hessam wept.

"You are my hope, Hessam. Please be strong."

Zulaikha held him and let her brother cry freely.

"I couldn't see him. Do you know who identified him?"

"No. Who?"

"Gholam, our brother. I peed my pants when I heard. I called him. I don't know how he got here so fast. He went to identify him, but he passed out. Can you believe it? Our macho police officer brother fainted at the sight of Abbass's dead body."

Her stomach was cramping. She had been bleeding since the day she heard the news. The sky was soft, and the full moon shone in the courtyard. In the depth of such nights, she thought, a storm, flood, or earthquake would suit the inhuman injustice that defined Abbass's destiny.

■ ■ ■

Visiting Abu in the hospital, Zulaikha saw Najwa, wearing black, slimmer, and pale. Her eyes were swollen from sleepless nights crying. She was beside Abu's bed and said nothing but hello and thank you to the visitors.

When they were alone, Zulaikha asked her how she was coping.

"It's overwhelming—I didn't know Abbass had so many friends, young and old. Abu's old friend visited him last night—

he was—"

"Zulaikha knows Jamshid." Abu looked less disoriented than the night before. "It's my fault. I raised Abbass to be an artist and a warrior. My son, my warrior son, forgive me, my son."

The next afternoon when she visited, Abu's mind was far away. "Are you still mad at my boy?" he asked Zulaikha.

She kissed his hand and said, "I was never mad at him. Abbass will remain a true beauty to me forever."

"I told him to cut his hair. He didn't listen. Jealousy is a poison I was afraid of."

Abbass used to laugh at Abu for his superstitions and said, "A monkey is beautiful to his father, too." But Zulaikha feared that Abu's intuition could be true. Abbass's appearance would cause him hostility as much as it gained popularity among his friends or the school kids.

Najwa couldn't bear it anymore. She brushed past Hessam as he stepped into the room.

Zulaikha kissed Abu's hand and gave up her seat to Hessam. "I'll wait for you downstairs."

In the hall, she saw Najwa walking towards the elevator. She wanted to stop her and talk to her but changed her mind. Najwa needed a few minutes of rest. She had another long night in the hospital.

That evening, tired and thirsty, Zulaikha asked Hessam to stop by the telephone cabin and call Assef.

"Why?" Hessam asked dreadfully.

"I want him to know what happened to Abbass. I want to tell him what's going on here. He should know."

Hessam didn't argue.

The telecommunication office was almost empty. They got a hold of Assef quickly.

"Listen, Assef. I have some—some bad news—someone killed Abbass." She remained still despite her trembling knees. "Don't cry, Assef. I need you to listen. I want to tell you—I think Hessam's life is in danger, too—are you still there?"

"Let me talk to him," Assef said.

Zulaikha passed the phone to Hessam as she stood beside the booth. Hessam closed the door as he muttered, "I can't hear anything."

She only heard, "Yes—I know, no, I won't—Salem, sure I know him, thank you."

She took the phone back.

"Tell me about Sohrab," Assef asked.

She told him that Sohrab was going to a good school. He had found good friends, and her life in Tehran was getting better and safer. She lost the connection and left the booth with sweat under her *manteau* attire.

"What was he telling you?" she asked.

"Nothing. He asked about a few people he knew. He wanted to know if they were okay."

There was more to it. Assef must have given Hessam a hint to find a hiding place. But Hessam's despair prevented her from asking for more explanation

■■■

Two days before she left for Tehran, she woke up early and went to the market to see if she could find any groceries. She planned to prepare a few small meals for her brother and leave them in the fridge. She found local sour cream and prepared Hessam's favourite breakfast, sour cream and honey with fresh local bread and Darjeeling tea. The sky was peaceful without planes. The vendors in the market were saying that a ceasefire might take place. Ramadan was coming, and Muslims should not fight in this holy month, but no one trusted Saddam Hussein. Most people had lost faith in the Iranian regime's intention for an end to the war, too. Everyone anticipated the sound of an explosion or gunshots at any moment.

When she got home, Hessam was still in bed. She woke him up and told him how beautiful it was outside. Hessam got up and washed his face. After breakfast, Zulaikha got Hessam to move some of the furniture into one room so he would be more comfortable. She found the Persian carpet that Jamshid had sent them in a closet. She pulled it out and sat down, staring at it. It still looked beautiful though full of dust.

"The past still lives here," said Hessam.

Zulaikha shook the dust off the carpet.

Hessam stopped her by taking her hand. "I'll donate it to the mosque or a refugee camp," he said. "I should have done it years ago."

"Do you know where they are? I heard *Amu* Jamshid visited Abu."

Hessam let go of Zulaikha's hand. "I called him about Abbass and Abu's condition."

Why am I not surprised? Nothing seems to matter anymore.

"You did the right thing. Have you heard from Kia? Is he still in America?"

Hessam looked away.

"Is he okay?"

"I've heard he's engaged to be married."

"Really? To an American woman?"

"No, to an Iranian—I think a classmate."

She didn't ask him how he knew. She didn't need to. The look in her eyes spoke for her.

"*Amu* Jamshid still calls me from time to time. He tells me about him and asks me about you, too."

At least one of us is happy and safe.

She put two books in her bag, "I'm going to take these for Sohrab."

"Don't think Kia has always been happy. He's also had his share of hardship."

"People's unhappiness never makes me happy, Hessam. You should know that."

"He came back to Iran when you and Assef were living together, around when Sohrab was born."

Suddenly she wanted to hear more.

"He couldn't find a job as an engineer in America. He didn't feel he belonged there, so he accepted a job offer in Kharg as an oil engineer."

"Did you go to see him?"

"I couldn't tell you at the time. It was right after *Amu* Habib's accident. You weren't happy. I didn't want to upset you."

"It's a strange time with this war. It feels too stupid to hold anger."

"Really? You okay with—"

Zulaikha nodded, but saying she was okay with their resumed friendship was a lie. That anger had nested in her—only fresh pains, Abbass's loss and Hessam's despair topped the old wounds for now. She was still bleeding—her cramps made her bend over this time. She ignored Hessam's concerned eyes and went to the bathroom. When she returned, the carpet was not on the floor or in the closet. She didn't ask Hessam about it. She didn't want to know where it was.

That evening, after Mrs. Sara gave her a painkiller for her cramp, she sat in the courtyard. The air was steady and quiet, with no gunshots, like a calm ocean before the storm. It had been two days since any anti-aircraft guns were shot, and any red sirens were heard as if there was a ceasefire, a break for mourning Abbass, their young fallen warrior.

Hessam was inside ironing his uniform.

"Are you also leaving tomorrow?" she asked.

He nodded.

Abbass's *oud* and drum were in the corner of the room. Hessam said he wished that he could keep them forever. He gave her a tape recorder. "Keep this for me. It's his voice," he said. "He sang a Vigen song. I can't listen to it, but maybe one day I can—I can't listen to any music he used to play." He wept again.

Shortly after dawn, before getting a ride from Parviz and Mrs. Sara to the bus stop, she found Hessam packed and ready in his uniform to return to his post. "I've got to go—they're waiting," he said.

"Remember that you promised me to transfer to Tehran. Mother will kill me if you don't."

She got the chance to share the longest hug she could with

Hessam. When holding him, she smelled his odour. It was different than ever, nothing like his Old Spice shaving cream. His body smelled like sweat. She touched his cheek. "When the war ends, and we are no longer in mourning, we will celebrate again. We'll move back here and renovate this place. We'll wear nice clean clothing and invite all the neighbours. Don't you think we should?"

"And I'll shave that day and wear my Ray-Bans again." Tears flashed in his eyes.

They both chuckled amidst their tears.

∎∎∎

Back in Tehran, in their dorm room, only minutes after she arrived home, Madineh asked her about Hessam. Her stomach started to cramp again, distracting her.

"I'm talking to you," Madineh yelled.

She told Madineh that Hessam would join them soon.

"Why didn't he come with you? That monster who killed Abbass will be after him, too."

Zulaikha's explanations were not convincing. She sat behind Madineh and combed her silver hair. "You look like you could use a bath," she said. "When was the last time you washed your hair?"

∎∎∎

The gynecologist receptionist gave her a form to fill out. One question always made her mouth dry: how many times have you given birth? She never wanted to hide her first child. She had managed to hide her mental wounds, but she speculated a doctor would be able to tell if it had damaged her body. The gynecologist, this time a young woman, asked her, "You have two children?"

"No, one. My first baby—"

"Oh, sorry to hear that." She wrote down her speculation

without waiting for Zulaikha to clarify.

Zulaikha didn't want to verify that she had given birth to a premature baby by force, which was then taken away and left to die. She felt as if she was protecting a criminal—her mother more than anyone—for a crime committed so long ago. *Let my poor child's murder file remain closed.*

"It's a mild uterine fibroid," the doctor said. "Are you okay to do the procedure now? It'll take just a few minutes."

"I prefer to get rid of it right now, yes."

The doctor asked her to relax her muscles. Zulaikha exhaled and stared at the ceiling—all she knew about relaxing.

"Avoid sexual intercourse for at least two weeks," the doctor said.

She had just turned forty-one. After a few years of sexless life without Assef, sleeping with Abdul had awakened the senses she was avoiding. But now this bodily malfunction arrived just in time. Pain was her peculiar ally, granting her the space she needed to mourn her loss.

■ ■ ■

A week later, once she was feeling better, she washed Madineh's hair and made tea. Three bearded men in green uniforms appeared at their door.

"We're looking for Hessam Bakhtiari. Are you his sister?"

She opened her mouth to answer, but one of them said, "May we come in?" He let himself in—his elbow almost hit her.

Madineh's hair was wrapped in a towel. "What do you want here? Get out."

One of the men walked around with his hands behind his back. Their place was too small to hide a person, so he ordered his men to search all other dormitory rooms.

Madineh became angrier by the minute, but Zulaikha held her hand and made her sit down. After twenty minutes of searching, the same man said, "You will hear from us soon. Brother Hessam has not returned from his last assignment. There's a chance that he was captured by Iraqis, but we don't know. The circumstances around it are very unclear."

Madineh fainted.

"Your mother needs medical attention." He glanced at Madineh, who leaned against the wall behind her as she slid down breathlessly. "We'll be in touch," he said.

Zulaikha screamed Sohrab's name, then Abdul's. None of them were around, but a neighbour, Sohrab's age, said, "I'll go get him—my mother called for an ambulance."

Sohrab returned, panting. He sat down beside Madineh and kissed her hand. "This can't be happening. We'll find him." He looked at Zulaikha. "Right, *Maman*?"

A medic measured her blood pressure.

Zulaikha's look drifted between Sohrab and the worried neighbours watching them as though they made a scripted spectacle. Abdul thanked the neighbours and asked them to give the family some privacy.

■■■

Madineh had been diagnosed with diabetes recently. For the most part, she had remained strangely quiet with the news about Hessam's disappearance. She had lost her appetite and a lot of weight. She begged for cigarettes, but Zulaikha refused. "Don't wear black," she yelled at Zulaikha. "No one died."

Zulaikha was afraid of Madineh's glare. "What's your problem with me, Mother?"

"Your scarf. Take that stupid shit off."

"Are you kidding? The guards may come anytime."

"Change it. Buy a blue or a brown one."

Sohrab startled her as he opened the door. "Look, *Maman*." He showed her a newspaper article with a young man's picture. A war's missing person, a University of Tehran faculty member. The announcement said the university had a *tajlil* for him. "We should hold one for *Amu* Hessam."

"What? He's alive," Madineh yelled. "Stop acting like he's dead, or I'll—"

"Look. He's a missing person, too, Bibi."

Halfway through reading the article, Madineh stopped him. "Call your good for nothing brother. Tell Gholam to do it."

Gholam said he was already thinking about it. "Leave it to me. Just be here next week," he said.

Sohrab took the phone and spoke with his cousin, Mousa, about what they could do and how they would help. Zulaikha didn't get a chance to tell Gholam she was short of money in front of Sohrab. Gholam didn't offer either. Abdul was there for her, though. He lent her money to buy their tickets.

When they arrived in Abadan, Gholam arranged a tribute in a local mosque. He was dressed in his national police uniform, a black blazer and hat, standing at the door welcoming people. Two soldiers with guns were guarding near him. His son, Mousa, distributed printed templates with Hessam's picture in his borrowed white navy uniform and a note underneath:

Pray for our missing brother and son and his safe return. He heroically went to the frontier but has not returned yet.

Sohrab joined Mousa instantly.

Sitting in the women's section, Zulaikha recognized Najwa in an aisle seat. She waved at her as she pointed at the door. They found a spot beside the stairway in the hall.

"I was dying to tell you something." There was a smile in Najwa's eyes. Suddenly Salem, her brother, appeared between them, glaring at his sister as he muttered her name. "Never mind—I shouldn't—" Najwa stopped talking.

"Wait," Zulaikha said.

Does she know anything about Hessam?

"Okay, don't tell me if you can't," Zulaikha said, "But is it bad?"

"No, no—I'll write to you."

"Just be safe."

"We will be, Zulaikha. We will be."

Hearing Najwa's confident tone made that day more tolerable. She did not know who was in attendance in the men's section of the mosque until they came out onto the street. Jamshid was waiting for her. "Have faith, Zulaikha," he said.

She glanced at Madineh, expecting her to mutter something vulgar, but she stared at an object on the ground. Mrs. Sara was by her side all day.

"I heard that you're caring for Abbass's father," Zulaikha said.

Jamshid cleared his throat as though embarrassed. "It wasn't easy to convince him, though."

"Does he know about Hessam?"

"No, he isn't himself after his own loss. I didn't want to add to it. But he asks about him. He asks me to go and get him. I tell him he is at work or went to Tehran to join his family."

Tears collected in her eyes as she asked Jamshid to give Abu her regards.

"You all have a safe trip back home," Jamshid said. "Your son is such a handsome young man, Zulaikha. He seems to be very sad for his uncle."

Anti-plane guns started shooting, followed by a loud red siren and a power outage. One of Gholam's soldiers approached her and asked her to follow him to the mosque's refuge zone. She found Gholam and the boys there. Madineh sat down on the floor like a robot. Mrs. Sara left her to sit with her husband. While waiting for the white mode, Zulaikha asked Gholam if he knew anything.

"Just leave it," he said.

"What do you mean?" she muttered. "You're a police officer, for heaven's sake. Can you not ask around?"

"I have. They said he had gone on an assignment with two men. Both were returned—one of them wounded, and I think he died later. They had said that Hessam disappeared as soon as the bombing started—he didn't help the others, something like that."

"Hessam told me that the man who killed Abbass may have hired someone. Can they be related?"

"I tried to investigate it, but they didn't let me. That student went missing shortly after Abbass's death. I think Hessam heard about that and just planned to escape. God knows." He glanced at Madineh. She was staring at them.

"We have to act and claim he's a missing soldier of war. We have to, Zulaikha. It's better to be missing than a fugitive. They're searching for him, so it looks like they haven't captured him, but they are on to us all."

"Hessam knows Khuzestan like the back of his hand," Madineh said. "It's better this way. Surely, better than being murdered."

Finally, she agrees with Gholam.

His presence, uniform, and guards convinced Madineh that he knew better. Zulaikha could use his energy at that moment.

Sohrab and Mousa were laughing at something in a corner. Suddenly Sohrab met her eyes and stopped his smile as if he shouldn't have been happy. She looked away.

The power came back. Gholam's Jeep with a driver was ready to return him and Mousa to their town. He sat in the front seat, all others in the back. On their way home, he told them that the Basij force would integrate with the national police soon.

"What will happen to you then, Gholam?" Zulaikha asked.

"Nothing—I'm thinking about retiring anyway," he said. "All of it is for making us believe they're something different."

"They are different, Gholam. We used to feel safe near the police." The sight of the guards terrified her.

Gholam shook his head as he looked out the window.

When they said their goodbyes, as Zulaikha walked away, Gholam pulled down the car window and called her name. "Be very careful. We have our boys to keep safe. Remember that."

It was funny how safe Gholam's presence made her feel that day. She touched his face. "You too, Gholam. You scared the hell out of them today. You may be in trouble, too."

Before bed, Sohrab played a bit with Abbass's *oud*. "How could anyone hate him so much?" He touched Abbass's drum. "I'll never forget him and his songs."

She allowed him to pack Abbass's musical instruments and

take them to Tehran. As Sohrab was experimenting with the *oud*, Madineh broke her silence and sang a Luri elegy:

> *When will you return, you, my red and white flower?*
> *My clover, my willow leaf*
> *You said you would return when the flowers grow back*
> *But the whole world ran out of flowers,*
> *When will you return?*

■■■

Zulaikha was reluctant to leave Madineh alone. She seemed too quiet and depressed. Sohrab visited her almost every day after school. On the weekends, when they gathered again as a family, they no longer talked about Hessam and Abadan. Madineh's cat-like eyes no longer flashed. Her swaying walk and flirtatious glances were things of the past. Zulaikha did not complain to her about not cleaning up after herself. On the weekends, after doing the laundry, she vacuumed the room and gave Madineh a nice bath. Madineh was only in her late sixties, but when Zulaikha dried her with the towel, Madineh's weak body was alarming. Troubles had worn her out too soon, too fast.

In those days, people entertained themselves by renting VHS tapes from a man who visited the tenants of the dorms with a suitcase, which he carried as though it was full of important documents. He rented copies of smuggled videotapes of American pop stars like Michael Jackson and Madonna and the most popular Bollywood movies. Zulaikha rented a few movies for her mother every weekend to keep her entertained when alone. Abdul's mother sometimes kept her company—they would watch Indian films together. On her good days, Madineh still played cards with her neighbours.

But a Revolutionary Guard could interrupt all of their creative entertainment.

Zulaikha had just arrived from the Alipours with a basket of herbs and vegetables. She went to the kitchen downstairs to put some leftover food and grapes in the shared fridge when she heard the mumbling of the neighbours coming from upstairs. Someone rushed through the warren of rooms and came to warn Madineh that the guards were looking for her daughter. Zulaikha stayed in the dark and damp kitchen without making a sound. What was she doing? Every thought in her mind cautioned her about how to behave, to cover her hair and button up her *manteau* to avoid confrontation.

One of the neighbours had seen her coming in.

She heard Madineh shouting, "What do you want from my daughter? She's not here."

Zulaikha could see the guard from the bottom of the stairs.

"Nothing, *Madar joon*. We just want to ask a few questions about your missing son. Hopefully, we can find him and return him as quickly as possible."

Madineh hissed, "You liars!"

"Maybe you can give us some information then." His tone was threatening.

"I haven't seen my son for over a year," she snapped.

"Your daughter was with him the night before he returned to his post, wasn't she? Where is your grandson? Is he in school? Do you want me to take you and him together until she shows up?"

Zulaikha climbed the stairs slowly but stumbled and paused at the third step. The man noticed her.

"I'm here," she said. "I just got here."

"This way." The Guard led her toward the yard.

At the top of the stairs, Zulaikha glanced at Madineh. "Call Mrs. Alipour."

Now, in the year 1984, an interrogation at Evin prison had evolved into a terrifying ordeal, surpassing its already-horrific history.

Zulaikha turned, knowing she might be away for a long time. "Cut the *sabzi* on the counter. Have Sohrab help you or the neighbours. Will you?"

Madineh nodded with frantic sorrow in her eyes. Zulaikha had grown to adore her mother's white scarf covering her silver hair.

An SUV was waiting at the gate. Their destination was Evin. They did not talk to her, and she did not ask anything. They blindfolded her in the car when they left the city and drove toward the notorious prison.

Once inside, they took her to a room and ordered her to sit. She could feel that she was in a big room, and she heard the presence of three men, two sitting and one standing.

She said, "Salaam," politely, with a shaking voice.

A woman from behind her removed her blindfold. She glanced at the woman in a chador who sat in a corner the entire time without saying anything.

The two sitting men greeted her simultaneously. "Salaam, Sister, how are you today?"

She muttered, "Not bad."

"Do you know why you are here?"

"No, sorry, I don't."

"It's about your brother, Hessam."

She stood up. "Did you find him?"

"Calm down, Sister. We want to ask you some questions about him, that's all."

"My brother may be a martyr or captured by Iraqis. You want to question me about what?"

"We suggest one more time that you calm down. We know your position, Sister, but we've heard rumours about Hessam's friendship with an anti–revolutionary clown, a drum player called Abbass. His disappearance took place right after Abbass's death. That seems strange, don't you think so?"

"I don't know what you're talking about."

"You don't know?"

"I asked him not to tell me anything about what happened at the front. I could not take it."

"You did not even have a funeral for your brother. Was that because you knew he was alive?"

"We hope that he is. We had a small ceremony in Abadan."

"He was the only person from his group that went missing."

"And that is strange?"

"Yes. That is not strange to you?"

"These days, everything and nothing is strange."

The man glanced at his fellow interrogator and smiled. "Oh, this sister is giving us some philosophy lessons, don't you think?"

"Yes, she seems to be a wise lady," said the interrogator.

"So, wise Sister, you know everyone who acts against the revolutionary forces gets punished?"

"Yes, Brother, I'm aware of that, but I have done nothing," she replied, distraught.

"We've reviewed the list of war captives—his name hasn't been found in any list from Iraq."

Tears welled in her eyes. "What do you expect me to say?"

The two men glanced at each other again. "Listen, we respect you as a war refugee, but you should think carefully. Can you remember anything he said about his friends in your conversations?"

"What do you mean? What about his friends?"

"Friends helping him escape."

"No, I can't."

"What about a schoolboy? Omid?"

She swallowed hard. "I had been living apart from my brother—and Abadan—for a long time. I don't—"

The interrogator shifted his head toward the woman sitting behind Zulaikha. "Where do you think is the best place for our sister to think?"

She answered with a northern provincial accent. "A solitary cell would be the best place to remember things."

Zulaikha interrupted them. "Oh, please, I have a son and an elderly mother to take care of. I have asthma—I could die in a cell with no air."

The other man said, "So you'll think deeper and faster."

Half an hour later, she was in a small cell shared with another woman. She was an older woman who slept for the most part.

Didn't they say they would put me in a solitary cell? I don't want to see others' torments on top of mine. I am losing it already.

Excessive stress might induce an asthma attack, so she tried to picture Sohrab, even her good days with Assef. When the woman woke up, she asked, "When are they coming for me? Do you know?"

Zulaikha could see that she was in a state of shock. An hour later, one of the guards came and asked the woman to get up. She mechanically moved and followed them.

Where are they taking her?

Now alone and frightened, she paced the room and muttered Sohrab and Assef's names. *What happened to us, Assef?* Then she hummed "*Esmaony.*"

It's a shame and a thousand shames.

Short of breath, she started coughing. When she knocked on the door and asked for help, two women came to check on her, one of which was the same woman from the interrogation room. She gave her a glass of warm water. A few seconds later, Zulaikha heard the woman guard behind the door asking her if she knew Arabic.

"A little bit."

"Your voice is beautiful. Where did you hear the song?"

"From the Kuwait TV, when I lived in Abadan."

"I'll bring you a Quran. You should use your voice and Arabic to chant the Quran verses."

Zulaikha pressed her hand against her mouth, attempting to hide her weeping.

After a few moments of silence, the woman said, "It's okay to sing that song, too. I won't tell anyone."

Zulaikha closed her eyes and put her hands on the sides of her head. "Thank you."

On her next meal tray was a small Quran. The female interrogator came to say hello. "I think I left something in the holy book. Can you check?"

Zulaikha picked it up, kissed the cover and searched the pages. She found a picture of a teenage boy with blue eyes.

"That's my nephew," she said. "Your brother killed him." She took the picture from her and walked away.

Undoubtedly this woman was playing mind games with her. Zulaikah opened the book and read a verse she remembered from her childhood, a declaration of gratitude to the Creator, the same prayer she read with Aliah's children the night Sheikh Ahmed died. The woman had left the door open. Zulaikha could see a cell opposite her occupied by two women. They appeared to have separated the elderly from the youth. One of them had green eyes and a lighter skin tone. They greeted her.

The green-eyed woman said, "Where did they take her? Do you know?"

"Who?"

"Your cellmate."

"I have no idea. She was not feeling well, maybe to a clinic."

The women looked at each other doubtfully.

"They had killed her son and husband. Maybe she's in a better place now," the green-eyed woman said.

"Do you mean she's dead?" She swallowed.

The woman refrained from answering her question. "Why are you here?" she asked.

"I don't really know. My brother is missing in the war, but they think someone helped him escape. What about you?"

The green-eyed woman spoke again, but the other one ignored them and lay down.

"We were family members of a colonel in the Shah's army," she said. "We're waiting for our death sentences."

Suddenly a hand pushed her to a wall and slammed the door. The world around her became darker as a hissing sound in her ears filled the room.

■■■

She woke up and found herself on a bed in a brighter room. The female guard was sitting on a chair near her bed, reading a book she could tell was the Quran. The intravenous drips and the curtains around her bed indicated she was hospitalized. The last thing she remembered was knocking on her cell door asking for help as she struggled to hold herself up.

The woman greeted her and put aside her Quran gently.

"What happened?" Zulaikha asked.

"You collapsed. Don't you remember?"

"Do I know your name?" she asked.

"You can call me Sister Matlab. Funny that I never told you my name." She approached Zulaikha with a strange smile on her pale round face. Her body, covered in black from head to toe, reminded Zulaikha of a nightmare she kept having, a crow flying over top of her bed.

Matlab called for a nurse to check on Zulaikha and pulled her chair closer to the bed. "I'm happy you're feeling better."

"Do you know what they want from me?"

This woman was playing a game and Zulaikha had no other option but to play along.

"They're keeping you to get to your brother."

"How? He doesn't know where I am right now." Zulaikha wished Matlab's smile would disappear—a smile driven by power.

"Your mother says he's alive. We have interrogated your other brother, too—"

They have interrogated Gholam. They haven't brought Mother here yet. Perhaps she's under surveillance, and she has no idea.

"If your Hessam knew the trouble he has got you all in, he would surrender. That's what a wise man would do in this situation."

"But what has he done?"

Her response was another disgusting smile.

"What if he is in captivity?" Zulaikha continued.

"We're looking into that, too." Sister Matlab placed her book in her bag.

■■■

When Zulaikha went to the bathroom before her transfer from

the prison hospital, her reflection in the mirror startled her. Why were her lips bluish? Her fingertips, too—as if she had been physically tortured.

They relocated her to section 209, where the prisoners were young women, high school kids, university students, teachers, and professors. Some had been beaten, and some were awaiting execution.

Sister Matlab continued to take an interest in her, offering her private Quran lessons. Three weeks later, she told Zulaikha that they had contacted her mother. "We'll send you home soon, but she needs to find you a guarantor."

"Can I call her? She might not know what to do."

"I'll see what I can do."

When she told her cellmates the news, some were happy for her and gave her their family's addresses and asked her to let them know their daughters were alive. Others looked at her suspiciously.

"Why are they letting you go?" a girl in her twenties asked. "It's not easy to get released from here. You must have given them information."

"I'm here because of my brother—he may have been killed in the war. I am just a housekeeper, nothing more."

One of the other girls said, "Leave the poor woman alone. She has no ideas, no ideologies or anything. Look at her highlighted hair. Obviously, she hasn't touched a book or newspaper in her life. They have no mercy for anyone anymore."

Part of her wanted to tell them about her reading sessions with Abbass and Hessam. But she said nothing.

"She's here because of her brother," another girl joined in, "Didn't you hear what she said?"

A young girl who could not be more than sixteen said,

"Your brother joined the Mojahedin in Iraq. That's what I heard."

Mojahedin allied with Saddam Hussein. I would have killed Hessam myself if he did. But would I? Who did help him, though? What the hell has happened to him?

She burst into tears. "No, he did not. You have no idea who he was. Have some respect."

"Didn't they beat you at all?"

"What is this? Another interrogation?" She pressed her shoulder and the back of her head against the wall. She couldn't remember if she was hit before she collapsed—or was that a nightmare before she woke up in the hospital?

"Why do you look so sick then? You weren't lashed or sexually assaulted?" the girl asked incredulously.

"I had an asthma attack when they pushed me into the solitary cell."

The girls, obviously from different political groups, argued with one another over everything when the Revolutionary Guards were not around. They were all confused—but they had one thing in common: everyone hated the guards and the theocratic regime. But no one, it seemed, had a clue about how to defeat them.

When a young woman with an infant joined them, a different atmosphere began to emerge. She'd given birth to her child in the prison hospital. The child had been her mother's saviour—although sometimes they would kill pregnant girls, too. Together the captives had to share in the care of that baby girl. One of the inmates unknitted her sweater as she muttered, "Maybe we can ask for something to knit." A proposition that left Zulaikha pondering how she could contribute in the days to come.

The next time Zulaikha needed a doctor, she noticed paper clips on the doctor's desk. She explained why she wanted some, and the doctor gave her a fistful. The prisoners created needles from paper clips and began to take turns knitting baby clothes.

When it was her turn to go to the yard, Zulaikha tried to listen to the voices of nature, the birds, and even children's laughter coming from somewhere far off. She asked one of the girls if she could hear the laughter too. "Yes, it's coming from Luna Park."

Zulaikha remembered the park. Life and love, which they were all deprived of feeling, continued beyond the prison walls.

Sister Matlab let her make a call. She called Mrs. Alipour and told her that she needed a guarantor.

"*Beh rooye chashm*, Zuli *jan*—we'll be there right away, but what will we be signing?"

Sister Matlab took the phone from Zulaikha to explain. "She won't leave Tehran without official permission." She hung up abruptly.

■ ■ ■

Her cellmates told her she should not expect to leave the prison on her own on the release day. "No car is allowed on the premises and no one can know what this place looks like from the outside. "They will take you to Luna Park and leave you there."

She did not believe this story until it happened.

She sat with Sister Matlab in the back of a car who only allowed her to remove her blindfold once they approached the park. They dropped her off, and as she got out of the car, the woman guard said, "I beg for your prayers."

Zulaikha couldn't believe what she had heard. She turned back and whispered, "Likewise."

Birds were singing, and as she walked along the road, she looked up and saw two crows flying after each other. All the beauty of nature, tall willow trees, and soft blue sky seemed ignorant to her plight. How could this beautiful park, with its trees and birds, bear the secrets of the damned fort on top of the hill? She could not know the direction to the prison, but those tall trees and birds nesting in them could see the path to that fort of pains for decades—they stood tall and remained silent. What could they do? Trees burn and birds migrate, leaving those young men and women without hope, without the sounds of laughter and birdsong. That park was the end of all the worldly beauty. After one passed Luna Park, it was crossing a borderline to darkness and hatred.

■ ■ ■

Zulaikha had been in Evin for almost three months. Eleven-year-old Sohrab and his close friend Reza were waiting for her in front of a car outside Luna Park. She recognized Abdul's taxi. She hugged both Sohrab and Reza. Abdul got out and said hello, walked toward her with his limping long legs and opened the car door humbly. She did not expect him to be there. She noticed all three of them were dressed nicely as though they had come to pick her up from a trip. Abdul was wearing a green shirt and was clean shaven. This man was good to her. But Assef was still there in front of her and in her dreams. She blamed Sohrab for his resemblance to his father as though it had blinded her from seeing Abdul the way he deserved to be seen. She beamed at Abdul.

Suddenly she felt an itch on her scalp. Her black chador was adding to her discomfort. She wanted to scratch her hair, but not in front of the boys. She needed to wash her hair with good shampoo when she got home. The last time she and her prison mates could take a shower was five days ago, when one of the girls had shouted, "Water is warm, ladies."

"You all look so nice," she said. "Look at me. I'm a mess."

All three of them said "no" simultaneously. Their voices screamed their sincere attempt to convince her that things would be alright.

She glanced at Sohrab and Reza and observed a bond between them. Reza was the kind of close friend she had wished for her son for a long time.

■■■

She stayed in the dormitory sick and useless for a few days. She wrote to Aliah:

> I dreamed about you last night. I want to sleep all day and dream about my awful life in freedom. The things that happened to me in the past year have been more horrific than my nightmares…

As her gaze settled on her words, she hesitated briefly, then tore the page apart. A minute later, she commenced anew, the words echoing the same sentiment as before.

A knock on her door provided a timely diversion.

Her first visitors were Abdul and his mother. They brought her a big pack of pastries and flowers. Other neighbours came afterward as if supporting her return was their duty. When they asked her what happened in Evin she refused to share any details. Talking about it would bring back the moments she wanted to leave behind.

A week later, she had had enough of useless days. She asked Abdul if he would give her a ride to a couple of the addresses she got from the prison mates. In one day, they went to two houses. Abdul parked outside and waited for her. She went inside for a few minutes, told them that their daughters were fine, prison food was not that bad, and a bunch of other lies. She carried a list of the items they needed or gave them small notes the girls had written on paper.

One night she dreamed of a long passionate kiss. This time it was Abdul's. Thankfully, Assef was fading from her mind. Abdul's kiss and touch liberated her from a man who never belonged to her. With Abdul, she discovered a new woman rising inside of her, as though the pain she had endured since the war had given birth to another Zulaikha, one who had been living there inside of her for a long time, quietly hidden, and who could now rise up and speak. The shyness of her youth was gone—she now demanded more and commanded her young lover. But why was she crying? Where were those tears coming from, at the climax of her pleasure? She did not understand. She only knew that this pleasure, this satisfaction, would not fill the emptiness of what she had lost. The tears, the urge for crying, came from losing dignity, from the humiliation and fear of returning to that same place where she had no control, no power.

Madineh silently made it possible for her to spend more time with Abdul by inviting his mother over to watch old Indian and Farsi movies, make Turkish coffee, and show off her coffee fortune telling talent.

A curtain separated Abdul's bedroom from the living area of their place. Abdul's mother's bed was on the other side of the curtain. Abdul didn't want his mother's little space to distract their lovemaking. He closed the curtain and laid a blue velvet bedspread on the floor. Zulaikha sensed that Abdul was confused about her change in sexual behaviour. "Where did that come from?" he asked her several times. She now understood how oppression changed people—not only their minds, but their eating habits, sleep pattern, dreams, and sexual manners.

One evening, when she was lying on her side with her naked back to him, he told her, "Marry me, Zulaikha. I will be good to you."

She turned her head around and said, "Are you out of your mind? Don't make me call the whole thing off."

Abdul hated Tehran. In Khuzestan, the enemy had injured him, and a countryman had slapped and humiliated him in Tehran. He told her that he was done with Tehran. His relatives had moved to Shiraz, and they were happy there. "We can start a new life there in Shiraz," he said.

"What are we going to tell Sohrab?"

"Nothing—if you prefer. We'll get married now but move in together when he's old enough to understand."

"I can't leave Sohrab again. I've told you before." Last week when one of the dorm's tenants moved, Sohrab told her he wouldn't change schools anymore—he refused to be far from Reza. "Not ever again," he said.

"You deserve better, Abdul," she said. "I'm not the right person for you."

Abdul could not convince her that she deserved to be happy. They argued about their age difference, moving from Tehran together, and what they should do about their mothers. But how could she tell him that the main reason for her resistance was that she wasn't in love with him? Love was like a visitor who had left her heart a long time ago.

■ ■ ■

One day when Zulaikha was about to leave for grocery shopping, she received a letter. She thought Aliah had responded, but the letter was from Germany—from Najwa. Zulaikha put her basket down and opened the letter with excitement.

> **Germany accepted us as refugees. We are very happy and busy learning the German language. I am sure you heard about Abu. He had another stroke and died a few days after we saw each other.**

She glanced at Sohrab, then Madineh.
"What's wrong, *Maman*?"
"Nothing—Najwa and Jalal are in Germany—"
"Why do you look sad then?"
"Abu—"
"We know *Maman*—he passed away—we didn't want to tell you until you felt better."
The pain that the guilt scattered inside her body was a different kind. It burned. "We should have brought him with us—he died away from us."
Madineh finally sobbed.
"We couldn't, *Maman*—he was very sick."
She blinked her tears away. Sohrab had his share of adversity for a kid.
"Look, *Maman*—I have a surprise for you."
Sohrab showed her a few toman bills.
"Where did you get this from?" She glanced at Madineh. This was no surprise to her. Things had happened while she was in Evin.
Sohrab had contacted his father and told him about his mother's arrest. "We had no money left while you were away. Bibi didn't want me to call Baba at first, but I told her it's better than borrowing from neighbours."

"He asked what we do for food and other expenses. I had only one word, *Maman*—nothing."

"And?"

"He asked me to go to a bank and open an account and tell them that my father wanted to send money," Sohrab said. "The bank didn't want to open an account without my parents' consent. I gave Baba the bank manager's phone number, and he called and convinced them."

"How?" Zulaikha asked.

"I think he told him where you were. I mean—Evin—"

"Stop it, Zuli," Madineh yelled. "Don't question the child. I was there, too."

Hearing Assef's name echoed in her mind. She tied her scarf around her neck. "I'm sorry you had to contact him for the money."

"Let him help, *Maman*. He should." Sohrab spoke like an adult. It was comforting and terrifying at the same time.

Abdul offered to give her their regular ride that day. No other addresses from the girls in Evin remained for her to visit. She was not ready to return to work, socialize, or serve her employers for weeks after her return. But now she needed to work and keep busy.

Today, she gave him the direction to the Alipours' house. They were both quiet for the most part until she broke the silence. "My mother said you are moving to Shiraz. Is that true?"

"Yes, my mother and I have been thinking about it."

"When were you going to tell me?"

Abdul slowed down his speed and looked in the mirror. "I wanted to tell you on the day we were leaving, so I could see if you feel anything about me. I wanted to see the expression on your face."

"You're being unfair." She looked out the window. "You deserve someone happier, someone with fewer troubles."

"Let's stop talking about it then. Let it be."

That would be her last ride in his taxi.

■■■

On a day four years later, she was vacuuming the master bedroom when she heard Mrs. Alipour's scream from the dining room.

"It ended—the war ended!"

Car horns blared. She turned off the vacuum cleaner, sat on a chair, and stared at the wall in front of her for a few long minutes. That day was the twentieth day of August, 1988.

CHAPTER 4

The House

KHUZESTAN IN THE 1990s

MADINEH DIED IN HER SLEEP in the spring of 1994 when she was seventy-six years old, losing her long-time battle with diabetes. After the government evacuated war refugee dorm tenants gradually, Zulaikha and Sohrab began renting two rooms in an old house whose owners lived abroad. For the last few years of Madineh's life, while Zulaikha worked at the Alipours' house, Sohrab visited his grandmother almost daily around lunchtime.

That day, twenty-one-year-old Sohrab called Zulaikha to tell her, "Bibi passed away, *Maman*. I found her in bed under the animal print blanket she loved so much."

For Zulaikha, Madineh's death did nothing to solve the complexities of their relationship. In fact, her mother's passing brought still more confusion. In her youth, Zulaikha had periodically wished for her mother's death, once before their appointment at the clinic to abort her baby, or earlier, when Madineh used self-harm to force Zulaikha to obey her. In her final years, though, Madineh had become a harmless, quiet elderly woman with shiny silver hair. She had become dependent on Zulaikha's care to the extent that she once told her, "I wonder what I will do without you on the other side. I don't know if I can manage." But she never asked her for forgiveness. Zulaikha had been waiting for that day to come.

Death, she found, was so vulgar. It arrived uninvited to spread its familiar, creeping numbness through her veins, drinking away the red wine of vitality with a menacing laughter at the confusion left in its wake.

For the first six weeks after Madineh died, Zulaikha visited her grave every Friday, even though the cemetery was two hours away. She washed her tombstone and spread flowers and rose water over her grave as if again giving her a nice bath. She cried at her burial place but did not utter, "My Mother, I know you've forgiven me. I forgive you, too."

Gholam was now a retired police officer. Barring the year that he gave his mother and nephew, Sohrab, a roof and, later on, his efforts to find out about Hessam's disappearance, he'd had little to do with her. When Zulaikha called to give him the news about their mother's passing, he reacted indifferently. He refused to attend her funeral and, a few days later, called and asked about the house in Abadan. "What do you want to do? I think we should sell it and cash in our shares."

It took Sohrab and his generation longer than usual to graduate from high school. During the war, and when Tehran was under attack, schools closed repeatedly. Sohrab graduated when he was almost twenty years old. After his high school graduation, as the only son of a single parent, he was exempt from mandatory military service. He worked in a dried fruit export company as a customs clerk, a stressful underpaid job responsible for issuing shipping documents. A few days after Madineh's funeral, when Sohrab was helping to clean the dinner table, Zulaikha asked him to accompany her to visit Gholam in Aghajari, but he was reluctant.

"This is the worst time to visit them, considering how he didn't come to the funeral. Don't you think?"

"Of course, but I must settle the estate with him. I need you, Sohrab. You know I rarely ask you to do anything for me, and if I do, it's because I really do need you."

"Okay, *Maman*, I'll take a few days off," he said. "Can we go to a hotel and not to their house?"

"He'll be offended."

"No matter what we do, he'll be offended. But—" He needed a minute to think it through. "I don't want to offend Mousa."

■■■

Sohrab and Zulaikha sat on the very back seat of the bus to Aghajari.

"These mountains used to scare me, *Maman*," Sohrab said, looking out the bus window.

This was another part of Khuzestan with agricultural landscapes she had almost forgotten. A little boy who was herding sheep waved at them. She waved back, leaned back and closed her eyes to rest.

"Why did *Amu* Gholam hate Bibi Madineh so much?"

Hearing this blunt question, she opened her eyes and sat straight. "Believe it or not, I never got it either. Gholam never forgave her for our father," she said. "Gholam was older than us, and our father's separation and death were the hardest on him. Bibi was a young single mother, and Gholam was tough like her. Each wanted to control the other—he couldn't tolerate it, so he didn't return home after his conscription. Then, he got used to his life away from us—out of sight, out of the heart."

"I think you were both unfair to her."

Is he giving me attitude today?

She glared at him. "Really? Why?"

"In those years, when she took care of me here, we sometimes trail walked as she talked about her life, about the migration of her ancestors to Khuzestan. She would get tired quickly and sat on a rock to catch her breath, but she'd insist that we should keep walking, reminding me that hiking is in our blood. As I got older, I heard her telling me her memories repeatedly, but I didn't mind. I always listened to them like it was the first time. She was trying to keep them alive. If I complained about your absence, she would defend you, picture you as a Bakhtiari Lur superwoman fighting to earn a loaf of bread," he said. "She saw your side, but neither you nor Uncle Gholam tried to understand her circumstances. Did you?"

Zulaikha was quiet. If her mother were alive, they would have had another fight. *How dare you talk to my son without my knowledge? He should learn his history from me, not you.*

But death had intervened and opened a new angle for her to see. Madineh had cherished devoting the remainder of her life to Sohrab.

"She used to sing a lot, too—that Luri song, *"Shir Ali Mardoon."* Remember? She had a good voice. Did you know that?"

She sighed. She remembered the song very well:

> *I'm a Lur who eats acorn,*
> *Seven years a shepherd,*
> *I never learned marching…*

Zulaikha took her son's hand. "Do you think about her a lot?"

He wiped his tears with a tissue. "If Uncle Gholam or anyone in his house says one thing, even one bad thing about her, I won't stand it."

Death was a flood washing out Madineh's flaws. Ill speaking of the dead was stupid. She pressed her head on her mourning son's shoulder.

Gholam was waiting for them at the bus stop. He was older but still looked tall and in shape, with the same moustache, though now it was gray. He held Sohrab and kissed both cheeks, but with Zulaikha, he was distant. They shook hands like strangers. Guiding them to his old Paykan car, he drove them to his place, a journey of only fifteen minutes. He was proud that he had recently renovated several rooms. He had a three-bedroom house with a beautiful lawn. "See how neat it is. It's all Kobra—my back doesn't let me do too much gardening."

Kobra held her. "I'm so sorry for your loss. I couldn't leave the house. My heart was there with you all the time, though."

Her son, Mousa, was shaking Sohrab's hand when his mother told him to help to get their luggage. "Welcome, welcome. You must be starved by now."

A big table of saffron rice and an eggplant dish was ready for them. Sohrab once told her, "Mousa has inherited all the good things—it's like he has perfectly sorted out his parents' best habits."

Zulaikha helped with the dishes.

They heard someone knocking at the kitchen's back door. It was the shepherd boy who had waved at them earlier. Gholam let him in as though he were a regular visitor. Kobra spread a small tablecloth on the porch floor and asked the boy to go and wash up. She put out some leftover food as Zulaikha readied a glass of ice water. His sheep fed on the lawn grass, and for a moment, Zulaikha expected Gholam to object or say something to the boy, but they all looked content.

When the kid returned from the bathroom, Kobra glared at his shoes. "You're wearing torn shoes again. What did you do with the last ones I gave you?" He sat with his head down.

"Do you realize how much he walks?" Mousa asked. "Those are the same ones you gave him. I'll give him another pair."

After lunch and a quick bath, the boy left with his new oversized trousers and shirts.

Before they went to sleep, Zulaikha shared her strange observations with Sohrab at night.

"When you lived with them, were they this nice, like they were with that boy?"

"They were busier and sometimes tired, but yes, for the most part. Why?"

"Bibi always complained about them. I never knew how much of it was true."

"Bibi got bored easily," Sohrab chuckled. "Perhaps living so remotely in such a small town for a long time had made them more receptive to other people.

Gholam worked on his car almost all day to prepare it for their journey. The next day, before sunrise, Zulaikha went outside with her bags. Sohrab and Mousa were still sleeping. Gholam was washing his car window. "My car is ready to roar."

Zulaikha put the bags inside the car and stood beside him.
"Why are you staring at me?"
"You look like her. Did you know that? Especially your eyes."
He stopped wiping the car window. "Did she suffer?"
"No, she passed while sleeping but was sick for years."
"God bless her soul," he said as a stranger would have.
The smell of fresh bread wafted outside. Kobra had prepared sour cream, honey, and tea. Zulaikha sat at the table and had a small bite. "This was Hessam's favourite breakfast, too. Remember?"
Gholam nodded. "I still think he's alive, living his life somewhere."
"It's been ten years," she said. "So he's abandoned us?"
"Pretty much." He dipped his bread into the sour cream.
"Do you know something, or is it just a feeling?"
"I know our brother, Zulaikha," he said.
They were in contact all the time. Maybe he knows things about Hessam I've never known.
"It's been a long time since we've seen each other," Kobra distracted them. "But it's like it was yesterday, don't you think?"
"A very long time indeed."
"Bibi Madineh, God bless her soul, may have told you things about us, Zuli *jan*, but please believe me, she could be very difficult sometimes," she said. "She always found something to complain about—once I asked Sohrab to help with something, she screamed that she had not come here to be enslaved—in front of the children."
Zulaikha felt a lump in her throat. Sohrab had become all of Madineh's children.
"No need to explain. I know my mother, and it's all in the past." She drank some tea to clear her throat. "I should have thanked you earlier for caring for them during the war."
Shortly after sunrise, they began their journey back to Abadan. Sohrab was sleeping for the most part, but Zulaikha could not keep her eyes off the road—the city in its state was like standing over a wounded man about to die: bombed buildings, still-closed

shops, and broken palm trees.

When they entered the old, empty house, Zulaikha's legs trembled. She sat down and put a shaking hand on her stomach.

Gholam, examining the damage on the courtyard wall, shouted, "Damn the bastards. Look what they did to us."

It was not only from the war's vulgar intrusion—thieves and thugs had broken into the house and taken most of the items. Even the water taps and electrical fuses had been stolen.

Mrs. Sara still lived next door. She must have heard their voices in the yard and came to the open door.

"Is this Sohrab? Oh my God, I thought time had stopped and Assef was visiting. He's so like his father." Her eyes filled with tears as she held Zulaikha.

"You haven't changed, though," Zulaikha said.

Mrs. Sara rolled her eyes and invited them back to her house. She brought them lemonade and cookies.

"We finally decided to renovate." The wall paint looked and smelled new. "Sorry for the paint smell. We waited a long time—we thought another war might start."

Parviz, her husband, still a plumber, complained about business. "Who wants to live here?"

Gholam asked them about the housing market.

"These days, nobody wants to invest in anything," Parviz said. "Just leave it. You can sell it someday when things are better here."

"You may be right, but we have plans for my son, Mousa." Gholam explained that he wanted to use the money to send his son to Japan. In those years, many young Iranians who hadn't been admitted to universities made good money working in Japan.

Mrs. Sara saw them off at the door, where Sohrab surprised Zulaikha with another question. "My Uncle Hessam never phoned your house. Did he?"

"No. Why, my child?"

"I don't know. I've just wanted to ask you all these years."

"He may have when we went to Isfahan. We went away for a

while, too."

Sohrab glanced at Zulaikha. His eyes gleamed as if he heard what he had hoped for.

As they drove to downtown Abadan, Gholam searched for an open real estate agency.

Zulaikha and Sohrab did not want to return to Aghajari the same day. They stayed with Mrs. Sara and her husband in Abadan. Gholam left but let Mousa stay with his aunt and cousin.

"We should go and see what we can find in this ruined city," Mousa said. "We might as well have some fun."

Sohrab glanced at Zulaikha.

"Go have fun, boys," she said. "Just be safe."

"Yes, if you see vandals, just let them do their thing," Mrs. Sara said.

Sohrab and Mousa chuckled.

Back in the old house, as Zulaikha boxed some of the old items left in Hessam's room, she noticed that the carpet had disappeared.

Finally, thieves took it.

Someone had thrown Hessam's books off the shelves and collapsed the bookcase savagely.

"Guards searched the house a few days after that *tajlil* ceremony," Mrs. Sara said. "Sorry, I only stacked them in a corner. We had to evacuate—"

"It's okay. Feel free to give away anything else in this house."

"Thieves will be happy that you made everything ready for them to pick up," Mrs. Sara said. "By the way, those guards stole one of your carpets, too—I saw one of them putting the roll in their car. He yelled and asked how this family got a rug like that. I went to tell them it was Bibi Madineh's carpet—well, I'd seen it in her house when she lived with Habib. Parviz didn't let me say anything. They said they'd take it to a mosque."

A mosque became the home of that damned carpet. If only Mother knew.

"Enough of this dusty crime scene," Zulaikha said. "Let's go to the fish market."

As they browsed, Sara asked Zulaikha about Assef and if they were still in contact.

"Assef?" She sighed, "No, but he's in contact with Sohrab."

"Really? How did that happen?"

"Long story." She then told her the stories of her troubles after she moved to Tehran, the dorm, cold winters, and what had happened to her after Hessam's disappearance. At the dock, a fisherman greeted Mrs. Sara. They watched him cut a giant tuna on a stand.

"Why didn't you re-marry in Tehran, girl? Are you still thinking about Assef, or are men a bunch of losers in that big city?"

Zulaikha put her bag down. "It just didn't happen."

"It didn't happen, or you didn't let it happen?" Zulaikha's hands were crossed as she looked toward the palm grove. "I wonder if my first house with Assef is still there. Do you know?"

Mrs. Sara crossed her arms and shook her head. "I don't think so, darling."

There goes the house of my dreams.

■■■

When Sohrab and Mousa returned, they looked hungry and excited. Around the meal, the boys talked about their little adventure in the city. "It's like a ghost town, *Maman*—nothing but stray dogs."

After dinner, Mrs. Sara offered that they stay the night. Only Mousa accepted. Zulaikha and Sohrab stayed in the house.

Mother and son both could not sleep. Zulaikha, who had found their old radio earlier that day, tried to find an Emirate station. The connection was weak, so she gave up.

"What are you reading?" She sat beside Sohrab.

"Don't you remember this? I found it on the floor." The book belonged to Hessam. It was a small children's novella by Samad Behrangi, *The Little Black Fish.*

"How could I forget? He made me read this and then made me read it to you. Like this was an essential book everyone should read."

"I'm remembering so many things here that I didn't think about in Tehran."

"Really? Like what?"

"In this room, after that tribute, I caught Bibi Madineh staring at a picture of her boys. When she saw me watching her, I told her I would have found him for her if I were an adult. She said she knew I would've. I was a child, and in my mind, I wanted to be a superhero and bring him back for all of us."

And how I needed a superhero, my son. I really did.

■ ■ ■

A week after they returned to Tehran, Zulaikha got a call from Gholam. She was busy frying fish for dinner and wanted to ignore the call, but it kept ringing. She turned off the stove and ran for the phone.

"I have a proposition to make," Gholam said.

Zulaikha didn't know what to say.

"Hello? Are you there?"

"Yes, I'm listening, Gholam."

He offered that he would buy her share and send his son and Sohrab to Japan at his own expense.

"After seeing them together, I thought they could be good friends. I was never close to my brother or you. I never had a cousin, either. I think it will be a good idea for both of them. Do you agree?"

"I like to see them like that, too, but you've caught me off guard."

"How much do you want for your share of the house?"

"How would I know how much it's worth? Plus, I want to keep a share for Hessam."

"You think Hessam will be back for the house?"

"I don't know, but I can't touch his share."

"Okay. I'll pay you one hundred thousand tomans, fifty thousand for each of you, and I'll pay for Sohrab's ticket and three months' expenses, but then you'll officially sign your shares over to me, and I'll be the sole owner of the house. Okay?"

"Let me talk to Sohrab. He's an adult and doesn't like me to decide for him."

"Okay. Be quick, though, before I change my mind."

Sohrab did not find it a bad idea. He had no intention of studying for the Iranian university entrance examination. Japan was a country open to Iranians. "I think this is a great opportunity for me. I don't know about the house, though. I'm sure he's ripping you off, but I have no idea how much—"

"Wait a minute," she said. "Gholam hasn't even brought up one word about being one of the sons—you know what I mean?"

Sohrab shook his head in confusion.

"According to Islamic laws, Gholam and Hessam—the sons—each get more shares than me."

"Right, he either forgot about it or—"

"Gholam forget about money?" She chuckled.

Maybe my mysterious brother is showing his gratitude for my taking on the sons' duty of caring for our mother.

"Never mind that. What were you saying about Japan?"

"Right—by working in Japan, I could send you money, *Maman*. Forget about that house."

"I wish I could."

"Japan can open other doors for me, too."

"What do you mean?"

"I can go to Europe after I've earned some money. So many people are doing that these days."

"Now, you'd better stop overwhelming me, Sohrab."

"I think I should consult with my father about this opportunity. You don't mind, do you?"

"No, but don't give him too many details about Gholam's proposal or anything he doesn't need to know."

She didn't want Assef's sympathy concerning her ruthless brother, for he had been ruthless to her, too.

■■■

Sohrab and Mousa left for Japan in the winter of 1994.

A month before Sohrab left, Zulaikha had no time for melancholy or hesitations. His son was emigrating—to accommodate the transition to this new chapter with more grins and less frustration, she arranged a garage sale, and they sold many of his unwanted items.

In a final farewell to Madineh, the family went to the cemetery the day prior to his departure. Zulaikha overheard her son's quiet words, "I never found Uncle for you when you were here. I am sorry for everything, but you have always had me, Bibi." Sohrab kissed her stone, and they spread rose water and flowers over her grave.

When Sohrab left her in the airport, gravity was not powerful enough to anchor her feet to the ground, as if she were adrift in air. In late spring, she went with Mrs. Alipour to their villa near the Caspian Sea. The saltwater, green woods, and humid climate rejuvenated her soul. Gravity began to work again, and she put her feet on the ground and felt the beauty of being alive once more. Walking along the shore through the forest, she cried a lot. Back in the villa, she took a shower. When she looked in the mirror, the wrinkles under her eyes reminded her of her aging face more than ever.

But Mrs. Alipour had a different opinion. "You're still young and beautiful," she said. "Open your heart. Something good will happen, and you deserve it."

Returning to Tehran by chartered car, she gazed out at the green forests and mountains.

"There's an acquaintance, a widower—he lost his wife two years ago. He's in his mid-sixties but in excellent shape. I'll arrange an afternoon tea with the three of us. Would that be okay with you?"

Drops of rain hit the car windows harshly. She heard herself answering Mrs. Alipour, "Sure."

As she opened the door and entered her place, she was as drained as when she had left. Sohrab was not there—his room and his closet were empty. She noticed the answering machine was blinking. She had a short voice message from Assef.

"Zulaikha *jan*, it's me, Assef. Sorry I didn't call before about your mother. Well, I never had a mother. I know I acted pretty stupidly by not calling. I hope it's not too late to express my condolences. I also wanted you to know that I'm in touch with Sohrab. He's fine. I wonder how you are these days, without your mother, without Sohrab. You have raised a good boy. Take care and—and don't be sad, please. Bye."

She listened to the message, his voice, and his charming accent more than ten times until she fell asleep on the floor beside the answering machine. He had not left a phone number. Perhaps he had assumed that she had it. She could search for his contact information in her old notebook, but there was no point. She saved the message, but it was automatically deleted after six days.

■ ■ ■

Zulaikha kept the money from selling the house in an investment account with a high-interest rate. Gholam sold the house in 2000 when people began to move back to Abadan to renovate their beloved city. Mrs. Sara's brother-in-law, who had lost his son in the war, used his grant from The Foundation of War Martyrs to buy the house from Gholam. Gholam never revealed the house's selling price, but Mrs. Sara volunteered to tell Zulaikha if she wanted to know. She didn't. It did not matter. The house was not theirs anymore.

PART 3

Her Return

LATE DECEMBER 2007 TO LATE 2008

> *In an empty ventless room,*
> *A reflection was floating,*
> *And I fell asleep in the dark.*
> *In the deep end of my sleep, I found myself,*
> *And this awakening interrupted the serenity of my sleep.*
> *Was this awakening my new mistake?*
>
> **–Sohrab Sepehri**

TEHRAN'S STREETLIGHTS GLITTERED LIKE STARS on earth. The city below her had been her home for over twenty years. Tehran had changed for her after the war. Through its suffering, Tehran became kinder to outsiders and finally found a way into her heart.

Before baggage claim, men and women from the Revolutionary Guard walked around talking on wireless phones in the passport check line-up. The anxiety made her breathe more heavily. She used her inhaler as she approached the customs officer's desk to hand over her passport. Funnily enough, she had almost forgotten the inhaler when she packed for her trip to Amsterdam. The woman on the other side glanced at her as she matched her face with the passport picture. She picked up her phone and asked Zulaikha to wait.

"Is anything wrong?" she asked.

She received no answer. In less than five minutes, two bearded young men with Basij uniforms approached the customs desk. The woman handed them her passport.

"What's going on?" she asked them one more time.

One of the men asked her to follow them. "Just a procedure, Sister. Not to worry." He directed her to the parking lot, where an SUV with a driver was waiting.

They climbed into the SUV, and one of the men reported their status on a wireless phone. "Yes, she's here. We'll be there in a couple of hours."

A couple of hours? Are they taking me to Evin? Seriously?
"We heard it was freezing there in Europe this year."
They chatted with her as if they were taxi drivers or random passengers socializing with one another.
"Yes, it was—oh, sorry," she yawned. "I'm exhausted."
"That's understandable. Get some sleep, Sister. It's a long way."
"To where? Where are you taking me?"
"We have our orders. You'll know soon."
She looked out her window. The sun was rising when she saw the sign on the highway showing the Exit to Sa'adat Abad. The car switched lanes to exit when the man beside her passed her a blindfold without a word. She covered her eyes, inhaled with all her heart, and visualized Madineh.
Time for you to step in, Mother. Protect me from their harm. I'm not young anymore.

∎ ∎ ∎

The car had pulled over—she heard two women greet the men in the car. They delivered her like she was a package.
"This way, Sister. Just lean on me," one of the women said. "It'll be over soon—there, you can take it off now."
Two women in chador entered the room. One wearing large prescription glasses carried two green and yellow folders. She could see that they had pinned her passport inside the green one. The other woman said her name was Sima and didn't bother to introduce her colleague.
"Can you tell us why your flight was cancelled the day before yesterday?"
"They told us there was a security issue," she said. "I thought there was something wrong with the plane."
It was not easy to break through. Both women had poker faces she failed to read.
"What's the status of your son in Holland?"
"He's working there."
"Is he a refugee or does he have a work visa?"

"He was a refugee but now a resident." She swallowed with fear. "He works—"

"His source of income?"

"He works in a shipping company."

"You have been here before."

Was that a question?

"A long time ago, Ma'am—what's this about?" Zulaikha asked.

The woman with the large glasses pulled out the yellow file and looked inside.

Sima put her elbows on the table. "Who is Kia Chaharlangi?"

"He's an acquaintance—it was a coincidence—"

"What's his profession?"

"I didn't ask him."

"What about in the past? What did he do?"

"He was an oil engineer as far as I remember."

Sima looked down at the file with an expressive arch in her eyebrows.

"Anything wrong?" Zulaikha asked.

Someone opened the door. "Sima *joon*, there's a call for you."

Sima joon? Not Sister? Times have changed.

She waited a few minutes, paced the room, then gave up, put her head on the table, and quickly fell asleep.

The creak of the door startled her.

"What time is it?" Zulaikha asked. "Do I need to call my son or a lawyer?"

"We'll let you know. Come with me," Sima said.

Shortly after sunrise, they walked through a tunnel with windows. Zulaikha remembered this tunnel—they were taking her to Section 209.

She was hungry but did not care for food. Every inch of her body wanted her ordinary life back. She coughed as she approached her cell. "I may need a doctor."

"Just get some rest—I'll check on you in a few hours." Sima closed the sliding door.

The cell looked as she remembered—only the mattress sheets had flowery patterns attached to funny bed skirts. Two other women were inside. They were both sleeping. In the room's silence, the woman who liked her Arabic singing came to her mind. She couldn't remember her name.

How can I still remember that malicious smile, even her nose with a sloping tip, but not her name?

One of the girls woke up. "We have company," she said. "They released six inmates today—we thought we'd be lonesome."

She was Farah, a university professor in her late forties with dual citizenship in Canada. She taught Middle Eastern studies at a university and had lectured about theocracy before her trip. They had arrested her as soon as she stepped off the plane at Tehran's airport. She had been in that cell for six months.

Neda, the reporter, seemed hopeful that she would be released soon. Her family and lawyer worked round the clock to secure her release, and in the process, "They paid them a whole lot of money."

"I don't have money—I'll probably rot in here," Zulaikha said.

"But you said they asked your son and your friend's profession—they smell money—don't you think, Farah *joon*?

"Who knows?" Farah said. "But didn't they tell you why they're keeping you?"

"Maybe it's because of my brother. This is my second time here. I was also here twenty-five years ago."

"What about your brother?" Farah asked.

She sat on the edge of one of the ugly beds. She explained her history—in a nutshell and with caution—from Abbass's assassination to Hessam's disappearance to how they escaped Abadan and lived in Tehran since then.

Sohrab's last question echoed in her mind as she searched for words to depict the chronological order of her brother's vanishing after so many years. "Could Hessam reach out to Kia?"

"They can't be still looking for him after all this time," Farah said.

"I didn't think they were." Zulaikha leaned against the wall and hugged her knees.

"I used to watch a show in Canada," Farah said. "It's called *Cold*

Case. They'd reopen a case if they accidentally dug up a file."

Hessam is my cold case.

"You must have seen many things here," Farah said.

"Yes, in this very same spot—but things are a little bit better now."

"Really? You think things are better now?" The journalist, Neda, looked amused and sounded as though she were interviewing Zulaikha for a television report.

"Better? Compared to that time—yes, things are better," Zulaikha said. "This section was full of kids as young as fifteen. You were not here, were you?" Zulaikha looked at Farah.

"No, not here, but I was still in Iran. I guess I was one of the lucky ones," she said. "My parents were wealthy. They sent me out of the country after the mass killings started."

"Why did you return when you knew you might be arrested?"

"To see my elderly parents. I was foolish enough to think nothing would happen to me because I was a Canadian citizen."

Zulaikha shook her head.

Her cellmates were friendlier and more mature than the ones she'd had years before. They did not fight with each other and treated her respectfully. Zulaikha looked at the writings on the wall behind her left by a past prisoner.

Ey kash midoonestam keh montazeram mimooni (I wonder if you will wait for me)

She touched the words with her finger, connecting to the person who'd written them.

Farah stood beside her. "Where could she be now?"

"I hope she's visiting her son or daughter somewhere in the world like I was."

"Or time had stopped for her here in this corner," Neda sighed.

■ ■ ■

She asked around to find out the whereabouts of the interrogator who had liked her singing. Finally, a middle-aged guard in the laundry room told her she knew who she was talking about.

"Dr. Matlab is a member of parliament now."

"Yes, that's it—Matlab." She snapped her fingers. "Sorry, I got too excited."

"I think she was a martyr's relative," she said.

"She was?" She remembered the picture Matlab had hidden in the Quran when she said Hessam had killed him.

"Everyone claimed they were," The guard said mockingly. "She got a grant and studied philosophy. Good for her. Look at me. Still here."

Neda nudged Zulaikha. "Ask her address," she muttered.

After they were back in their cell, Neda insisted that such an influential person might be helpful.

The guard allowed her to write a letter. Farah and Neda crafted the content, summarizing how they'd met—anything that could remind Matlab who the sender was, the asthma attack, the hospital, and the Arabic song.

"It would work better if you said you learned the Quran from her," Neda said, "And you never ever sang a song again."

Farah chuckled.

Shortly after, the guard who brought them their mail and messages called Zulaikha to a corner. "Keep this to yourself. I heard you'll be out of here soon."

"Really? How soon?"

The woman looked around to make sure no one was listening.

"I don't know when exactly. I think maybe as soon as tomorrow."

"Did you hear someone saying that?"

"It doesn't matter how I know. Don't forget my tip."

Zulaikha tried to remember how much cash she had in her wallet. Sohrab had given her three hundred Euros, and luckily she had put it in her suitcase, which was still at the airport. She still had enough money in tomans for the taxi fare and grocery shopping. "Thanks a lot, Sister." Zulaikha put her hand on her chest to show her gratitude. "I'll pray for you."

"Don't thank me yet. I'll bring you and your friends some good food tonight. Thank me tomorrow with a good tip."

They might have opened her purse and wallet by now. She would have to deal with it later.

Neda was sure that Dr. Matlab had a role in her release. "I told you—in this country, we all need to know someone in the system." She lay on her stomach on the carpet to browse a magazine the guard had brought them.

Farah lay beside her playfully to take a peek at the magazine. "What if they want something in return?"

"Then we have no choice but to sell our souls to the devil. Do we?"

"I just did," Zulaikha said. "I told that woman guard I would pray for her for giving me the news."

They laughed and enjoyed their greasy eggplant stew and sticky rice dinner.

The next day when Zulaikha returned from the bathroom, Neda was gone.

"Where did she go?"

"You inspired her, Zuli *joon*." Farah picked up her towel.

"What do you mean?"

"I guess she learned how to trade," she said. "She told me she knew things about important people."

"You don't say." *I am learning from these young women.*

The guard came in the afternoon with a grin, Zulaikha's release paper and seven new inmates behind her. "Don't forget my *shirini*." She winked as she led Zulaikha toward the office.

Zulaikha turned to glance at the women.

"Well, hello," one of them said to Farah. "Looks like we got here to keep you company—fresh out of a closed publishing house. Let's pick our beds. Shall we?"

The guard's grin disappeared as though she transformed into a werewolf. "Shut the hell up, or next is solitary," she shouted.

Zulaikha looked away from her—she waved goodbye to Farah.

"Hey. You. Are you coming with me?" the werewolf guard yelled. Zulaikha sped up until she was walking alongside her.

"Don't look at me like that. She was asking for it."

The release counter had a secured window with a male soldier behind it. The female guard stood beside Zulaikha as she passed him her release paper and got her purse back.

"You can use this paper at the airport for your luggage," he said. "Your passport wasn't released." He stamped the paper.

Zulaikha opened her wallet and gave the female guard ten thousand tomans. "Sorry. I need some money for the taxi."

It had been eleven days since her arrest.

■■■

Zulaikha's taxi turned left toward the old Pepsi-Cola factory on Jayhoon Street, where she had lived for ten years. Three street cats scattered as she went up the stairs to the doorway. She recognized Tony, the black and white fluffy one. He was much bigger now. He had forgotten about her or was just giving her attitude—it had been too long since he had last seen her.

She had a few pieces of mail, mainly bills and an early New Year's card from her nephew, Mousa. The card was a picture of the *haft-sin* with a kind note wishing her a happy Nowruz. Since the year they reunited in Abadan, Mousa had never forgotten to send his aunt New Year's cards.

She opened her window and let the fresh air disperse the stuffiness. Snow, like shreds of cotton, began falling. The sky appeared white, but she could still see stars between the clouds and snow. The windows could not stay open for too long. Soon, she would need to turn up the heat.

She had four messages on her phone. The first one was from Reza Alipour, saying he was in Istanbul but was checking to see if she was back and would call again. The second said her baggage was still in the airport, waiting for her to pick it up.

The third one was from her friend Nasim. "I thought you'd be back by now. I guess I mixed up the dates. Call me."

Zulaikha missed Nasim the most when she was in Holland. Nasim was a few years younger than her, but they had some interests in common, like favourite books and movies. She was a widow, and both her daughters had moved to Canada. She had used her inherited money and leased her small shop on Jeyhoon Street. Part of the shop sold contemporary romance novels and poetry, and the rest of the store was filled with stationery, Persian DVDs, and government-approved CDs. They met a year ago after Nasim noticed Zulaikha's frequent visits to the store searching for romance novels and asking for "something engaging and easy to read."

Nasim recommended Zoya Pirzad novels—like Zulaikha, Pirzad was from Abadan. Reading her stories was like traveling back home. After Zulaikha paid for the books, Nasim invited her out for tea. They began to meet regularly. On late afternoons, Zulaikha walked to the bookstore, browsed the books, read several poems, and waited for Nasim to close. Then they would walk or visit a new coffee or teashop.

The last message on Zulaikha's machine was from Dr. Matlab's office.

"This is Dr. Matlab's assistant. Call us back to arrange a meeting at your earliest convenience."

She took a long shower and made herself a cup of tea. She had longed for these moments alone. Reza Alipour had given her a second-hand computer last year. He had taught her about using Skype to communicate with people overseas. She clicked on Sohrab's name.

Sohrab answered the Skype ring immediately. "Hello, troublemaker."

Sheila was staying with him. She had her hat and coat on. "So sorry for what they put you through," she said. "Did you lose weight, or is it the camera?"

Her pants had been looser since she arrived in Tehran.

"It's been stressful—were you two going out?"

"Just for a walk, *Maman*—not to worry," he said. "Did they ask you to sign anything?"

"Yes, and they kept my passport."

"What are you going to do now?"

"I have to see someone I know about that."

"Who?"

"A woman I know from those years—" Zulaikha trusted Sohrab would recall her first time in Evin. "She's now a member of parliament."

"Oooh—" Sohrab glanced at Sheila. "My mother's made important connections. By the way, we Google searched your friend—Kia—we found him on the internet."

"You did?"

"Let's leave that for some other time, *Maman*," Sohrab said. "I'll have Reza check up on you when he's back. He'll help you with anything you want. Please don't be shy to ask him."

"Look. I got a Nowruz card from Mousa." She displayed the card in front of the screen.

"That's so thoughtful, *Maman*. We've got to go, but we'll talk soon. Okay?"

They sent her a kiss and logged off.

Sohrab did not ask her about her experiences in the prison this time—only if she signed something.

Maybe he didn't want to say anything in front of Sheila. Who wants to be with a man with baggage like that? Young women are smarter these days.

She walked to a corner store for groceries before closing time. The shopkeeper recognized her. "Welcome back, Ma'am. How is your son?"

Zulaikha told the shopkeeper about her wonderful time with Sohrab and let him assume she had come back from the airport, not detention.

On her way back, the pavement was gleaming with a white layer of snow. At home, she made some eggs and potatoes and ate them with a better appetite, then turned on her television and switched it between Turkish and Dubai TV channels. The reception was weak. Perhaps a storm had shook up the satellite on her small balcony. She tried to adjust it, but it was no use. Maybe the neighbour's son could fix it tomorrow.

The next morning, she called Dr. Matlab's office. Her assistant told her that the earliest time would be within two weeks, in the middle of February.

"That works for me," she said.

"Be here on time. Dr. Matlab is very busy."

"I understand—"

The phone clicked, but it rang as soon as she put it down. Reza greeted her warmly. "I just got back from Istanbul. Sohrab told me what happened."

"You're my guardian angel. After you rest, let's pick up my suitcase from the airport—or you won't get your *soghati*." Sohrab's gifts, a chocolate box and a winter hat, were in the suitcase.

"How about tomorrow afternoon? I'll bring some pictures from Sohrab—he just emailed me."

Later the next morning, she visited Nasim at the bookstore. It was around Persian new year and the store was at its busiest.

"Did you get my message?" Nasim hugged her. "I totally mixed up the dates—"

"No, you didn't."

"What?"

"It's a long story. You look too busy. I'll call you later so we can go for coffee."

She left the crowded bookstore and Nasim's puzzled expression.

Reza had parked his car in front of her building and was standing beside it. "How long have you been waiting? I thought you—"

"Not to worry. I was in the neighbourhood. I was about to call you. Don't we need to show them your passport to get your suitcase?"

"I have a memo from Evin about my baggage."

Reza rolled his eyes. "Let's try their letter then."

In the car, they looked at Sohrab's pictures together. In one photo, Sohrab looked adorable with his helmet on, standing beside his truck. In another one, he and Sheila stood beside their bikes. The last photo was taken in an internet café with Sohrab staring at a monitor.

She put the envelope in her purse but peeked at the pictures again on the way to the airport.

"He's looking for something in this one." Sohrab's deep stare at the monitor disrupted the peace she had managed to find.

"He didn't want to share that one—Sheila took that as a joke," he said. "Since I've known him, he had told me his uncle is alive—now his girlfriend finds this amusing, so—"

"Sheila told me they found Kia's whereabouts—you know—the man I ran into in Amsterdam." She looked out the window. "Hessam's old friend."

"I know. Sohrab told me about that," Reza glanced at Zulaikha. "With the internet and all the new platforms, finding people is not that hard anymore."

They merged into the exit for international flights.

"Don't worry too much," Reza said. "Actually, because of Sohrab, I've read a few books about the families of missing people. Once that man—I mean Mr. Kia, once he tells Sohrab he has no idea where Sohrab's uncle—I mean your brother is, Sohrab will give up. But he needs closure."

Hessam's disappearance was the unsolved puzzle she had learned to archive. Now, after so many years, Kia's connection was added to the riddle.

■ ■ ■

In mid-February, the spring breeze returned to ever-sunny Tehran, and corner stores sold hyacinth flowers with their mesmerizing smell.

Dr. Matlab's office was near the historical parliament building in the centre of old Tehran, which had been drastically altered in the past ten years. The traffic was restricted near the parliament, so she got off the bus and walked a few blocks. On her way to Dr. Matlab's office, she went to the famous Lurd Café and bought a box of fresh *shirini*. Abdul had taken her there a few times. He knew the Armenian owners. Today, she recognized the man who sorted the pastries into a box for her. She waited for him to show a sign that he knew her, too, but no such luck. She paid without saying anything.

When Abdul used to drive around town in his orange taxi, he would tell her, "This street was once Tehran's *Campos Eliseos*." He said the same thing about another street until Zulaikha's chuckle stopped him. Now that she had been in Holland, she found a resemblance in the landscaping and cobblestone streets between here and in Europe.

Outside of Lurd Café, a young Afghan girl, hardly in her teens, begged her to buy the bouquet of *narges* she was selling.

Dr. Matlab will think that the flowers are for her. Shirini is more than enough.

Zulaikha couldn't resist the girl's pleading eyes. Tehran could still be unkind to outsiders. She bought a bouquet.

The receptionist directed her to the sixth floor. As she waited for the elevator, some memories of her encounters with Dr. Matlab returned to her. From the times she sat in the corner of the ventless interrogation room, in a black chador, so quiet like she was a thing, not a person.

She sat there in that corner, watching my humiliation. Her voice was confusing, never harsh, but hurtful. "You sing a song in Arabic better than you recite the Quran. Try to be better at the latter."

The elevator rang.

She faltered as she followed the signs to Dr. Matlab's office. She was letting that strange woman back into her world voluntarily.

Dr. Matlab greeted Zulaikha with the same infuriating smile. "Why so much trouble?" She glanced at the box of *shirini* and flowers. Her assistant took them off Zulaikha's hands.

"No trouble at all," Zulaikha said. "I heard you're now in the Parliament—my congratulations."

Dr. Matlab had a stately oak desk and a wide bookshelf with tidily organized books. Two large pictures of the country's leaders were behind her on the wall and a wall-to-wall Persian carpet draped the floor. The room smelled of rose water, which reminded Zulaikha of the cemetery. She had to visit her mother's tomb soon. Madineh would have shouted at her for arranging this visit. *"What the hell do you think you're doing, giving presents to a malicious woman? Don't forget that it is in the scorpion's nature to sting."*

"You haven't changed much," Dr. Matlab said.

The Armenian baker did not even recognize me.

"Neither have you," she said.

"I still remember the song you sang in your cell."

"Really?" Her heart pounded faster.

"Yes. In fact, I have watched Warda's performance on YouTube."

She watches music videos on YouTube! Times are really changing.

"It's a beautiful song indeed. I hope you still keep reading the Quran, too," she said.

"Did you receive my letter? I wrote to you from Evin."

"I don't remember—I receive thousands of letters from all over the country." She signed a paper as she glanced at her monitor. "How have you been? Did you get married again?"

"No, I haven't—raising my son didn't give me—" She breathed heavily suddenly. "He lives in Holland."

"Oh, what does he do there?"

"He's in the shipping industry—he drives a big truck."

"Well, he could have driven a truck here, couldn't he?" She glanced at Zulaikha, expecting a positive response.

Zulaikha crossed her ankles. "The most important thing is his health and happiness." She prepared for a preaching response.

Dr. Matlab put down her pen. "Yes, I know. I have a daughter, and she wants to be an actress." She glanced at the right corner of her desk and picked up a picture frame. "Children do strange things."

Suddenly Dr. Matlab looked vulnerable.

"But health should not be just in the body. The mind and soul need to be healthy, too." She turned the framed photograph, a girl with *hijab* but a lot of eye makeup, toward Zulaikha. "My daughter will be married soon. What about your son? Aren't you looking for a wife for him?"

"Oh, no," she replied. "My son wants to choose himself, and I think he already has a candidate."

"You used to have his picture with you all the time. You even asked for it in the hospital. Remember?"

"I still do." She was giving more power to this psychopath every moment.

"Let me see." Dr. Matlab strolled toward the bookshelf behind Zulaikha's chair.

Zulaikha turned her head to follow her as Dr. Matlab picked up a notebook from the shelf. Zulaikha reached for her purse from the table beside her. The bag dropped from her trembling hand, and the envelope of photos slipped out of the bag. One photo peeked out. Zulaikha bent apologetically to put the picture back in the envelope. Dr. Matlab was faster. She picked it up. It was Sohrab and Sheila's picture.

Dr. Matlab returned the envelope to her but kept that picture. "Oh, he has grown. Is this the marriage candidate?"

Zulaikha looked up and nodded.

"Ah. Have you met her?"

"Yes, I met her briefly in the Netherlands on my last day."

"How did they meet?" she prodded.

She is interrogating me again.

Drops of sweat broke out on her forehead. "Why do you ask?" she muttered.

The receptionist in a black chador came in holding a silver tray with two cups of tea and a bowl of sugar cubes.

Dr. Matlab showed Sohrab's picture to the young woman. "I think Mahmood, my nephew, would have been a couple of years older than her son. Don't you think?"

The woman took the picture and peered closely at it. "Yes, God bless Mahmood's soul."

Mahmood must be the blue-eyed boy then.

Zulaikha gazed at the assistant's long brown pants and a pair of expensive-looking leather shoes. How she carried the tray of hot teas while keeping her chador on looked impressive. The assistant put Sohrab's picture on the side of the desk and left the room.

Dr. Matlab sat down and folded her arms in front of her. "So, how may I help you today?"

Zulaikha's throat was dry. She had to remember how to word her reasons for being there. She'd practiced it the night before. She explained what happened after her return from Amsterdam. "They asked about what happened in Amsterdam and then my brother. You know it's been a long time since the war and his disappearance. They're keeping my passport—"

"So, you think it's my job to sit here in this office and make recommendations about my past acquaintances when they're in trouble?"

Maybe it was premature to ask about the passport. "I didn't mean to imply that at all. Forgive me if I offended you."

Her desperation brought back a smile to Dr. Matlab's face. "I'll look into your case and see if they can make any changes in your status. Someone will call you."

There wasn't any reason to stay there any longer.

"Thank you for your time. I'll wait for the call."

There was an "Out of Order" sign on the elevator. As she descended the stairs, she remembered the picture of Sohrab and Sheila. She rapidly went back up the stairs, anxiety flooding her body. When she re-entered the office, the young woman who'd brought the tea handed her the picture with a smile. "I knew you would come back for it."

Dr. Matlab came out of her office to give a folder to the young woman. "Oh, you're back. I just got off the phone. Do you have any contact with your relative, Kia? You didn't tell me he's an important oil engineering consultant."

"He's not my relative."

"Right. Your brother's friend."

"I separated from him at the airport. I have no contact with him."

"Well then. We'll be in touch," Dr. Matlab turned toward her office. "Something came up, Sister Sussan. I must leave for an important meeting."

Powerful people could make things worse or better. Leaving the office, Zulaikha no longer felt so clever.

∎∎∎

On the twentieth of March, the eve of Nowruz in Iran, Sohrab called to congratulate his mother on the Persian New Year and tell her that Kia had responded to his message.

"Your message?"

"Yes, we found his contact information on the internet, but he didn't respond until a few days ago. I was right, *Maman*. I mean about Uncle Hessam."

"Does Kia know where he lives?"

"I'd rather not talk about it here. You're in a sensitive situation after Evin." Their phone could be tapped, especially after she met with Dr. Matlab.

"Just say yes or no, damn it," she yelled.

"Probably," he said with his head down.

She sucked in her breath and put her hand to her mouth with a shudder. "Oh, my God." Tears filled her eyes.

"I'm having some second thoughts, *Maman*—believe it or not."

"Why?"

"Suddenly, when I found out he was—you know—"

Zulaikha stared at the screen, allowing Sohrab to find the words he seemed troubled to use.

"I now realize why you wanted me to stop."

An alive Hessam meant he abandoned them. He had cut them out of his life just like she feared he would whenever they had a sister-brother fight. Occasionally he threatened her that he would leave them like Gholam. But that was unbelievable. They had been through so much together.

"I think you want to know his side," she said.

"I know. He doesn't know about me yet."

"I'm confused—you just said—"

"I'll talk to Reza," Sohrab said. "He'll come to tell you everything in person. How does that sound?"

It was as if their conversation had to be coded.

"That's good. Please do it quickly before Reza goes to Turkey again."

Sohrab nodded. "Be patient for now. I should be as well. I also told my father."

Sohrab's hard work had paid off—he should enjoy it. But strangely, Sohrab seemed disappointed. She refrained from asking more.

She called Reza a few minutes later, but he didn't pick up. "Reza *jan*, call me as soon as you get this message. It's important."

It was new year's day. Everyone was visiting their families. Waiting for Reza could take all day. She needed to keep busy to let time go. *Haft-sin* decorations would help—she had almost done it last night—flowers and greens were already on the table. She placed a mirror and two candles beside them.

It was a tradition to wear something new. She showered and changed into a new purple dress she had bought in Holland. It was a little cold, so she wrapped a new shawl around her shoulder and brushed her hair in front of the mirror.

What does Hessam look like now? Does he have a family?

The phone's ring startled her.

"Nowruz mobarak, Zuli *jan*. Did I catch you at a bad time? This is Assef, by the way."

"I know—no, it's good that you called." She sat on a chair and ignored her numbed hands and feet.

"I'll redial by Skype so that I can see you. It's easier to talk that way."

"I need a minute," she said.

She glanced at the mirror. Good timing, but she was thirsty. She poured herself a glass of water and waited for Assef to call her.

The Skype ringtone was new to her.

He was on the screen, an older, grey-haired Assef with a light green shirt and a pair of jeans. He, too, seemed to have prepared himself to face her on camera. He was standing in an open kitchen. The window behind him showed the Dubai landscape with palm trees and high rises.

"Zuli, oh my Zuli—there you are—as beautiful as always."

Zulaikha raised her eyebrows. "You don't look so bad yourself. Did Sohrab tell you to call me?"

"He did—he couldn't get a hold of his friend," Assef said. "He says we should meet soon."

"I don't have a passport anymore."

"I'll figure something out. Give me some time. He said we should be careful with this—"

The connection became weaker and Assef's image froze. A few seconds passed and he appeared again. "He had met with that man, Kia, in Amsterdam airport. Apparently, he travels a lot," Assef said. "Sohrab said he was going to Baghdad and then Iran. He wanted to visit his mother in Ahvaz."

"I don't care what Kia is up to. What about Hessam?"

"Be patient, my lady. Kia hasn't told Hessam anything yet."

"Why?"

"I know—just bear with me—"

"You're killing me."

"Hessam's daughter—"

"Daughter?"

"Yes, he has a daughter—her name is Natasha. She tells Kia about—"

"It's a nice name," she said, eager to learn more about her.

"Yes, she seems to be so. Listen. So, I was saying—Hessam has some health issues—I think it's his heart. Kia wants to approach him about Sohrab gently. He has said that Hessam's wife has been upset—she doesn't believe that Kia met you in the airport by accident."

"What is that supposed to mean?"

"It means because Hessam was going to have heart surgery, Kia may have wanted to reunite his family before it was too late—stories you women are good at making." He drank a glass of water and put it down firmly. "There, I said it all in a nutshell—and all in Farsi. Sohrab is a good teacher." He grinned.

Zulaikha's focus drifted from the monitor. She was trying to digest what she had just heard. "Is Hessam that ill? I don't believe it."

"It's not like you saw him last year, and he was okay. Think about it."

Zulaikha tried to grasp Hessam's wife's resistance. She had never seen her brother with a girl when they were young, so she hadn't the slightest idea what type of woman would attract Hessam. "Do you ever remember Hessam with a woman?" she asked Assef.

"He wasn't close to me, but let me think." He looked up. "Yes, I think I did. Why?"

"He was too private. I never knew what type of woman he liked."

"I think he had casual flings. Once, I saw him with a girl downtown—he told me they worked together—I think she was buying him a pair of Ray-Bans."

"Ray-Bans—so typical of an Abadani man." Hessam was obsessed with those sunglasses.

A bad connection scrambled Assef's image on the screen. She tried to call him back, but it was no use. She lay on the couch for a few minutes. A stray cat's meowing distracted her. She looked down her window and saw Tony, her favourite black and white stray. She took some food for the cat and his kittens downstairs. A few more joined.

She had just heard her brother was alive but ill with a heart condition. And his wife didn't want to welcome them to their family. Should she be celebrating? What should she feel? Her mind was with Sohrab more than anyone. How hurt he looked.

She had not thought about Hessam in the past five or six years. She couldn't remember the last time she had dreamed about him—it might have been over two years—but she remembered how he appeared in that dream. He stood beside their door at the end of the dark alley in *Istgah Haft*. He was calling her name. She would dream about him again, with no face, and ill. Watching cats playing, pausing to look at her, always helped her fall asleep, hoping she would only dream about them, not the dark alleys of her past.

When she woke up the following day, she checked the clock

on the night table. Sohrab would be at work, but Reza or Assef would call her soon. She made breakfast and started a new crossword puzzle. Time was passing sluggishly, and words were slipping her mind. It was still the new year's holidays, but Nasim would keep the store open for reduced hours. People were still last-minute shopping for gifts and cards. She walked to the bookstore.

"What's wrong?" Nasim asked.

"Do I look that bad?"

"You look stressed—what's the matter?"

"I haven't heard from Sohrab. That's all."

"I've got something to cheer you up. Just wait two minutes."

Khomeini pronounced music *haram*, like opium in the eighties. His attempted murder of the music never worked. The laws had loosened up—they now allowed artists to perform publicly, provided they adhered to certain conditions. While women were forbidden to sing or dance, many male and female musicians continued creating.

Nasim invited her to a concert by Shajarian's son. The father was a legendary singer of traditional Persian music. His son had followed in his father's footsteps. Although Zulaikha wasn't in the mood for a crowded concert, Nasim was persistent.

"I don't have enough cash on me," Zulaikha said. "I'll go get some and will be back."

"No rush—"

"No, I'd better go. I want to see if there's a message."

Nasim said she would take her to a new coffee shop after she closed the store.

At home, she washed the few dishes left in the sink and put a load of laundry in the machine. She was just about to leave to pay Nasim and get her ticket when someone rang her buzzer.

She pressed the intercom button. "Hello?"

Dr. Matlab's voice answered her. She was at the door.

An intense fear turned her stomach. Was Dr. Matlab there to take away what was left of her freedom? She covered her hair with her scarf and opened the door. "Wow, how great of you to visit me," Zulaikha said.

Dr. Matlab brushed through her door, causing Zulaikha to step aside and let the woman in.

"Nowruz Mobarak—I brought you *eidi*," she said. "I thought you might like them." She handed her two books about women in Islam, a Fatima Al Zahra biography and an Islamic Solidarity text. "I've been visiting some of my female voters for the new year—well, you're not in my district, but I'll put my cards on the table here—I need votes—you and your friends want to vote for women, don't you?"

Zulaikha couldn't tell her she had never voted for anyone. "Why so much trouble?" Her samovar was cold. She turned it back on to make some tea. Somewhere she had heard that a samovar boils water faster.

"No trouble at all—you brought me flowers," Dr. Matlab said. "I'll call you within three weeks or so. Can you finish reading those by then so we can discuss them?"

Zulaikha brought her tea and cookies. "Are you lending them to me? I thought they're—"

"No, I was joking."

What a relief. She hoped her terror did not show on her face.

Dr. Matlab had taken a seat in her dining room. Her eyes were examining all the walls and shelves in her apartment. "I didn't know you had a computer."

Zulaikha leaned on the kitchen counter. "A friend showed me how to use Skype to talk to my son. I use it for that—nothing else." She had just admitted to using Skype and she wasn't even standing appropriately. She fixed her posture. "I think it's permitted to use Skype. Isn't it?"

Dr. Matlab ignored her question. "Any news from your son—or your oil engineer acquaintance?" She looked comfortable sitting on the dining room chair, flashing her strange and annoying smile.

"No, my son is busy, and I told you I'm not in contact with that man." Zulaikha's hands trembled. "How about my passport? Have you had a chance—"

"It's the holidays—so no." She put her cup of tea down and walked toward the door.

Zulaikha saw her downstairs. A car with tinted windows was waiting for her. She had come with her driver on the new year holiday like this was one of her assignments.

She's going from house to house. Perhaps she tells her driver she is guiding women in the right direction. Now next house. It was hard to believe that a member of parliament had nothing better to do.

Zulaikha called Nasim to apologize for being late. "On my way—I'll explain." But she could not tell Nasim all the details in the store. Once Nasim closed up, they walked a few blocks and picked a coffee shop in a new mall.

"That woman I told you about, Dr. Matlab, visited unexpectedly," she said. "She gave me two books as *eidi* and talked a lot of nonsense, like that she's visiting voters. She's keeping an eye on me, Nasim."

"How awful." She frowned. "Ignore her—she'll leave you alone eventually."

Coffee time with Nasim was pleasant, but she usually wanted to avoid unpleasant news, and Zulaikha tried hard to avoid a "What's the matter this time?" question from her.

"You should buy a mobile phone," Nasim said. "It'll help your connections, like when you want to check your messages."

They went to a shop nearby. The shopkeeper showed her a few options, but Zulaikha couldn't decide. She would deal with it later. She was exhausted.

At night Zulaikha opened one of the books left on the kitchen counter. Two wordy paragraphs later, she picked a romance novel for bedtime reading.

After she returned from grocery shopping the next day, another surprise was waiting for her. This time two young Basiji guards were at her door, showing her a search warrant for her apartment. Though they wore Basiji uniforms, she couldn't tell if they were conscripts until she spoke with them. She asked them because conscripts were less frightening than the volunteer Basij force.

"Yes, ma'am, we are conscripts." One was tall and young—the shorter one ordered him around. The tall one unplugged her computer.

"But I use that to communicate with my son. Why do you have to take it?"

The shorter soldier pointed at her TV. "How about her satellite?"

"Never mind the satellite," the tall one said. "They didn't tell us anything about that."

"What could I possibly have in the computer?"

"We don't know, Ma'am," the bossy one said. "We just have to do our jobs."

The younger soldier grinned as he carried the desktop. "We may even clean it for you," he said. "Try to hide your satellite better, though. Cover it with a blanket or something, at least for the next few weeks."

"Right. They may not send such nice soldiers as us next time."

Outside, the younger soldier put the computer in their trunk. "One more thing—be careful using your landline," he said.

"Do you think they—"

"Just be careful, Ma'am." He started the car. "Take care."

Her neighbour's son put down a big garbage bin. "Is everything okay over there?" he asked from across the street.

"I think I'm in trouble." She walked toward him. "Can you do something about the satellite? They just warned me about it."

The neighbour commiserated with her, which was a relief.

He uninstalled the satellite and took it to his own house, but gave her a temporary connection so she would still be able to receive her Turkish and Emirates channels.

She called Reza the next day again but couldn't reach him, so she called his mother and told her about the computer.

"Reza left for Istanbul yesterday," Mrs. Alipour said. "Why don't you come here? Use our computer to talk to Sohrab if you need to, darling."

She asked Mrs. Alipour to leave a message for Sohrab. "Please tell him my computer needed repair. I'll buy a mobile phone and will give you the number as soon as I have it."

She put down the phone and looked around. Her desk without the desktop meant she could not access Skype or Sohrab. Her mobile phone looked like a device from a different planet. In her isolated world, watching satellite TV—showing pop stars lip syncing and dancing—was like holding on to something. Something useless but enlightening.

■■■

The soldiers returned the computer to Zulaikha after two weeks. They hooked it up for her and left. An hour later, Dr. Matlab called. "Can you meet me today? I have a meeting in the mosque beside Mellat Park. Be there in two hours."

"What's this meeting for?"

"Never mind that—be there—you owe me, Zulaikha. Always remember that."

"What do I owe you, Dr. Matlab?"

"You need your passport. Don't you?" She hung up.

The park was on the city's north side and more than one hour from Zulaikha's place by taxi. She sat on a bench beside willow trees and listened to the sound of the fountain nearby as she waited. A few minutes later, she suspected she might have the wrong address, so she walked around to assess her whereabouts. She had been here with Sohrab and Reza a few times—this bench must be the exact meeting place. She could go to a shop, ask permission to use their phone and call her office. Instead, she returned to the same spot. Ten minutes later, she gave up and walked toward the crosswalk to catch a bus or taxi across the street when five green guard patrol cars passed the red light with their sirens. She gripped her scarf tie to prevent it from sliding off in the wind, wondering if this fuss had something to do with Dr. Matlab. She was suddenly in front of the modern Safavieh bazaar. She bought a water bottle and glanced at a glamorous and too-expensive jewellery store before catching the next bus.

At home, there was no message on her answering machine. She turned the television on. The news was about next year's upcoming presidential election with Ahmadinejad running again for the role. She changed the channel and watched a new Turkish TV series about a girl who had lost her memories and couldn't even recognize her husband. Thanks to the neighbouring country, Turkey, for making so many entertaining TV series, Zulaikha and her friend Nasim now could comprehend basic Turkish dialogue. After the show, she made herself a cup of tea, picked up a magazine, and turned to the crossword puzzle. All of the questions seemed too hard. She lay down on her couch and stared at the ceiling, crossing her arms and holding the magazine to her chest.

The landline in the hall rang. She couldn't catch it before it went to the answering machine. It was Nasim reminding her that the concert was tomorrow.

They dressed up for the concert the next day in colourful scarves, coats, and a little makeup. The singer started the lines of his lyrics from Rumi's popular poetry:

> *Listen to this reed how it complains,*
> *It tells a tale of separations*

The performance was melancholy and dramatic, making them cry during many songs.

"What's wrong with us?" Nasim said as they exited the concert hall. "We should find something more cheerful."

"We pay our performers to rub some salt into our old wounds—that's what's wrong with us," Zulaikha said. "I could use something cheerful."

They went to a crowded coffee shop. Tehran was a sleepless city with young people driving around, or in coffee shops and pizza places late at night. A sleepless city among these strangers was safer than her apartment, where an intruder might knock at any minute. Zulaikha was undecided about whether to open up and tell Nasim about her fears. She would say that if Zulaikha was being watched, her friends were, too. To share too much could cost her Nasim's company.

Once they had their coffees, Nasim leaned in close to her. "I have good news," she said.

"I'm longing for some good news."

"I got my visa." Nasim was leaving to visit her daughters in Canada within a few weeks.

This happy news meant more detachment. There goes fun coffee time. "Sounds wonderful."

"Why the teary eyes, Zuli *joon*?"

"Ignore them. See? I blink them away for you."

Nasim was an intelligent businesswoman. Zulaikha had never had a chance to learn how to invest her money. She had given up her hairdressing skills. She often wished she either owned a small bookstore or rented a chair in a hair salon, yet she had never taken any steps to turn that wish into reality..

"Don't worry. I'll be back soon, and this time we'll look for a couple of good men for you and me."

They chuckled.

At home, she tried some crossword puzzles before going to sleep. Except for the name of an actor in a recent movie, everything else seemed as unsolvable as the mysteries in her life.

■■■

In April, Zulaikha had called Sohrab a few times, but he had been distant. Once Sheila picked up the call. "Give him time, please. But wait—I don't know if I should tell you this," she said.

"What is it? Please tell me."

"I don't want to upset you, but a few days ago, he got a phone call, the number was from France—a woman with a French accent was trying to speak with him in poor English, so he gave the phone to me. It was Karmen—I mean—Uncle Hessam's wife."

"France? I thought they lived in Canada."

"She's visiting her family in France," Sheila said. "I speak French a little, but I could tell she wasn't that nice Zulaikha *jan*. She said this was the worst time for her family, and we should stay away until her husband is recovered—"

"Is it because Sohrab keeps calling them?"

"Not really. I think Kia had told her he met Sohrab here. She feels more like we are real."

"Don't feel bad that you told me. We should stay away from them. I'm used to it now—Sohrab should be, too."

■ ■ ■

On Friday morning, she heard her landline ringing from the hall. She let it go to the answering machine as she put the groceries in the fridge. Dr. Matlab's voice filled the room.

"Call back as soon as possible. I have important news that I want to share." No apology for not showing up in the park.

Zulaikha munched on a handful of almonds. *What would they do to me if I didn't call her back? Perhaps they would send another group of Basiji guards to arrest me for something idiotic this time. Or I'll never get my passport back.*

She called the number after half an hour.

"Are you at home?" Dr. Matlab asked.

"I'm calling you from home." She rolled her eyes.

"I'll be there in fifteen minutes."

Zulaikha made sure everything was in order. She hid her novels and ensured her television was set to Iranian channels. She put together a basket of fruit, tea, and pastries to keep up appearances.

This time Dr. Matlab was on time. She took off her chador like she was visiting her friend's house—though she still had her scarf and *manteau* on. She asked Zulaikha how things were. Something was different. Dr. Matlab's peculiar smile had disappeared.

A tense silence reigned in the apartment.

"I waited a long time in Mellat Park," Zulaikha said. "Was everything alright?"

Dr. Matlab frowned as though she had forgotten about the missed appointment. "Oh, there was a fire in my building—I left the fundraising event early. Didn't you hear?"

What game is she playing this time? Was she in one of those wailing

SUVs?

She put a small plate and a knife on the coffee table. "Please, help yourself." She pointed at the tray of fruits. "No, I didn't watch the news—what was the fundraising for?"

"To build a bike lane for women in the park," she said. "Now, some people want me dead."

Perhaps she wants to build a massive wall for women, but they won't give her money.

Nasim had told Zulaikha about tensions in the regime between hardcore Islamists and the reformists. Some joke if this manic was a reformist. "I thought you had a bodyguard."

Dr. Matlab glared at her. "That may have to change."

She poured a cup of tea. "If you're asking for a donation, I could help with a few tomans—"

"I need to hide for a few days."

"What do you mean?" Her hand holding the silver tray trembled. She had been too obedient with this woman—it wasn't working.

Dr. Matlab sipped the tea. It was too hot and gave her discomfort. "Wow. It's boiling."

Zulaikha had never felt joy from another person's suffering except for this moment. "Why?"

"Watch the news a bit more. I thought you would at least offer some support."

"What support can I possibly give you?" she asked scornfully this time.

Dr. Matlab glanced at her books in a case beside the dining table. "You owe me, Zulaikha." She picked up a book of Hafez poetry.

"Please sit down and tell me what I owe you. I want to know."

"Don't you remember? We could have killed all of you with the file you had. You, your son—"

Zulaikha's heart began to beat faster as she stepped forward. "My son? He was a child."

"Mahmood was not much older than your son when he died." She held the Hafez book up to her chest. "He didn't even get a chance to be a martyr."

Anger overcame her sympathy for the dead boy. Teenage boys went to the frontier, killed and sacrificed for the promise of a piece of heaven. "How am I to blame?" Zulaikha asked. "Now that we got to this point, why don't you tell me about my file?"

Dr. Matlab put down the book. "Your brother tricked everyone. They trusted his directions, but he left a soldier to die."

Hessam left someone to die. This was a new terror adding to those she had already endured. "How do you know all this?"

"My nephew, Mahmood, went to the front so proud, but your brother took it away from him. Mahmood killed himself soon after he returned to his family." Dr. Matlab's pitiful expression had replaced her self-righteous smile. She looked at her watch and walked toward the door.

Zulaikha froze without noticing Dr. Matlab was near the door wearing her chador. *She was full of revenge and hatred for my family and me the whole time.*

"Wait a moment. What about my passport? When can I get it back?"

Dr. Matlab put back on her shoes. "Oil engineers earn a lot of money. Don't they?"

"What's that got to do with me? Are you asking for money to return my passport? How much do you want?"

Dr. Matlab mumbled a Quran verse and looked up at the sky as if asking for forgiveness from the Creator. "I'll look into it and have someone contact you."

How come her nasty smile is back? A minute ago, she needed a hiding place.

"But they won't be as easygoing as I am." Then she used the exact phrase she said many years ago in Luna Park when she dropped her off. "*Eltemas e Dua* (I beg for your prayers!)"

Zulaikha watched her walk toward her car. No chauffeur waited for her this time. She drove herself away in a little Toyota.

■ ■ ■

Zulaikha went shopping with Nasim almost daily during their hot and dry May to shop for her daughters in Canada. They carefully selected every package Nasim's girls might need or had missed.

Nasim asked the shopkeeper to bring her a yellow purse sitting on display.

"That's the last one," the shopkeeper said. "Let me check if there's another one in the back."

Zulaikha picked up a man's bag. "I now have a family member in Canada, too."

"You don't look very happy about it."

She rolled her eyes. "I don't know how I feel or should feel."

Nasim came closer and touched her arm. "Give yourself time."

"Sorry, that's the last one," the shopkeeper returned.

They continued browsing the mall.

"Am I making you tired?" Nasim asked.

"This is fun, Nasim," she said. "Lately, I want to stay out as long as possible, and I used to be a homebody."

"Why don't you come give me a hand in the store?"

"That would be wonderful, Nasim." She hoped she would replace her friend temporarily while she was away.

Zulaikha began working in the store every afternoon then she went shopping with Nasim after they closed the bookstore. Nasim needed a lot of things for her trip.

Nasim didn't offer formal paperwork to assure Zulaikha she was on the payroll. Instead, she kept saying, "I owe you," or that she would bring her a great *kadu* from Canada.

Zulaikha's first week was productive. She communicated with customers, learned some merchandising, and received the shipments. Before the weekend, while helping to move some stationary boxes to storage, a young woman in a black chador entered the shop.

When Zulaikha returned from the back of the store to place a few notebooks on a case, the young woman was at the cashier paying for a poetry book by Hamid Mosadegh.

Zulaikha recognized her. She was the same young woman in

Dr. Matlab's office. It crossed her mind to hide in the storage, but it was too late. Their eyes met.

"How are you, Zulaikha *jan*?"

Behind the counter, Nasim glared at Zulaikha as she finished her transaction.

Zulaikha stepped closer to the woman. "All is well—I hope."

"All is well." She repeated mockingly. "Dr. Matlab was sick for a few weeks. She went to the North to her villa at the Caspian beaches with her family for vacation, but she is back now."

"That's good." She refrained from saying more.

"Why don't you come to the office one of these days? I think she brought you a souvenir from the North. What a coincidence. Have you been working here?"

"Oh, no. Just helping for a couple of days."

"That's nice. We'll be in touch."

Zulaikha nodded.

"Who was that?" Nasim asked.

"She works with Dr. Matlab."

"This is not her first time here," Nasim said. "She's been here a few times in the past three weeks, Zuli."

"I don't mean to cause you any trouble."

"I know." She placed two books from the counter on a shelf beside Zulaikha. "But you realize—I mean—they close bookstores all the time."

"I'll leave if you want me to." She stepped toward the back to pick up her purse.

"Don't be silly." Nasim passed her an envelope with money in it. "This is for you."

"What's this for?"

"Your wage—you've been a great help."

Zulaikha stared at the envelope. She needed it badly.

"Come on, don't look so sad. Let's have tea and talk about it."

Later on that evening, the two women tried to solve the mystery. They reviewed the conversations and their interactions.

"No question that they're terrorizing you, Zuli. They want you to know they're watching you."

"But why?"

"They want to know who you would contact or see your reaction to fear."

"You said it, Nasim."

"I think you should be careful about communicating with anyone around you and abroad."

"I can't get Matlab, the snake. One moment she threatens me. Then she says she needs a hiding place—someone is trying to kill her."

"It's a corrupt system, Zuli. She's probably been threatened by someone and needs money," Nasim said. "There are many groups and oppositions within the regime."

"Can her rival be worse than her?"

"Who knows? People are vying for power. Many are outing each other for past mistakes."

"I must admit that she had fooled me. I had sensed some emotions in her." Zulaikha's finger traced the rim of her glass. Her tea was cold. "I think you don't need me tomorrow, Friday. Right?"

"I'm going to be open till noon. What's on your mind?"

"I'm going to do something this time," she said. "And don't tell me to be careful. I'm tired of being careful."

Nasim leaned back and drank her tea, shaking her head in confusion.

Since the soldiers returned the desktop, Zulaikha feared the equipment as if they had inserted something deadly. She had not even touched it. But now, she didn't care. She was worried for Sohrab and could ask him how he was or how the weather was.

Sohrab was in his pyjamas when he answered the Skype call.

"Were you sleeping?"

"I wish," he said. "I can't sleep—too much in here, *Maman*." He tapped his scalp. His hair was messy and he hadn't shaved.

"How is Sheila? Is she with you?"

"She's mad at me—she just left—I'm a mess."

Now I'm going to mess things up even more, son.

"I need you to give me Kia's number." He was in Baghdad a few weeks ago. He could be in Ahvaz by now.

"Sure, write it down, but if you want to know about him and Uncle Hessam, he wrote me everything."

"Everything?"

"About the past—never mind—I understand why you didn't tell me about him."

Kia couldn't have shared everything. Or maybe he has no shame. I wanted to ask him to help me get my passport from that woman. But what now? "I need you to read it to me."

"It's a long one, *Maman*. I've read it five times already."

"Email it to Mrs. Alipour. Now go shave and get some sleep. You need to keep that job—your girl, too." She hung up to let the coming cough clear her throat.

For the past fifteen years, Zulaikha had managed her asthma with healthy eating, daily walking, and physical housework. She had barely used her inhaler—her doctor had reduced her medication dosage and told her he didn't see anything wrong with her anymore. Somehow Kia's name or mentioning the past with him caused mild symptoms in her body. Most of it was her mind's defence mechanism.

I'll need this inhaler in Alipour's villa tomorrow. No, I won't read his email there. I'll print it and bring it here. I'll need to be alone for this.

Last week, Mrs. Alipour held her and told her she was worried for her. "I was there when it all happened, Zuli *jan*. Remember?" she said. "Honestly, I never thought your brother survived—well, what do I know? I know it's hurtful that he never—but—if I can do anything, let me know—stay here a few days, or we can go to the North together."

She put her inhaler on the night table and opened her bedroom window to watch the street cats while she read.

> **Dear Natasha and Sohrab,**
> I am in my hotel room in Baghdad. I have been thinking about both of you the whole day, and I think I should share what I know with you two.
>
> Hessam was my high school friend. How I knew Hessam and his family sounds simple now, but it was

complicated in those years. Hessam was a friend, but I was also interested in his sister, Zulaikha. Things got serious, and my father intervened because he wanted me to move to America and become an engineer. My father's approach was wrong, and Zulaikha's family took it as an insult.

I last saw Hessam in Abadan in 1977, two years before the revolution. This was the time I returned to visit my parents. My father did not want me to stay. He believed something was happening. A new movement! Not exactly the same as when Dr. Mosaddegh was a leader. He said communists, nationalists, and a new Islamic group were growing. He talked about assassinations and an underground movement in the forests of the North. He told me the country would not be the same. It wouldn't be safe until the political movements died down. A few years after I graduated from university, I don't know why, but I couldn't find a job as an engineer. Maybe I didn't try hard for it, but they wanted work experience in every interview, and I didn't have any. I worked in a gas station near my apartment in Tulsa, Oklahoma.

When I returned to visit my family in Abadan, my father insisted that he would do anything for me, but he did not want me to stay. I arranged to meet Hessam in Hotel Karevansara, his nightly routine in those days. He said he did not want anyone in his family to know about our meeting. I thought maybe it was because he understood me. We were both young men, and maybe, like any other person around me, he blamed his sister, too. Perhaps he thought it was the woman who deceived the man. Did we talk about it? Not much.

He said, "Let's forget the past. We were too young and shouldn't be held responsible for our parents' actions." I only wanted him to know that I did not have a role in my father's decisions.

We talked about our lives. Hessam spoke about *Hezb e Tudeh*, the People's Party, political prisoners, and possible strikes in the National Oil Company. He talked about Abbass, that he worked hard, played music, and wrote songs. He said Abbass had ambitions. He wanted to become a prominent musician and dreamed of someday playing in an orchestra in Egypt. Sometimes I felt Abbass—his art and intellect—influenced him. Hessam wanted to impress Abbass. I didn't take Hessam seriously when he spoke like a revolutionary. That was not the Hessam I knew. I talked about my American girlfriends—tall, blonde American girls who threw themselves at me and my empty life away from Abadan. He told me the country needed engineers like me, something my father used to say. With all my confusion, I applied for a job at the National Oil Company. They hired me quickly with a good salary at that time. The position was based on Kharg Island. I went back to the US, packed all my stuff and told my friends in Tulsa that I was an actual oil engineer now and would be returning to my home. Home felt glamorous in those years.

It was around the time when I had just moved to Kharg that I heard about an accident in Hessam's family. Hessam visited me in Kharg while Zulaikha was in Ahvaz visiting her husband's family. My resumed friendship with Hessam was still kept as a secret, a secret from my own family and a secret from Zulaikha. Hessam told me that Zulaikha was in love with her husband but that the man was not right for his sister. Sorry Sohrab, if you are reading this. I felt bad for her. Believe me. I wanted her to be happy. It was such a pity her marriage to the man she loved didn't last. Hessam was protective of you, Sohrab.

I remember I took him to the market and he bought you this big toy car, a red Mercedes. He said, "I won't let him feel any shortage in life without a father the way I did."

After hearing about Cinema Rex's mysterious fire, I decided to leave Iran forever. Hessam told me that he or Abbass could have been burned there. That catastrophe was very eye-opening for me. The atmosphere was getting intensely political. I'd made good connections with American Shell managers, who soon offered me a job. I remember the day I called my father and told him about it. It was like I was giving him and my mother the world. I could hear his voice calling my mother, "Come, come, listen to this."

I knew Abbass's address and wrote to both of them. They replied to my letters until the revolution happened. Then we wrote less and less. They were busy being involved with protests and their jobs.

On both occasions, I got sick when I received my father's letters about Abbass's death and, shortly after, Hessam's disappearance. I was ill and could not go to work for a few days. When I called home, my father was in tears. He said, "It's so bad. Just be happy you are not here."

I dreamed about Hessam a lot. I wore black and stopped shaving for a few weeks. My American friends understood that I was mourning. I wasn't socializing and couldn't handle any crowds, especially when I saw friends together laughing or playing sports on the playing fields. I became a young boy missing his friends again. *What happened there? What am I doing here?* I asked myself many times. And every time I called my father, it was to search for answers without asking anything. I needed my parents' kind voices in those days, and they genuinely showed me love and support. How did they know how I was feeling? I wonder sometimes.

I vomited when I got Hessam's letter from Egypt. I thought someone was making a bad joke when I saw his name on the envelope. In his letter, Hessam sounded very desperate. He was ill and out of money. We did not have the luxury of internet access in those days, and when I saw that he had left me a phone number in the letter, I realized one more time in my life how smart he was. I called him immediately and started my conversation by shouting at him, "Do you realize what you have put me through?" Then he told me why he had escaped, and I knew I should not have blamed him. I arranged to send him two thousand dollars right away. That money was not much for me, but he told me a million times that it saved his life. We were in touch by letters and phone, and I sent him small amounts until he told me to stop and that he had a steady job as a restaurant owner. He fell in love with a woman with an Algerian father and a French mother, and he wanted to marry her. I promised not to tell a soul about him and his new life. We both knew how dangerous it would be for his family if the regime found out that Zulaikha, his sister, or his mother knew about his escape. At first, it was for his family's safety, but then years went by, and he adapted to a new identity, and he talked less and less about reconnecting with anyone from his past. Then one day, he wrote to me that a relative of his wife in Quebec had invited them to go and work with them in his restaurant.

After I saw Zulaikha at the Amsterdam airport, and as soon as I returned to Vancouver, I called Hessam to tell him about my encounter with his sister. Natasha told me he was in the hospital preparing for a scheduled surgery. I flew there immediately, and when I saw him, I realized I should wait. I left it to his

family to find a suitable time.
   I would be happy to answer more questions if you have any.
   Yours Truly,
   Kia

Hessam was alive and didn't give a damn about her all those years, so be it. The best thing about it was that she could be mad at him. Zulaikha read the line about Assef a few times. Hessam had confided in Kia about Assef, the father of her child. After all that happened, he had allied with Kia. Hessam told her about Kia on their last visit, but she said nothing to him because Hessam was always right. He was a "supportive" brother in his own way. He took her to the notary for the divorce and bought her a purse afterwards. When she needed him, he sat with their mother and blamed Assef for Habib's accident.

She put her fingers on the keyboard to dial Assef. She missed his face. She wanted him to tell her jokes and ask her to snap out of this madness. She wouldn't call him in that state, though. Instead, she paced the room, sat again, and stared at the monitor. The top of the email showed Kia's email address. She typed a response:

   I read your email to Sohrab and Natasha. Sohrab said you would be in Ahvaz soon. Let me know when we can meet in Khuzestan.
   Zulaikha

A frequently used clue in her puzzles was: "in the law of the universe, nothing can travel as fast as—" Easy to answer: *nour*, the light.

Emails travel fast, too, and so can people's reactions. But Kia responded four hours later, during which she read ten pages of a book, returning to the first page ten times.

   I am glad you reached out. I won't be in Ahvaz until

the fall. I'll let you know as soon as I am there. I can't wait to meet with you.
Kia

The light from the monitor had been bright enough to make her forget that night had enveloped the streets. The edginess was leaving her body, giving space to fatigue. *Hessam is alive, but he's ill.* She put her head on the table and closed her eyes.

She dreamed about Madineh and Habib sitting on a picnic blanket beside the Karun River. Zulaikha had put her head on Assef's legs. He was touching her hair. Young Hessam was beside a palm tree in front of them, glaring at Assef. "Why don't you leave her alone?" Hessam yelled.

Before sunlight, she called the twenty-four hour taxi service. She had to go to Behesht e Zahra Cemetery. No one could be as comforting as Madineh.

"Sohrab found Hessam, Mother. He's alive." She sobbed as she scattered *narges* on her tomb.

"Didn't I tell you?" Madineh's voice echoed in her mind.

■■■

A week later, Nasim introduced Zulaikha to Mitra at the bookstore—a new girl Nasim had hired temporarily. Mitra was a friend of one of her daughters.

Nasim looked at Zulaikha and gestured toward the back room. Once out of Mitra's earshot, Nasim asked, "Do you like our new girl? She used to work in a clothing store before. What do you think?"

"You picked her. She must be good."

"I'm worried, though. Look at her outfit, her showy makeup—" Nasim mumbled.

"I guess you had to choose between troubles like mine or hers." Zulaikha turned to leave.

"They could close my store, Zuli *joon*."

"Right," she said. "What's new in the store? Give me a good

book."

She picked a new novel and her weekly magazine. Nasim didn't let her pay.

Later that night, she attempted to solve that week's crossword. She had trouble finding a word for "self-contradictory, like a tree in the desert." The word irony crossed her mind, but it was too short. Words were hiding from her that night.

■■■

They met at Nasim's the night before her departure. Nasim told her about the beautiful summer in Vancouver, Canada she had planned. Her daughters had taken time off work, and they would take her to a few islands in British Columbia. Nasim's flight was very early the following day. Zulaikha helped her with the last of her packing and tidying up her apartment.

"You'd better go to bed early. You'll have a long journey tomorrow."

"What will happen to you?" Nasim looked worried. "Be careful with that woman. I'll give you my key." She opened her purse.

Zulaikha put Nasim's suitcase near the entrance door.

"Oh no. You shouldn't."

"Yes. You never know. Plus, my plants will need you to water them."

She put the key in her wallet and picked up her scarf from the console's hangers.

"I hate that I make everyone worried."

"Take any CDs or books from the shop. Don't stay in the house for too long. Find a tour and travel—maybe to Syria or Greece. There are many cheap tours these days. Show the enemy there's nothing to worry about."

Zulaikha wrapped her scarf around her neck, looked in the mirror and applied lip gloss. "I have my crossword puzzles. Life is good."

Nasim stood in the entryway next to the console. "Wait. I want to show you something on my computer."

Zulaikha and Nasim looked at a profile with Nasim's picture on it. "This is my Facebook page."

"What?"

"Kids do this these days. I did it so I could be in touch when I'm away. I'll put my pictures here. Whose profile do you want to see? Sohrab, for example?"

And there he was. There were a couple of pictures with Sheila, too. She had no idea. "Can I see this one?" It was Natasha's profile.

"This is a private one. You can ask her—click here—then you'll be able to see it. Do you want me to?"

"No, not now." She tilted forward to see her picture better. "She doesn't look like us."

"She's stunning—look at those hazel eyes—perhaps like her mother's side?"

"Sohrab says she sings." She glanced at Nasim. "Like my mother."

"I'm making you a profile. It takes a minute, easier than your puzzles."

"Speaking of a crossword puzzle, there's one word I'm dying to find."

"What is it?"

"Self-contradictory, like a tree in the desert."

"Paradox?"

"You're the best." she hugged Nasim. "I'm going to miss you. Come back soon."

"Think about it. Standing in a desert doesn't mean you won't find a tree." Nasim's eyes were filled with joy as she spoke. "Something good will happen to you, Zulaikha. I am sure of that."

When she got home, her feline friends played outside her door like they were waiting for her. She sat and petted them.

■■■

Zulaikha recovered from a brutal cold in late spring. Sheila was in contact and had emailed her some pictures and told her Sohrab was fine. They heard Hessam and his wife would be in France for the summer.

The news was all about the upcoming election. Today, Zulaikha saw Dr. Matlab on TV—a woman reporter interviewed her about women in Islam. Zulaikha stared at her without noticing her lecture. "Creep," she muttered and switched the channel.

She was cutting vegetables when Assef called. She struggled to speak through her coughing.

"Hello? Are you okay?"

She nodded and asked about Sohrab.

"Sohrab is fine. It's just—"

"What? Tell me."

"I'm worried for him, Zuli."

"Why?"

"He says he might go to Canada after summer—"

"But I thought—"

"I know. I did, too, but it's in his mind. He wants to meet his cousin and then find a way to face Hessam."

Zulaikha was quiet.

"I want to go with him, but he refuses—he says I should be with you when he's in Canada—can you hear me?"

"Why doesn't he give up?"

"I've been thinking—about this whole thing—I'm sorry, but your family hurt you and me, and we moved on, but now Sohrab? No—"

It's like he reads my mind from a distance.

"I want to see you, too, but you have another family now, don't you?" She rolled her eyes.

"I want to change things between us."

"Maybe you should go and visit your son then. How many years has it been since you've seen him?"

"I will, but we need to visit first."

The connection became spotty.

She anxiously waited for him to redial her number, but nothing. She finished cutting the vegetables and had a glass of milk with her cough medication. She made up her mind. Where else than Abadan would be better to unravel a few riddles with Assef while Sohrab finally met his uncle? It was close to Ahvaz, and she could also plan to meet with Kia.

The phone rang again.

"You may be right," she said. "I'm losing my mind here. They took my passport, but I can still," she paused. "Why don't we both go to Khuzestan?"

"That's a good idea. I have to visit my sister anyway," he said. "How long will it take you to get there?"

"Let's sync our schedule with Sohrab's of visiting Hessam—let's wait until fall." *I should tell him about my plan to meet Kia.* "I have another plan in Abadan that should wait for the fall anyway."

"What plan?" Assef asked.

"I'll let you know soon. Stay tuned."

Nasim could be right. Going to Khuzestan and seeing Assef again was as unreal as finding a tree in a vast desert.

PART 4

Velgard the Dog

TO THE SUMMER OF 2009

Go on, go to her, why should I bother
You are the sun, she is the earth, I am the sky
Shine on her for I sit gently on the shoulder of stars.
Shine on her for my heart cries for her.
This is the perfect love, this forgiveness
Your heart is mine, your body is hers.

–Forough Farrokhzad

Zulaikha arrived at Abadan Airport in the late afternoon. Like a newcomer, she followed the airport workers toward the baggage claim. She asked the information desk to keep her suitcase for a few minutes.

She checked her purse to make sure she had put her inhaler somewhere accessible. It was in the tiny pocket. She looked outside on the boulevard. The wind and the humidity hit her face before her eyes met Kia. He was out beside the sliding door.

"You made it." He had a grey pullover and jeans—and, as Sohrab had described him—expensive sneakers. "So we are meeting again—at another airport. What's up with that?"

"I know. But I couldn't think of anywhere else. It's a shame, but I no longer remember many places in Abadan."

"No, no, it's all good," he said. "Where can we go to talk?" He looked around.

Zulaikha glanced back inside at a juice stand with two empty rows of chairs in front of it. They sat next to each other. "How's your mother?" She coughed.

"She's fine—well, for her age. Are you okay?"

"I'm fine. Ignore my coughing."

"She's stubborn. She doesn't want to live with me in Canada."

"Has she been out to—" She coughed again. "—to visit you there?"

"Are you sure you're alright? I know about your asthma, Zulaikha."

She used her inhaler. "My asthma is under control—it comes

back only when I'm stressed. But you keep talking, please—stress will go."

"Yes, my mother visits but mostly hates it. Too cold."

It was November, and Sohrab had told her Montreal was one of the coldest cities in Canada.

"I'll get you some water."

"No, no, I'm fine," she said. "You must forgive me for not treating this as a social call—more a mission I've had in mind for a while." She had practiced her lines.

"No worries. Same here."

Oh, same for him.

"When we ran into each other in Amsterdam, I got into trouble only because I was seen with you. I must give you a backstory." She debriefed him about her first arrest after Hessam disappeared and how she met Dr. Matlab. "I was foolish to think she would help me this time, but she began harassing me, asking about you. They took my passport as—"

"Collateral?"

"I don't know—to control me—" She craved carrot juice as she heard the blender from the juice stand.

"You think I can help?"

"Yes, I do. You can at least see what Matlab wants so I can get my passport back. I can't tell what's on her wicked mind—she talked about fundraising for a bike path."

"She could be short on money or is thinking about a business overseas. I have triple citizenship and have built relationships with suppliers in Asia and Europe—I can bid on oil equipment tenders, buy and sell to them, things like that could be interesting to her."

"But she's a philosophy professor—I don't understand how she—"

"I've heard from my partners that a few Iranians with no education have become rich by bypassing sanctions. The Iranian side didn't know about me before those Americans questioned me in Amsterdam. Now they do."

"And I thought Amsterdam only changed my life."

"No, it hasn't changed my life as much as it did yours," he said. "I can check if she wants to open an overseas bank account or register a business to transfer her money. I can give her some hints, but I don't want to get too involved with them, Zulaikha, sorry."

Zulaikha looked up disappointed. "I want my life back, Kia—I want to see Sohrab again, and God knows—maybe even Hessam."

I may be selling my soul, reaching out to him, though.

"Let me see what I can do. Give me her information."

She had that ready, too. A business card Dr. Matlab had left in her apartment.

"Don't call her from Iran. She's dangerous."

"I know. I'm leaving Iran soon, anyway," he said. "Now I have something for you."

She just noticed an envelope in his lap.

"After I returned to Canada last year, I contacted Hessam and his daughter. Natasha said Hessam was hospitalized, so I immediately flew to Montreal. It was before his heart surgery—" Kia took a white handkerchief from his jeans to wipe the sweat off his face. "I understood I shouldn't tell him anything about running into you, but I told Natasha and his wife outside of his room. Karmen, his wife, told me to leave it alone. She took it rather strangely as if I was preparing for—you know. It's even hard just to say it. She said what's going on? She screamed that Hessam is still alive—that he would be fine soon and he didn't need to make a last wish for an estranged family reunion."

"I can understand. I've also been confused."

"But strangely, months ago, Hessam asked to be alone with me—I think it was when the doctors told him he needed an operation. He gave me this." Kia glanced down at the envelope. "I know he meant it for you and Sohrab, just in case—you never know what will happen with a heart problem." Kia leaned forward and lowered his voice as he looked around. "It's about how he escaped. So, be prepared."

The man in the juice bar was putting the garbage out. He was humming a familiar song.

Kia straightened his posture. "I wanted to mail it to you, but—there you have it."

"I'll read it with Assef. He'll be coming from Dubai." She looked at her watch. The numbness attacked her hands, spreading into her arms as she put the envelope in her purse.

"I know that flight may arrive in a few hours. If you have time to kill, hire a guide to drive you around town—they're in the side street as you walk in the boulevard."

"I have to get my luggage."

"I'll go this way to catch a flight back," he said. "But one last thing—I want you to know how sorry I am for—"

"Don't. Not today. This is too much already. I don't want to cry in front of you." She let him go in a different direction. "Wait," she said and stepped toward him. "Don't ask me for forgiveness. Ask him."

"Who?"

"He was a boy. He moved his toes."

"I have. All my life, Zulaikha." He walked away.

She was cold and unsteady—a familiar hissing sound in her ears was the sign of her blood sugar dropping. She went to the juice stand and asked for carrot juice.

Dragging her luggage, she strolled along the boulevard until she saw a stop sign. A slim man in his sixties was waiting for passengers. He greeted her sombrely, grabbing her suitcase like they had a long-standing agreement and he knew exactly where she was going. She followed him.

She put her purse on her lap and rolled down her window to watch the drive into Abadan. Rows of palm trees passed her, but her mind had drifted.

The driver glanced at her in his rear-view mirror. "Life is peaceful now in Abadan, isn't it?"

She shook her head in regret. "Would you drive me through Farah Abad? What's it called now?"

"Who cares? I still use the old ones."

"It's heartbreaking to see the fall of something that was once so proud."

"People don't even come back to see this place anymore," he said. "If your loved one gets a disease that deforms him, don't you want to see him anymore? He won't be the same, but his soul is still inside. Right?" He sighed.

What does Hessam look like now? Has his illness deformed him? What about his soul? Is it still there? Sohrab said he had changed. He probably sounds like a stranger with a French accent.

The driver pulled over as the car approached *Labeh Shat*, the Karun River.

Zulaikha got out and looked down at the water. "Aaaah, Karun!" Down there, on the grass having picnics, she had the best and worst days with her family.

The driver lit a cigarette and grabbed a piece of paper from his dashboard. He told Zulaikha that he wanted to read a poem to her that his son had given him. "I always read it to returning visitors, if they let me," he said. "This is by Forough. You know her, right?"

"Of course, I know her. Where's your son now?" She wrapped her purple scarf around her neck, making sure it was not revealing her hair.

Like many others, the driver's children had also immigrated to Canada. "My son is an engineer, but he loves poetry."

Zulaikha sat on an old rusty bench waiting for him to recite. The poem was "Remembering the Past." He knew it by heart—he only held the paper as a prop.

There is a city beside that effusive river
With twisted palm trees and incandescent nights
There is a city beside that river
Where my heart
Is spellbound in the hands of a proud man
There is a city beside that river
that for years
opened its arms to you and me

Atop the sandy beaches and behind the shadows of the trees
He has stolen kisses from my eyes and lips

The moon has witnessed
how I have softened his cold heart
By casting the spell of my empathetic heart
The moon has witnessed
The shedding of excited tears
from those two wild, unfamiliar painted eyes

We sailed into the heart of moonlight
On a boat that hit the chest of those eternal waves
The white glance of stardust, our feast
Blossomed in the disturbed, scattered silence of midnight

He fell asleep in my arms
Like an infant
I have kissed those two eyes
Entangled by the waves of my skirt
He has pulled
My sinking gown from bottomless waters

Now, it's me who remembers you
In the heart of this silent solitude
O' the roaring city, it's you I retain
I have kept him in my heart, and you hold him dear
I grant joy to my heart, envisioning him.

Zulaikha clapped her hands and wiped away her tears. "Oh *Amu*, you killed me with this poem."

"We all have someone to remember, right?" he said. "Hop into the car, Sister—it's getting late!"

"What's your name *Amu*? I am Zulaikha."

"What a name. I haven't met a Zulaikha since—I don't even remember when. I'm Qassem."

Zulaikha chuckled. "No one wants my name for their daughters, *Amu* Qassem."

"Even better. You'll be our one and only."

The sun had already set, and darkness would settle in soon enough. She glanced at the river one more time. A river is the only thing that stays intact after a city goes through a war. Rivers did not show bomb craters or bullet holes. Rivers were not ruins. But this river did not seem as crystalline as it used to. It murmured something was still wrong, even in peace.

∎ ∎ ∎

Zulaikha looked up at the sky. The full moon was shining. Myriad stars were woven together like an animal pattern in a fabric. Assef was waiting for her in front of the old Hotel Karevansara, smoking in a corner. He noticed the car pulling over, put his cigarette out, and approached the vehicle. He winked at Zulaikha as he helped the driver take her suitcase from the trunk. Assef paid the fare and asked the driver to return to the same place tomorrow morning.

No one was around but the driver, so they dared to hold each other. When she turned, Qassem waved at them. Zulaikha waved back at him as they walked toward the entrance door.

"You look stunning. Purple has always been your colour."

She had picked her shawl that morning after trying five of them. She gazed at his toned body. "Skype doesn't do you justice," Zulaikha said. "You look stronger."

"Really? Because with Skype, you see me sitting," he said. "Driving was killing my back. I take care of myself more—I lift weights." He raised his arm to show off his arm muscles.

"Still smoking, though."

"Only when I see you."

She rolled her eyes.

"Look at it—our Karevansara—still glamorous, still glimmering. Don't you think?" The hotel looked intact—no sign of the brutality that hit its vicinity since the first days of the war. The arched windows shaped a curve against the green roundabout. Long ago, she had asked the newcomers in the dormitory if they knew what had happened to the hotel. Nobody had noticed. They drove on other roads—it was in the red zone. Who cared about that hotel like she did?

"I would keep my expectations low," Assef said. "Let's first see how it is inside."

"Forgive Iran for not offering you Burj Khalifa, Mr. Dubai."

Assef shook his head as he approached the hotel reception. He got his leather bag from the man behind the desk and hung it over his shoulder.

He had booked two rooms—Islamic rules did not allow unmarried couples to share a room. Mousa, her nephew, had offered her a new studio apartment, but she wasn't prepared to take Assef there or spend the night under one roof with him yet.

"I need to freshen up," she said. "Come knock in ten minutes, will you?" The elevator took them to the fourth floor.

"Only ten minutes?"

She wanted to go to the bathroom. "Just do as I say for once."

Assef raised his hand slightly to his right eye in a military salute.

■ ■ ■

When Zulaikha opened the door to Assef, her hair had been tightly ponytailed since the morning. It was easier to manage when she had long hours under the scarf.

"Your hair." Assef took a seat in front of their window to the balcony. "You look like a flamenco dancer in this dim."

Zulaikha had put her shawl and *manteau* on her bed. The envelope was still in her purse.

"How did it go with Kia?"

"Stranger than I expected."

"Why? Did he refuse to call that woman?"

"No, Assef." She leaned forward and finally opened her purse. "He gave me this. Hessam wrote this before his last year's

surgery—he had open heart surgery."
"Is it a will?"
"No, it's about how he escaped."
"Did you read it?"
"No, I'm scared to—there may be something horrific in it—"
"Like what?"
"Dr. Matlab kept telling me something—that he was the reason her nephew killed himself," she trailed off. "What could he have done to him?"
"Stop it, Zuli. You know that woman is not in her right mind—don't let her—"
"Read it aloud."
"With my accent? My Farsi is even worse than before—"
"I don't care—"
Assef put his glasses on. "Let me see—it's his handwriting."
"I'll help you if it isn't legible."
"Things you make me do, Zuli."
The night had scattered its shadow into the room. Zulaikha reached for a lamp beside Assef's chair. The touch of her finger dispelled the darkness. She swallowed hard and sat on the edge of the bed with her eyes on the window.

∎ ∎ ∎

Dear Kia:
If you are reading this, it means either I have died, or someone from my family has found me. I have raised Natasha here in this part of the world. I have told her about my life and my youth. I wrote the story of I how I left Iran years ago. I wrote it so I wouldn't forget it. Then, later on, I wanted to pretend it was just a story, to share it, or have it translated. But I didn't want anyone to tell me it needed to be edited and sounded impossible or unbelievable. When you read it, you will know why.
When they invaded our twin city, Khorramshahr, in

September of 1980, I was working as an accountant in the naval force office, and although I was not a militant, I admit that the military atmosphere had influenced me. Soon after the bombings started, the media announced that the Basij force would train people free of charge. I signed up, like many other men who thought that skills with guns would be necessary to defend our homes. When the Iraqis invaded Khorramshahr, my house was bombed. My family moved to Tehran, and working in the navy facility was unsafe, so they let me and most non-militants take an extended leave or work part-time. I kept up my training with the Basij and the naval office, which allowed me to work in a Basij building and kept me on the payroll.

Eventually, I went to the front line, near Shalamcheh, in the northwest of Abadan. By 1984, most people had left Abadan—my best friend, Abbass, his father, and fiance had lived in Ahvaz, in a school. He taught music lessons and wrote songs, and he was very popular with his pupils. One of his students, Omid, had a father who was some big shot in Sepah, the Guard. That man had asked Abbass to stop teaching music and reported him as an anti-revolutionary. After Abbass was dismissed from his janitor job, they moved back to Abadan, where Abbass tried to repair their house and make a living there.

One day, when I was at their house, government soldiers took me to the city jail. They interrogated me and asked me why I was always hanging out with Arabs. I knew they meant him. They kept me for a couple of nights. They frightened me and made me watch as they beat prisoners in front of me. I was horrified.

When they released me, I told Abbass about it,

and we decided it would be better for me to keep my distance. I remember he told me that he felt someone was following him sometimes. They suddenly called me for an assignment, and I left to the front with the Basij. A few days later, I returned to town for my days off and was told that Abbass had been shot to death. They executed him on the street in front of his neighbours.

I stayed with Abbass's father for a few days. Abu was in deep mourning over his son's death. I wanted to give up the war and find his killers. I was full of hatred and did not return to my duty for a while.

Basiji soldiers came to our door and saw that I wore black. I told them that I was grieving for my friend. In those days, mourning was as common as a cold—people called and asked for the day off because someone close to them had been killed by a bomb, in an attack, or in jail. I stayed in my ruined house, surrounded by collapsed walls, and started renovating a room. I removed the loose bricks and washed a couple of carpets, a blanket, and a mattress—neighbours came to help me. Thanks to Khuzestan's climate, I could sleep in my roofless room. I worked like a construction worker all day, so by night, I could sleep and not think about Abbass and his short life. But even so, nightmares woke me up almost every night. When my sister, Zulaikha called our neighbour one day, they told her I was not doing well. Soon after that day, someone knocked on my door. It was her. She had come to see me because she knew I might do something crazy. She sat with me in the roofless house and tried to convince me to move to Tehran with her.

By then, the regime had destroyed their opposition brutally in Tehran and other large cities. Iraqi missiles had reached Tehran, so it didn't seem to be that safe, but I told her that I would join them soon. After Zulaikha left, I requested a transfer to Tehran and arranged with Jamshid to move Abu to Ahvaz and look after him. A few days later, when I returned to Abadan to check the status of my transfer request, that boy, Omid, Abbass's student, was sitting outside my house. When I asked him what he was doing there, he told me his father was looking for me. He warned me to find a way to escape before it was too late. His father had hired killers. Omid seemed to be hysterical, and then he ran.

After I saw that boy, I contacted someone I knew. Abbass's fiancé had an older brother who was resourceful. He suggested I escape to the Emirates and go as soon as possible. What an irony that was. My life was more in danger from my own people than from the Iraqi army. A messenger working in a committee in downtown Abadan came to me and said they would arrange for my escape from the country. He told me to volunteer again and return to the front and move toward Ahvaz the first chance I got. Ahvaz, in the middle of Khuzestan, was rather far from Iraqis. I did not have too many options. He had me memorize a phone number and an address of a house near Andimeshk. I would become missing-in-action, a missing person.

When I returned to my post, the local Basiji gave me the cold shoulder. They all knew about my friend Abbass and wanted to keep their distance from me. I even heard them saying mean things. "That pretty Arab faggot got what he deserved." They were disgusting, but I ignored them. I had a mission I could not endanger.

They had me organize the shipping of water drums to the front, near Shalamcheh, because I knew the roads. I don't even remember the locations now, but at that time, I was young and knew exactly where I was going. Although they did not trust me, the shortage of human resources was a problem for them, so they had to rely on my help regardless. I left in a Land Rover with the water and two other men, the driver, a guy from Tehran I'd seen before, and a young soldier, hardly sixteen years old, still dumb enough to be excited to be in the war. His name was Mahmood, and he was from Rasht near the Caspian Sea. He had blue eyes and light brown curly hair. Both men were unfamiliar with the place, which was lucky for me. If I had been with a local Basiji, my plan to escape might have been jeopardized.

After an hour of driving, Iraqi planes attacked us. I told the driver to drive into the palm groves, but the driver was hit as we drove parallel to the river, heading for the forests. He stopped the vehicle in the middle of the road and fell unconscious. The kid panicked and began sobbing and praying loudly. I yelled, "Get a hold of yourself. We can't survive if we are weak." The kid continued whispering his prayers. I ordered him to be quiet, but he didn't listen. He was transferring his fear to me too. I needed his help, and he was making the situation difficult for all of us. A minute later, he asked me to forgive him and tell him what to do. We slowly climbed out of the Jeep and lay on the ground behind the road's high pavement.

The driver was still alive but bleeding heavily when the Iraqi airplanes left us. We laid him in the back seat. I directed the kid to drive alongside the river. "Where are we going?" he asked.

"Just keep going," I said. "There's a sign ahead of us. We must get him to medics, or he'll bleed to death."

Suddenly the planes came back. I told the boy to get off the road and hide in the trees until the planes completely disappeared.

"Come back when they're gone, no matter if you find me or not, drive along the river, and you will come to a town with a hospital."

"What about you?"

"I can find my way. I'm from here, but you should go back to your town and live your life. This is not a place for you. There is too much death here. Do you hear me?"

Before he could answer, a terrible explosion shook the ground and sent concussive waves pulsing through the air. I ran into a different clump of trees and hid myself. The boy started screaming my name. "Brother Hessam, can you hear me? Are you hurt?"

I didn't answer. The poor kid ran in circles calling out my name and looking for me. Iraqis had cut some of the palms when they captured Khorramshahr. I tried to jump over one of the cut trees but fell into a hidden hole. I stayed hidden, silent. Then the Iranian guns started firing at the Iraqi planes. I stayed hidden. The boy could not keep searching for me. He knew he couldn't wait because of the wounded driver. When I heard the car engine start again, I felt better. I hated to leave him on his own, but I had no other choice.

I walked and limped for two more hours until a car came up behind me—I'd heard it coming from a distance. I knew it wasn't a military vehicle. I looked muddy and dirty—the driver took pity on me. He asked me to get in and offered me some water. His car was an old Peykan, and he told me that he just got it back from the mechanic and hoped that it would get him as far as Ahvaz. "Sorry, but I'll take you to Ahvaz only if this piece of junk gets us there." I chuckled—I still remember it because it was my first smile in weeks.

"How is the battle going?"

"Horribly," I said.

"My family left three weeks ago. Would you believe that they walked most of the way? They could not find a bus or a driver to take them. People have been lining up for buses for days."

"Good that they could escape." I thought about my nephew Sohrab, Zulaikha, Abu, and my mother.

The driver still talked while I contemplated what everyone else might be going through. "Yes, they are in Tehran now. I'll join them, too, if *Khoda* allows me."

I might still have been safe. It was too soon for anyone to question where I was. I had to find a phone and call my contact. Three hours later, I was still in my Basiji uniform when I asked a shopkeeper in Ahvaz to give me some water and let me use his phone to call my family in Andimeshk. He granted my request, under the impression that I was a war hero and not a deserter. I called the contact I had memorized and talked to someone who would come and pick me up. I went to the bus stop, bought a ticket for Andimeshk, and slept on a bench until I heard someone yelling for passengers to board.

Two hours later, a man, a Lur from Haft Tappeh, was waiting for me. He took me to his house. He worked in the sugar cane factory, and after a few days, a messenger delivered an envelope to him containing my new documents. I asked him how much he wanted, and he told me all was looked after. I made my way to Andimeshk, took a bus back to Ahvaz and then to Bushehr and a barge to Kuwait. I stayed with an Iranian family there, and they helped me with money, a suitcase, and a ticket to Cairo. I was rescued, but there was a catch: I could not tell anyone I was alive, not even my family. I knew that the government officials might go to my mother and Zulaikha, and maybe even take them for interrogation. I had to act like a machine, accepting the conditions for my freedom, even though it meant my family would believe I was dead.

I have never forgiven myself for pretending that I was killed. At that moment, I couldn't stop thinking about my ruined house in Abadan, *Istgah Haft*, the wall that I'd started renovating, and all my childhood memories. I contacted Mrs. Sara's house once, but no one answered. Perhaps they had also evacuated. For me, Abadan and Khuzestan meant the whole world. But the city, once more beautiful than many famous cities, had become a ruin. I had no country anymore.

Egypt became my new country in 1986. I'd changed my name in Andimeshk to Habib and met Karmen while working in construction. She owned a small coffee shop. Through her relatives in France, we moved there, and when she received some inheritance money a few years ago, we moved to Canada and opened a small restaurant, slowly expanding it.

I was lost, but I still could have tried to find one of my family members sometime during all these years. Partly out of fear for people's safety and partly for the comfort I built in my new life—and partly simple procrastination or depression. A part of me had died there.

I don't deserve to be blamed for escaping from the horror and the contagious hatred spreading everywhere. The animosity toward a beautiful soul like Abbass was too ugly. I never wanted to feel that extent of hate and anger ever again.

■■■

She put aside the glass of water Assef had just given her without drinking it. She wore her scarf and opened the door. Assef called her name. "Where are you going?"

"Give me a few minutes." She did not know what she was doing or where she was going. She heard a quarrel from a room. A man was saying, "I told you, didn't I tell you? You never listen to me!" There was no response—the man was having a phone conversation. She climbed down the stairs and went to the lobby. A very young, bearded man was sitting away from the reception desk, reading a book. He got up and approached the counter.

"Is everything alright, ma'am?"

She faked a smile. "Yes, I couldn't sleep. I have a headache. Do you have an Aspirin or any other painkillers?"

The man fetched a small first aid kit and gave her two pills and a glass of water. She gaped at a large poster of the city in black and white on the side wall. It was Abadan, in the sixties perhaps.

"There's a small war museum we have made in that corner. Help yourself if you want," the receptionist said. "It's more an exhibition of pictures."

"War museum?"

"Yes, you said you couldn't sleep."

She stepped toward the room but then stopped and turned to him.

"I don't want to."

"Excuse me?" He put aside the glass of water.

"Why would I want to look at those things? They freak me out," she said. "I hate all of it."

We were this museum for Hessam, a place to never look back, a place to never re-enter.

The young man wiped the sweat from his forehead with a tissue.

"My brother went to the frontier and never came back. Perhaps you weren't born then."

"I'm so sorry. Yes, my parents always tell me about the war and those years. Sometimes I want them to stop," he said. "Unfortunately, the restaurant is closed—otherwise, you could have a tea or coffee." The young bearded man was unexpectedly pleasant despite the hostility she had anticipated from men looking like him.

"I was never able to afford to stay in this hotel. I was never allowed to go to a casino," Zulaikha said.

"Even back then?"

"I mean my family didn't let me," she said. "Even back then, we were a bunch of idiots."

"Some people think those days were heaven compared to the hell we live in now," he replied.

"On the weekends, my brother Hessam and his friend Abbass—" She refrained from mentioning Kia's name, "—they used to come here to play, drink, and meet women until around four in the morning."

"Did you come back to see what this place looks like? It shocks most people. Sometimes I think about making a documentary of people's reactions, seeing this city again."

That's how he sees me. Shocked. I am behaving like a lunatic. I should pull myself together.

"I may want to move back to Khuzestan. Do you think I can get a job here? I can help in the kitchen or clean. Imagine my brother's face if I tell him to guess where I work."

"I thought you said you lost your brother."

"I said he never came back."

The phone rang, and he went to answer it while looking at her with concern.

Zulaikha heard Assef calling her name. "What are you doing here? Let's go back upstairs."

Zulaikha glanced outside toward the roundabout and its flowers.

"Help me, Zuli. I don't know what I should do, to be honest with you—"

"Yes, welcome to my life. Not so easy, Assef. You can run away again if you want."

She turned and looked at the receptionist, who was still talking on the phone, giving someone directions to the hotel.

■■■

Zulaikha stood by the window, exposed to the motionless street. She stared at the green roundabout's small pool with a playful dolphin statue swimming under the fountain.

"Say something, Zuli," Assef said. "I'm terrified but won't run away—not anymore."

She closed the curtains.

"Hold me."

"What?"

"Don't be afraid, Assef. Come near me. I want to feel something."

He pulled her gently toward his chest.

She put her head on his shoulder. "Why can't I feel anything?"

He undid her ponytail and let her hair fall on her shoulders. How in need of his touch her tired hair had been. They kissed and crawled onto the bed. She closed her eyes and let her body comprehend the moment. It had been months. She was one moment angry and another moment numb. This chemistry could only bring back natural emotions. Only this touch, this passion she had missed for so long, had the power to stabilize her.

Zulaikha woke up two hours later from a dream. She was walking toward Nasim's bookstore in Tehran, when suddenly, someone pushed her from behind. She tripped and fell on her hands.

It took her two seconds to remember where she was. Assef was snoring, and the air conditioner had made the room very cool. She got up as quietly as she could and went to the bathroom. The moon was shining in the middle of the sky. It was too humid outside, and she did not want to open the window. She turned the fan off.

"Are you cold?" Assef's voice quavered. "I'll go take a shower."

Zulaikha nodded.

"Will you pass me my towel? I don't like hotel towels."

He had become so fancy, or we had become too inferior to outsiders.

His bag was open. A large unsealed padded envelope fell out as she reached for a yellow towel. It was filled with US bills.

Assef's cell phone ringtone and vibration made her almost drop the envelope. She placed it inside the bag, picked up the cell phone and knocked on the bathroom door. Assef was shaving.

"Don't worry about that." He glanced at the phone. "Do you need anything here?" He wrapped the towel around his waist.

"I need to shower, too." She stepped into the bathroom and glanced at the hotel towels. They looked clean. The bathroom walls were marbled tiles, and the shower had good pressure.

When she returned to the room, Assef was nicely dressed and sat reading a newspaper.

"I'm getting hungry," he said. "I wonder if their kitchen is closed."

"I think it is—the receptionist told me. Thanks for your trouble, by the way."

"Oh, you Zuli, no trouble for me. Are you feeling better?"

"Not really." She took the newspaper from him. "How are your wife and daughter, by the way?"

"They're fine. My daughter is twenty-seven now."

"I don't even know her name."

"Malak is my wife," he swallowed. "And my daughter's name is Salimeh."

"Nice names." She didn't want to dig into his personal life further. The more she acknowledged his other family, her being there with him became pointless. "What time is it? Can we call Sohrab?"

"Sohrab met with his cousin and uncle last week. You know all about it, don't you?"

She nodded as she remained seated on the bed. Outside, stray dogs were barking. It seemed that loose dogs were everywhere on the streets. The sound of a gunshot made them bark even more.

"I hope they aren't shooting the dogs," Zulaikha said.

"They think they can change the situation here by bombs and armed attacks."

"Who, Assef?"

"I don't know, maybe separatists, maybe the government itself."

"I thought you were a separatist."

Assef sneered. "Many of them are my friends, but I have a different way."

"What is your way?"

"Can we talk about what's bothering you, Zuli?"

Yes, let's put the pieces of the puzzle together.

"Do you remember in those years when I called and asked you to do something for Hessam?"

"Barely. Why does it matter? Someone had helped him, and he lived his life," he said. "To be honest, the news about Abbass shook me more than anything—me and everybody—"

"Who's your everybody?"

"Many people knew Abbass back then—his father, too. People loved him. I was surprised nothing happened when they killed him—no retaliation," he said. "And when I heard about Hessam, I suspected he escaped."

"Did you ask anyone?"

"No, Zuli. I was never that close to your brother. You know that." He looked away.

No kidding. He still remembers.

"I wanted to tell you not to worry many times, but we weren't on good terms."

"I should've known. Najwa tried to tell me something—" She sat on the bed again. "Then she wrote me a note and told me they had escaped and took refugee status in Germany. I thought she wanted to tell me that. Why didn't I ask you?"

"I sent some money to her brother, Salem, but what difference does it make?"

Zulaikha remembered something. "I wanted to call you. But I thought, what if your woman answered the phone?" She picked up Hessam's letter. "Until a decade ago, I didn't think he was dead. I thought he would have made contact. How come he was so cruel to us?"

"It was a terrible time, Zuli. People turned their back on—"

An explosion shook the room. They looked at each other.

"What was that?"

"A bomb." Assef looked out the window. "This province is never safe—you shouldn't consider this place your haven."

She stood beside him. The street still seemed calm. "I already miss Tehran."

"*Hala volek, Tehrani shodi baram?* (Now, buddy, have you become a Tehrani lady for me?)" He held her in his arms.

"Poor boy. The blue-eyed boy. Hessam had no idea what happened to him," Zulaikha said mournfully.

"Why did Dr. Matlab let her nephew go to war somewhere they knew nothing about? Were they distributing cookies there? No. I would've told the kid the same thing. That woman is more responsible than anyone else," Assef said.

"When can we call Sohrab?"

"You look exhausted, Zuli—get more rest. I'll go to my room. I should see who called me. We'll do it when you look rested. I don't want to make Sohrab more worried. He's as confused as you are."

"Okay—for Sohrab," she muttered.

Assef kissed her forehead this time.

The ambulance and fire truck sirens broke the silence. But she closed her eyes and went to sleep with the hotel towel still in her hand.

■■■

In the morning, she awoke to ferry horns on the river. It was her last day with Assef before he left to attend a wedding. Qassem was waiting for them beside the roundabout. "Are you ready for a good breakfast? Our fall is the best season to be out."

In a local café with straw arbours on their patio, they ordered eggs, local sour cream, honey, and tea. Zulaikha enjoyed watching Assef eat. She had more energy today. When she returned from the bathroom, Assef was paying the bill.

"All done?" he asked. "Let's go then—we have an important task."

"What task?"

"Let's get married."

"What?"

"Yes, Zuli *jan*. We can't get a room in the hotel or go anywhere without a marriage licence, and I'm too old for sneaking around and getting into arguments here. Let's get a temporary marriage licence."

"Are you serious?"

"It's easier to smuggle goods into this country than to hang out with a woman."

"Smuggling goods may be easy for you, Mister."

"Don't be upset—just an option for us. We can have a temporary marriage and keep extending it."

"I was enjoying our time together. Now you're doing it again—doing your own thing without—"

"Do you want to answer to the guards when they ask how we are related? At our age?"

"Why not a permanent marriage then?" she said archly.

He paused for a moment. "Permanent?"

"Answer my question—why not a permanent, respectful marriage?"

"I didn't think you'd want me as a permanent husband."

"You find this funny?"

"No, I'm serious! How would I know?"

"What if I do want it?"

She heard her own voice demanding to be a second wife again. Last night she let Assef take charge in the desperate hours, putting pieces of her missing brother's puzzle together when she was losing her grip. As much as she longed for a secure life—even a part-time life—with him, Assef didn't belong to her. She was putting her dignity at stake. But love and dignity didn't always go hand in hand for her.

"Let's go then," Assef said. "They may be going to close at noon for the prayers."

Qassem was smoking hookah under another straw arbour.

"Do you know a notary public who can marry us immediately, *Amu*?" Assef asked.

"Oh brother, you have first to do a blood test and—"

"Blood test? Why?" Assef asked. "Give me a puff, *Amu*."

"For drug tests and genetics," she said. "It's the rule. Don't you remember? We had done that when we—" Zulaikha shook her head.

"Hurry up," Qassem gave up the hookah and his arbour. "We may still have time."

Sitting in the back seat of Qassem's car, she glanced at Assef's neck and toned shoulder blades. He glanced back and winked at her. She wanted to go with this flow. This day, the blue sky and the fall breeze.

They waited outside for the office to re-open after the noon prayers. Three other couples were waiting, and by four in the afternoon, they had married again—not a temporary marriage, but a permanent one. They still had time to kill before Assef's trip to Ahvaz.

They drove past the ruins of the Cinema Rex, then to Farah Abad from *Istgah Yek* to the neighbourhood of the old house in *Istgah Haft*. The old house with its poor exterior was still standing.

Mrs. Sara and her husband had passed away five years ago. Mrs. Sara died in her sleep—her husband couldn't last more than six months without her.

"I want to say hello to Mrs. Sara's brother-in-law, Pirooz," Zulaikah said. "He's the new owner."

Pirooz recognized her. "Are you Zulaikha? Where have you been?" he asked. "Welcome, come, come inside." He called his wife, Narges. Qassem waited for them in the shade.

They had renovated the interiors. The courtyard and the garden were almost as Zulaikha remembered. But when they entered the house, it had a large living room and an open kitchen. Her knees began to tremble. She leaned against the kitchen counter and asked if she could have some water. The atmosphere sank her deeper into a muddy lagoon with each moment.

"I shouldn't have let you go inside," Assef said in the car.

The day was too beautiful to dig up the lost past.

"Let me cheer you up," Qassem said. "Do you like Tajik? Let's listen to some music."

Qassem pressed the car audio, but the radio was broadcasting a report about the upcoming election. When they mentioned the president's name, Ahmadinejad, Qassem pressed the tape button tightly. "They talk about him all day long," he said.

"What's going on, by the way? I'd like to know." Assef asked. "Funny, even the Emirates radio talks about him."

"He has some guts—I admit," Qassem said. "He questions things in the UN, like the veto right—perhaps foreigners think he's on to something, but he's just crazy."

"I don't see any difference in any of them. More control—more fear—that's how I see it," Zulaikha said.

"But are these guys in the regime now against each other?" Assef asked.

"Yes, his opponent party is The Reformists. Some joke. Anyone *Rahbar* Khamenei backs up will be the next president."

"We're going to have a bumpy summer, *Amu* Qassem, won't we?" Zulaikha teased.

The car cruised between the National Oil Company of Abadan and the workers' cottages. Smoke and fire were still pouring out of the refinery's giant pipes. An Arab worker biked alongside their car. He was bony—his skin was cracked by the sun, like the refinery had sucked his blood dry and given nothing to him in return. Qassem honked at the biker, and he waved back. An old Tajik song was playing in the car.

They stopped for dinner in Khorramshahr near the Karun River. Qassem knew the owners. He told them this was a special spot and left the couple to eat alone.

Zulaikha wasn't used to this all-day sightseeing excitement. And with Assef by her side no less. She needed to remind herself that it was only for today. *He lives in Dubai, and his wife doesn't know anything about what's happening here.*

She searched in her purse for something to use as a fan.

"What's wrong?"

"Nothing—a bit hungry—food will make me feel better."

Knowing that it was only for today, the care he showed her didn't feel real.

The restaurant was not busy. The servers and most of the patrons were local Arabs. The server brought them chicken kabab and rice with saffron on top. When Assef saw the food, he was as happy as a hungry child. "Don't go back. Come with me to Dubai. We can live there together."

"Can you stop it?" She frowned.

"You'll like Dubai."

"No, I get along with damaged places more." She looked out of the window beside her at the view of Khorramshahr bridge. "Abused, invaded, and attacked places attract me more. I feel connected."

"You feel connected." Assef drank his Pepsi.

"Never mind what I say—I just mean that a part of me wants to stay here."

"Your choice, Zuli. I take care of you, anywhere you—"

"Yes, why not? With your US bills—"

"My US bills can be used to rescue someone like your brother."

"I'm sorry," she said. "I know you work hard for your money."

"I've tried to make things right between us in any possible way—but—never mind."

"You want me to thank you for supporting Sohrab?"

"No, just don't remind me I'm a loser all the time."

The server came to check on them. Zulaikha asked him to pack the rest of her meal.

"Still not feeling good? You didn't eat much."

She stroked his hand. "I never thought you were a loser—I love being with you—it's just always temporary, though."

Assef rested his fists on his chin. "I'll think of something. Give me time."

He held her hand as they walked toward the car until his cell phone rang. He picked it up and spoke with a woman briefly in Arabic. She only understood a few words—something about tomorrow, and the wedding.

In front of the hotel, she shook Qassem's hands warmly. Assef hugged him and gave him money and a business card. "Anything you need, just call or email me here."

They checked out of the hotel. Assef picked up a rental car to drive to Ahvaz for his old friend's wedding. He offered to give her a ride to Mousa's place.

"No, I'll ask the receptionist to call a taxi for me. It's getting late—you're going that way." She pointed in the direction of Ahvaz.

"So, I'll see you in a few days at your nephew's place—we have our mobile phones now—" He carried her luggage to the door.

"I want you to do something for me."

"What?"

"I don't know how my internet connection will be at Mousa's place. I want you to tell Sohrab I'm not ready yet. I'm not ready to see Hessam or talk to him. I know it's been months, but I want to be sure he wants us in his life—his family, too."

He held her. "I'm sure he'll understand."

"Do you remember when Sohrab was born and I told you why I wanted to name him Sohrab?"

"Yes, you read me a poem from his namesake poet."

She nodded. "I can feel that poem more than ever. I'm used to this space you all left me to live in—I wish I could find the poem again—something like—be gentle not to fracture my thin glass space."

I should ask Nasim to send me the book when she's back.

"Believe it or not, I get it," he said.

Everyone would understand a fraction of how it had been for me.

"I'll tell Sohrab you said something about his name, glass and fracture. How does that sound?" Assef teased.

She chuckled. "You drive safe tonight. I know she's there, too."

"How did you know?"

"I heard you talking to her."

"That was my daughter, you bluffer. Rhianna has invited them. I have no control over any of my women."

■ ■ ■

Zulaikha spotted a big black dog walking beside the slowing car. It was getting dark—she was used to being alone or walking home in the dark, but not near stray dogs in an abandoned city. The dog must have sensed her being new—it kept looking at her from afar. She was missing her cat friends in Tehran as she got out of the car.

"Maybe I could befriend you one day," she muttered.

Mousa's studio apartment was above a grocery store on a corner of Amiri Square near downtown Abadan. She turned on the light. The place was almost empty. There was a single bed next to a window that opened onto the street, and a note from Mousa on the desk next to the bed was waiting for her.

Welcome to Abadan, Aunt Zulaikha.

Feel free to use the computer. Sohrab told me that you would need to Skype him (Well, if we ever get an internet connection). Please call me if you need anything. The shopkeeper downstairs knows about you. They are my tenants and will help you. I will see you soon.

Mousa

A knock on the door startled Zulaikha.

"I brought you some groceries," a man said from behind the door. "I'm Rahim—from the store downstairs. Mousa asked me to."

She cautiously opened the door and let him in.

"Do you know where Mousa is?"

"Yes, ma'am." He put a large water bottle on the counter. "He must be in Ahvaz visiting his father."

The bag of groceries contained teabags, bread, butter, eggs and cheese, but she still had her leftovers from dinner with Assef. First, she needed to freshen up.

She undressed and stared at her reflection in the wall-to-wall mirror above the sink.

Maybe I should darken my hair. Assef said I looked like a flamenco dancer last night.

She turned on the faucet in the shower and whispered a song beneath the stream—the old Palm Grove song by Tajik. Qassem was playing it in the taxi while cruising Abadan.

When I was with you,
The sound of my oud, my poems, my songs were luminous.
Now, without you, my only hope,
At nights,
I am the moon's companion
Venus's confidante.

She watched the running water wash off the lather from her body. She was used to these moments alone—this silence. She had learned to live in her unwanted solitude for years and made it her own. To fracture her thin glass walls was crude and invasive. Maybe it was the same for Hessam or Karmen, his wife. They were used to having only each other without his family around. She wrapped a towel around her head and pulled open the curtains. The gleaming full moon brightened the room.

She went to the kitchen and picked up a frying pan. She was about to turn on the oven, but changed her mind.

How much does Gholam know? He has also suffered from this charade, this disappearance.

She dialled Mousa's number.

"Aunty Zulaikha, welcome. Is everything all set? Did Rahim bring you the groceries?"

"Yes, Mousa *jan*. Listen. I need to talk to your father. I want to—"

"Hello?"

"Yes, I'm here. I want to tell him—"

"I know, Aunty. I've told him about Uncle Hessam already."

"Really?" *This would make things easier.*

"I'll tell him to come and visit you tomorrow first thing. He's not here right now."

"Where is he at this time?"

"He keeps himself busy, Aunty." Mousa chuckled. "He'll tell you."

"Please tell him I'll be waiting. If he can't come, will you let me know? I hate waiting."

"Of course. Get some rest. Do you want me to tell you how to connect to the internet or watch movies?"

"I'm tired. I'll try the internet tomorrow." She went to bed with her book and a cup of tea.

■ ■ ■

A dog barking at an approaching car woke her up. She looked out the window. It was Gholam parking his Peugeot. She put on her scarf and *manteau* quickly and ran downstairs. She had no idea how much she had missed him until that moment. She couldn't even wait until Gholam had locked his car to hold him.

"You look good, you old man," she wept.

"You too, Sister. Our dickhead brother has been living a fancy life. Can you believe this?"

Zulaikha chuckled. She had been looking for swear words to call Hessam, but nothing felt right.

"I just woke up. Come up. Let me fix you breakfast."

They walked upstairs. "This place doesn't even have a carpet—just one chair and two stools?" he said. "Go freshen up. I'll take you to Minoo Island for breakfast."

"What keeps you busy these days? Mousa laughed when I asked him last night."

"He always laughs at me. I'm a consultant for the police. He calls me Lieutenant Colombo. Can you believe it?"

She covered her mouth to avoid laughing as she exited the bathroom. "You look like Colombo a bit. What sort of consultant?"

"Crime scenes. I retired and opened a real estate company—the one Mousa is managing," he said. "I missed my old job and asked my old friends if there was anything for me. They offered me a contract, and I took it."

"How's Kobra?"

"She's in Isfahan. Our daughter is pregnant."

Zulaikha congratulated him. She had to find a suitable time to share Hessam's letter.

"Kobra lives there most of the time. She says she hates Khuzestan. What made you come back?"

"I'll tell you all of it in the car, but before that," she said. "You need to sit down for this. I have a letter from Hessam."

After reading the letter, he kept his head down for a few seconds. "Bastards," he muttered, and handed it back to Zulaikha. "Let's get out of here," he said.

He must be as numb as I was.

They cruised around Minoo Island and stopped in the marina. The breakfast was simple, just tea, bread, and cheese. After their breakfast talk, they sat on a bench in front of the harbour.

"I want you to know something, Gholam."

"I know what you want to tell me."

"No, you don't."

"You want me to ask you to forgive me but—"

"No, that's not it."

A young man approached them and spoke directly to Gholam. "Brother, if you want to paddle in the river, I'll charge you only five thousand tomans."

"Not today. Maybe next week." Gholam dismissed the man without asking her, but he could be too distracted. Zulaikha's eyes followed the man who was going toward his canoe.

"What then?" Gholam asked.

"Back then, you were a scary brother, Gholam. I was not sad that you left us. It was a relief—"

"Here we go again—"

"Let me talk, Gholam."

He leaned forward with his back to her.

"But we always knew where you were, what you did, whom you married. I want you to know how and when I stopped being scared of you."

Gholam turned his head to the side to be able to see her.

"When I saw you in front of the mosque distributing flyers about Hessam in your uniform—when you assured us that he was alive. It was you who kept that hope alive in all of us, including our mother." She needed her inhaler again. "They told me in Evin, that they had questioned you about Hessam's whereabouts—"

"Those bastards tried to break me—"

"That was the first day that I felt we were connected—I'll never forget that feeling I had in that dark place."

"I felt the same when they told me about you. They disarmed me first—then they told me, 'We have your sister.' I could have killed them." He clenched his fist.

"I've been so confused, Gholam. I don't want us to be mad at Hessam. Even if he ignored us, he was not the reason for what they did to us after him. But I can't help it—"

"Yes, it's ironic we should feel lucky, but—"

"Nothing about it is lucky or happy. I don't feel lucky that I had to learn to live without Hessam and explain it to Sohrab either."

"What if they gave you his body? Have you thought about that?"

Gholam's insensitive comment made her heart pound faster. She gazed at the young paddler, still sitting in his canoe waiting for customers. "No. How can you say that to me?"

"Because I identified Abbass's body." He faced Zulaikha and looked into her eyes. "Remember. Nothing can top that, Zulaikha. Nothing."

She shook her head and covered her face with her hands for a moment. "It's getting windier. Can you take me home?"

"Let's go. I need to be in a meeting this afternoon."

As they drove, Gholam pointed to locations they'd been before that had been badly hit by the war. "I want to ask you a favour," Gholam said.

"What is it? Anything."

"There will be some commotion in Khuzestan closer to the election. Mousa is a bit pigheaded. Keep an eye on him. Will you?"

"Of course." Outside the car window, palm trees were swaying in the wind. "You raised a good boy."

"I know. I wish Mousa left Iran like Sohrab, but he loves what he does here. Too much manual labour in Japan threw him off." He pulled over and let Zulaikha get out of the car.

She waved at him. Gholam turned around his car, stopped, and glanced at her. "One more thing."

"What is it, Lieutenant Colombo?"

"If you get to see Hessam, tell him I said I was a shitty brother, but back then, I was prepared to take a bullet for him to keep him alive."

He didn't wait for Zulaikha to say anything. His engine roared as he drove away.

■■■

Since Assef took off to Ahvaz, he had been sending her texts asking how she was. The internet was down, and she could not get a hold of Sohrab. She was only a few days away from Tehran. Nasim must still be away, but Zulaikha called the bookstore anyway. Mitra picked up and said she hadn't heard from Nasim lately. Zulaikha went to the store downstairs to pick up mayonnaise for her egg salad, when a small crowd of protestors passed by. "What's going on?" she asked Rahim.

"We don't want Ahmadinejad. He has to go." Rahim said as if it was that simple.

"When will Mousa be here?"

"I don't know. I haven't heard from him."

After lunch, she walked along Amiri Street and looked for bath and kitchen items. When she returned, Mousa was moving boxes to the store. At first, she didn't recognize him. But Mousa recognized her. "Aunt Zulaikha." He hugged her. "It's so good to see you again. Is everything going well?"

He looked bigger than she remembered—taller than Sohrab, with the same wavy black hair.

"Thanks to you, everything is fine. It was quiet until the protest this morning."

"How did it go with my grumpy Dad?"

"Better than I thought."

He chuckled as he handed her an envelope.

"What is it?"

"Sohrab asked me to print this and bring it to you," he said. "He said it's almost impossible for him to Skype you. He's trying to call, though."

"What are they doing to the internet?"

"They're filtering it. There's a huge movement on Facebook about the election."

Nasim had told her about Facebook, but Zulaikha didn't remember it exactly. Mousa kept explaining. "They don't want us to connect to the world, Aunty." He looked at his watch. "I have to visit a client shortly. He may buy a complex—good money for me. Wish me luck. People are coming back to this place."

"You will do it. With your charm, they won't be able to resist. Are you sure you don't want to come upstairs?"

"Yes, I'm sure. I forgot to tell you about the roof. Go up and check it. It has a good view. It's open."

"I'm scared of opening this," Zulaikha said, gesturing at the envelope. "Do you know what it's about?"

"It's all good news," he said. "I'll come back and take you to dinner, then show you a few tricks about working with the computer so you don't get too bored. I'll take you to a good seafood restaurant. My stingy father treated you to bread and cheese. I'll show you our city is not as bad as it looks. How does that sound?"

"That sounds wonderful."

Upstairs, she opened the envelope anxiously.

> Dear *Maman*,
> I am glad you settled in Abadan. My mission is finally accomplished. I am back in Holland. I met Uncle Hessam and my cousin, Natasha. I want you to know that I had been thinking about you and

Bibi Madineh every minute of it. But Baba said you are not mentally ready yet. He even told me about Sepehri's poem you had told him about. I had a lot of fun hearing him talking about the fracture of the thin glass.

But my wonderful news, which I am sure will make you happy, is that I have asked Sheila to marry me, and we will be engaged soon. I want us to reunite in Dubai for my engagement. And from now on, I want to focus on my life with Sheila.

By the way, Baba told me about you and him getting back together. You are an adult, and it's your decision, but be careful with him. Try not to get too attached. He'll leave you soon to go to his job and other things, you know.

Warmest hugs to the best *Maman* in this world.
Sohrab

When Mousa returned, he looked excited. The sale had gone through. "You brought me luck, Aunt Zuli. Let's get out of here."

"That's good news, but can you first show me what to do with this internet? I'm not that hungry yet."

"What's wrong, Aunty? You look a bit pale."

"Nothing—it's too hot for the wintertime, or have I become too Tehrani?"

"Did Sohrab tell you anything that upset you?" He was met with silence. "I bet he did."

"How long have you known that he's getting married?"

"Only for a couple of days. I swear to God."

"I'm just overwhelmed," she said. "You'll have to come to his engagement. We have to tell Gholam." She had to adapt to the idea that life for her loved ones away from her would carry on and arrive to her as news every now and then. It had always been like that for her, as though people around her plotted to push her away. And now she was so used to this reclusive life, she wanted to be the one to push them away.

Mousa unplugged her modem a few times until she was connected. He began typing a message to Sohrab.

> **Good job, man. Your mother looks shocked. Her internet is running. Now don't just email. Call her!**

Zulaikha read the email and chuckled.

"I just remembered there may be a storm. Let's postpone our dinner plan after all."

"A storm? Of course," she said. "I've been thinking—could you find me a one-bedroom apartment in a good area? I might eventually make a second home here." Lately, she had been dreaming about Tehran—she often walked from Jayhoon Street to Nasim's bookstore, with a few cats following her, until some dark object or a woman in chador hit or pushed her. She was used to such dreams. They would go away eventually, like they did when she moved to Bahrain. She hadn't called Aliah for years, but Assef told her about them. She had retired, and her daughter, Saba, had expanded their business.

Mousa offered his studio. "It's a small flat, but you're only one person. It should be good for you for a little while. Don't you think?"

She was too shy to say she needed a place big enough for herself and her new husband—if Assef ever reappeared. "I'll think about it, but I want to see some places myself."

She saw Mousa off downstairs. The grocery store was jam-packed. People lined up for groceries like an extended holiday was coming.

"Is this because of the storm, Mousa?" she asked.

"Right. Not any storm, Aunty—a sandstorm." He raised his eyebrows.

Zulaikha had heard about the increase in sandstorms in Khuzestan. Nasim blamed the regime for everything—even the sandstorms or the drought that caused big rivers to shrivel pathetically.

"Listen to the radio, please. It's important. Don't worry about groceries." Mousa waved at Rahim.

"Hey, Mousa, pick up anything you want for your aunt now—we're closing soon," Rahim shouted from the cashier's stand.

"I can manage, Mousa," Zulaikha said. "Go home." A text had come. Assef was on his way to Abadan with a sandstorm in the forecast.

■ ■ ■

As night approached, Zulaikha sensed something was wrong. It shouldn't have taken Assef this long to arrive. She paced the room and looked out of the window. Finally, her phone pinged.

> **I am okay, don't worry. I had a little accident on the way. Please call me. I can't get a hold of you.**

She called him from the landline. "I'm in Khorramshahr—" he said. "At this clinic—are you writing this down?"

She called Mousa for help. They drove to Khorramshahr to visit Assef. One of his eyes was bandaged, and his leg was cast. Assef was never steadfast facing hardship. He always disappeared when bad things happened. Now she saw him lying on a hospital bed, weak, and wounded. His humourous tone was gone.

Zulaikha froze in front of his bed. "What happened?"

"Can you believe this happened to me, with all of my driving history? I couldn't see the road clearly. I was near Khorramshahr, a crazy pedestrian—a woman in a black chador crossed the highway. Who would do such a thing? Only in a crazy place like this." His mouth was dry. "I tried to stop, but my car veered and then rolled to one side. I pulled myself out, but it was too dusty. Clouds of dust and sand got in my eyes."

Zulaikha glanced at Mousa as she poured Assef a glass of water from a jar.

Mousa was beside the door, possibly aware that they were remarried, perhaps through Sohrab.

"Okay, now. Calm down," she said. "You'll stay with me. You

can't go back to Dubai in this condition." She glanced at Mousa.

Mousa stepped forward and shook Assef's hand. "Looks like the storm has changed its path. We'll get you out of here, Uncle," he said. "Wait for me to ask them what we can do."

"I can't let you stay here." Assef sipped some water. "You'll move to Dubai with me."

"Another time, Assef," she said scornfully. "Did you have a good time in Ahvaz?"

Assef rolled his eyes. "Yes, the wedding was fun."

Mousa came in ten minutes later with a wheelchair and two crutches. He gave them a ride back to the flat and helped Assef to go up the stairs using the crutches.

"Come with me, Aunty. I got a mattress—actually, a comforter—downstairs."

They went to the parking lot, where Mousa opened a storage locker and handed her a comforter in a bag.

"I haven't seen this type of storage before," she said. "It looks like a big cage."

"Don't you like it? They were less costly to install."

"Do I owe you money for his hospital bill?" Zulaikha asked.

"No, he had paid everything already," Mousa said as he approached his car. "By the way, don't be shy about him, Aunty—you've lived alone for a long time. He should take good care of you, or I'll kick his ass this time."

She held her nephew and kissed his forehead. "You have no idea how proud I am to have you in my life."

Zulaikha spread out the comforter and a couple of pillows on the floor for Assef.

His cell phone pinged. "They're worried for me," he said. "I want to tell them where I am if you don't mind."

Zulaikha needed a moment. There weren't many options.

Assef called her name.

"I don't mind. Go ahead."

The dog she had wanted to befriend earlier was still barking. She could feel the animal's presence from her bathroom window, which opened to a field. Lately, the dog had been sleeping near her wall at night. She started feeding him her leftovers. That night she took some food outside. The animal came closer.

"Here is your dinner," Zulaikha said.

The dog smelled the plate and ate it up.

"He never told me where he was, but his other woman should know."

The dog stared at her.

"I wish I could read your mind—or that look in your eyes."

She was not used to being so close to an animal as large as that dog. She warily turned her back and went upstairs.

The next day, Assef was sleeping when Zulaikha heard an approaching car. A taxi dropped off two women.

"Wake up, Assef," she said. "They're here. I mean your daughter and—" She refused to mention the wife.

Assef remained on his comforter as Zulaikha opened the door.

Malak had a pretty, round face. Her soft, olive-coloured skin, large brown eyes with long black eyelashes, and shiny black ponytail resting on her right breast underneath her *aba* attire made Zulaikha feel insecure and jealous. Assef's bond with this other family was now on display before her. Before this, it was possible to deny their existence, but now they were right here. They spoke Arabic, and Zulaikha spoke Farsi—Assef's daughter tried translating her mother's Arabic into her broken Farsi.

"So, you want to stay here, Father?" asked Salimeh, his daughter.

"I'll go back to work soon. My eyesight is not good yet, love."

Assef excused himself to the bathroom to change his bandage. He was cold to Malak. Perhaps he didn't expect her to come this far.

In an awkward moment, Malak looked at Zulaikha head to toe. "You—younger than me?" she asked.

"I don't know." Zulaikha smiled shyly, trying to comprehend the other woman's point.

"I am fifty-six," said Malak. "How old are you?"

"A lot older. I'm in my sixties."

"You look younger, though. It's because of your dark skin. Dark skin doesn't wrinkle as much."

There was a silence between them.

"Or maybe because you have only one child, and he's away. You live like a single woman."

Zulaikha remembered Malak had other children from her first marriage.

"Would you like sugar and milk with your tea?"

"You are his *Ajam* wife," Malak said. "I know he loved you very much. I was a poor girl from Palestine when we moved to Kuwait. He took care of me. My children need him. Do you understand that?" Malak seemed to be in pain.

"Yes, I do," she said.

How about asking you all to leave me alone right now— including Assef?

"We just came back from his relative's wedding. Did you know that?"

"*Ommi*, talk to my father about it, not her." Salimeh interrupted her mother in Arabic.

"I'm going to go back to Tehran soon." Zulaikha wanted to say that she had a life in Tehran—she had friends who cared for her. She didn't need this. She said nothing.

Malak began to cry.

Her daughter hushed her. "Pull yourself together. You promised."

Malak was like a mirror reflecting Zulaikha's same sorrows. How do women keep a man? Why was it so hard with Assef? Neither of them knew. But Zulaikha was done trying.

When Assef returned to the room, the women had tea and biscuits quietly.

"We're going, Baba," Salimeh said. "Can you call us a taxi to the airport?"

"We shouldn't have done it, Assef," Zulaikha said the moment they closed the door.

"No, don't let it get to you."

"How can I not?"

"We got married again because there was a reason—that reason is still there."

"What was the reason?"

"We love and need each other."

"I know why I need you, but why do you need me?"

He held his hand over his heart. "Because you've lived here all these years—I want to feel you close. What is in Tehran or Khuzestan? You don't even like it here or there."

"You don't like Tehran or here. I do. Tehran has been my home for a long time now, Assef." She shook her head. "I'm too old for games and competing with your other woman. No one knows but me at this very moment how good it feels to be too old for this, not to be hurt like before."

Assef stepped forward to hold her. "For once, please try to remember how I was when I left—young, angry—I needed a rebound, but—it has been you and you always."

Zulaikha refused his hands. "It was never only me, even this time, you came to Abadan for the wedding—I was just on your way."

Assef interrupted her. "Not true. I told you my sister invited them." He limped toward the comforter.

It was painful to see him in that condition. "It doesn't matter—get rest."

"I hate arguing." He glanced at his leg and grimaced as he sat down. "This pain is bugging me." His phone rang. It was Sohrab.

"I need some fresh air," she said. "I'll call him back." She didn't want to explain her stressed voice or face to Sohrab.

Downstairs, the stray dog was resting in front of their door. He got up and followed Zulaikha along the path toward the marina she had viewed from the roof. She focused on the dog as they walked, wondering what he had seen in her. When she returned, the dog took his station next to their building once more. She put out a bowl of clean water for him. She was thirsty too.

Assef was standing in front of the counter, playing cards. She hadn't thought about their argument.

"Are we good?" he asked.

She nodded and poured some icy water in a glass. "Let's Skype Sohrab," she said.

Sohrab had shaved his head and wore a yellow shirt that Zulaikha liked. "Is it me, or has Abadan made you more aloof, *Maman joon*?"

"Neither—it's because I got a new friend here—a dog."

Assef, still beside the kitchen counter, stuck his tongue out and imitated a dog.

"Really? I knew about your affairs with cats—that's so cool, *Maman*—What type of dog?"

"It's a big black dog. I call him Velgard. What's up with the baldness, *pesar joon*?"

"Oh, just a change," he touched his head. "Don't you like it?"

Sheila appeared from the back, showing off her new boyish haircut. "Look at me," she said. "We did it together."

"I love it. Both of you look like hot celebrities."

"Tell her about your trip," Sheila said. "Don't keep her waiting."

Sohrab looked at his mother. "Should I?"

Zulaikha nodded. "I think I'm ready."

Sohrab described Montreal's weather and its icy roads a bit too long, making Zulaikha impatient. "Where did you meet?" she asked.

Sohrab described Hessam's restaurant, and the flat above his restaurant with a red velvet couch.

Zulaikha leaned on the counter, her hand under her chin, and absorbed all of it. "Did he ask about me?"

"His first question was about you—about where you live now," Sohrab said.

Zulaikha tilted her head as a funny childish joy warmed her cheeks.

"I showed him a couple of pictures we took while you were here."

"What did he say?"

"Something you wouldn't like," he glanced at Sheila.

"Don't be like that," Sheila yelled.

"Okay, he said you look fit for—"

"My age." Zulaikha frowned.

Assef raised his eyebrows and cut a piece of cake on the

counter.

"I told him you live in Tehran but you're now visiting Abadan. He said something interesting that made me think about Bibi Madineh."

"What's that?"

"He said we're Bakhtiari Lur—we're restless—we migrate all our lives—that's what Bibi Madineh used to tell me, too."

Zulaikha remembered that also.

"Then he looked at your picture again and said that the Hessam we knew had died after Abadan—a different man lived on. He had been dealing with trauma and nightmares about Abbass's murder. Uncle Hessam couldn't do anything for his friend, except plotting an escape from the war zone."

Sheila put her arm around him and kissed his cheek. Her presence was comforting. She had told Zulaikha that she had an estranged relationship with her mother and stepfather. She barely talked about them.

"I think we should cut him some slack, *Maman*." Sohrab blinked away his tears. "Honestly, sometimes I feel that I should put that country behind me and never look back," he said.

"None of us are the same person, Sohrab—we have all dealt with nightmares," Zulaikha said. "Have you met his wife?"

"Not yet," Sohrab said. "We mostly met in his workplace, but I think she's not ready to admit we exist."

Zulaikha shrugged. Karmen's reactions had made Zulaikha suspect that Hessam had intended to cut his ties with them after all. Karmen knew he had escaped a war, but what about after a few years had passed? He had shown no sign of missing his family. Otherwise, she would have asked him. Women can feel these things.

"How did he get the heart condition?" Zulaikha asked.

"Didn't Bibi Madineh tell us your father died of a heart attack?"

"Oh," she said. "I thought my mother made that up."

Sohrab rolled his eyes. "Poor Bibi," he said.

Yes, poor Mother. How harmless she became to Sohrab.

"How long are you going to be there, Baba?"

"Four more days, son." Assef sat beside Zulaikha. "Now go have some fun, don't think about the past too much. We have lots of parties to plan."

They all sent each other long-distance kisses.

In the remaining days, Assef and Zulaikha ate, played cards, and searched for their friends on Facebook. She found Aliah and viewed pictures of Nasim with her daughters in front of a beautiful marina in Coal Harbour, or Canada Place. At night the couple bathed and cuddled on the comforter. Assef got rid of his cast on his last day.

On the way to the airport, the taxi driver played an old Googoosh song in his car. They were sitting in the back seat as close to each other as possible. Assef was holding her hand tight.

> *Why are you silent and cold?*
> *Why bring coldness?*
> *Why act so bad, oh why,*
> *towards my exhausted heart?*

Assef still limped slightly. They parted beside the taxi outside the airport.

"So this is it again," Assef said. "Not a goodbye, though—I hope not."

She gave him a wry smile. "No, we'll see each other again—our son is getting married."

"What was my score on this trip?" he asked. "Did I fail badly?"

"There's room for improvement, but at times, you were even terrific—especially the first night at the hotel when I went cuckoo—you read Hessam's letter."

"Right! Hessam's handwriting was awfully hard to read. You should give me more points for that."

She chuckled and held him.

"Let me go first," she said. "I can't watch you leave."

"Okay—I'll stay right here."

She got in the taxi and sent him a kiss from the window.

■■■

She met Mousa that afternoon to view a brand-new, ground-level apartment in Amiri Square, only two blocks away, but adjacent to a field she had used as a walking trail. The construction and the noise meant the site was not done yet. "A developer is building a complex here—Aunty, people are coming back," Mousa said.

She had second thoughts about moving from Mousa's condo—she had fallen in love with the roof and the view of the marina, but Mousa had spent time finding this new place.

"I hope they don't want it to look like Tehran," she said. "Having a park would be nicer."

"Nah, Tehran's mess was Ahmadinejad's work." He was referring to the president's background as the mayor of Tehran.

She suddenly saw the stray dog outside the fence. A conscript was pulling the dog, and another one walked beside it, blocking the animal's way.

"Stop, no no no." She ran toward them.

Mousa called after her, but she didn't stop.

"What are you doing? This dog is harmless."

"We have orders, ma'am. These dogs can be dangerous."

"No, not this one. Please," Zulaikha begged with a shaky voice. "I'll pay you for it. Don't harm the dog."

She screamed Mousa's name.

"I'm here, Aunty, right behind you," he said. "What's going on?"

"They're taking my dog."

"Your dog? You can't have a dog."

Owning the dog was against Islamic beliefs, but the laws were not clear. Because the origin of the belief was about the dog being dirty, keeping the dog outside or as a guard could be acceptable. "Yes, I can," she said. "It's a guard dog."

"We'll make it up to you, man," Mousa said. "Release him to us. Come to my shop—take anything you want, we have nice ice creams and Fantas."

The soldiers glanced at each other. "Okay, just this time," the conscript said. "If we see it running in the field, we have no choice. We must take the stray animals." He let go of the dog.

The stray dog walked away, but he turned his head and looked at Zulaikha.

"You go, Mousa." She ran toward the dog. "I'll walk him to our place. I know how to."

"If you're sure," he said. "Do you remember our plan to visit my mother? She's excited about it."

She couldn't wait to see Kobra and Gholam in Ahvaz for the weekend.

She was still scared of touching the dog. They stared at each other for a few moments. "What am I going to do with you, you dirty dog? Come with me. I have to wash you."

The dog walked along with her toward the condominium. Zulaikha pulled the water hose from the front yard and slowly approached the dog. He let her wash his dirty fur.

"What should I call you? How about Velgard? But you shouldn't stay a *velgard*. They'll kill you, do you know that?"

From Velgard's stare, it looked like he had accepted his new name and life. From that night on, he slept outside their door like he was guarding her territory.

■ ■ ■

Their weekend plans were a blast. On the way to Ahvaz she finally received a call from Kia about her passport. "I'm calling from Kuwait. Can we talk?"

"From an airport again?" She was partly teasing.

Kia chuckled. "Not this time, but believe it or not, you're on my mind at every airport," he said. "But listen, I managed to get a hold of Dr. Matlab. You're all set, Zulaikha. She said she would have your passport mailed to your address in Tehran."

"Good," she said.

"I didn't tell her where you are."

"I'm glad you didn't. What did she want from you?"

"She was going to Singapore. She got a job with the consulate or ambassador—she asked me if I could meet her there for potential business. I said I would on one condition—then she laughed and said she knew what I wanted."

I bet she had that same menacing smile when she said that.

"I've got to go, but I hope to see you somewhere soon—and not in an airport this time."

"Safe travels, Kia." She heard her voice calling his name. This time without needing her inhaler. She glanced at Mousa and asked him to put back his music on.

Kobra had made various dishes, from eggplant appetizers to chicken and rice with saffron and *zereshk*. Zulaikha hadn't cooked or hosted guests like that for a long time. She enjoyed being a guest for a change. Mousa teased her new hobby, the stray dog. "We rescued a dog by offering Fanta and ice cream," he said.

Kobra visited Isfahan often. "I heard about an animal shelter there in Isfahan."

Kobra sparked an idea in Zulaikha. "Find out more about it when you go next time. Will you?"

What would Velgard be doing now without her? He needed a leash. She should ask Sohrab to send her one. She should learn more about how to take care of a dog.

■■■

By mid-May that year, the early morning sight of Zulaikha and Velgard walking along the trail to the daffodil field had become familiar to the locals.

Nassim had extended her visit to Canada until after the election.

Zulaikha had finally become her niece, Natasha's, Facebook friend. Through an awkward Skype video call, they became acquainted. Natasha was a performer and dance teacher. She danced and sang in Hessam's restaurant. "He's with my mother in France," she said. "We haven't told him about our reunion plan yet. We have to be very careful with him after his surgery."

She finally looked at two pictures of Hessam taken in recent months. He looked like an older Omar Sharif, with silver hair and wrinkles around his eyes. She stared at his picture for a few long minutes.

I know that they killed my Hessam on that battleground. Someone else was resurrected to live on—someone without a country, without a name. I even know their deadliest weapon that destroys the soul, hatred. I know he had done things he may not be proud of to save himself. Hessam left that boy on that last road. I now want to know who he became.

■ ■ ■

Assef had been sending her short emails—sometimes just forwarded jokes—that he missed her. She wrote him back about her days. Sometimes, she'd shared a picture she took with Velgard.

After her morning walk, she showered and read Assef's latest email. Today's was longer.

> I am bad at writing love letters. I wish I could send you a song instead of this letter, the song you loved, the song you danced to. The song made me realize I was in love with you. I was your guest. *Amu* Habib invited me to join him and your mother at your house, and that night you cooked, while your mother ordered you around. She kept yelling—more tea, more fruit for our guest, take away this glass, bring a clean one—and you were smiling and doing all the work until the Emirate channel showed a singer performing, and you became rebellious and told your mother not to yell anymore because you wanted to watch the show. You stared at the TV screen and whispered the song in Arabic. You sang Arabic with a Farsi accent, which made me laugh, and you looked at me and whispered something that I couldn't hear, and I was all eyes

for you when you started dancing to the music. We dined and drank till late that night, and the next day I was on the road thinking about you, your curvy body, your full lips, your hair, and I was out of my mind for you. That image of you dancing stayed with me. That image may have saved me on those foggy nights when I drove exhausting roads with an exhausted body. You may have let me go, and I went, but you stuck to me, Zulaikha. You really did.

So many years have passed and we have gone through so much, but I never told you how I felt. I know I never even asked you what happened to you when they took you to prison in Tehran. I didn't have the courage to ask about it. Thinking about them having touched you sickens me.

My eyesight and broken leg are better now. I am back to work. I'd like us to meet soon. Have you received your passport?

Noises from outside distracted her. The presidential election debates caused more tension. She didn't follow them, but every time Ahmadinejad said something that irritated people more—something laughable, like he supported freedom of speech—they were out on the streets. Lately, the protests were happening more in Tehran. But last night in the store downstairs, she heard people talking about a protest.

A crowd of protesters was approaching Amiri Avenue. Two giant military vehicles, identical to Jeep trucks, blocked their way. The security police began shooting in the air. Zulaikha kept her head down as she sat on the floor away from the window. "Velgard," she muttered.

Velgard was barking.

Desperate to figure out how to manage the situation, she led Velgard toward the parking lot. The cage-looking storage was perfect for hiding him. She sat beside him and held him. His heart beat fast.

"You're safe here. Calm down, you good boy."

She dialled Mousa's number and got the answering machine.

The sound of smashing windows in the shop made her run to the store. The air outside was dusty.

The shopkeeper had a mask on. "Ma'am, go back upstairs and close all the windows and doors. They used tear gas."

"I need Mousa immediately," she sat on the stairway. "I feel sick."

"Wait here then." He called Mousa's number.

Within a few minutes, Mousa rushed in.

"What happened, Aunty?"

"Come inside, Mousa. Don't go out there. You have your parents to look after."

"Don't worry." He didn't listen and rushed back out.

"Wait!" Zulaikha shouted.

Upstairs, she rinsed her burning eyes.

Velgard's barking had changed to howling. The crowd had broken up. She could hear men running and yelling.

When she passed the store to get to Velgard, she saw two men hiding in the shop. "Mousa went home, ma'am. Don't worry," Rahim said.

She nodded.

How can we control this hatred from growing and passing on to the other generations?

She rinsed Velgard's eyes as she coughed, then used her inhaler.

She lay her back against the wall and rested her head on her knees, waiting for the outside aggression to calm down. Velgard looked calmer. They were both hungry. She was in control of this little part of her cosmos.

■■■

In mid-June 2009, finally, presidential elections were held. Before that year, Zulaikha had always gone to the poll, inserted a blank paper pretending she had voted. She could skip it, but there was a risk in not voting. People said fingerprinting was for tracing them. She could be questioned if there was no stamp on her birth certificate. All candidates must have passed the supreme leader's approval, so most people voted for who could be a lesser evil. For Zulaikha, the election was a charade—the president was already selected—not by the people, but by the supreme leader.

The ballot boxes for her neighbourhood were kept at a nearby elementary school—a newly opened one. Walking to the school, she passed the soldiers blocking traffic. The national Islamic music and the banners of both candidates filled the atmosphere. The voting station was in a classroom. People around her were arguing. She had no desire to interact with people or share her beliefs. She just wanted to be done with it fast. But the lineup was long—she could be there for over an hour.

A young Basiji woman fingerprinted her and asked her to go to the voting cubicle. She wrote **Nobody** folded the paper and returned to insert it inside the box before the woman.

"Your button!" The woman pointed at Zulaikha's button above her chest.

"What?" She looked down at her buttons. A small part of her skin was showing. She covered it immediately as if someone had caught her baring her naked breasts and rushed outside.

On her way home, the protests had already started. "Get lost, Ahmadinejad," people chanted.

She looked at her watch. It was around seven on a hot, damp evening. She looked down at her buttons again.

I need a new manteau. I shouldn't let this humiliation happen again.

Mousa and Rahim were on the street wearing green to support Mousavi, the other candidate.

"If there's going to be another protest here tonight, I have got to do something for Velgard," she said. "I don't want another fearful night for him."

"Tomorrow is victory day, Aunty," Mousa said. "We'll be celebrating."

Mousa and Zulaikha had built a large straw arbour shelter beside the daffodil field, where Mousa's friend planned to construct a community centre next year. Zulaikha walked her dog there that night. She sat and stared at the clear sky, ignoring the screams and shotguns.

The next day didn't turn out as Mousa had wished. The supreme leader announced Ahmadinejad as the president for another five years.

The news enraged Mousa and his friends downstairs. She heard him complaining when she went to buy milk. "They'll pay for this fraudulent election."

Basij motorcycles maneuvered along the street, intimidating people.

"So what time are you going to protest tonight?" she asked.

"Around six or so, if you want to hide Velgard, do it. There will be bloodshed tonight."

Zulaikha shook her head. She called Gholam and asked him to drop everything and be on his way. "Give the phone to Kobra." She made plans with Kobra and asked her to be firm with Gholam. "There's no time for childish stubbornness," she said.

As dusk approached, she walked Velgard to his shelter. The security man recognized her.

"Would you keep an eye on him, please?" She offered him money.

"No way," he said. "Be careful out there tonight, Ms. Zulaikha." He made it sound like an ancient-style Persian war was on the horizon.

Night brooded over the streets as she kissed Velgard's head and walked away from his gaze in disbelief. She had missed calls from Sohrab and Assef but had no time to reply. She walked a long way and knocked on some doors. "We've got to stick with our sons and daughters tonight," she said.

Two parents closed the doors on her, but fifteen others followed her to Amiri Street.

Gholam and Kobra were waiting in the parking area. They took out four boxes of white carnation flowers and four trays of raisin *shirini*. "Is this good enough?" Kobra asked.

"We'll know soon," Zulaikha said.

"I can't believe I'm doing this," Gholam muttered.

"We're open to suggestions, Brother." She tasted the crunchy raisin *shirini*.

When the military vehicles blocked Amiri Square, parents linked arms in the formation of a human chain before them. At the same time, Zulaikha spread flowers on their cars as Gholam and Kobra stood beside each Basiji guard, offering them *shirini*.

"These are our kids and this is just a peaceful protest," Gholam told one of them with terror in his eyes.

The Basiji glanced at the cookies and looked away. Behind them, the protestors chanted, "Where's my vote? Cheaters, cheaters—"

Suddenly Gholam was not in Zulaikha's sight anymore.

The guards broke the human chain with a water cannon as the young protesters scattered around. The water pressure pushed Zulaikha and her box of flowers, causing her to hit a shop door. The muscles of her neck tugged as she collapsed. She looked up and saw two hands from two heads—one wearing a Basiji helmet—offering help. Still light-headed, she randomly gripped one of the hands and got up. The guard ran away.

"He wanted to help you," Kobra said. "At least one of them—" She burst into tears. Mousa and Gholam ran toward them from across the street. "What happened? Are you hurt, Aunty?"

Zulaikha shook her wet head and glanced at the floating white flowers.

"Let's get out of here," Gholam said.

When Zulaikha got home before midnight, she emailed Sohrab and Assef and told them she was alright.

> It was a night to remember, but we are all fine.

Sohrab Skyped Zulaikha everyday, even with the weak internet—only for a few minutes. "Iran is all over the news, *Maman*. Something will happen this time."

Sheila and Natasha's Facebook pages became full of pictures from the human chain protests in Europe and Canada.

Five days later, Neda Agha Soltan's killing was broadcasted live all over the world.

Zulaikha was clueless about how to resist violence without violence.

"How can we not hate them, *Maman*?" Sohrab asked.

She shrugged and looked up as if the answer was somewhere high in the universe.

Someone somewhere must know. This is a piece of the puzzle the next generations should put together.

■■■

On cool and dust-free September nights, Zulaikha went up to the roof to watch the boats down by the marina. To her left, the refinery lights were shining. The air smelled like petroleum, and she couldn't stay there for more than a few minutes without covering her mouth with her shawl.

She called Mrs. Alipour and asked her about Tehran.

"The protests about the election died down here. Life is back to normal," she said. "I'm glad you weren't here for the most part. It was bad."

You have no idea how bad it was here.

"I miss Tehran. I never thought I would."

"Well, it's your home. Come back."

She had been in Abadan for over nine months. Sohrab and Sheila's engagement party was in Dubai for the 2010 New Year. The reunion they had talked about was happening. She received an intriguing invitation from Assef via email.

> You have given me our son, Sohrab. And he is not just a son, he is my friend. And now I am over the moon that he is getting engaged. Hessam and his family are coming to Dubai for the 2010 New Year. It will be spectacular here. You will see.
>
> I am writing this to tell you that I will be booking a one-way ticket to Dubai for you for next month, a few weeks before they arrive. Once you are with me, we

will talk, and you will see how you feel about staying with me. I want you to stay. But I want you to want it. I will buy your return ticket if you decide to leave.

I am sorry that I always disappointed you, and that you had to face so many things on your own. I lived my life on the road, running away from attachments. I work hard here in Dubai and love that I am a part of this place's growth. I still run from attachments. But it's the first time in my life that I want to stay, to be attached. I will take you to different places here. We will go to the top of Burj Khalifa Tower and watch the world underneath us.

Please say something. I am helpless, or don't say anything—just tell me, my Zulaikha, I am your Yousef, your Assef. They have written our love song in holy books.

She stared at the monitor for a few minutes. She had written a response, an unsent draft that she would revise soon to be suitable for an RSVP to a wedding invitation.

You have changed for me, my Yousef. Our separation cast a spell on me. I became the queen of my own world. I was drowning in the deepest sea of guilt after the forced abortion of my first child, my first son, whom you never knew about. You walked into my life and gave me a new son, our Sohrab, and life returned to me. But then you became one of those who let me down. You disappeared and then re-appeared. I learned to live with that, too.

You are my friend and companion now, but my heart does not have a place for love any longer. Maybe I should be more patient because love hides sometimes, and perhaps I am just incapable of finding it in my heart.

I dream about my small apartment in Tehran,

Bahrain, and the cities I have left. And lately, you have been in my dreams more than ever.

There is no better news than Sohrab's engagement and reunion with Hessam. But I wish you would stop expecting me to live with you in Dubai. It means ignoring Malak and your daughter. That is disgraceful. There was a time that I would do anything and dive into disgrace to be with you. That time is gone. It is lost. I will wait some more, though. I will wait for love to sneak out of its hiding place in my heart. Where will that be? I don't know. Maybe on top of that tower, the Burj Khalifa? Who knows?

She heard the sounds of a lift truck readying the neighbouring field for construction. She looked out her window. Her eyes met Velgard's. He seemed to be waiting for her.

Her phone rang. It was Nasim from Tehran.

"Where have you been, girlfriend?" Nasim said excitedly.

"Well, hello to you too."

"I'm back here," Nasim said. "And they tell me you moved to Abadan. I can't believe it."

"Didn't you tell me to go cruising? So, I've been cruising my hometown."

"Good girl. When are you coming back? We have so much to talk about."

"I—hold on a moment," Zulaikha said. "Can I call you back?"

Velgard was barking outside. He was demanding food and her company. His life depended on her.

AUTHOR'S NOTE

This novel is a work of fiction. Actual events inspire some parts, and some character names are taken from my family members. From my mother's side, our ancestors were from the Bakhtiari Lur tribe, and Chaharlangi, a branch of the Bakhtiari, was my mother's maiden name. Most locations, towns, and street names are based on real locations. I have tried to match historical events, timelines, and locations with the narrative.

The dialogues and setting in the Evin prison from the 1980s chapters are based on my friends' experiences.

I have translated all the Persian poetry and song lyrics in this novel. The translated poetry is from the following books:

Sepehri, Sohrab. *Hasht Ketab*. Tahouri Publication, Tehran, Iran, 2004.

Moshiri, Fereydoon. *Gonah e Darya*. Nashr e Cheshmeh Publication, Tehran, Iran, 2001.

Farrokhzad, Forough, *Another Hello to the Sun*. Sokhan Publication, Tehran, Iran, 2002.

Mosadegh, Hamid. *Majmooeh Ashar*. Negah Publication, Tehran, Iran, 2008.

The name Velgard for the dog is my salute to Sadegh Hedayat and his body of work, including The Stray Dog (*Sag e Velgard*).

The following books helped me remember the locations in Khuzestan during the war:

Dehgahn, Ahmad. *I Am Your Son's Murderer*, a short story collection (in Farsi), Tehran, Iran, Ofogh Publication, 2004.

Ahmadzadeh, Habib, (Translated to English by Paul Sprachman). *A City Under Siege*. Mazda Publishers Inc., Cosa Mesa, CA, 2010.

I have translated the small pieces from Luri folk songs just as I remember the lyrics my mother used to sing them. There are several classic and modern versions. The reference to Shir Ali Mardoon/Mardan is a tribute to a Lur Bakhtiari warrior (1892–1923) who fought against tyranny.

DISCLAIMER

All reasonable efforts have been made to obtain the copyright to publish the translated poetry from Sohrab Sepehri. Readers who know how to credit the estate of the poet appropriately are invited to inform us, and we will obtain their permission if there is a reprint.

ACKNOWLEDGMENTS

My gratitude goes to our beloved Luciana Ricciutelli (1958–2020). She read two previous drafts of this novel before she accepted it. She called *Zulaikha* "important" in one of her rejection emails, and that word encouraged me to keep revising and rewriting the story until it found its home.

Thank you, Maria Meindl, Inanna's excellent substantial editor. You truly helped *Zulaikha* to be more itself/herself. Rebecca Rosenblum, thank you for your leadership and the hard work of facilitating and proofreading. It has been a pleasure working with you. Thanks to Mel Mikhail for copy editing and Courtney Hellam for the beautiful book cover. My best regards to Meg Bowen and Inanna's sales team, and special thanks to Renée Knapp for your passion, hard work and for being there for us writers.

To Karen Connelly, my mentor during the Humber Creative Writing program, who continued working with me through writing several drafts; it gives me so much joy that you still remember Zulaikha after so many years.

A previous draft of this novel was shortlisted for the 2019 Guernica Literary Award. I am forever grateful to the judges, Sonia Saikaley, Anita Kushwaha, and H. Nigel Thomas. The news about being shortlisted boosted my will to keep going incredibly. So, I take a bow.

My special thanks to Eileen Cook for mentoring me in learning the craft of writing and for all the positive vibes you always give me.

I am forever indebted to Sonia Saikaley, Anita Kushwaha, Naben Ruthnum, and André Forget for generously giving their precious time and reading *Zulaikha*. You all must know that I am an admirer of your works.

To Zulaikha, my cousin, for trusting in me and being a part of my life during the war and for some unforgettable years.

I am thankful to my late aunt and uncle, my beloved Zan Daiee Ezat, and my cousins for their hospitality, for hosting us all those springs or summers in Abadan and Ahvaz, and for all the memories that shaped the landscape and setting of this novel.

To my sister, Shahin, and niece Delaram for the support, inspiration, and insights. To my friends for giving me space when needed and tolerating my introverted nature.

And Nina, my daughter, you were the reason I wrote this novel in English. I always felt that with our immigration, I failed to tell you about Khuzestan and our history. You read two different versions of *Zulaikha*. You even proofread it before I submitted it. My mission is accomplished because now you know about your roots and ancestors' birthplace. And that you are a restless Bakhtiari Lur too. Thank you Nima for inspiring the artwork and providing input about the cover.

To you, my reader, wherever you are, thank you for not only reading this novel but for trying to hear a different voice and giving it a chance because I know how foreign it might have felt.

Niloufar-Lily Soltani (Lily) is a literary and crime fiction writer and poet. Her poems have been published in literary magazines such as *Strange Horizons* and *Dissident Voices*. *Zulaikha*, a 2019 short-listed Guernica literary award candidate is Lily's debut novel. Lily lives in Vancouver, BC, Canada, and works as a senior supply chain specialist in the power and energy sector.